NIGHT GAMES

Also by Marilyn Harris

Marilyn Harris

————◆————

NIGHT GAMES

Doubleday
NEW YORK
1987

Library of Congress Cataloging-in-Publication Data

Harris, Marilyn, 1931–
    Night games.

    I. Title.
PS3558.A648N5 1987   813'.54   87-629
ISBN 0-385-18817-X

"Night Games scare the hell out of me always have.

"Don't trust them never will. We used to play 'Punch-the-Ice-Box' beneath the street lamp and nothing you ever saw was so except old orange peels and upside down movie marquees spelling John Garfield bass-ackwards in slanty angles of slippery neon.

"I used to wish for something real and everything was . . ."

Joe Bobbity
HOMING PIGEON
1941

NIGHT GAMES

Logan Airport
Boston
October 10
1986

"Keep up!"

Zoe saw Clay glare over his shoulder at her. She was lagging behind. In his voice she heard the same anger and hostility that she'd heard for the past month, a savage confrontation of wills that had left them seriously wounded.

The Mannings, Clay and Zoe, entered Boston's Logan Airport led by their two young sons. The three Manning males were catching a night flight for Los Angeles. Zoe should have been going with them. But she wasn't.

All the way down the long concourse, they formed an imprecise but recognizable procession. The two boys, Robert, ten, and Rick, seven, were in the lead, their little gray faces staring moodily out over the collars of their adult clothes. They knew where they were going.

Next came Clay, head erect, shoulders back, his face grim from the ravages of the intense domestic war.

Last came Zoe. She wore a foolish smile on her face which somehow suggested that she might be in physical pain.

Again Clay called over his shoulder. "For God's sake, keep up!"

Zoe struggled to obey, but still she lagged behind. As they approached the boarding area, she stopped altogether. Beyond the wide expanse of window, she saw night and an immense silver plane waiting. Beyond the wing of the plane she saw multicolored dots of light outlining the end of the runway where they were still picking up the debris from the afternoon crash. According to the car radio most of the passengers had been decapitated. All the way down the long concourse she had heard screams of protest and weeping.

Clay scolded her for her lack of attention. "What in the hell—Zoe!"

She looked at him and vaguely shook her head, finding no connection in her ideas. She regained her composure and walked to his side, eyes down.

The boarding area of Gate 45 was crowded and noisy. Their two young sons contributed to the chaos by encircling them, shrieking, arms outstretched, imitating the airplane they would shortly board.

In an attempt to make himself heard above the noise and at the precise moment when the boys fell silent in order to draw breath, Clay shouted, "What will you do now? Go home and wait for your lover?"

His voice carried over the crowd as though amplified. Heads turned. Eyebrows lifted. Mouths went sliding into smirks and grins.

Zoe did not answer. Bending her head a little, she looked inquiringly at the floor. Her hand shook as it played with the clasp on the navy blue purse.

Then slowly, blessedly, the noise built again. The boys, their faces animated by tension, resumed their high-pitched shrieks. A pockmarked woman in a black wool coat with an immense shock of white hair moved close to listen, then moved away, clearly disappointed.

Zoe's discomfort seemed to soften Clay. He moved close and coldly apologized. "I'm sorry," he said.

"No need."

He continued to look intently down on her. "You should be coming with us, you know."

Zoe's absorption with the floor continued. "Not this time."

"Why not this time?" he demanded. "You've gone before. How am I to explain?"

She did not look up. "Why should you have to explain anything? To anyone?"

He glared at her as though this were old ground that had to be gone over until they got it right. "Because Mother will ask. She'll wonder."

"Not for long she won't," Zoe replied. "If the truth were known she'll be delighted. At least be honest, Clay." She saw the expression in his face and caught her breath. He looked as though he could kill her, could effortlessly place his hands around her throat and squeeze the life out.

At that moment, a uniformed man with a tired face strode into the waiting area. He called out, full-voiced, "Sorry for the delay, folks. Just a few minutes longer. Please be patient. Have your boarding passes ready when I call."

Clay turned away and took his look of death with him. Zoe knew he was dreading the ordeal of explanation that awaited him in Los Angeles. She felt sorry for him.

Now there was a groundswell of movement as the passengers pushed close to the boarding door. They all seemed desperately intent upon preserving their balance. Most faces appeared engaged in strained efforts to look casual. For the moment, the weary uniformed man who had stirred them all into action had disappeared. Clay still stood with his back to her. The two boys, clutching their small travel cases, stared out of the window. For now, they were blessedly still.

Zoe considered leaving at that moment, of simply turning and walking back down the long concourse, out into the night air and home. But she couldn't. Instead she stood, still obedient, waiting to play out the remainder of the scene.

At thirty-two, she had long auburn hair and wore a simply tailored, rather plain navy blue pants suit. Her face, oval-shaped, had a taut, unseeing air about it. She was accustomed to dealing only with those problems which did not require visibility or identification. Unlike Clay, whose head turned constantly, attempting to see and record everything, Zoe stood anchored, her feet together, her small hands and slender ringless fingers locked over the rim of her purse. Even when standing erect, she still appeared bowed. Her nose was small and slightly pulled down by the inward clamp of her lips over her teeth as though she had sealed her mouth against the necessity of speech.

Now, as she fumbled in her purse for red-cellophane-wrapped cinnamon drops to give to her sons, her eyes lifted, then fell, formed an opinion as a condemned man might weigh the merits of death. As yet she had not even discovered that she was not ugly. Her red-brown hair was pulled tightly back and fastened with a gold clasp at the nape of her neck. The neck was smooth and firm. Age, as though it were a process capable of pity, had thus far been kind to her. Suddenly the silence within her became intolerable. To break it she reached and touched Clay's sleeve.

Her expression was a combination of timidity and anxiety. "I hope you didn't mean that," she began, "about the lover."

He shrugged. "It was a poor joke. I've apologized."

"I didn't mean that you had to apologize. I just meant—"

"What in the hell are we waiting for?" he interrupted, glancing around.

She tried again, wanting a reassurance of his trust in her. "Do you really think that I have a lover?" she asked.

"I don't think it makes a damn bit of difference what I think on any given subject."

"That's not true, Clay, and you know it."

He looked down on her. "What have I said in the last month that has made the slightest impression on you? Apparently you have made up your mind. Why waste breath?"

The subject was closed. Zoe watched him as he walked a few steps away from her as though she were a contagion.

The delay stretched on. Robert complained. "What are we waiting for, Dad?" He stood on one foot, then the other, twisting the travel case behind his back, clearly bored.

"The man told us to wait," Clay said with a smile.

The boy accepted this without protest and conveyed the message to his younger brother, who leaned against a near post, slid down it and sat dejectedly on the floor.

Clay tried to comfort them. "It won't be long now," he said, and the three of them, father and sons, exchanged a warm, exclusive agreeable smile.

The male alliance suddenly aroused Zoe from the helpless condition in which she found herself. She must be calm. The thought of being by herself was frightening and yet hopeful. She saw Clay staring at her now with that expression of intense concentration that she knew well, a particularly severe expression. She tried to stare steadily back. It was at this very moment of increasing power that the precise image of her husband appeared to her. It always provoked a mood of weakness in her, some inner imbalance, some exaggeration of deeply buried fears.

He appeared now in the crowded waiting area of the airport as a fixed point in space. He had dark hair and a trim body. He jogged. He had a strong face and a calm bearing even when annoyed. His height made him easily visible in any crowd. Like most tall men, he carried his head a little bent, with something serene in his face which gave the impression of prayer. She had no snapshot of him playful and reckless, few even smiling. All about him was the passive air of a listener, an arbiter. His good alert face saw problems and dealt with them immediately. Everything, everything, had always been here. It was simply a matter of dealing anew with the world.

Her husband's persistent control both impressed and annoyed Zoe. When she had first met Clay Manning, he had been a bachelor just over thirty. He was president of his own firm, Evergreen Electronics, located in that jungle of technology which flourishes on a strip of Route 128 outside of Boston. His electronic genius had been working at peak capacity, a top secret operation for NASA, planning the first civilian space satellite, hopefully operational by the year 2000. The intense mental activity had given him affecting mannerisms of vagueness. He had been living in an attractive English-style red brick house in Newton with a tree-filled fenced backyard. He had purchased the house for himself, apparently with no wife in mind.

Zoe's past had been a bit more complicated. A bright student from Whitney, New Hampshire, she had applied for admission to Radcliffe, Wellesley and Brandeis and been rejected by all three on the grounds that she had required a full scholarship and money was tight. She never quite had the courage to share her three rejections with anyone, so when the time had come to leave for college, she packed two bags and moved to Cambridge. Within the first week, she'd taken a small walk-up apartment on Freeling Street, Number 212, and acquired a job at Mrs. Wickey's Catering Service. The nature of the job permitted her to work irregular hours, sometimes in the mornings putting pink rosettes on white cakes, sometimes at night in a black silk uniform serving the cakes to an assortment of professors. The rest of the time she illegally attended classes, at Radcliffe, occasionally at Harvard, now and then at MIT and Brandeis, and if the professor of the moment had seemed to be viewing her with suspicion, she left the classroom and caught the bus to Wellesley and there had taken up approximately where she had left off. By the end of four years she had become skillful with the pastry tube and had acquired a fairly decent though unrecognized college education.

Being illegal for all that time had taken a toll. She had made no close friends except perhaps for Mrs. Wickey, who thrust upon her the role of surrogate daughter to take the place of the one she had lost in 1974 to a faceless rapist-murderer.

The boarding area continued to fill with restless, impatient people. Next to the window Zoe saw a young couple in close embrace; the boy's hands were cupped around the girl's buttocks, pulling her closer, closer, in defiance to the obstacle of clothing.

Zoe watched fascinated, remembering the night, years ago when there had been a panel discussion at Harvard on "The Imperative Scientific Question." In the large, wood-paneled seminar room, there were many faces and voices but none so fascinating and contradictory as Clay Manning. Within three weeks, their courtship, if the word would do for a shared illness, moved from superficial intellectual sparring to intense and grotesque lovemaking. He demanded and got incredible performances out of her. Their days and nights in the red brick house in Newton introduced them both to the insulating exclusivity of passion. Like a great illness, a love affair of that degree had not only made them oblivious of the ordinary standards of decent or sensible behavior; its devouring egotism had made them oblivious to the surrounding universe itself. Two months later they awakened to find themselves dangerously humiliated, Zoe pregnant, her mother and father dead, and inflation on the rise. They were married by a justice of the peace in Concord, Massachusetts. Now ten years later Zoe still felt worn out. The intervening years had dealt them the cruelest blow of all. They had grown polite.

Suddenly Clay turned angrily back to her, picking up the old refrain. "You should be going with us," he said, flatly, as though it were a complex problem that he had just solved. He looked down on her almost pitifully as though she were punishing him by making his life unduly complicated.

It was a different tone from the one he had taken with her for over a month, since she had first announced she did not want to make the annual pilgrimage to Los Angeles. She wondered briefly how a man of his intelligence could not understand her need for one week alone. But then she did not fully understand it herself. She looked up at him, ready to try again for both their sakes. She said quietly, "We've discussed it, Clay. Your Mother wants to see you and the boys. And I need the time."

"For what?"

She shook her head. "I'm not sure, but please don't worry. I will be all right."

"We could put off going for a while," he offered. "We could go at Christmas time."

"You're expected tonight," she said.

"I could phone."

Again she shook her head. They stood together in a little circle, imprisoned by luggage and their sons who were clearly listening.

Now the waiting area was totally congested. The flight

to Los Angeles would be full. Zoe felt claustrophobic. She longed for the quiet darkness of the car. She tried again, out of courtesy, to give him an explanation that she herself did not fully understand. "Please don't worry," she began, keeping her voice down. "I'll go home, straight home. I *will* lock the doors. And tomorrow I will drive up to New Hampshire. I know the road. I've made the trip for years, long before I met you. I'll be perfectly safe. I'll look over the old house, see if we can't salvage it for weekends. Then one week from today, I'll be standing here waiting for you."

It had sounded so simple, so clear. But she was mistaken in thinking he understood. "Please," she whispered. "Please let me do this."

She was openly begging for his permission, for his understanding for one week's freedom. But he merely stared down on her with something resembling contempt.

Her two young sons look frightened. Rick moved close. "Mama?" he inquired.

She saw the alarm in his eyes and was sorry for her part in causing it to be there. "You take good care of yourself," she said, cupping her hand around the back of his head and drawing him close.

"Do you have a present for me?" he asked, in a tone as simple and natural as though it would never enter her head not to have a present for him.

"No," she said.

"Grandmama will," he boasted, and pulled away from her.

She tried to remind herself that he was very young and very spoiled. And he was right. There would be presents, expensive, breakable toys. The nature of her thoughts caused her to turn in the opposite direction toward the crush of people clutching their tickets in their hands and still waiting for the tired man in the uniform to reappear.

Of course there was always the possibility that she was wrong, that she should be boarding the plane with her family.

But remembering what was in store for her if she went, scenes terrible even in memory, she decided again and for the final time no.

She had made the annual autumn pilgrimage to Malibu for the last ten years, and she had tried very hard to behave herself, had endured the cliché-ridden relationship with her wealthy mother-in-law, a stern, slim, fashionable, coping, slightly older female version of Clay who viewed Zoe as an unalterable and tragic mistake. Zoe knew intimately Knott's Berry Farm, Disneyland, the Farmers Market, the wonders of Universal Studio and the exclusivity of the Malibu Beach Club. She knew that the house next door had once been occupied by Hedy Lamarr, and that Errol Flynn had occasionally gone to Clay Manning, Sr., for legal advice. Five years ago, Clay Manning, Sr., a man whom Zoe had come to love, had taken the easy way out and died suddenly of a heart attack. He alone with his warm easy ways had made the annual sojourn bearable. He had always greeted her, red and perspiring with an unbuttoned collar and a sympathetic warning in his eye.

She bowed her head, feeling the sensation of old grief flowing through her. The passengers were growing increasingly restless. She saw her youngest son sitting on the floor beside a post amid a forest of legs. His hand was shaped like a gun; he aimed his finger at certain feet and his lips moved in a silent "Bang-bang."

Then suddenly the uniformed man was there again, standing beyond the roped-off area, a clipboard in his hands, thanking the passengers in a dull unenthusiastic voice for their patience and inviting them to line up for boarding. The jammed area became alive with movement. Clay motioned for the boys and they obeyed instantly. For a moment Zoe felt that they would all simply leave without a final word of goodbye. The pockmarked woman in the black wool coat was standing very close to her. "Aren't you going, deary?" she grinned.

Zoe shook her head and tried vainly to push through the crowd. She could still see Clay, but she had lost sight of the boys. She felt frightened. She must not let them go without final goodbyes.

Her ears were filled with the incessant roar of voices. She felt drenched through with effort. It was no use. She had lost sight of Clay. Passengers continued to flow around her, all glaring at her as though she were an annoying obstacle.

Dropping back into a corner, her face suddenly bore the solemn rigidity of the dead. Her expression did not change for the next few moments, so intent was she on looking normal. She held a dialogue with herself inside her head. It helped to make her look normal. She said, "They're calling your flight! Take good care of the boys for me. And take care of yourself as well."

Suddenly Clay was before her, reaching for her almost violently. He scolded, "I thought you were right behind me."

"I am separated," she said and the words sounded curiously wrong. But before she could correct them, he reached for her in an entangling embrace. Her hands convulsively clutched at his shoulders and she held her breath. As a child who has been hurt skips about, putting all his muscles into movement to drown the pain, in the same way Zoe yielded to his embrace with subtle pressures from her own body.

Then someone was pushing her leg. A son. She disengaged herself from the curious embrace. The harsh lights overhead cut new lines into Clay's strained face. He was aging, as she was. She murmured politely, "Thank you."

He said nothing and turned away.

She reached out for a son and drew back Rick, the objector to their recent embrace. She bent down, wondering if she should kiss him or not. Her lips were still moist. She was aware of Clay's eyes fixed upon her from one side. "Look," she said lightly to the boy, "you take care of yourself. Promise? And help Grandmama whenever you can. And send me a postcard from Disneyland."

The boy was a miniature, an exact duplicate. The large original stood to one side discreetly rubbing his groin.

Rick nodded solemnly and solved her dilemma of whether to kiss or not by awkwardly, almost shyly putting his arms around her neck. The gesture, so vulnerable, disarmed her.

Then Robert was there, slightly taller, his face appearing hurt, as for the first time he sensed separation. He responded mindlessly to the spectacle of kisses and embraces, nudging Rick to one side and slithering in against Zoe, embracing her, pressing his hand against her breast, then moving it down against her stomach, searching for a quick easy entry back into the womb.

She stood up to receive him, lifted his head and looked him squarely in the eye. "You, too," she said simply, assuming that the boy had already heard her last-minute instructions.

Quickly she reached into her purse and withdrew two handfuls of red-cellophane-wrapped candy. She gave them to both boys and watched as they shoved them into their pockets, each taking time to unwrap one and pop the sweet into his mouth.

The crowd in the waiting area was dwindling. She stood up and looked at Clay. "You'd better hurry," she said quickly, noticing the last passenger disappear.

Clay gave her a curious look. "Did you lock your car door when we left the parking lot?"

"Yes," she replied. "Now hurry."

He shook his head a final time, trying to understand. Suddenly he reached for the hand luggage at his feet, motioned the boys forward and turned abruptly away.

The boys waved goodbye. Clay did not. Robert was the last to disappear. He turned back and threw her a kiss. She'd never seen him do it before and wondered vaguely where he had seen it. And while wondering, she stared at the cavity of the door and watched it blur as though she were viewing it underwater.

Suddenly she ran to the large expanse of window, pressed her hands against it, wanting to reach through and draw them back. But she saw nothing except night and the immense silver plane, pointed nose, waiting. Finally she saw the last three passengers start up the steps, one tall figure, two smaller ones.

"Keep them safe," she prayed. She could still taste his tongue inside her mouth. A sticky circle of candy was on her cheek. She pressed her forehead against the cool glass and watched the gigantic door close. All the impressions of the day, beginning with the feverish packing, the veiled and exhausted battle, now threw her into a deeper depression. For a moment she saw nothing but death, or the advance of death in everything. Even her cherished scheme to be alone for one week seemed a bid for death. Pressed close against the window, she could hear and feel the tremendous vibrations from the plane. Then the plane shuddered forward, turning its bulk awkwardly like a beached thing out of its element.

Zoe leaned closer into the glass. The plane was now moving across her reflection. She would have to plan a triple funeral. Cut roses died so quickly. Gladiolas were cheaper, showier. The double funeral had been bad enough.

"Your parents were suicides. There were problems you did not know about. No reason to blame yourself."

She closed her eyes. Inside her head was a jerking marionette. "Keep them safe," she prayed. When she opened her eyes, the plane was gone. The people were gone. The once crowded waiting area of Gate 45 was deserted. The door leading outside into the runway was closed. Every door that she saw was closed.

She raised her eyes to the night outside the window. Off in the distance at the far end of the runway, she saw the whirling red lights of emergency vehicles. She watched the lights with a cold, almost haughty expression. She felt abandoned. But this was absurd. She had wanted it this way.

Behind her she heard a faint noise. She looked over her shoulder. A young black man was making a large flat broom whisper across the floor. Her fingers pulled self-consciously at the strap of her purse. She walked carefully around the pile of rubbish.

As she passed, she looked down at the collection of discarded items and carefully catalogued each one; an assortment of cigarette butts, used Kleenex, two candy wrappers, several crumpled and discarded airline envelopes, a green comb with teeth missing, and there to one side, a small square piece of red cellophane. She stared at it and quietly bent over and picked it out of the rubbish.

The black man stepped back, eyeing her suspiciously. He had a prominent gold tooth and a fierce scar puckering white down the left side of his face. "Lost something, girlie?" he grinned. He held the broom out at arm's length, reclining acrobatically on one hip. His fly was unzipped.

She enfolded the red cellophane in her hand, shook her head and walked away. Beyond the waiting area, the concourse stretched ahead.

Shortly she was in the midst of intense foot traffic. Her

eye made contact with every passing face as though she were searching for someone in particular; businessmen with brief-cases, sailors home on leave, retired couples on holiday, kids going from nowhere to nowhere. She tried to stand erect. Voices passed by. Her ears attempted to follow them, to fo-cus on specific words. Perhaps beyond the uniquely human sounds and the steady stream of faces was a vanishing point through which she might pass if she would only persist.

There were a few fairly amiable thoughts; Robert's al-lergy medicine. She'd forgotten to remind Clay. But he would remember. She was certain. She was the one who al-ways forgot. And she should have said something about their preferences for breakfast, their peculiar bedtime rituals. Where, she wondered, was the pockmarked woman in the black coat going?

Gate 41 was crowded with a departing flight. She stepped out of the flow of foot traffic and watched the passen-gers file through a door which was identical in every way to the one through which Clay and her sons had just passed. She felt irrationally that if she went through this door with these passengers, she might encounter the three of them some-where in the night.

She continued to watch until the last of the passengers disappeared. The planes in the night had insatiable appetites. She had watched them devour two waiting areas filled with hundreds of people. Where had she left the car? The vanish-ing point was drawing closer. Most amazing of all was the fact of her nonidentity. She was no one, had no legitimate place beyond her relationship with the three who had just de-parted.

She stepped to one side and leaned against the railing that separated the waiting area from the concourse. She half shut her eyes. Her purse slipped off her shoulder and swung crazily about her wrist. Overhead she heard Musak, a full orchestra with every violin in the world whining.

A flight attendant, pretty with red hair and smooth skin and violet-shadowed eyes, drew close. "Are you all right?" she asked, her voice filled with concern through habit, training.

Zoe looked up, startled.

The flight attendant moved closer with professional curiosity. "There's a comfortable lounge just up ahead at Gate 36, if you care—"

But Zoe shook her head and moved quickly away. The volume of Musak increased, the violins screaming. She thought with a wave of black humor that she couldn't even get out of this airport.

A few yards ahead, she saw a large brightly lit newsstand, a safe haven, a legitimate excuse to stand still, gather herself together, patch up whatever new had been torn within her, and then continue on to the parking lot.

There were a number of people milling about as she entered the area and confronted a large display of current magazines. She saw *People* magazine, Joan Collins aging, *Newsweek,* a hooded faceless terrorist, *Playboy,* a pretty girl with a self-absorbed smile. The Muzak seemed louder here, as though she were nearer to its source.

Two young girls in tight blue jeans and bare midriffs came in and two boys in Epcot T-shirts met them, and they laughed and paired and went off arm in arm. A stolid woman in a pink flowered hat passed by leading a beautifully brushed red setter dog. Behind her, a pale nun prayed past.

Zoe tried to turn her attention back to the assortment of magazines, but safe inside the harbor of the newsstand, she found the passing parade fascinating and in a strange way healing. It was like being in a theater, seated comfortably, safely out of the line of action, but witnessing a variety of tragedies, comedies and melodramas. Nothing was required of her but to watch.

"Can I help you, honey?" The voice was slightly nasal and came from behind the cash register.

Zoe glanced up over the pyramid of mints and gum. "No, thanks," she murmured. "Just looking."

She was held in some mechanical observation of the woman who was staring back at her. The heavily mascaraed eyes were seeking to enclose her, frowning at her as though Zoe had offended her in some way.

Then suddenly a long clawlike red fingernail was pointing at her. The woman's face arranged itself into a foolish, false girlish angle. The black pencil-thin eyebrows lifted, the eyes bulged. The shadowed eyes and red mouth were endeavoring to work in conjunction with the brain. Some form of recognition was dawning.

"You're—you're—" she stammered.

Zoe felt as though all life in the vast concourse had now stopped and was watching her. Through a stint of will, in spite of her embarrassment, she kept her head raised as she tried to turn away.

"No, wait!" the woman protested. She was grinning now, one hand curiously rubbing her left breast, which was visible beneath a pretty, tightly fitting short-sleeved lavender sweater. Then finally, triumphantly, "You're Zoe!" she announced. "Zoe—Zoe—" The red fingernails hung suspended and snapping in midair. Suddenly a eureka expression crossed her face. "Blaine!" she shrieked. "Zoe Blaine from Whitney, New Hampshire." Instinctively Zoe backed away. She shook her head as though to deny her identity.

All the time the woman was wildly talking, eagerly reaching out as though Zoe might turn and bolt at any minute. "Don't you remember me?" she grinned. "Runner-up in the Miss New Hampshire Contest, 1974." Her face glowed with pride.

Still Zoe held her distance, refusing to recognize and identify the strange woman. There was a brief silence. Zoe continued to stare fixedly at the painted face, the blond Shirley Temple wig, the short-sleeved lavender sweater pulled down tight over bra-less breasts. No, there was no recognition.

Finally in shrill enthusiasm, the woman shrieked, "Isn't it marvelous? I mean that we should just bump into each other?" Her hands gestured wildly on either side. "I mean, after all these years and all that."

But still Zoe struggled. It occurred to her to simply turn and walk away, but there was some quality of hope in the woman's eyes which prohibited this. "I'm—afraid that I—" she said hesitantly.

Now in mock exasperation, the woman stood with both hands on her hips. The red lips were glistening and protruding, as though she were pouting. "All right for you," she grinned in the manner of a five-year-old child. Then the blond curly head lifted as though she were approaching one of the happiest moments of her day. "Mary Lisa," she announced, an expression of intense pride on her face. "Mary Lisa Fletcher." Now she leaned so far over the display case that both her breasts were pressing against a neat stack of Mr. Goodbars. "Class of '73, Whitney High."

Zoe held her position and took another closer look. "Of course," she said, almost to herself. "Of course," she repeated. "Mary Lisa Fletcher," she said, dumbly.

"Well, it used to be Fletcher," the woman grinned. She looked heavenward as though playfully ashamed. "It's been a few other things in between." The red fingernails on both hands joined each other for the counting process. "First it was Fuller, then Biggs, then—" She hesitated, eyes lifted, struggling to remember. "Oh, yes," she giggled, "then Mc-Murtry." She leaned close to share a confidence. "He was swell, my truelove. But he got himself killed in a motorcycle accident out on Cape Cod." Her face went through a softening effect as she spoke of death.

Zoe continued to watch and listen, spellbound. The woman went on counting. "Then it was Polanski, a real bastard. And now it's Mosely." She stood on one hip. "But he is gone now," she added. "Split about six months ago. So I guess just Mary Lisa will have to do."

For the first time Zoe smiled. She tried to imagine the emotional trauma of five husbands and five marriages and could not. She still could not place the woman accurately, but it seemed unimportant. It had been an interesting interlude. It had given her a chance to gather herself together; she felt strong now, or at least stronger. And the extraordinary light on Mary Lisa's face fascinated her.

A middle-aged man stepped up on Zoe's left. He wore a soiled gray overcoat and a scruffy, predatory expression. He whipped out a copy of the Boston *Globe* and slapped it on the counter with some change. Mary Lisa scooped up the coins. "That's exactly right," she smiled, as if praising the man for some difficult feat of accomplishment. "And thanks," she said.

He lingered, paper in hand, in close examination of the bare breasts beneath the lavender sweater. Mary Lisa jerked open the cash register, deposited the money and pushed the drawer closed, every movement enhancing her totally unrestrained body. Zoe watched it all, still fascinated.

When the man showed no inclination of ever moving on, Mary Lisa looked at him almost apologetically. She whispered kindly, "Your coins buy a paper and a quick look, honey. I'm sorry, but you've had both." There was nothing at all flippant or superficial in her manner. She seemed to imply that if she had the time, she would oblige him in any way he saw fit.

When he was out of earshot, her manner changed again, as though she were now seeing Zoe clearly for the first time. "Isn't this marvelous?" she repeated, her face crinkling and glowing with what was either sincere pleasure or an excellent imitation of it. "It's been a few years. You're looking great. You really are. Marvelous, just marvelous. Someone's been taking good care of you."

For the first time, Mary Lisa pulled self-consciously at the lavender sweater. "Me, I look like hell," she murmured. "I know it." But the painful reflection lasted only a moment. "You know what I've decided?" she asked eagerly, the warm grin back where it belonged. "I've decided that life's easier on brains than on looks."

Zoe started to offer a mild protest. But Mary Lisa didn't give her a chance. "No, I mean it," she said, her face mock-stern. Her hand adjusted a blond curl. "Five husbands and look at me. Here I am pushing papers and lifesavers at Logan Airport. Thirty-two going on sixty-two." Her face brightened. "I *was* the second runner-up in the Miss New Hampshire contest. You *do* remember, don't you?"

Zoe said, "Yes, of course I remember." And she did. She was on the verge of saying more when three white-haired ladies stepped up to the counter in search of candy bars. Mary Lisa greeted them with simple kindness and indicated to Zoe that she was to wait.

Reluctantly Zoe agreed because she wasn't absolutely certain how to get away. She had the strong feeling that if she simply turned and walked down the concourse, Mary Lisa might run after her and that was a scene that she would just as soon avoid. Somehow it seemed important that she contain the woman here within the limited area of the newsstand. She vowed to herself to be alert for the first opportunity to leave.

Still not fully comprehending why she was staying or how she could escape, she turned away and began to flip through a copy of *Newsweek*. She saw a picture of Cher dancing with an Indian.

Mary Lisa Fletcher. Zoe remembered her, had not known her well. She remembered gossip on the school bus. On a crisp clear autumn evening in the seventh grade, there had been a class hayride, and while Zoe and the others had been singing their hearts out over "Shine on, Harvest Moon," Mary Lisa had crawled beneath the hay on the tailgate with Malcom Mabry and had "done it." Or at least that's what Zoe had heard whispered.

Quickly Zoe looked back toward the cash register. The old ladies were having trouble deciding between Milky Ways and Butterfingers.

Zoe continued to thumb through the magazine. A hollow-eyed cocaine addict stared up at her from one of the pages. If Clay and the boys were to walk up at this moment, how would Zoe explain Mary Lisa? Determined to seize the first pretext for leaving, she replaced the magazine on the rack and bumped softly against a young black girl with Whoopie Goldberg curls, coming from the opposite direction. She murmured her apology and moved a safe distance out of the way.

The hand clutching the strap of the navy blue purse suddenly opened. To her surprise, she discovered that she was still holding the small piece of red cellophane.

As she put it in her pocket, she remembered a metal dance pavilion painted green on the edge of Red Moon Lake. Zoe saw it clearly as she stared across the crowded concourse, her eyes not moving. She remembered pink tulle and gardenias and music coming from a small dance combo. Mary Lisa had kept disappearing into black woods with one boy, then another, Mary Lisa obliging, laughing as though it had never occurred to her not to oblige. Not that she had been the town tramp. For a town the size of Whitney, population 5,030, there had been a surprising number of obliging females. Zoe with her brain and insane parents had been the exception.

Zoe turned away. She felt weary and somehow vexed. She could not understand why she was standing here, waiting for a woman she scarcely knew, why she could not muster the strength of will to simply walk down the concourse, out into the night, find the car and go home.

Then Mary Lisa was searching for her again, her face arranged in that perpetual, mindless smile. "There you are," she exclaimed. "My goodness, why are you hiding?" She reached out and gently dragged Zoe forward until they were once again standing in the center of the crowded newsstand. "Now," Mary Lisa ordered. "Tell me about yourself. It's been ages. You look great, you really do. What are you doing out here? Going someplace? Meeting someone?"

Zoe shook her head to everything. "No," she murmured. "I just put my husband and sons on the plane. They're going to California for a week."

"Hey, sons!" Mary Lisa smiled joyfully. "That's great. How old?"

"Seven and ten," Zoe replied.

Mary Lisa hitched up her slacks, still looking extremely pleased with the thought of sons. She reached behind the counter and withdrew a pack of cigarettes. "You know, I would have bet my life right off the bat that you had sons. Isn't it marvelous?" She extended the package of cigarettes to Zoe.

Clay got angry when she smoked, yet it was impossible to say no to Mary Lisa. She took a cigarette, then asked, "And you? Do you have—"

Mary Lisa shook her head. The perennial gaiety on her

face faded. She lit Zoe's cigarette, then her own, and breathed the smoke deeply. She stared at the cigarette.

"I've had three collapse in the oven," she said softly. And Zoe assumed that she meant miscarriages. She inhaled deeply and blew the smoke out between pursed lips. A policeman gave her a bill for a copy of *Playboy* and walked rapidly away. She called after him, still slightly subdued, "Thanks, Harry. It's a good issue. You'll enjoy it."

Zoe held her cigarette stiffly down at her side and hoped that Mary Lisa wouldn't notice that she wasn't smoking it. Somehow she felt that if she smoked it, Clay's plane would crash. And she would be responsible and guilty and she would have to plan a triple—

"Where're you living?" It was Mary Lisa again, fully recovered.

"In Newton," Zoe replied.

Again Mary Lisa looked so pleased. "Isn't that marvelous? I could have guessed that, too. I mean, that you live in Newton or Wellesley or one of those places." Suddenly she extended her arms broadly on either side. "See? I told you. God looks after those with brains. The rest of us just have to muddle through the best we can."

The two women gazed at one another. Neither seemed inclined to speak or to offer consolation or to ask further questions. Zoe felt embarrassed but could detect no similar feelings in Mary Lisa. Rather she was like a child, warm and affectionate and staring because she wanted to see. Finally she laughed abruptly, "I never was much."

Zoe graciously protested. "Just the prettiest, most popular girl in the whole class."

Mary Lisa's eyes darted up, then down. She creased the half-burned cigarette with the sharp tip of a fingernail. Without looking up, she said, "There was just one thing that I did well."

The crowded newsstand seemed suddenly dry and arid. The melancholy crowds became motionless, all were listening. Zoe looked down on the burning cigarette, which she had yet to smoke. Moved by the strange silence coming from Mary Lisa, she could not, would not, walk away. She wanted to distract her, wanted to leave the woman as she had found her, fairly whole and intact.

But before she could conceive of a subject or a plan of action, Mary Lisa glanced up at her, smiling, "I didn't mean to embarrass you."

"You didn't," Zoe said. A large man just entering the newsstand bumped against Zoe and pushed her closer to Mary Lisa. Zoe dropped the cigarette and stepped on it and felt obliged to carry the conversation for a while. "Do you go home often? Back to Whitney, I mean?" she asked.

Mary Lisa shrugged. The light was returning. Her shoulders lifted. "Oh, now and then," she said. "My old man's still alive." Suddenly her face clouded again. She took another long drag on her cigarette, then stomped it out on the floor. She reached forward with extreme familiarity and put her arm around Zoe's shoulders. "Listen," she said softly, "I really was sorry to hear about your parents. My old man told me. I was sorry to hear about that. It must have been hell for you, having them go together, I mean. I'm so sorry."

Looking at her at such close range, Zoe had the feeling that she really was sorry. Still under any circumstances it would have been difficult for her to talk of memories so intimate; now it was torture for her. She bungled a few sentences, could not find words. What made it worse was that Mary Lisa continued to stand with her arm around her, in silence, as though her closeness would please Zoe. Again the crowded area seemed filled with sleepwalkers.

With her eyes half closed, her fingers burning as though

she still held the lighted cigarette, she said, "Well, I must be going."

"Where?" Mary Lisa asked flatly.

Zoe felt intimidated. "Home," she said. "I'm driving up to Whitney in the morning."

"Isn't that marvelous?" Mary Lisa exclaimed and at last stepped back. She stared at Zoe. "You going alone?"

Zoe nodded. She thought she saw a quick look of disapproval pass over Mary Lisa's face. "Why?" Zoe asked.

"Oh, I don't know," Mary Lisa smiled. "It's just that I don't like to do anything alone. I don't even like to go pee alone."

Zoe laughed in spite of herself. Besides, it seemed a good way to exit. Laughing. In a way, Mary Lisa had been an effective tonic, strange but medicinal. Now Zoe began backing away. In her mind she ran through the amenities of leave-taking. None seemed quite appropriate, so she settled for honesty. "I was feeling very lonely a few minutes ago," she said. "Thanks for being here. It was good to see you again."

"Wait!" Mary Lisa started after her, her face alive with movement. "Do you really have to go? I mean, well, what do you have to go home to? It's been years and I was wondering if—" A decision of some sort was struggling mightily beneath the blond wig.

Zoe wanted to avoid all of it, both the conflict and the resolve. "No, I really must be going. It's late." She hesitated, then laughed casually. "I'm not even certain I can find my way home. Clay does all the driving."

Then Mary Lisa was following her, a long-legged, slightly faded beauty in clinging slacks and sweater, reaching out as though she meant physically to restrain her.

Instinctively Zoe moved quickly away from contact. If Mary Lisa saw it, she gave no indication of it. The words came fast now. Her face was alive with the results of her decision. "Look," she began, as if a matter of monumental importance had been settled. "Well, what I mean to say is, well, why do you have to go home at all? I mean, well, I get off here in a few minutes, and I'm having some people over, just old friends, and I'd—"

Zoe backed further away, sensing what was coming. "No, I really must be—"

"Why? You said yourself that there's no one at home." Mary Lisa continued to draw closer, her hands reaching out, her eyes moist and blissful with excitement. "Look, I live just up the way, in Marblehead. It's kind of a run-down place, but it isn't bad. My second husband was in TV repair. He gave it to me before he split." She ran around behind Zoe now, literally blocking her exit from the newsstand. "Oh, please," she begged, the blond curls jiggling. "I've got so much to tell you." Her head lifted proudly. "Don't think for a minute that I work here all the time. In the summer, do you know what I do? I perform with the Merrywood Music Tent out on Cape Cod. You've heard of it?"

It seemed so important to her that Zoe nodded, indicating she had, although in truth she hadn't.

"No big parts, you understand. Florence Henderson gets all those. Just chorus work. But I had two lines last summer in *Guys and Dolls* and the producer said that next summer I could try out for a bigger part in *West Side Story.*"

Mary Lisa seemed to be waiting for a reply of some sort, so Zoe murmured, "How nice," and hoped it would suffice.

Apparently it did, for she went right on, her hands waving excitedly, drawing in the air a picture of the party that was waiting in Marblehead. "All these people are really great. They're all from the Music Tent, all actors, and I know you'd love them." She leaned close as though to share a confidence. "You simply have to meet Bubs. There's no one like Bubs in the whole world."

Zoe's brain yielded up a leaden image. The adventure was difficult to imagine. Every nerve, every response, every reflex in her being said no.

Still she tried to find a way around the persistent woman. A group of children all dressed alike in dark blue suits and white shirts suddenly flooded into the newsstand. Shrieking, upturned faces headed toward the arrangement of candies. Zoe was certain that the surge of business would distract Mary Lisa, but she was wrong. She stood before Zoe now, one hip thrust out, her hand behind her head, a pose. "You didn't know I'd had theatrical experience, did you?" She beamed. "Ta-dah," she sang. And thrust her hip farther out. She slipped out of the pose now and gave Zoe a smile of childlike delight. "Oh, no formal training, you understand. But Bubs says I have natural talent that formal training would just screw up."

Three nuns entered the newsstand and made futile attempts to gather the children together and herd them out. Mary Lisa bobbed her head to them, crossed herself and murmured softly, "Good evening, Sisters." Then within the moment she turned her attention back to Zoe. "You'll come, of course," she said, tossing her head as though she were physically shaking off a negative reply.

But Zoe was adamant or tried to be. "No, I really can't. There are things I've got to do."

Still Mary Lisa stalked her. "Look, you just told me that you dumped the husband and kids for a week. Now what has to be done?"

Suddenly Mary Lisa stepped forward and grabbed her shoulders.

"Look," she suggested, "you can come to the party, stay the night with me, then drive up to Whitney in the morning." The more she talked the happier she became, as though standing before her was the one ingredient to make the party complete.

Zoe could neither understand nor conquer the humiliating feelings that were pressing against her. Why was the woman so insistent?

She lowered her head. "I must go to Whitney tomorrow," she began. "It seems I have to decide what to do with the house. I had a letter from someone, a man with the town council. Anyway, they want me to clean it up or sell it." Zoe hesitated; she wanted to say further that she had absolutely no desire to go to the party, that most social contact had become insufferably painful for her and that she could not meet people without hideous conceptions rising in her imagination. "Well, at any rate, I have to do something with it. The house, I mean," she concluded lamely.

Mary Lisa took a step forward, her eyes narrowing. "It seems like a creepy thing to do," she said, sympathetically. "I mean, walk through the very room where your father actually—"

Suddenly a man standing at the cash register called impatiently, "Hey, you in business or not?"

Mary Lisa called back full-voiced and quite pleasantly, "Be right with you, sir." With mock ferocity she warned Zoe, "Don't move an inch, I mean it. I'll be right back."

Zoe massaged her forehead and glanced down the long concourse toward freedom. The feeling of entrapment was now apparent on her face. Marblehead. A few friends. Actors. Merrywood Music Tent. Ta-dah. Dear God. She looked longingly down the concourse.

"Now look, honey, I don't mean to be pushy, but—" It was Mary Lisa again. "Ten minutes and my relief comes on and we're on our way. What do you say?"

Zoe felt a sudden sharp pain in her lower left side; ovulation made difficult by tension. Another egg waiting. She walked slowly to the outer edges of the newsstand. The persistent shadow that was Mary Lisa followed her.

Finally, painfully, to make up for past crimes of omission, Zoe nodded her consent and immediately regretted.

Mary Lisa's high laugh rang out. She actually jumped up and down, then did a little turn around. "Wow!" she exclaimed. "Me giving a party for Zoe Blaine." She caught herself up short. "Well, it isn't Blaine anymore. But whatever it is, who cares?" Finally, "Isn't it marvelous?" she squealed, her expression totally blissful. Suddenly she reached out for Zoe's arm, her attitude now a combination of joy and concern. "You're not worried about your husband, are you? I mean, what he'd say?"

Zoe shook her head. An unpleasant sensation gripped at her throat when she met Mary Lisa's glance. At the mention of her husband, the feeling increased, and although she was certain that Clay would care a great deal about her attending the party in Marblehead with Mary Lisa's friends, she still managed to shake her head and laugh lightly, "No, of course not."

"Well, that's good," Mary Lisa went on in a voice which seemed to be almost deliberately high-pitched. "I mean, I don't want to be bitchy or anything like that, but I don't think there is a man in the world who can stay virgin pat for a week. So if *they* can't, why should we?" She hurried to add, "Not that it's going to be that kind of a party, but still I don't want you to worry. You hear?"

Zoe nodded. Virgin pat. A curious phrase.

Now Mary Lisa put her arm around Zoe's shoulder and began to propel her back into the area near the cash register, to secure her in the event she changed her mind.

"Oh, God!" she gasped, her face filled with almost slavish adoration. "What a great time we're going to have tonight." She leaned close. "You and I must find a private corner and catch up on all the years. I want to hear everything, everything. And then it will be my turn and I will tell you everything." As she talked, she applied constant pressure to Zoe's shoulder, drawing her still closer. "Isn't this marvelous?" she exclaimed again. "I can't believe it. I really can't believe it."

She looked at her watch and reached for her purse beneath the counter. "If my relief isn't on time tonight—" She withdrew a tortoiseshell compact from her purse and proceeded to powder her nose. "Dempsey and Rich will meet us outside in a few minutes," she announced, spitting on her finger and smoothing down her eyebrows. "They're great guys," she went on. "Mechanics from downstairs. You'll love them. They always go home with me on Friday nights." She giggled. "Sort of traditional, you might say. Of course, they've been busy as hell today what with the crash and all."

Zoe tried not to see or hear, tried instead to concentrate on stilling the panic rising within her. Nothing would happen. What she had agreed to do was perfectly reasonable. There had been a random encounter with an old acquaintance and an invitation to a party in Marblehead with a few friends. Nothing would happen. She was an adult, other opinions to the contrary. She could take care of herself. It might even be interesting for a little while. She would insist upon taking her own car. That way she could leave whenever she wanted to.

As though Mary Lisa had read her thoughts, she came close again. "You got wheels?"

Zoe looked blank.

"A car. You got a car?"

Zoe nodded.

"Good. I don't. I usually ride with Dempsey, but we'll all go with you tonight. That way you can leave anytime you want to."

Zoe managed a grateful smile.

Mary Lisa studied her closely for a moment. "Hey," she scolded softly. "Relax, we're going to have a great time tonight. I promise." Again she touched Zoe's arm. "You know, you're tighter than all get out. You really are. I've got a stash of great grass. That will relax you." She drew a deep breath and placed one hand directly on top of her head, a curious position like a little girl. Quite earnestly she said, "God didn't put us here to be uptight. He put us here to hang loose." She smiled. "I'm a hang-loose person. It's simply the only way to survive," she pronounced calmly.

Suddenly an elderly, heavyset woman in a plaid wool jacket appeared in the newsstand. Without a word she shuffled behind the counter past Zoe and Mary Lisa. She shoved a brown worn purse beneath the counter and crawled awkwardly up onto a high stool near the cash register.

Mary Lisa greeted her warmly. "Flossie," she grinned and went instantly to the woman and tried to put her arms around her.

For a moment the old woman struggled to disengage herself. "Keep your goddamn hands to yourself," she muttered, almost falling off the stool in her attempt to escape Mary Lisa's embrace. The old woman righted herself, then eyed Mary Lisa angrily, shrewdly. "How much fucking you planning to do tonight?" she muttered.

An expression of genuine hurt crossed Mary Lisa's face. "Flossie," she mourned. "You're not feeling well."

The old woman exploded. "I feel goddamn okay and I'll feel a hell of a lot better just as soon as you get your cheap ass out of here."

Mary Lisa looked weary and Zoe noticed that there was not that play of eagerness in her face. For a single instant there was a flash of something else. Zoe saw it but could not identify it.

Now she saw that Mary Lisa was again trying to make overtures to the old woman, encircling her on the stool, her hands reaching out as though she longed to touch, but dared not. "Did you take your medicine?" she whispered, as though she didn't want anyone but the old woman to hear her.

The old woman's anger was now approaching rage. She turned on the stool, flailing at the air. "Goddammit, leave me alone, you hear? I'm not one of your lost souls or pimps or jocks." She lifted her shaggy gray head. "I was a lady before you ever crawled out from under your rock, you hear? So just leave me alone, just goddamn leave me alone."

From where Zoe stood a distance away, it seemed that Mary Lisa was suffering actual embarrassment. She seemed terribly concerned for the old woman. She smiled now, as people smile at the weaknesses of those they love, and putting her hand over the old lady's hand she said, "I'm just worried about you, Flossie. You know what the doctor said."

"Slut!" muttered the old woman and reached for a candy bar.

Mary Lisa gave her a final sad smile. She lifted her head and indicated that Zoe was to follow her. Almost resignedly she walked ahead, but her manner had changed to something sorrowing and dejected.

Zoe felt herself moving along the concourse. The absence of Mary Lisa's enthusiasm joined the discomfort of Zoe's new freedom in an unholy alliance. The concrete walls on both sides of the corridor seemed inadequate to contain the press and weight of so many bodies.

The concourse widened as it passed the rows of ticket desks and car rental agencies. The human congestion increased. Now they were moving faster, bobbing and darting their way through the crowds, Zoe falling back, but now being dragged forward by Mary Lisa, who had recovered from her sorrow. "You had dinner?"

Zoe nodded.

"Good," she grinned, the fire completely rekindled after the rebuff of the old woman in the newsstand. She threw both arms up in the air in the manner of an old-fashioned evangelist. "Then it's on to the party," she exclaimed.

Zoe recorded everything. The only problem was that she couldn't deal with it. The wide bank of glass doors was ahead of them now, and beyond that, night.

Suddenly Mary Lisa shouted, "There they are!" The voice so close and loud startled Zoe. She looked in the direction that Mary Lisa was pointing in.

Beyond the glass doors, she saw two men, one stocky, one tall, both in windbreakers and shivering slightly in the cold, both carrying metal lunch boxes, both with stubbly faces and dark heads that now glowed red from the whirling light of a nearby emergency vehicle.

Without willing it, without wanting it, not certain what exactly was causing it, averting her head to hide it, Zoe began in fear and confusion to cry . . .

———◆———

The man named Dempsey sat in the backseat, staring out of the window, his dark eyes sullen. Mary Lisa sat close beside him, a talking machine, directing Zoe through hazardous Friday-night Boston traffic, interrupting her own instructions to gleefully call the roll of those who would be waiting for them at her party.

In the rearview mirror, Zoe saw Dempsey eyeing her, as if she were an intruder. Once he whispered angrily to Mary Lisa, "Does Bubs know she's coming?"

Mary Lisa replied full-voiced. "Of course not. How

could he? We just found each other, just like that," and she snapped her fingers, grinning, suggesting that the chance encounter at the airport carried with it immense meaning.

Zoe had been given to Rich, like a gift. He was a short, stocky, slack-jawed, small-chinned male, heavily built like a wrestler with reddish, curly hair. He had freckles. He sat as far over against the door as he could without falling out and glanced longingly now and then into the backseat. His rejected love for Mary Lisa weighed heavily on the enclosed air of the car.

The tears which had so inexplicably plagued Zoe had not lasted long and had gone blessedly unnoticed by the others. She had not wanted to cry anyway; it was someone else within her who had done the crying. The first cool blast of October air, the comforting sight of her trusty dark blue Ford station wagon, the sight of Robert's baseball cap on the dash —all these familiar signposts had for the moment stilled the unhappy dissension within her and had now left a vacuum. Her predominant opinions at that moment were "Well, it's too late now. I'll take them where they want to go, then I'll excuse myself and leave."

Rich jauntily crossed his legs and withdrew a cigarette from the pocket of his windbreaker. He stuck the unlit cigarette in his mouth, then reached for the baseball cap on the dash and slapped it on his head. Undersized, it perched comically on top of the red corkscrew hair.

"You play?" he asked.

Zoe tried to concentrate on the traffic. For the moment, all of her attention was being channeled into the question of which lane. Once out onto the immense and crowded highway, she answered, "No. It belongs to my son."

"You've got kids?" Rich asked then, idiotically.

Mary Lisa answered for her from the backseat. "Two sons," she said proudly. "Zoe and me, we grew up together in Whitney, New Hampshire. Did you know that, Dempsey?"

Dempsey apparently knew nothing. In the rearview mirror, Zoe caught a glimpse of his face, taut, almost grieving, his head turned sideways, his hand moving slowly over the front of Mary Lisa's lavender sweater.

"Of course, we didn't know each other too well then," Mary Lisa went on, apparently impervious to the hand that was now cupped about her breast. "Zoe there was always the brain, and I was—"

From the front seat, Rich snickered. "Yeah, what was you then, Mary Lisa?"

"I was the class idiot," she giggled, almost prettily. "But look at us now. Isn't it marvelous? That after all these years we find each other and take up just like there were no years in between, like nothing at all happened and we were still back in school. Isn't it marvelous?"

Dempsey was now lifting her sweater, his mouth angling down toward the bared breast. Still Mary Lisa talked on, impervious. In the rearview mirror, Zoe saw that she had merely lifted herself slightly as though to better accommodate the open mouth and the black, shaggy head.

"Whitney wasn't much of a town," she went on, rocking gently with the sucking motion of the mouth that was pressed against her. "But we still managed to have some pretty good times. I liked summers best when school was out and we used to live down at the Red Moon Lake." She laughed softly. "God, that was fun. I hate cold."

As far as Zoe could tell, the woman was not even aware of what was being done to her. Her face, light-splattered by passing cars appeared nostalgic. She leaned back against the seat and stared out of the window.

Rich was gazing longingly over his shoulder at the activity in the backseat. His eyes appeared blind and furry. He looked ridiculous with Robert's baseball cap on his head. "Way to go, Dempsey," he muttered, his rate of breathing increasing.

The car was silent. Zoe tested her emotions with one clear honest thought of her husband and sons. They were on the way to the beach house in Malibu, where the widow of Clay Manning, Sr., would look after them, would be secretly delighted by Zoe's absence.

In the rearview mirror she saw that Dempsey was now trying to guide Mary Lisa's head down between his legs. His hand on the back of her neck was applying strong pressure. The pain and urgency on his face had increased. Clearly he felt unutterably wretched now. Rich was still watching from the front seat; his body angled around. His glittering eyes were wide open, gazing with envy at the two in the backseat. A dumbshow was taking place in the rearview mirror. Zoe saw Mary Lisa shake her head and at the same time try to shake off the hand against her neck. Dempsey's mouth formed a silent but gigantic "Why?" Mary Lisa shook her head again, magnanimous even in her rejection. The blond curls jiggled on either side of her face. Suddenly, violently, Dempsey straightened himself in the seat, pushed against Mary Lisa's head with such force that she bumped against the side of the car. The blond wig slid to one side. She straightened it.

Rich snickered. He slapped his hands against the back of the seat and turned around, looking very pleased. Obviously Dempsey's defeat had been his victory. Now Dempsey sat well over on the other side of the car, clearly looking for relief of his suffering elsewhere. Mary Lisa readjusted her sweater and went on chatting merrily about Whitney, the cold red brick high school, the smelly cafeteria, certain classmates.

Zoe gazed silently at the highway before her. She was

grateful in a way. They were making it easier for her simply to drop them off and avoid going to the party. Clearly she was cramping their style. She thought this from habit. Never had her presence anywhere failed to cramp the style of the moment.

A car coming from the opposite direction refused to dim its lights. The brilliance struck her eyes with such force that she winced. The world for a moment looked liquid.

Rich cursed, apparently suffering the same discomfort. "Goddamn motherfucker—"

From the backseat Mary Lisa begged almost sadly, "Don't, Rich, not tonight, please—"

As though offended, Rich muttered, "Who asked for her to come along anyway?"

Zoe felt herself vanquished on all sides. For some curious reason, she felt a certain need to win Rich over. "Talk as you like, Rich," she said. "I don't mind." Then she wondered if she could say anything that would make sense to him, anything that might stimulate an answer. Carefully she guided the car into the slow, outside lane, and began musing on a quite different matter other than traffic. "What do you do at Logan?" she asked.

He braced himself with his hand flat on the seat between them. Beneath his breath he muttered something, but she couldn't hear.

"What?" she asked.

"Wheels," he said, full-voiced.

"You work on the wheels of the airplanes?" she asked.

"Now where else would I work on wheels?" he sneered.

From the backseat Mary Lisa interrupted. "He's just the best wheel man at Logan," she smiled.

Immediately after this came the delicious slow rise in his confidence. With his hand adjusting the collar of his windbreaker, Rich took a deep breath and looked about at the long string of cars passing them in the other lanes, and at what was happening all around him in this world in which he now had a place. He elaborated. "The mechanisms in the little gizmos that make the wheels go up and down beneath the plane?" He seemed to be waiting for her acknowledgment. She nodded. "Well, that's my department. Very tricky. Very, very tricky," he announced.

From the backseat Dempsey grumbled, "Shit, a monkey could do it."

Again Mary Lisa objected. "Be nice, Dempsey," she begged. "Please. Let's make tonight a marvelous night. Not like some of the others."

Dempsey looked out of the window, as if for a moment he were undecided whether to honor her request or not. Rich sat up straight, pleased with the reprimand.

Zoe continually shifted her eyes back and forth from the traffic to the rearview mirror to the man sitting beside her. She felt as if she were in the presence of three children. She'd never known people like this.

Suddenly Rich leaned over. "You ball?"

Zoe shook her head. "No, the cap belongs to my son. He's the one who plays base—"

Rich giggled. He spoke slowly for a dim-witted child. "I didn't ask you if you *played* ball. I just asked if you balled."

Instantly Mary Lisa's face appeared between the two of them. "Look, I'd better get up in the front seat so I can direct Zoe. Rich, you get in the backseat with Dempsey." She looked at Rich from under a veil of disappointment.

"Well, what in the hell did I do?" he protested.

From the backseat, Dempsey laughed outright. "You dumb son of a bitch," and the laugh dissolved into a low snicker.

Again Mary Lisa insisted that the change be made. In fact she was standing up now, her neck and head bent over, one knee raised. "Come on, Rich," she begged. "The roads get tricky up here what with all the rotaries. And Zoe doesn't know the way."

Finally, reluctantly the man raised himself up in the seat. "You can say that again," he grumbled.

The awkward switch was made, a tangle of legs and arms, both men taking full advantage of Mary Lisa's upended body, she protesting only mildly to the hands cupped around her buttocks in mock assistance, hands squeezing her breasts. Finally, breathlessly, she settled into the seat beside Zoe. She adjusted the blond wig, stroking the curls. She turned earnestly in the seat and apologized to Zoe. "They're acting up to impress you. They know better, they really do."

"Screw you," said someone from the backseat.

In the cool night, Zoe smiled. She felt she had wandered into a zoo with wild and exotic animals. Clay would not approve. She wasn't certain that she approved. But approval seemed a weak tool when confronted with the three sitting around her. If things got out of hand, she could always leave. At least she felt less wretched here than she did in the airport. Something was improving.

In a small voice, Mary Lisa asked, "You're not sorry you came, are you?" Her face creased with concern.

Zoe tried to reassure her. "Of course not." She even found the courage for one small lie. "I'm looking forward to it. I've never known actors before."

Mary Lisa beamed. "You'll love them, I know."

From the backseat came a muted conversation. "What was the final body count this afternoon?"

"The whole goddamn plane, except for a guy in the rear who got his legs cut off. They took him away in a basket, but I hear he's still alive."

"Seawall?"

"Sick pilot, I heard—"

"Probably both."

Again Mary Lisa protested. "Please, you guys, don't talk about it." She looked back at them so simply, so brightly.

"Well, what in the hell can we talk about?" demanded Dempsey in a low voice.

"Nice things, happy things," beamed Mary Lisa.

"Shit."

For a few minutes there was nothing from the backseat, although Zoe could see pieces of their faces dispensing judgment. Dempsey's dark, swarthy face had gone slack now with dead desire, and Rich's face, ruddy and freckled, gazed out of the window at the passing cars like a prisoner. They seemed totally pliable and passive, not unlike her two young sons after a scolding.

Even though they had left metropolitan Boston far behind, the traffic was as congested as ever. The towns blended with each other, a continuous stream of shopping centers, a glut of urban sprawl. Zoe stayed in the safe slow slot of the outside lane. It was easier than flipping back and forth and she was in no hurry. Stiffly her fingers gripped the wheel. She felt, at moments, in the continuing silence of the car that she was locked within a dream. She felt that she knew why she was here, why she had finally accepted Mary Lisa's invitation to attend the party. She had felt guilty over abandoning her husband and sons and there was nothing left for her but to humiliate herself.

She lowered her head and rubbed with one hand a mild but persistent ache in her right temple. In the interim of silence, she reaffirmed her earlier decision. She would take these people to Marblehead, deposit them at the appropriate place. Then she'd drive home. There was a good possibility that Clay would call from Chicago. They changed planes there with an hour's wait. It was like Clay to call to see if she had arrived home safely. He was blameless. She was the one.

She felt dead with her thoughts. She drove in the slow lane, unaware of the speedometer dipping. There was no need to go to Mary Lisa's party for humiliation. She could accomplish that at home all by herself.

"If you go much slower, someone's going to shove a bumper up your ass."

The voice came from the backseat.

She glanced into the rearview mirror. Eyes stared sullenly back at her.

Predictably Mary Lisa sprang to her defense. "I think the whole world is going too fast. I think it's marvelous to drive slow for a while, to look around and really see the world where we live."

"Shit."

Unfortunately the world where they lived at the moment was a dirty string of used-car lots, automobile graveyards, pawnshops and dimly lit bars. Zoe said nothing. She stepped on the accelerator. The car shot ahead. She swung out and around three cars, not bothering to look back. A horn honked angrily. She ignored it, still accelerating. She was going fifty, then sixty, over now into the fast lane. The two men in the backseat sat up, an expression of excitement and approval on their faces.

"Atta girl," Rich grinned. "Now you're moving."

Mary Lisa giggled. "You drive good. You really do."

Ahead was an intersection. The light was turning yellow, but Zoe shot across, impervious to the traffic starting out in the opposite direction. She sat erect now, gripping the steering wheel with both hands. The center white line of the highway seemed to be beckoning to her. The sooner she got there, the sooner she could turn around and go home.

Her thoughts were now moving with the speed of the car. Home was that complicated maze of corridors and rooms with old food odors and dying plants and dirty carpets. The tuna fish can from the macaroni casserole was smelling up the kitchen . . . Do your floors suffer from wax buildup? . . . Yes, all her floors suffered . . . The roof leaks in the pantry . . . Call the roofman . . . Ring around the collar . . . Needs paint . . . Ring around my throat . . . Our great American home . . . I'm sorry, Clay, I tried to call the plumber . . . Use the mud room, Rick . . . Must shop . . . Dinner at 6-30 . . . Vaginal spray will save a marriage . . . Avoid the bedroom until the sound of snoring can be heard . . . Weep in the bathroom for what was avoided in the bedroom . . . Mother never told me about Summer's Eve Douche . . . Mother is dead . . . Incredible, loathesome, mind-killing, soul-deadening, heart-stopping, sob-rendering, nerve-annihilating, blood-draining, muscle-paralyzing, eye-blinding, ear-deafening, tongue-severing, God-defying Shit . . . The brain is dead . . . The tongue moves, but nothing comes out . . . Take Alka-Seltzer, that's all you can do . . .

She took advantage of a long empty stretch of highway to accelerate to ninety.

Mary Lisa sat up uneasily. "Honey, maybe—you'd better —I mean, we're not far now."

"Jesus Christ," someone cursed from the backseat.

But Zoe, under the duress of speed, could no longer separate the voices. There were those coming from the backseat, those from inside her head. They were all like a constriction which prevented her escape.

Again Mary Lisa suggested meekly, "Honey, maybe we'd better slow—"

The speedometer was moving effortlessly past ninety-five. Speed was a pleasant sensation. If there were obstacles of cars ahead of her, Zoe merely slipped around them. On either side. It made no difference. Horns honked ceaselessly at her. Narrow passages. Narrower escapes. They had wanted to go faster. She was taking them faster.

Suddenly someone in the backseat shouted, "For Christ's sake, slow down."

Ahead was an intersection with a red light and three lanes of waiting traffic. No way out or around. Two courses of action: one, to slam on the brakes. Or to crash.

Zoe felt stirred by a sort of sullen anger. Blocked again. Mary Lisa was screaming something at her. The two behind in the backseat were pressed backward like astronauts in a lift-off. The barrier of cars was coming up rapidly. That unreasonable humiliation which she had felt earlier had completely vanished.

Suddenly at the last minute she slammed on the brakes, pushed them to the floorboard. The car swerved, shimmied, veered crazily from one side to the other, vibrated. The air was filled with the smell of burning rubber. Still she held fast to the wheel, pumped the brakes up and down, battled with the highway for balance and finally brought the car to a halt inches behind a large furniture-moving van.

A stronger smell of burning rubber permeated the car. The silence coming from the other three was nearly like peace, but not quite. For peace, you need a total lack of human company.

Zoe glanced outside the window at the hostile faces in the cars around her. They looked flat somehow, a bearded, saintly-looking man over there shaking his head in complete censure, and there, a woman with a white lace scarf on her head, talking angrily to the old man sitting beside her, and there three children, their faces pressed against the car window, mouths agape, eyes wide, obviously listening to the lecture that was being delivered from the long-haired woman in the front seat on how not to drive. Their features seemed to be without dimension, as though they had crawled out of the Stone Age and would shortly crawl back again.

Rich, in the backseat, cursed. "Crazy goddamn bitch."

Slowly Zoe turned around and faced him directly. Her voice was even. "Slow or fast?" she asked pleasantly, willing to give him all the time he needed to fully comprehend a decision that was basically his.

Mary Lisa sat up from the curled position she had assumed, obviously in preparation for a crash. "How about in between?" she smiled, a marked strain on her face. She retrieved her purse, which had fallen onto the floor. Raising up, she studied Zoe carefully. "You okay?"

It seemed a simple question, but for the moment there was no answer. Zoe stared out at the light, which was just beginning to change. The sensation of speed had been pleasant. Of course she knew that she could have killed all of them. And thinking this, she experienced a delayed reaction. Her hands trembled. The muscles in the back of her neck tensed into a cramp. Now she drove obediently across the intersection, trying to still the hubbub within her. The steering wheel felt like flesh in her hands, as though it were something human she was gripping. She angled into the middle lane and settled the car into a safe forty-five miles per hour. If she had killed them all— But such thoughts were useless. Newton was still there. Clay and the boys were on their way to Chicago. Mary Lisa was putting on lipstick, and the two in the backseat seemed to be viewing her with new respect.

Dempsey asked, his voice taut, "Where'd you learn to drive like that?"

She shrugged.

"You handle a car pretty good," he added.

Mary Lisa chirped from the front seat, "Zoe was the smartest one in the whole class."

Still the seconds passed. If she had killed them—

Now Dempsey leaned forward, laid a beefy hand on her shoulder, more than laid it there, began subtly to apply pressure. "You ever been in a bad car accident?" he asked, his voice low.

She shook her head.

"Ever *seen* a bad car accident?" he asked, his fingers squeezing her shoulder as though they wanted to meet in the center of bone and muscle.

She winced slightly and shook her head, trying to pull away.

"Then I don't care what kind of a smartass you are, you hear?" he muttered, his face now close to her ear. "You keep this car under fifty in this traffic, or Dempsey will come up there and show you how smart *he* is."

Mary Lisa pushed his hand away and tried to smooth his ruffled feelings. "No harm, Dempsey," she smiled. "She just wanted to go fast for a while."

The big man leaned back again in the seat, his dark face still creased with anger. Rich announced glibly, "Well, she got us here in record time. There we are," and he gestured out of the window toward the lights of Marblehead.

From the moment she had reawakened out of her momentary madness, Zoe had tried to prepare herself to face resolutely what was before her. She knew somehow that she would not be permitted simply to drop them off, that Mary Lisa would insist to the point of embarrassment as she had insisted back at the airport that Zoe leave the car and join the party.

Marblehead was a string of lights around a half-moon bay, all drawing closer. Mary Lisa took a vial of spray perfume from her purse and liberally sprayed herself and the car. It smelled like dying gardenias. Zoe breathed deeply. It was good in a way, helped to cancel the smell of burned rubber.

"Almost there," Mary Lisa squealed excitedly.

Zoe shivered. Her forehead felt damp. There was no one at home in Newton. No reason, really, why she must hurry back. This thought surprised her, lifted her, as it were, out of her fever before it dropped her back again.

Mary Lisa was pointing now. "Up there, at the McDonald's, see? Okay, take a sharp left right there."

Zoe nodded. She still could feel Dempsey's hand on her shoulder, although the man had long since leaned back into the seat and was now staring blankly out of the window, his face grotesquely colored by passing neon lights.

"Here! Here!" screamed Mary Lisa. "You turn left here," and she pointed sternly up at the two golden arches.

Zoe did as she was told. From the backseat she heard Dempsey muttering to Rich, "Dumb bitch. If *she's* smart, I'm king of the brains."

Rich snickered and said something too low to hear.

As Zoe took the turn, she half closed her eyes, and so it was through faulty vision that she first saw the street. It was lined on both sides with tall, weary perpendicular white frame houses, two-storied, precisely slotted about twenty feet apart with sagging wood front porches, tall sooty windows and identical red brick chimneys. The street pavement was cracked and full of chuckholes. The headlights of the car caught specifics: there an abandoned tricycle pushed against the curb, a ragged hedge of dead bushes, an overturned trash can halfway out into the street, and there a black couple in heavy coats sitting on a concrete stoop. The two black faces looked up and stared blankly at them as they passed.

"Damn niggers," cursed Rich from the backseat. "Taking over the world."

"Don't," Mary Lisa protested gently. "They're good neighbors, they really are." Zoe glanced over at her and at that moment Mary Lisa gave her an ingratiating smile. "Near the end of the block," Mary Lisa announced. "Here we are. Just pull in anyplace you can near the curb."

There was an empty slot directly in front of the house. Zoe pulled forward and angled the car in.

Mary Lisa was apologizing. "It's not much, I know," she commented, leaning close across the seat. "Probably nothing compared to what you're used to. But I'm so glad that you've come. I really am. And I know you're going to have a marvelous time. So come on. Let's go." She reached for Zoe's arm and missed.

At that moment, Zoe pulled away. The uncertainty and feeling of aversion for the new experience which was coming was awful. But in the next minute she found herself moving across a cold, dead, weed-infested yard, going deeper every minute into a foreign country. One of the windows of the house was open, and from it came the continuous sound of a strong voice, someone reading aloud or making a speech. The voice was sometimes interrupted by a chorus of ringing laughter.

"Bubs is here," Mary Lisa giggled. "And everyone else for that matter. They know to go ahead and start without me. We're all old friends," she concluded with pride. "Very old friends."

Suddenly unable to rise to the occasion, Zoe turned around and would have gone back to the car except that the two men following close behind her, carrying their metal lunch boxes, blocked her escape. Dempsey stamped his foot at her as though to add to her alarm. Rich giggled, "She don't look like she wants to come to our party."

Again Mary Lisa sprang to her defense. "Oh, for heaven's sake, leave her alone, you two." To Zoe she added, "Pay no attention to them."

Now Zoe found herself moving again, being guided by an insistent hand steadily toward the sagging front steps.

Somewhere in some direction, there was Newton. There were streets there, and a house, empty but safe. She tried to remember precisely where she had left the car. Was it her imagination or were the two men closing in behind her? Now she heard music, a stereo or radio, the wild insane beat of punk rock. There were six wooden steps, a row of empty milk bottles to one side, a bicycle of ancient vintage propped up against a wall and, nearby, a large window through which she could see people, many people, a constant flow and ebb of movement, laughter, voices. Inside her head, a woman was screaming.

Mary Lisa was talking continuously, pointing out the dead honeysuckle and the bed of marigold seeds that had never come up. One foot was moving before the other. Before Zoe now was the open cavity of the front door. She took a final look over her shoulder in the direction of her car, then stepped inside the house.

Inside, there was a small dim entry hall which led into a large, high-ceilinged living room. This was the room filled with people. As they caught their first glimpse of Mary Lisa, their attention shifted, rose, grew into a din of greetings. Faces and bodies swirled around them as they were dragged into the center of the room, all hands reaching out, a few women embracing Mary Lisa in obvious affection, all eyes seeming to gleam more brightly in her presence.

Suddenly Mary Lisa clapped her hands to signal that she wanted their attention. The tag ends of laughter and voices faded as all heads, all eyes, turned toward the two women, Zoe and Mary Lisa, standing in the middle of the room.

Zoe had the sensation that her face was windburned. She was unable to distinguish specific features about her. It seemed strange to her that the conversations which had been flourishing before she had appeared should have been broken off so suddenly.

Now she felt Mary Lisa's arm pressing tightly around her shoulders, heard her announcing, "Listen, everyone. I want you to meet an old and very dear friend of mine from Whitney, New Hampshire. Her name is Zoe—" She stopped and leaned close for help.

"Manning," Zoe whispered, keeping her head and eyes down, feeling as if someone had cut her throat with one stroke.

"Manning!" Mary Lisa parroted at the top of her voice. She went on. "Now I want you all to be nice to her, you hear?" A peal of male laughter came from the kitchen. "Because she's my friend and she's feeling very lonely tonight." She added brightly, "She's smart. She was the smartest one in the whole class at Whitney High." In silence at last, Mary Lisa took Zoe's hand and stood for some time, clearly unable to decide what to say further.

A voice, scarcely audible, whispered behind them, "Is she the one?"

Someone replied, equally low, "Ask Bubs."

A bent old woman in a flowing red robe bowed low to Zoe and without waiting for an introduction walked off into the kitchen, where laughter still could be heard. The others began drifting away, some looking closely at her, others walking past her. Rich leaned against a far wall. Zoe noticed that the same mistrustfulness, the same bitter, almost ironical smile, lingered on his face. A middle-aged man, dapper in a gray suit, nodded at her. A young girl with long silken blond hair smiled and said, "Hang in there, honey."

Others were moving past her now, conversations were being rekindled. Someone shouted, "You'd better tell Bubs." A young man in faded blue jeans came toward her, carrying a drink in his hand. "Who did she say you were?" he asked and extended the drink to her.

She took it and gave her name again because she had no choice and because it seemed the thing to do.

"Married?" the young boy asked.

She nodded and he walked away, without comment. At that moment she discovered that Mary Lisa too had disappeared. The room seemed to be emptying, the party drifting off into other parts of the house. She moved mechanically to a near wall for refuge. The drink was strong, orange juice and vodka and something else, a bitterness that she could not identify. Safe for the moment against the wall, she looked about at the surroundings. The room was furnished neatly with some effort at style. It contained two large dark brown sofas and a round coffee table, a gold clock under a glass case, a narrow oblong mirror on the far wall and a small old-fashioned chandelier hanging by a bronze chain from the ceiling with low-wattage bulbs which seemed to cast shadows over everything. There was a mixed assortment of other furniture of all sorts. It was a nondescript room.

Zoe noticed books lying on the coffee table, their titles indistinguishable in the dim light. On the walls there were a few reproductions, romantic landscapes in tarnished gold frames. One full-length portrait attracted her attention. It was the portrait of a man, middle-aged, wearing a long black priest's robe, European-looking somehow, with a crucifix around his neck. He had a very trim black beard and long black hair, a strong face with suspicious, secretive and melancholy eyes.

Rich was beside her, his arm about her waist. "That's Bubs," he grinned, bobbing his head toward the portrait. "You'll meet him soon enough."

Suddenly Mary Lisa reappeared. She had changed clothes and was wearing a flowing lavender gown, belted at the waist with a gold cord, the fabric sheer enough to permit visibility of the body beneath.

Rich whistled.

Mary Lisa curtsied prettily. "You be nice to her, you hear?" she smiled, pointing at Zoe. "Did I tell you that she and me went to school together? She's smarter than all the rest of us put together."

Rich nodded blankly, still concentrating on the bare body beneath the sheer lavender gown. Slowly he moved forward, one hand reached out.

Mary Lisa moved back, scolding. "Oh, for heaven's sake, Rich, you act like you're fourteen years old." In the next minute she swirled away, locking arms with a passing couple dressed identically in leopard jump suits.

Zoe watched her, fascinated. The only image that came to mind was that of a slightly demented queen holding court. In the next minute she looked back at the portrait, to the mock dignity of the man posing within the gold frame. A large mother-of-pearl shell of white fleecy clouds rested directly over his head in the middle of what otherwise resembled a night sky. A curious light came from the bottom of the picture. The face itself seemed too remote, as though it had just undergone some intense emotional disturbance and had been asked to pose for the portrait immediately thereafter.

Rich was beside her again, asking coolly, "Do you want a joint or do you prefer to snort?"

Zoe shook her head and took a sip of the bitter drink in her hand to indicate that one canceled the need for the other. In addition she murmured, "I can't stay. I really must be—" and to demonstrate what it was she must do, she took a step backward and collided with a large man with a ruddy face wearing a baker's apron and chef's cap. He grinned at her, then engulfed her, putting his arms around her and drawing her close. "You just got here," he exclaimed. "No one leaves Mary Lisa's party before dawn."

She pulled free, more exasperated than alarmed. She

constantly reminded herself to deal with any and all events with the least amount of disturbance, to read nothing into anything, to maintain, despite her inward agony, a semblance of balance.

Rich had lit a joint now and was waving it at her. "Ever doped before?" he asked, almost kindly. Then he grew very instructional. "Just drag deep and hold it." He forced it at her, still urging, "Go on."

She took the cigarette between her fingers and held it for a moment. She wasn't frightened. The people seemed harmless, very much at ease with each other, a curious mix of old and young, a few in business suits, others in jeans, still others in robes and costumes as though they had stepped out of one role to play another. Laughter penetrated the air on all sides, nothing of weighty or suspicious consideration going on, merely friendly and good-humored intercourse, just a Friday-night bash for the restoration and salvation of their souls.

Rich scolded her. "You're wasting it, for God's sake. Go ahead and smoke."

Unable to think of one good reason why she should not, and pleased with the imagined effect that such an act would have on the grim, self-righteous little group gathering shortly at the Malibu beach house, she put the joint to her lips and breathed deeply. A gush of hot, sweetish smoke filled her lungs. She bent over in a paroxysm of coughing.

Rich giggled. "Not so fast."

As she recovered, Zoe lifted her eyes, water-filled now, to the portrait hanging on the wall opposite where she was standing. The unfathomable eyes gazed down on her. Insufferably insolent and challenging was the effect of the black light around the head, admirably done by the painter, the black hair and smooth white hand with one finger lifted displaying an enormous ruby ring.

A little group had gathered around her now, all offering

their advice concerning the joint which she still held in her hand.

"Drink something," someone said. "Helps to cool it off."

Another invited her to "Try it again, honey. It takes some getting used to."

The large man in the chef's cap demonstrated for her with an imaginary joint. "See?" he beamed, exhaling slowly nonexistent smoke.

The old woman with thin gray hair, shriveled and lost inside the red robe, stepped into the center of the group and took the joint from her fingers and gestured for the others to move back. "See, sweetie?" she grinned. "Do it slow. Do everything slow and you'll live longer." She placed the joint between toothless gums and inhaled deeply. The old woman stood so close that the little red circle of ash was merely inches from Zoe's face. As Zoe closed her eyes, the old woman leaned still closer. She whispered, "Never mind those who have gone away," she hissed. "You're here and they're there, and never the twain shall meet."

When the smoke had cleared, the old woman was nowhere in sight. The others still stood about Zoe, their eyes shining particularly brightly, their various faces revealing a confident and happy frame of mind.

"Try it again," someone urged. And again she was the center of attention, all eyes fastened upon her. She did as she was told, certain that a refusal on her part would somehow diminish her value in their eyes. The smoke went down easier this time. She held it in her lungs as she had been instructed to do, then slowly exhaled.

Her accomplishment was greeted by a round of applause. Even the eyes in the gold frame seemed to beam at her with a continual radiance of approval. Rich kissed her lightly on the cheek and the aura of acceptance was an elixir almost as potent as the joint in her hand.

Briefly Zoe tested her reflexes. She was still in control and there even seemed to be a mild cessation of anxiety, of thought for the house in Newton and the three who had flown off into the night. Her throat burned, and in order to soothe it she took a long swallow from the drink in her hand.

Then Mary Lisa was at her side again, a stern expression on her face. "You should leave her alone," she scolded the others mildly. "All of you, I'm ashamed. You really should just leave her alone."

They listened attentively to her, but they seemed not so much interested in the meaning of her words as in her attitude. Slowly they drifted off, a few looking back longingly at Zoe as though she was a new playmate with whom they had been forbidden contact.

Even Zoe considered protesting, but by the time the thought processes of protest had fully organized themselves in her brain, Mary Lisa had her by the arm steering her toward the staircase. Then, to apologize for the scolding, Mary Lisa called back lightly over her shoulder, "Pizza's on the way."

A few in the group heard and nodded and still looked longingly toward Zoe. "Don't keep her too long," someone called out. "Give us a chance at her."

"It's not fair," another added. Then they disintegrated into smaller groups. Conversations were resumed. Someone laughed.

Mary Lisa guided Zoe up the stairs. She was moving past wallpaper that was vivid; huge, orange-colored water lilies floated disembodied without stems in a sea of bilious green. In one hand, Zoe still carried the joint, almost burned out now, and in the other hand, the half-filled glass. The upstairs hall ahead was dimly lit. The air against her face seemed cooler. She heard, behind closed doors, voices.

All the way up the stairs, Mary Lisa seemed extremely protective. "I'm sorry I left you," she murmured, leaning so close that Zoe could feel the unencumbered movement of a breast against her arm. "But I had to order the pizza and I thought maybe that you might have to do something as well." She giggled. "I don't mean order pizza. I mean pee."

With fresh force, Zoe felt conscious of herself from the springy motion of her legs to the movement of her lungs as she breathed. She glanced sideways at Mary Lisa and decided that the woman looked rather like a blond wolf with her black brows and flared nostrils and big red hungry mouth.

They reached the top landing now, slightly breathless. Zoe giggled, distressed to discover that she sounded like Mary Lisa. "As a matter of fact, I do have to go to the bathroom," she said, still trying to catch her breath.

Mary Lisa pressed her arm tightly and guided her down a corridor which seemed to be listing to the left. In one spot the water lilies were peeling off the wall, falling down in ragged strips. Zoe noticed two doors on one side, three on the other, all closed, all with light coming through the cracks.

"Here we are," Mary Lisa said in front of the last door at the end of the hall. She turned the knob and started in.

A man's voice, deep, angry-sounding, called out, "What the hell?"

Quickly Mary Lisa slammed the door shut, still giggling. "Sorry," she called back. "We'll wait." An exaggerated expression of mock embarrassment covered her face.

Zoe leaned back against the peeling wallpaper. The drink was there in her hand so she finished, making a wry face at the bitterness in the bottom of the glass. The joint was burning close to her fingers. As she glanced about for an ashtray, Mary Lisa indicated the floor. She looked saddened somehow. She whispered, "Do be careful. Please. Sometimes it's dangerous to mix those things."

Zoe looked at her with a questioning expression. This was the whole point, wasn't it?

Mary Lisa still watched her with what appeared to be deep concern.

What was she supposed to have done? Refuse the drink? Refuse the good-hearted instructions from all the experts downstairs? In the waiting silence, she took a quick inventory of herself. She felt relaxed. All the feelings she had passed through fell into three separate trains of thoughts. One was the absence of her husband and family, of her minor disintegration upon their departure. Another series of thoughts related to the safe dark house in Newton. But a third series of ideas turned upon the question of where she was now, and where she would be tomorrow. After that, nothing took shape for her.

In the mental vacuum, she glanced about. The hall was dark, lit dimly only by bare bulbs hanging at either end of the corridor. In the semidarkness, she felt relatively safe. But the silence seemed to be stretching on too long. The talking machine beside her was strangely quiet, still passing a judgment of some sort, watching her carefully, vigilant for the first sign of weakness or incapacity. Shrinking from the look, Zoe walked rapidly a few steps away. She pretended to examine a large orange water lily. From downstairs she heard the sound of laughter. The silence in the hall weighed so agonizingly upon her that she felt compelled to break it. "Who are all those people down there?" she asked.

Mary Lisa answered slowly as though she had been jarred out of deeper thought. "Most of them are from the Merrywood Music Tent out on Cape Cod?" And she took the statement up and left it there like a question. She added, her eyes glowing with pride, "There's a lot of talent down there.

We're the ones who back up the big stars and make them look good." She said this mechanically, as if she had heard it said time and time again.

From inside the bathroom came the sound of a toilet being flushed. Suddenly Mary Lisa reached out and grabbed the empty glass in Zoe's hand. "Look," she said, eagerly, "I'll go on down and get rid of this for you, see how the others are getting along. When you're finished, come on down. Pizza's coming." She added, as an extra inducement, "Pizza Supreme. With everything on it."

She moved rapidly away, incredible and dauntless energy coming from somewhere. One minute she was there in the semidarkened hallway, the next minute she was gone.

Zoe stood at attention before the still-closed bathroom door. She heard the toilet being flushed again. Her bladder was beginning to cause her mild discomfort.

Behind the door on her left, she heard voices. She glanced up at the high shadowy ceiling. For some reason it was very difficult to remember why she had come and what she was doing here. In a way it didn't matter. She still felt like an imposter, the same feelings she had had when she had sat in on classes illegally. Remembering those years and the years before in Whitney where the imposter feelings had first started, her head sank and she stood silent. If things got out of hand, she could always leave. Her car was down in front of the house. Although she was on unfamiliar territory she could retrace her path back to the airport, then find her way home from there.

Out of habit she reached up to her shoulder to adjust her purse strap. But there was no purse. In the car, of course. She had left it in the car. As soon as she finished here, she'd leave. Clay would be in a rage if he knew. The boys mustn't ever know that she'd— She was thinking so quickly that she felt herself stammering, unable to articulate the words that were forming in her head.

The voices behind the closed door in the opposite bedroom seemed to have grown silent. She thought she heard a soft moan. Quickly she turned her attention back to the still-closed bathroom door. What was taking him so long? She stepped up to the door and knocked softly. "Are you all right?" she inquired, keeping her voice low.

No answer.

Downstairs she heard the high splintered laughter of the party. Predominant among all voices was Mary Lisa's, shouting, calling out certain names, warm and hospitable.

Perplexed, discomfort increasing, Zoe stared at the closed bathroom door. Should she knock again, or try to open it? Maybe someone was ill. She heard water running now and stood absolutely motionless. Oh, God, hurry. She leaned close to the door. "Listen, if you need help, I'll—"

Still she waited. Beneath the crack in the door, she saw a shadow, very black, moving back and forth. Someone was walking heavily with uneven steps. The entire darkness of the hall was alive and following her. The silence had become so great that the floor resounded each time she shifted her feet, slight, indecisive movements beginning to fill with dread. She kept her head raised. The door was still closed.

A sound of deep breathing, the same as that of sleep began to penetrate her hearing through the closed door, as though on the other side someone were breathing through his nose, his jaws clenched.

Then suddenly the door swung open. The man in the portrait appeared before her, long dark hair, deranged face, shaggy beard. He held a machete in his hand, upraised. His shirt sleeves had been pushed back and his arms and hands appeared to be covered with blood. His eyes contorted, bulged. He lifted the bloody blade high into the air and lunged forward.

Zoe screamed and fell backward. The air from the swiftly moving blade stung into her face, swirled around her body. She tried to move out from beneath the swinging blade. But someone had her by the throat now and she was falling backward. In the last instant she caught a glimpse of the shadow play on the wall. A monster was moving over her, pushing her grotesquely, silently to the floor, the bloody wetness from his hands now slime on her throat. It was impossible to struggle. The blade was arched across her neck, pressing downward. Light was fading, faded. She was dying or dead.

She lost consciousness, certain that she would never have to see Newton again . . .

———◆———

When she regained consciousness the light changed before her closed eyes, but changed so slowly that she did not at first notice any difference. In her imagination, she saw the man's distorted face, machete upraised. She looked dispassionately at the jumble of unsorted pictures that presented themselves to her at random: a tall man with two little boys under each arm flying through the air, a long gunmetal-gray corridor with no exits, a smiling, slightly pitiful doormat with a female face, bare breast and a blond wig, two disembodied airplane wheels, an enormous coffin in the shape of a house, and finally a grinning, shaggy man, death's face.

She groaned. Her hands moved down her sides. The mattress on which she was lying was concave and felt as if it were trying to swallow her. Someone was torturing her nose with ammonia. She tried to turn away, but the foul odor merely followed after her. There was still the silent inadequate creature that sat at the center of things in Newton, but even she seemed to have lost the knack of discrimination. Now and then the gate on the lower part of her brain would open against the bright light and the smell of ammonia, and words would try to come out. But each statement was so separated by the glassy images that continually passed before her mind that she did not know which was relevant to which.

A female voice, tragic and caring, asked urgently, "Are you all right, Zoe? Zoe? Oh, I'm so sorry."

The voice was close, hovering, heavily perfumed and perennially apologetic.

Zoe tried to open her eyes. The lids lifted for an instant. She saw a tightly packed semicircle of crowding curious faces; there, the old woman in red flowing robes, and there, Rich's flat, ruddy freckled forehead and slack jaw, and there the dark swarthy countenance of the man named Dempsey, and there, the man in the chef's cap, and there— She gave up. It seemed futile, a struggle with shadows. Someone insisted upon shoving the hideous odor beneath her nose. She pushed it away and tried to sit up so that the mattress wouldn't devour her.

A female voice greeted her expansively. "Zoe! Thank God. I'm so sorry. I really am."

The words were simply spoken, simply received. Mary Lisa was sorry. Zoe was now able to determine that the foul odor was coming from the perfumed hand. She felt obliging for being alive. But the odor was strangling her.

Again she tried to push the hand away and caught a glimpse of red claws holding a silver vial. She felt embarrassed and ashamed. Lying back down, she listened to the black floodwater that was covering her brain. It seemed important somehow that she pick up the pieces of her carefully guarded personality and at least make an attempt to put them back together again. But it was difficult with the chorus that was going on about her.

"You should have warned her," someone scolded.

"She should have known," someone else countered.

"He's harmless," muttered a third voice defensively.

"Not if you don't know him."

"What must she think of us?"

"It would really be so much simpler and better if she hadn't come."

"Open the window. Air helps."

"Where did you say she belonged?"

At last Zoe opened her eyes. This time they stayed open.

Mary Lisa was there, perched on the side of the bed, her face wrinkled with concern. Zoe experienced the sensations of a person just awakening from a drugged sleep. After a fearful agony and a sense of something huge being forced upon her, she felt all at once that the threat had been removed, that she could awaken and live and think again and take an interest in other things besides the threat. Directly overhead, she saw cracks in the high ceiling, brown water spots, peeling plaster and a bare bulb hanging from a long frayed cord.

It seemed an idiotic question, but she asked it anyway. "What happened?" she murmured, her tongue feeling immense in her mouth.

Mary Lisa leaned close. "It was just Bubs," she explained. "I should have warned you. He thought it was me outside the door. He's always playing tricks." She giggled. "Most of us are used to them. But you, poor thing—" Her voice drifted off into head-shaking, eye-squinting sympathy.

Zoe closed her eyes the better to assimilate this wealth of new and useless information. The only thing that interested her now was how she could extricate herself from this zoo into which she had inadvertently wandered.

With her eyes still closed, she heard Mary Lisa say, "He's right here. He wants to apologize."

She heard a shuffling then, the semicircle of faces adjusting themselves to accommodate a new body. With her eyes still closed, she heard Mary Lisa gently scolding someone, the frail admonitions of a weak-willed person confronting a stronger will.

"Bubs, you ought to be ashamed," she whispered. "You might have scared her to death."

It seemed to Zoe beyond doubt that she had to get out of here as soon as possible. With that goal in mind, she moved her head on the pillow and opened her eyes again.

The man was standing there beside her, looking down, the same intensity in his eyes, the same blood-red color smeared over his arms, the same hand that had held the machete over her. Suddenly she remembered everything, and in spite of her strongest efforts at control, she felt herself becoming frightened all over again.

Mary Lisa rushed in, continually soothing, continually repeating, "It's all right, it's all right, don't be afraid. He's harmless, Zoe, please. He is an actor." She giggled. "Only the best in the world, but then I don't have to tell you that." She giggled again. "He has a bad habit sometimes of just not telling you when the show is starting."

Zoe turned slowly on the pillow. She felt awkward and ashamed. What heightened this feeling was the fact that the entire room seemed suddenly to have gone silent.

She looked up, then looked away, then glanced quickly back. Upon closer examination she discovered that the man now standing beside the bed bore little resemblance to the one who had lunged at her in the hall. She stared searchingly at him. The man, if it was the same man, had changed clothes. There was nothing very notable or terrifying about him except a slight contrast between the holiday gaiety of his apparel and the remorseful gravity on his face.

He was now wearing a bright pink linen jacket, over-sized, a white waistcoat and a pale lemon yellow straw hat with a pink rose stuck in its brim. His lean, slightly livid face was dark by contrast, and the beard which had appeared shaggy and unkempt in the semidarkness of the hall now looked trimmed, Spanish-looking perhaps, or Elizabethan. He was smoking a cigarette with the seriousness of an idler. There was nothing about him to indicate that the white waist-coat covered a blood-stained shirt, which Zoe could see now, the cuffs of which protruded out from under the bright pink jacket. The dark hair had been pulled back and apparently tied at the nape of his neck. He had a great smooth brow, his lower lip drooped a little, his mouth looked bored and sulky. But the eyes were the same, impressive, ironical eyes almost totally lost in shadow. They appeared now and then to be winking. He continued to stare down on her as though he were sending some incomprehensible telegraphic message. Now his strange face seemed to be filled with a gentle melancholy.

Mary Lisa prompted him softly, "Go ahead, Bubs. She's waiting."

The silence became so great that it filled Zoe with a sense of mortification. The entire room crowded with faces seemed to be alive and breathing, yet frozen, waiting for the sound of his voice.

Finally he stepped forward and approached Zoe with an affable smile. He took her hand and, holding it for some time in his, looked into her face as if recognizing familiar features. He bowed graciously. "Madam," he said in a deep, polished, slightly artificial voice. "I'm sorry I frightened you. I thought you were the whore here, who is beyond fright." He inclined his head toward Mary Lisa, who smiled prettily back at him as if he had paid her a priceless compliment.

Zoe listened with a certain skepticism. At the moment he had bowed to her, he had briefly removed the straw hat and she had caught a glimpse of graying, filthy, matted hair. The way light fell upon his face, it appeared the bone was showing in places.

Without warning, his hands began to tremble. Within the instant his eyes had filled with tears. He now glanced at Zoe inquiringly. "Do you believe with conviction that I would harm you in any way?" He stared reproachfully at the others standing about him, but did not say another word.

Now he paced moodily up and down beside the bed, trying to regain control of his emotions. The tears disappeared as instantly as they had formed. He seemed impatient and slightly put out with the silent gathering.

"Christ!" he muttered under his breath. "I've apologized. Do we have to go into a third act?"

The others stirred themselves into sluggish action, shuffling, coughing, a few whispered exchanges. It was as though, having been reminded of boredom, they became bored.

Zoe too stirred herself out of a trance. She sat up, made an attempt to smooth the dark blue jacket, which had become hopelessly twisted. She felt gingerly of her neck; it was sticky, smeared, slightly sore. It had been an incredible incident, but now she was ready to put it out of her head.

Mary Lisa was still hovering, still concerned. "Are you sure you're all right?" she asked.

The man named Bubs answered from the foot of the bed. "She's fine," he bellowed, his anger increasing with every word. "She's probably never felt more alive than at the moment of her imagined death." Abruptly he crossed to the door and flung it open. "Now, out! All of you!" Then he was shooing them out of the room, using his straw hat to hurry them along. He stopped long enough to put his arm around the old woman in the red robe. His face seemed alive with growing enjoyment. He whispered, "You promised to give us a show tonight. Go on down and warm up your witch's ass, and we'll be there shortly."

The old woman grinned and stammered some answer. But no one was listening. They all left the room now, chattering softly among themselves, a few looking back almost solemnly at Zoe, scanning her from head to foot.

Zoe raised herself to the edge of the bed. Mary Lisa was still with her, assisting, patting, soothing. "I'm really sorry," she sighed. "I know you must have been terrified. I had no idea—"

From the door, Bubs ordered, "Stop simpering!" His face, in shadow, appeared distorted.

Zoe longed to join the others on their way downstairs, and to that end she murmured "I'm fine" and tried to stand up. But she still was shaky, still trying to rid herself of the effects of incredible fear. The palms of her hands felt wet. Opening them, she noticed they were blood-red. She whispered, "What in the—" The faintness returned. Weakened anew, she sat back down on the side of the bed.

Now the man was ordering Mary Lisa out of the room along with everyone else. Zoe tried to protest. The realization that she would be alone with him was one more unforeseen torture. But he would not permit her to speak. He glared at her, and with extraordinary courtesy he held the door for Mary Lisa and indicated that she was to pass through it immediately and without question.

By way of explanation, he said simply, "I caused the damage. Now let me repair it. Go on down. We'll follow when we're ready."

Mary Lisa offered one weak and useless protest. "But she's—"

"Mine!" he replied, not smiling. "Ancient law of Bedlam and Chaos states plainly that the woman you almost kill is yours. I must put her back together again. It will only take a few minutes. Now leave us."

Again Mary Lisa flushed terribly. "Bubs, I'm warning you—"

"Of what?" he asked broadly. "Don't worry. She won't hurt me."

Mary Lisa took a final and regretful look backward and then she was gone.

Zoe sat on the edge of the bed, petrified. "Please," she begged softly, "I'm really quite all right now. I must be going."

He faced her from the closed door, leaned against it, shaking his head in a mechanical way, the tiny artificial rose in the brim of his straw hat bobbing crazily back and forth. He picked up a hand mirror from a worn, dark brown, slightly lopsided dressing table near the door. Suddenly he was before her, holding the mirror directly in front of her face. "Anyone you know?" he asked.

She tried not to look, had no desire to look, but could not avoid the image that stared back at her. The face was smudged with red; an innocent, almost childlike expression looked out and around the red smudges; a gold clasp hung in a loose strand of mussed, totally undone hair. Just at the moment when she felt she had mastered her confusion and completely recovered from her fear, a new revulsion took place in her, increasing her embarrassment.

He laughed outright at the stricken expression on her face and sat down close beside her on the bed. From his back pocket, he withdrew a clean white handkerchief. Without speaking he indicated that she was to give him her hands for the purpose of cleaning them.

She did so because she suspected that it would be futile

to refuse. He took one hand and began moving the handkerchief back and forth over her palm. She tried to guess his age but couldn't. Up close he appeared younger. There was a mocking look in his eyes. He worked slowly, deliberately, moving the cloth between each finger, almost hypnotic movements, focusing all of his attention on the job at hand.

He said once, "It's just stage makeup. It comes off fast but it leaves a pink tint." It was a cultivated voice, the sort of voice that might belong to an actor.

Downstairs she heard the noise of the party as it gradually revived itself. Help was close by if she needed it. She felt childlike, having her hands cleansed. The need to speak was increasing, something to break the expanding silence. "What did you say your name was?" she asked, trying to assume a casual manner.

"Bubs," he replied and that was all he said for a minute. Then he turned her hands over very slowly, holding both of them now, his long, bony fingers searching. "Your hands belong to you," he went on. "Clearly yours. I've seen hands that did not belong to the person who owned them." He said one thing, but said it as if he meant something quite different by the words. Now he looked about uneasily. He was obviously muddled and had lost the thread of what he was saying at every word. All this, together with his appearance and glittering, almost frenzied eyes, held her attention.

When he reached out for her face, she quickly stood up and took the handkerchief from him. "I can do it," she murmured and went to the larger mirror of the dressing table near the door. A wavy distorted image stared back at her, pink-tinged as he had predicted. Apparently she'd covered her face with her hands, had reached out to protect herself, had touched the red substance on his arms and had transferred it to her face. She looked now like a burn victim.

She leaned in on the image, found a clean corner of the

handkerchief and commenced rubbing her face. Her dark blue jacket looked faded and wavy in the mirror. Her hands still tingled. She stopped rubbing and stood there for a minute, her eyes fixed upon his reflection.

The man appeared ghostlike behind her on the bed. There seemed to be an unspoken accusation of some sort coming from his eyes to her. His face was grave and slightly vexed. He looked at her as though she were a child. "Clean your face," he muttered, "or else let me do it."

Quickly she forced her eyes away from his reflection and rubbed again. Occasionally her eyes shifted across the mirror, bringing him back into focus. Each time their eyes met, she was disconcerted by the intensity of his gaze, the manner in which he scanned her from head to foot. Once she actually stopped short in bewilderment at the hostility in the eyes searching her. He appeared to be pleased by her growing agitation. Again she forced herself to look back to her own reflection and finger-brushed her hair smoothly back and fastened it firmly with the gold clasp. Moderately restored, she glanced across her image. She needed her purse, needed face powder to cover the pink tinge.

"You don't need powder," he said. His voice tapped against the back of her head, a skillful intelligence capable of reading her thoughts. Astonished, she turned and faced him. His face, on the bed, less than three feet from her, seemed brighter.

She felt ashamed of the new weakness, of being tongue-tied and red-faced. Her reserves of everything were perilously diminished. The only answer was escape, and with half-frightened yet curiously blissful indifference to everything but escape, she started toward the door.

"Where now?" he asked dreamily, almost absentmindedly.

She felt bone-tired. Her face burned from repeated rub-
bings. "Home," she said, not looking at him.

"Which is where?"

Suddenly she heard a sharp, shrill scream coming from
downstairs, a woman crying out continuously. Then it
stopped. Zoe's hand froze on the doorknob. In the yellow
dim light of the shabby room, the cry echoed and bounced
off the bare walls.

With considerable effort, she looked back at him, puzzled. He had stretched out full length on the bed, his hand
behind his head, the straw hat lying to one side. Now he
lifted his head to listen. He withdrew one hand and made a
hurried sign of the cross on his chest. "The witch is at work,"
he said calmly, matter-of-factly. "I wouldn't go down there
now if I were you."

At that moment the scream came again, a piercing, penetrating shriek, someone suffering unspeakable agony.

Zoe held fast to the doorknob, uncertain whether she
should keep it closed as protection against the dangers without or fling it open and escape from the dangers within. She
looked over her shoulder at him. "What are they doing?" she
asked uneasily.

He twisted sideways on the bed and propped himself up
on one elbow. He was so tall that he filled the bed from top
to bottom. He rubbed his eyes, then wedged his left hand
between his legs. "I told you. It's the witch," he said. "She
does it every Friday night."

"Does what?" Zoe asked.

He didn't answer. The screams started again. The vio-
lence of the noise seemed to be breaking down the door.
They came again and again and between the screams was a
grotesque silence as if everyone else in that large party downstairs had either gone home or else was content to merely
watch what was causing the agony.

Still standing by the door, Zoe felt herself on the brink of incoherency. Somewhere beyond this hideous house and these people was the safe highway that would take her home. All of her considerable defenses remained obstinately silent. The bridge of her nose burned. Gently she pressed her forehead against the closed door as if to pass the most important part of her being through the door and leave only a husk to endure the eyes of the man on the bed and the hideous screams coming from downstairs. She raised a hand to test the wood. Why had she come here? What in the name of God had possessed—

Suddenly with a convulsive movement he sprang to his feet. He was beside her, his hands on her shoulders, guiding her forcibly away from the door. "It'll be over shortly," he soothed. "Then you can go home."

Her left hand tried to push him away. There was a new kind of weakness moving over her. It started on her shoulders where he had touched her and was creeping down her back between the layers of clothing. She found herself straining to listen, and as though to oblige her, the screams downstairs increased, a series of high-pitched shrieks, more animal than human, a macabre crescendo climbing, splintering her eardrums. Actual vibrations from the screams seemed to reverberate through the room.

She listened with a combination of amazement and horror. Her head and shoulders were shaking. She backed away from the man, who stood in the center of the room closely watching her. Now and then a shudder rose from the pit of her stomach. She folded her arms about her body for protection.

He continued to stare at her and once reached out for her. But she moved quickly to one side until she was wedged into the corner near the door where the walls joined. She pushed into this crevice until she had no more strength to push farther. She was experiencing a degree of terror that she had never felt before.

Slowly he extended a hand to her, softly pleading, "Zoe, there's no need," he begged. "What's happening is harmless." When she did not respond, he began walking aimlessly about the room, glancing back at her now and then. There seemed to be concern on his face and to a certain degree remorse.

But Zoe was in no state to trust anyone. All feelings blended into the one predominant sensation of fear. She pushed farther back into the corner away from all threats, visible and invisible. She was vaguely aware that the screams were subsiding. But the silence that followed was almost as frightening. She was aware of her foolish position in the corner and aware that in order to escape she would ultimately have to leave her sanctuary of intersecting walls. But for the moment it seemed a safe place.

The man continued to stand alone in the center of the room. He looked at her almost mournfully. Abruptly he went to the closet door and flung it open. At the same time he jerked off the colorful jacket and white waist coat, stripped himself down to the play-blood-soiled shirt.

Zoe watched carefully from her corner, received impressions, tried to sort them out. He appeared to be changing clothes. Now the soiled shirt dropped to the floor. In its place he slipped a white T-shirt over his head. Quickly he loosened the long dark hair that had been pulled back. He reached again into the closet and withdrew a worn patched blue denim jacket.

The eyes from the corner watched closely. She heard screams again, but was unable to determine whether they were coming from inside her head or from downstairs. In her world, women did not scream like that.

Then the man who had tried to kill her was standing

over her, extending his hand to her. "Come on," he ordered. "Let's go."

When she refused to obey, he leaned close. He spoke patiently, emphasizing each word. "Ancient Law of Bedlam and Chaos says it's time to go," he smiled. "The same law says they're going ape-shit down there and that we'd better split. For your sake."

The voice eased past her, seemed to be speaking by an inspiration of kindness. The walls felt as though they were trying to eject her. Now the bearded man was tenderly drawing her out of her corner. "Come on, lady," he soothed. "I'll take you home."

With the force of movement, her head cleared a little. She knew again where she was. It was very difficult, however, to explain to herself in orderly fashion how she had allowed herself to fall into such company, how apparently for no good reason her fate was being decided in a worn, two-storied frame house in Marblehead by a bearded man in faded blue denim. There seemed to be questions in her head that required immediate answers, but not only was it impossible to answer them, however much she struggled Zoe could not even see the questions clearly. In her opinion, all that had happened was unpardonable, a sort of fantastic vision, at once stupid and absurd. She simply wanted the ordeal brought to an end and if it meant going with the bearded man, then she would do it.

She perceived now that the man seemed to be in a hurry. In an effort to oblige him, she straightened her shoulders, drew a deep breath and started toward the door, where he stood waiting for her.

Suddenly the dim bulb overhead blinked off, then on, then hovered for a moment between light and dark, hissing, then went out completely and stayed out. The black was an endless space before her. She gasped, looked blindly about for the remote face of the man in the room with her. Quickly she fell back again into her corner, which now felt massive and angled as if in the dark the house was expanding. She moaned softly, "Please—"

His voice was there, hovering close. "It's all right," he soothed. "Just these old houses. We can find our way in the dark."

She felt his hand covering hers. It felt chalky. His voice seemed to have no connection with the rest of his body. He seemed to be doing his best to urge her out of her fear. Yet the remembered image of him standing over her, machete upraised, still consumed her.

Zoe listened to everything he was saying with an astonishment that approached stupefaction. But she followed his directions because she had no choice, because the end to be desired was rescue, the ultimate necessity was survival.

He guided her slowly out of the door and into the equally dark hallway. Apparently the lights had gone out all over the house. She stumbled after him, staring blankly around her, listening to him constantly coaxing, soothing. They seemed to be feeling their way down one side of the wall. Now and then her hand brushed against a strip of rough, loose paper. The fallen water lilies, she assumed. Once he cursed, complained bitterly about a number of things, primary among them Zoe's presence in the house. His forward movement stopped; he jerked at her hand and roughly pulled her forward a few steps. "At least keep up," he muttered.

The mild scolding was familiar and caused remorse. She felt that something terrible was about to happen. She tried to do as she was told. In a way she was convinced now that her survival depended upon this strange man who was leading her down an unfamiliar corridor. But still she did not understand any of it. She wondered why the absence of light had not bothered the people downstairs. She heard no voices raised in protest against the darkness. No call for candles. Nothing. It was as if the house had suddenly emptied.

Then again he was leading her quickly down the corridor. For some reason now, he urged speed. A short distance this side of the staircase, he stopped.

"Listen!" he hissed.

His hand, still covering hers seemed to grow cold. She heard something then, a faint crackling. On the far wall of the staircase she saw a dim red glow. The realization of what she saw burst across her mind. Confirmation came in the form of acrid creeping smoke. Fire!

Instinctively she drew back. But he held her fast, cursing again, no meaning to what he was saying, just a string of obscenities. Against her wishes and certainly against her better judgment, she allowed him to drag her to the top of the stairs. Together they looked down. The major area of the fire seemed to be the downstairs hall. The path to the front door was completely obscured. The flames were spreading rapidly, slipping out in all directions, something feeding it, coaxing it to spread. There was no one in sight.

He looked curiously at her, then started down the steps directly into the blaze. When she saw that he intended to take her with him into the fire, she drew back.

He whirled around and faced her. "Then what?" he demanded. "There's no way out up here."

The blaze cast distorted shadows over his face. He seemed as frightened as she. Downstairs the fire was spreading. The flames were climbing, heading for the stairs and the worn rubber pads, which did not burn as readily but which sent a pall of gray smoke creeping up the steps.

She shook her head. "We can't," she said desperately. "Look!" She pointed downward to where the flames were already licking at the lower steps. The entire downstairs hallway resembled an open furnace. The smoke and heat began to force them back.

He seemed to listen to her, to study the fire. At least he was capable of listening to reason. There was no way they could make it safely through the inferno below.

Suddenly he stepped back up to the top of the landing and darted past her, running down the corridor in the direction from which they had just come.

It wasn't possible. That thought kept going through her mind. Nothing had happened to her. She was not trapped in an old house miles from home in the midst of fire. This was merely a nightmare of the worst sort. The heat was growing more intense. A burst of sparks landed three steps beneath her.

Terrified, she called after him, "Wait—"

But there was no reply. Not to be trapped here, that was the important thing. No one would know to identify her as Zoe Manning. She had no reason for being here. The fire in Marblehead in which "several unidentified people perished" would simply seal her useless unidentifiable existence.

She called out for help and received no reply, although she thought she heard doors opening and closing down the hall. The heat and smoke continued to beat her back against the wall. The flames were traveling fast.

Then he was calling to her from the opposite end of the hall. His voice was almost lost in the crackling, hissing fire. She heard him shouting, "This way. Come on—"

The smoke was enveloping her. She closed her eyes against the stinging fumes that filled her nostrils and tried to hold her breath. How quick, she thought. How easy it would be. The worst, whatever it was, could be over in a matter of minutes. It occurred to her that if she died here tonight, she would be entirely forgiven. For everything.

His voice came again, closer through the fog of smoke. "This way," he shouted. "Hurry!"

The thought of being rescued gave her strength to endure the suffocating fumes. She was certain she heard footsteps close by. They came near to her, then died away. Someone else must have taken refuge upstairs. This impression persisted for some moments, the feeling that she was not alone, that in addition to the urgent male voice at the end of the corridor, there were others moving past her. Yet every time she opened her eyes, the gray billowing smoke blinded her.

She cried out for help. But they seemed determined to separate themselves from her, to leave her alone, to save only themselves. The smoke felt like an actual substance now, like a thing of weight pressing against her. She could not hold her breath forever. She saw in her mind an image of herself horribly burned.

As she went down on her hands and knees, her husband's face appeared before her. Then there was the voice again, male, persistent, closer. "This way. Crawl toward me."

She pulled herself forward a few more feet until her lungs insisted on air. Her chest felt on the verge of exploding. Her right arm reached out in front of her. Fingers closed about her hand. Pulled.

The fire was taking over the hallway behind her. Through seared eyes she saw actual tongues of flame. As the unknown force was dragging her down the corridor, she thought of the death of saints at the stake, remembered reading how the eyelids burned first, forcing the victim to watch his own incineration, to hear the splattering of moisture in the flames which was the victim's own blood.

The thoughts were so horrible that she was up again on her hands and knees, trying to assist the hands that were pulling at her. She began to lift her head, searching for the face of her rescuer, but she saw nothing.

Incredibly, she thought she heard voices, closer now, Mary Lisa giggling, "Isn't she marvelous? She just got carried away. She's an old woman. If it makes her happy—"

And a man's voice, deep, angry, "She's insane."

Mary Lisa again, "Oh, not insane. She started it. She'll stop it. Don't worry, Bubs. You're such a worrier."

Zoe tried to lift her head to see the two in conversation. But she saw nothing. The uproar of the fire was directly behind her. When the smoke cleared for a moment, she opened her mouth and gasped in air. Then a fresh flame exploded behind her; heat seared her leg.

She seemed incapable of separating the crackling flames from the voices, which sounded so close. It was Mary Lisa, she was certain of it, somewhere ahead talking imperturbably. "Where are you taking her?" the voice asked.

A man replied, equally calm. "Where she belongs. You shouldn't have brought her here."

"Do you know the way?"

"Where?"

"To where she belongs?"

"North?"

"Right. Be careful. She's—"

"I know what she is."

Zoe groaned, collapsed. She was in a state in which thought lost its direction and started to circle, like a compass needle at the magnetic pole. Finally it cut loose from its axis and traveled freely in space until it seemed that all thoughts and sensations, even pain and joy itself, were only the spectrum lines of the same ray of light, all disintegrating. Solid clouds of smoke enveloped her. Her legs burned. Lying on the floor, her right hand went crawling. She pulled herself forward a few feet. What life was left was concentrated in the right hand. She lifted her body a few inches and hung there suspended. Ahead by not too many feet, she saw the outline of a window, felt a cool pure night wind. To one side of the window, she saw him lounging casually against the wall, hands in pockets, his long dark hair framing his face, red-colored in the reflection of the fire.

"A window," he smiled. "Are you ready?"

She tried to speak, but her throat and the inside of her mouth was parched. Dimly she saw him reach down for her. Some subtle interior balance was off. At first she thought he was lifting her up. Then she felt as though he were pushing her down.

A voice behind her warned, "Steady."

Then someone else was raising her arms, tying something about her waist. She felt the thing about her waist being pulled tighter.

Suddenly she felt herself being lifted bodily upward. She saw the edge of the window drawing nearer. Before her was a black cool cavity of space. She struck out in panic. In return for her resistance, she felt a blow against the side of her head. Night and the fire spun wildly in her vision. There were sounds that seemed every moment to be on the point of articulation, but instead lapsed into a liquid slapping against the edge of her consciousness. Over all this was one definable note, a singing hiss, and a continuous, unending scream.

When the scream was over, she was falling through pure, black cold air. She felt the earth's force of gravity slowly mounting within her. The thing about her waist cut off all breath. The monster from the portrait had tied it too tightly and had strained her arms while twisting them behind her back. How theatrical, she thought as she fell.

Then everything was gentle again, noncommittal and without offense . . .

———◆———

A sound was forming like a bubble behind her ears. She watched the sound for a timeless interval and decided birds. There were birds somewhere vocalizing, high-pitched trills in varying tonal patterns being passed from tree to tree to the steady refrain of a cricket.

In the beginning there were only the birds. Later a sound of deep breathing, the same as that of sleep, began also to rise in her hearing. She was breathing through her nose, her jaws clenched and sore. She had been grinding her teeth. She was unable to decide if she was alive or dead.

Her eyes began to blink open, then closed. She wanted to realize as quickly as possible how it could be that now she existed and was living, while at some time during the night she had died. She meant to investigate all of this in a matter of minutes. But a bright light, as from morning sun, caught in the corner of her opened eyes. All her senses stirred, the whole darkness of unconsciousness was alive and following her.

Screening the sun was a curtain of hair. She moved her head to one side, determined to communicate with the morning and birdsongs. She was in a bed. Lying on her side, she saw pale blue wallpaper with a deeper blue pattern of curious design, a cross configuration with green ivy intertwining. Whatever had possessed her to pick that pattern? She remembered a mournful female voice from years before, pleading, "Blue is for boys, Zoe. Pink is for girls."

"I don't care. I want blue."

Her eyes widened. She was half awake and couldn't take it all in and began objecting as though a sentence had been passed. Too late. She was fully awake and she left off protesting and saw clearly the white dressing table, the shattered mirror.

There was the female voice again, shrill and angry. "You did that in a fit of temper, didn't you, Zoe? Your father will punish you."

The terror that swept in with the voice and the cracked mirror shocked her into the use of her body. She lifted her head. On the edge of the dressing table stood a dusty line of Barbie dolls; the costume collection, there Cinderella and Scarlett O'Hara and Snow White, a solid row of tiny frozen blue-painted eyes, red circled cheeks. They appeared to be watching her closely.

She looked solemnly at the line of dolls and rubbed her eyes. It seemed in that moment that one of the dolls smiled at her. She struggled to lift her head, then caught her breath at the sudden pain in her neck. The angle of the room curved away from her line of vision. The brain was extraordinarily lively and working at a tremendous rate. She was aware that there was a continual throbbing of ideas of all sorts, always unfinished.

She knew where she was, knew that she was in her childhood room, knew clearly the feel and smell of Whitney, New Hampshire, knew without looking that behind her on the opposite wall was a scarred maple bookcase behind which at age eleven she had hidden a full-length picture of a naked man which she had found in an old magazine down at Red Moon Lake. There was a chest of drawers with a green net sachet of potpourri in the top drawer, a closet door that shrieked when swung shut, a blue-and-red patchwork quilt-covered wastebasket, and a cherrywood desk with uneven legs over which she had Scotch-taped a picture of Mick Jagger.

Her eyes hurt. She closed them, fully expecting the apparition of the room to be gone when she opened them again. But it wasn't. The room and everything in it was constant. She gripped the bedclothes and turned slowly onto her back. She was home. Her thoughts faltered and stopped. She lowered one hand beneath the blanket, turned the wrist, held the palm against the bare flesh of her stomach. Some convulsion erupted in the upper part of her brain. The hand inspected the body with the thoroughness of a child and sent back to the brain a blunt, childlike message. She was naked. Still the hand made indefinable pressures on the body while the mind battled for understanding. In the area of the waist, the hand stopped on a circle of discomfort. Raw scraped flesh, slightly damp. Bleeding? The hand backed away as though there were staring eyes in the fingertips.

Fully awake, her breath came quickly. At an end that was the beginning, she turned her head to the window through which she had watched years of seasons and saw that the sun was shining. She turned on her side. Separate realizations could be resolved into images, but other, more persistent questions could not be answered. There took shape from the darkness of her closed eyes an image of fire.

In a stray strand of hair falling across her face, she still smelled smoke. There had been a house and a party into which she had entered, begging, apologetic, had felt extremely silent among the noise and faces. But mostly there had been a fire.

Her mind kept coming back to the fire. She lay motionless, staring out of the window. She saw that the sun was on the rise. Dawn. In a glimmer of logic, she decided that she had left the party and had driven to Whitney. After all, those had been her plans. She'd rehearsed them often enough with Clay.

The name bore an image and both rolled heavily about in her mind. She sent both the image and the name away and drew the blanket closer about her as though to conceal her unexplained nakedness from the image of Clay.

Then the whole brunt of her logic fell in on her. Why didn't she remember the drive up, those hazardous, traffic-ridden miles which were difficult under the best of circumstances? She looked blankly about the room for an answer. The faded dusty white curtains hung limp at the window. She saw, directly above her bed an enormous, silvery complex spider web. Neglect everywhere, the silent disintegration of a house that had been closed for years.

Her head turned and the eyes tried to follow the ceiling to the closed door. She raised up, trying to see beyond the closed door to the rest of the house; the long corridor with imitation gas lamps on either side, guest room, never used on one side, bathroom where parents had died on the other. This image caused a jolt too sharp to deal with. She lay still, then moved steadily in her mind down the hall past her parents' room to the steep narrow staircase with rose carpeting and the inkstain on the third step from the top, her fault, on down the steps which led to the monotonous balance of the first floor; a hallway in the center, dining room on one side, a vile room of agitation and terrible ferment with its round oak table, scarred from beatings, living room on the other, study behind one, kitchen behind the other. She studied the image of what she saw beyond the closed door. The house was little more than a big white frame box sitting isolated in a grove of birch trees three miles from town. She felt abandoned. Meeting no resistance, she began to ponder objectively all New England architecture, monotonously balanced, perhaps to offset the imbalance which frequently resided within.

The house made her feel ashamed. She moved her legs up and down beneath the blanket and looked steadily at the closed door. Why couldn't she remember anything about the trip up, about leaving the party or the party itself?

The new day was fully light now. The sun came over the ridge of timber that separated her father's property from the occasional traffic of narrow Highway 41 and the timid outskirts of Whitney.

Moving around and between the chaos of her thoughts was a thread of reason. She couldn't stay in bed all day. Seeming all at once to function again, she sat up. The blanket fell away. She jerked the covering up and held it against her as if someone were in the room with her, witnessing her nakedness. Again, questions. Why couldn't she remember undressing and, more important, where were her clothes? With conscious effort to dispel the confusion, she made words to express her thoughts and spoke them softly: "Must find my clothes—"

She swung her bare legs out from beneath the blanket and touched cool wooden floors. A large blue jay near the window caught her eye. He circled, hovering, while another bird a distance away was signaling to him. Sitting motionless on the edge of the bed she watched them.

Quietly, along with the birds squabbling, she heard another sound. She looked back at the closed door and lifted her head, the better to hear. Confirmation, then. She heard a sound, the stealthy tread of footsteps on the stairs.

She pressed the blanket against her and tried to think in rapid coherent thoughts. But only a thick hiss filled her brain. Quickly she burrowed back into the bed.

Someone was in the house with her, perhaps had been with her all night. She might have adjusted to solitude. To be pursued by something and not be able to distinguish whether that something was a reality or a fantasy was disturbing.

There was a shuffling sound directly outside the door. Slowly the door was pushed open. For too long the shadows laid where they belonged. Nothing of substance disturbed them. Someone seemed to be moving with deliberate slowness.

Then the man appeared. In the next moment he was inside the room. Light and shadow caught on the specifics of his familiar face, neatly trimmed beard, long black hair, worn blue denim.

Zoe felt the crumpling of her voice as she considered screaming. She had never screamed before in her life. She lacked both experience and practice. Still the sensation of being trapped overwhelmed her. Something suggested to her that perhaps this was only a part of the same bad dream.

She saw him smile, saw grave deep lines about his mouth, saw him carefully raise his eyes from the tray he was carrying and look directly at her. She watched the face and the peculiar way he was just standing there, aware and considerate of her fear and ready to give her all the time she needed. All sense of the house, the town nearby and even her own name vanished. She felt cut off, adrift. She had no reason for being where she was, no relationship to her surroundings.

Finally, "Don't be afraid," he smiled.

She only stiffened and pushed backward onto the pillow.

He took a step forward. "You remember me, don't you?" he asked. "The party last night?" His eyes appeared impersonal and questioning, as though his identity must be confirmed before he could move on to the next step. He grinned broadly. "I tried to kill you. Remember?"

He waited for a moment, then she heard a long sigh break from his breathing. "Well, obviously, I didn't," he concluded. He continued to stare down at her and she found it exasperating to be gaped at.

He started toward the bed, extending the tray in front of him. "I thought you might want coffee," he said.

Her head began to swim. The indescribable odor issuing

from the long-closed and badly ventilated house felt stagnant about her.

He stood less than two feet from the side of the bed. He held out a tray filled with her mother's agonizingly familiar Haviland china, the blue teapot with the miniature Japanese bridge and tiny explosions of white cherry blossoms. Her recognition was immediate and sharp. All doors were shut and yet invitations to enter were to be deciphered in every object, every color. She ceased to look at the items on the tray and heard only the rasp and thump of words as they tried, without success, to surface from her throat.

Quickly he placed the tray on the table near the bed and hurried to her. She saw, coming closer, the white T-shirt, the blue denim jacket. He scowled at her, murmured an apology, then a plea, "Don't be frightened," he soothed, his hand reaching out.

He looked so deadly serious, the dark hair framing the gaunt, slightly lined face. Suddenly he moved away from her to the foot of the bed. He looked hurriedly about the room, searching for the proper place to stand. He raised his head and in the manner of a recitation announced, "My name is Bubs. Do you remember?"

He waited and then resigning himself to the inevitable, he lifted his face again. It had grown like a mask. There seemed to be a touch of coarseness about it, the skin and muscles were lax, the lids heavy, the hair unkempt, and two furrows had now formed on either side of the mouth. He seemed mildly embarrassed as he spoke. "Bubs breaks down into Bolar Ulster Bottoms," he pronounced with mock dignity, as though it was a curse from which he had been unable to escape. "My parents went to prison for it," he added, smiling sheepishly. He straightened his shoulders and walked a distance farther from the bed. "You and I got caught in a fire last night, Zoe." He looked back, almost begging her to remember. "Do you recall what happened?"

For the first time she was aware of herself cringing beneath the blanket. But there was an expression that was almost touching on his face. She relented then. "Yes," she replied. She released a long breath very slowly. "Was it—bad? The fire, I mean?"

He seemed pleased by her question, by the sound of her voice. "Not bad," he said. "Not good either, but not bad. At least we survived." He stood beside the window, hands behind his back, rocking slowly back and forth on the balls of his feet. Everything about him looked askew and the eyes he raised did not look straight but seemed to move around and above her. "Mary Lisa told me to bring you up here. She said this was where you belonged." He looked directly at her. "She knows you very well, Mary Lisa does." He ran his tongue over his teeth as though tasting something. He approached the foot of the bed, hands in pockets, relaxed. "Are you feeling all right?" he asked.

She nodded.

"The smoke got to you."

He laughed openly. "You should have seen yourself. We lowered you out of the window like a sack of potatoes." He continued to laugh for a few moments, then looked directly at her. "Do you remember anything at all?"

She did remember, although his appearance had not brought things back to normal. Rather it had made things worse. She listened to the dry silence that followed his question. "A little," she said and closed her eyes.

While her eyes were closed, she heard a sudden strong movement. She looked up to see him standing beside her, extending a steaming cup of coffee.

"Here," he offered. "Drink this. It'll help."

It smelled good but for some reason she dared not withdraw her hands from beneath the protection of the blanket.

"Here," he urged. "Go ahead. I made it myself." He
came nearer, bending over her, the cup shaking slightly in his
hands. When she did not respond, a bewildered expression
covered his face. He stood up as if trying to determine what
it was about the encounter that was so unsavory to her.

Slowly a dawning light covered his face. "How thought-
less of me," he murmured. "Your clothes were filled with
smoke. They are out airing. I had to remove them last night.
You were wearing the very fumes that were poisoning you."
His voice was matter-of-fact, his manner slightly amused. He
added, "I was only trying to help. Mary Lisa gave strict instructions to take good care of you. She views you as quite a
catch, you know."

Zoe knew nothing, but redoubled her efforts to speak,
convinced that her only hope of getting rid of the man was
somehow to communicate with him. "Could I have them
back, please?" she asked. "My clothes, I mean. Surely they
are—"

"Oh, they're not nearly ready," he interrupted. He
placed the untouched coffee on the table beside the bed.
"They should stay outdoors for the rest of the day at least."
He smiled again. "For your own good." He sat carefully on
the foot of the bed, his eyes downcast.

Quickly she pulled her feet away from all contact. "But I
must get up," she insisted.

"Then get up!" He uttered this command very loudly
and seemed to be exhibiting a certain pleasure in not coming
to her aid.

She tightened her hands on the bedclothes.

Slowly he stood and gave the appearance of surrender.
"All right," he agreed. "One step at a time," and abruptly he
left the room.

She heard him running down the hallway. For a moment she tried desperately to formulate escape plans. But there was no way out. She would have to wait until he returned with her clothes and then it would be too late.

A few moments later she heard him returning. She lifted her head, the better to follow the rhythm of his steps. She tried to calm herself, to convince herself that catastrophe was not possible, that things were bound, sooner or later, to arrange themselves.

He appeared in the doorway carrying a wad of soiled white material of some sort. He made a polite little bob of his head and extended it to her. "Here," he said, "put it on. It will do until your clothes are ready."

She looked first at his face, then at the curious garment he was forcing on her. It was familiar, a loosely fitting white robe with scooped neck and long sleeves which were covered with brown dried stains. Larger stains covered the front of the robe which he now held up for her close inspection.

"It looks comfortable," he smiled. "A bit soiled, but who cares?"

Suddenly she turned on her stomach. The trembling in her shoulders would not cease.

He was apologizing. "It was all I could find. Honest. You were the one who insisted on something." She could feel him moving closer, thrusting the garment down toward her.

She buried her face in the pillow. It was impossible to see anything except the memory that was so intense that it was like a pain. Years ago they had taken her into the cold room for the purposes of identification, to see the man and the woman slumped over the edge of the bathtub, their arms floating grotesquely in red water, the man in pajamas, the woman in a white robe.

"Go ahead. Put it on," he urged. "It's just harmless material." There was something mocking in the voice in spite of its efforts at kindness.

She had waited until they had taken the bodies out one at a time. Then she had stayed to clean the red water out of the tub, to return the razor to the medicine chest, as if neatness would somehow help. Then she had locked the house and had gone away. How had she overlooked the robe?

"Zoe, are you there?" He was calling playfully to her. "Believe me, it was all I could find."

With her face buried in the pillow, the realization gradually lost its fullest, most impaling concentration. More terrifying to her than the memory itself was the fear that he would see her reaction, would draw conclusions, claim victories. The point was, had been and always would be not to let him, not to let anyone know precisely what she was thinking, feeling, fearing. It was the isolation inside her head that kept her safe. Nothing more. Her fear was harnessed, back under control, and she turned to one side and looked at him. At the same time she saw, from her distorted sideward angle, the white robe crumbled on the bed only inches away.

She felt she knew now what he wanted. Mary Lisa had told him about the suicide of her parents. He was playing with her, trying to instill terror, trying to bring down all of her defenses. With the battle lines drawn, she felt certain that she had no genuine cause to be afraid of him or the house, or the curious circumstances that had brought her here. Nothing he could ever do or say could pierce the shell with which she had covered herself. To demonstrate for both of them the size and strength of her defenses, she raised herself slowly in bed. The blanket fell away. There was a slight tremor in the new coolness about her, but nothing very important.

She saw his face. He wore a look of faint disappointment, the chin bearded, straining upward, a slight impatience, a hope that she would yet crumble and require the strength of his will.

Contrary to what she had read in his face, he smiled broadly and praised her. "Good. Very good. What a paltry thing," and he held the bloodstained robe only inches before her face.

Before she could catch herself, she turned away and in the process ended up sitting in the center of the mussed bed. He reached forward and gently touched the bruised area around her waist. "One does so little," he murmured, "and we never know when pain will come." He shrugged and lifted his face, beaming. "Well, let all that can be, be. At least that's what I always say."

Suddenly he hurled the robe at her with mock ferocity. "Clothe yourself! Nothing ever happens exactly as one thinks it's going to." He reached behind her and hurled a pillow after the robe and within the moment started a crazy dancing jig around the bed. He was twirling before her through continuous cascades of sunlight and shadow, a madman shouting at the top of his voice, "Off to the New World! Print your foot upon virgin soil and take a flying leap," shouting it over and over again, spinning himself into a frenzy.

Finally breathless and appearing dizzy, he collapsed across the foot of the bed, arms outflung.

She watched him closely, saw his eyes closed, head tilted back, breathing heavily. In the sudden silence, she could still hear his voice bouncing across the walls of the room, could see him in his frenzy, twirling around and around. In her arms, she cradled the bloodstained robe, more than cradled it, hugged it to her as though it were life itself.

After a few moments, she became alarmed by his continuing silence. "Are you all right?" she asked.

With his eyes still closed, he countered, "Are you?"

When she didn't answer, his eyes opened. He did not

appear to be looking at her, but he was looking in her general direction. "I take your silence as assent," he said and pushed back the hair from his face. He stood up then, straightening himself, drawing a deep breath to satisfy his fatigue. He walked to the door. "Put on your robe, Zoe," he ordered. "We have company coming and things to do."

He did not look at her again or say anything further. But quickly he left the room and closed the door quietly behind him.

Still she sat foolishly in the center of the bed and kept her eyes on the closed door. She expected him to return at any minute and resume his madness. But he didn't. She wasn't even certain that she had heard his footsteps moving down the hall, and if she had, in which direction had he gone? The tiny mute Barbie dolls stared at her from the dresser. She felt the sensation of their dead eyes upon her.

In some bewilderment she left the bed. She held the bloodstained robe out a distance from her body. She had no choice. She had to get out of the room and downstairs to where her clothes were. After several moments of acute hesitation, she slipped on the robe, tied it firmly, feeling a momentary discomfort in the area of her bruised waist. Then she angled her face downward into the cracked mirror. What had been her punishment for the cracked mirror? She couldn't remember.

Company coming? For the first time the words penetrated her consciousness. She must go and set him straight. There would be no company here. Company never came to the house. Uneased by all that had happened and feeling that unless she was vigilant, she would slip into something that would bring her down, she moved away from the mirror and hurried out of the door. Several times she was tempted to slacken her pace in order to look around. But there was no time. As she walked down the corridor, she felt the folds of the robe about her, brushing against her legs, a warm sensation, not altogether unpleasant except for the foul and musty odor, the memory of blood draining out of severed arteries and running down the sleeve . . .

———◆———

She stood in the kitchen door, which still bore the hash marks put there by her mother, who had charted her growth for sixteen years. She felt remarkably under control considering the perilous journey that she had just completed down rose-carpeted steps, through the entry hall with her grandmother's hat rack adorned with carved wooden faces of the Seven Deadly Sins, past the living room and dining room filled with grotesque, white sheet-covered lumps of furniture. She had not taken the time to answer any of her own questions, as she did not want to arouse herself from the safe inertia of her mind. At the very moment when she had thought it impossible to disentangle dream from reality, she had lifted her head to a simple sound of life, an eggbeater. She had pulled her mother's robe more closely about her and had padded, barefoot, toward life.

He was in the kitchen beating eggs. The dark furred appearance of his face in the harsh morning light made him look older, as though he had aged within the last fifteen minutes.

Somehow it seemed necessary that she speak. "Was the fire bad?" she asked.

"What fire?" he said, blandly, having trouble shifting his attention from the rotary beater in his hand to the question coming from the doorway.

She felt impatient. "The one at Mary Lisa's house last night."

His silence chafed, grumbled. He stared at her as

though seeing her for the first time, his hands still holding the beater, poised now over a bowl of frothy eggs.

Vaguely he answered, "No. I don't think so." He plunged the beaters back into the bowl. Over the whir, he shouted, "You can ask her yourself if you like. She'll be here soon."

Zoe started through the door. "She's coming here?" She tried to raise her voice over the whirring sound. "Why?"

His face lifted. He stared straight at her. "Now where else would she go?" he asked, as though annoyed by her question. "This is her hometown too, you know. In fact, I believe she's bringing the entire party." He grinned. "Just for you."

The eggs beaten, he laid the beaters against the side of the bowl. Again Zoe decided not to deal with the foolishness of what he was saying. She wasn't absolutely convinced he was mad, but certainly his eccentricity verged on insanity. She had three goals: to find her clothes, then her car, then leave. If it took a while to accomplish those simple steps, she was prepared to wait.

Behind him on the stove, she saw a frying pan smoking. The stove itself looked clean, just polished. In fact the entire kitchen seemed to be in excellent shape compared to the rest of the house. On the counter next to the refrigerator, she saw bags of groceries, bread, canned fruit, fresh vegetables. Apparently he had been up early shopping, or perhaps he had never gone to bed.

"Hard or soft?" he called over his shoulder, pouring the frothy egg mixture into the hot pan.

She shrugged. "Suit yourself."

"I generally do."

The room was filled with the pleasant odor of eggs cooking. Carefully she took a seat at the kitchen table, noticed for the first time that it had already been set for two with the brown earthenware pottery that had belonged to her mother. The table used to have one leg that was shorter than the other. Gently she pushed against it. It still did.

He spoke not at all during the preparation of the meal, as if his concentration permitted only one activity at a time. He whistled now and then, strange, disjointed, unrecognizable tunes, like a man improvising. His lean face held a rapt expression. He appeared to be enjoying himself immensely, mildly amused by something and very pleased.

Zoe watched and waited and in a curious way longed to speak. She had a thousand questions but felt certain he would not answer any of them until he had cooked his eggs. It seemed to her, sitting in that bright, painfully familiar kitchen, that she was sitting instead in a cavern of night. It was a strange sensation, to be totally lost in the one spot on earth with which she was intimately acquainted.

"It's hot!" The warning came from close beside her. She looked up to see him standing over her, the steaming pan in hand. Carefully he spooned golden mounds of eggs onto her plate. She signaled enough with her left hand and noticed that the hand was trembling. He filled his own plate, then poured hot strong coffee into brown mugs, returned to the counter once again for a plate of toast, then took his seat opposite her, in what once had been her father's chair, she noticed.

He fell to eating immediately, his hunger deep. His eyes became piercing as he concentrated on getting the food from his plate to his mouth. She saw him more clearly now than ever before, saw how the upper part of his brow projected outward. His lips closed hungrily around the fork, and while he ate, his whole face seemed thinner as though the food was serving no purpose.

While he ate heartily, she ate not at all. He looked at her

with a stern glance. "Eat!" he commanded simply. "There's work to be done today."

Obediently she lifted her fork. But even as she ate, she kept her eyes on him. At any moment she might be called upon to defend herself. As she watched him, she saw with every second a quality she had not noticed before. He sat with his long legs extended out on either side of the chair, his head now resting in one hand, with which at the same time he held back the mass of black hair that fell over his eyes.

Near the end of the meal, as she watched him mop the residue of eggs from his plate with a piece of toast, she repeated his name, for confirmation as well as to get his attention. "Bolar Ulster Bottoms?" she murmured.

He looked sternly at her, the soggy piece of bread extended in a mock threat. "I warned you," he scolded. "I kill for less." He shoved the toast into his mouth and spoke with mouth full. "Bubs will do. Just Bubs." He smiled at her and settled back in his chair with his coffee. "It's Irish, you know."

"Were you born there?"

"Where?"

"Ireland."

He scoffed at the suggestion. "Are you kidding? That sewage pit of poverty and body odor and mindless Catholic superstition?" He grew expansive. "I'm American born and bred, like the Boss says. Born in the U.S.A. West Roxbury, Massachusetts. Just down the way." He gestured vaguely to the left with his coffee cup and spilled hot coffee on his leg in the process. He seemed not to notice. The meal had mellowed him. He appeared perfectly willing, even eager, to talk. "I've visited Ireland," he said with pride. "Have you?"

She shook her head and sipped her coffee, catching a brief glimpse of her own eyes in the shimmering black liquid.

"I took my old man once to the Mother Country," he

went on. "He was a Boston cop, corrupt as hell, who refused to go to his grave until he had set foot on the Holy Sod." He smiled reflectively and stared blankly at a patch of sun on the kitchen floor. "Begorrah, but it was a hell of a trip."

She looked up, impressed by his skillful Irish brogue. She was on the verge of asking what had happened to make it a hell of a trip when suddenly he leaned forward in a new excitement. "I've been to England! I worked there for a while. Did you know that?"

It seemed a foolish question. Of course she didn't know. How could she know?

He seemed not to notice and went on excitedly talking. "The Tintagel Repertory Theatre," he announced. "A British bloke said my Richard the Third was the best he had ever seen." He leaned back in his chair as though savoring a good memory and looked directly up at the ceiling. "But what in the hell did that bastard know? He was all of twenty-two. I mean, you have to wonder how many Richards had he seen?"

Suddenly an incredible light crossed his face. Abruptly he stood up from the table and twisted his leg into a distorted position; one hip swiveled outward, drawing his leg upward at a sharp angle, his shoulders hunched forward so that for a moment he appeared to be hunchbacked and hopelessly deformed. His left hand curled uselessly against the front of his chest. From beneath dark brows he looked menacingly at her.

He began to quote, his voice deeply sonorous and British. "Now is the winter of our discontent made glorious summer by this Son of York." He spit out the words and began to drag his distorted malformed body in a circle around the table. "And all the clouds," he proclaimed, full-voiced, "—that lour'd upon our house in the deep bosom of the ocean buried." He was standing directly behind her now. She sat still, listening. His voice exploded in a whine of ambition. "Now are our brows bound with victorious wreaths; our bruised arms hung up for monuments; our stern alarums changed to merry meetings, our dreadful marches to delightful measure."

He emerged on the opposite side of the table, a complete metamorphosis, a man changed instantly into a deformed and raging king. Suddenly he lifted his contorted face and shouted, in the throes of agony, "Grim-visaged war hath smoothed his wrinkled front; and now, instead of mounting barbed steeds to fright the souls of fearful adversaries—" he paused and looked out from behind the tangle of black hair, looked directly at her as if she were the cause of his deformity—"he capers nimbly in a lady's chamber to the lascivious pleasing of a lute."

His voice fell into deadly sarcasm. His crooked fingers went grotesquely dancing across the air. They paused there for a moment. Then abruptly he dropped the pose; his head fell forward upon his chest. He collapsed into the chair and looked upward, covering his face with both hands. From behind the barrier of fingers, she heard him mourn, "Oh, God, I *was* good!"

She didn't doubt it. With some effort, she forced herself back into the reality of the kitchen. She was sincerely impressed by all she had seen and heard. Less timidly now, she asked, "And this is what you do at the Merrywood Music Tent?"

He looked sharply at her through the fingers which still covered his face. "At the Merrywood Music Tent," he said acidly, "I powder faces and kiss asses." He removed his hands from his face and stared despondently at the surface of the table. "Mainly what one has to do to succeed at the Merrywood Music Tent is to suck cocks." He laughed derisively. "I'm eminently qualified. I just lack the appetite."

She felt almost sorry for him. Somehow it seemed important that she change the tone of the conversation. "How did you know where to bring me last night?" she asked.

He answered dully, without looking at her, his attention was still focused on past injustices, "Mary Lisa told me."

"Have you know Mary Lisa for long?"

Finally he looked at her and grinned. "Everyone was born knowing Mary Lisa. Didn't you know? She's the world's champion cocksucker." He shook his head. "Really remarkable."

A ray of sunlight struck Zoe directly in the face. The strong light seemed to extend through her eyes into her brain like a gentle intoxication. She lowered her head in an attempt to shade her eyes. "Did we drive up here last night?" she asked.

Suddenly he looked directly at her, his face flushed with anger. "Must you sit like that?" he demanded.

Shocked, she faltered. "Like—what?"

"Like all knotted up like that. Like you were wearing a straitjacket."

She glanced down. It was true. She had been sitting for some time with her arms wrapped tightly about her body. "I'm cold," she murmured in a weak defense.

"You'll get no argument from me," he muttered. He stood up and stretched luxuriously, reached upward toward the ceiling. When the stretching was over, he glanced blankly at the cluttered table. For a moment he seemed to have lost his train of thought. He pushed the hair back from his face and glared at her. "Of course we drove up last night," he snapped. "How in the hell do you think we got here?" He reached across for her plate. "Are you finished?"

She nodded.

He shook his head. "Wasteful, wasteful." He proceeded to eat with his fingers the cold eggs that remained on her plate.

She lowered her head and heard him smacking his lips. Apparently his hunger could not be satisfied. Finished at last, he gathered both plates and dumped them roughly into the sink.

He stood before her at the table, his hands gripping the back of the chair. His face seemed alive with energy now. The gloom was over at least for the time being. "We must get this place in order today," he announced. "And we really should make flags."

She glanced up at him. "Flags?"

"To chart the path for the others who are coming who don't know the way," he replied, speaking to her as though she were a child.

"What others?"

He grew impatient and roughly shoved the chair against the table. "Oh, for God's sake. I told you. Mary Lisa is bringing the party here. Where is your mind? Mary Lisa said you were bright. Then prove it."

Zoe felt a mild surge of anger. "What if I don't want the party to come here?" she demanded.

He seemed shocked. He raised his arms into the air and let them fall noisily against the sides of his legs. "We're doing you a favor," he said. He leaned across the table. "Mary Lisa said you needed us. We never turn our backs on a person in need. She's really very fond of you. Did you know that as a child, she used to stand out on that highway and peer through the trees just so she could get a glimpse of you? Did you know that?" His face was close, now so close she could smell the cold eggs still on his breath.

She looked up at him, but could not match the depth in his eyes. Still she felt it important that she answer him in some way. "I have work to do here," she said as firmly as possible. "I don't want or need—"

"Bullshit," he muttered. He lifted her face and forced

her to look at him. "We are going to do a play. Just for you.
We are going to play some games. Just for you. Night
games." He continued to look at her, his eyes communicating many things, all undecipherable. "No one in their right
mind would turn down such an opportunity," he added.
Abruptly he started toward the back door. His stride was
energetic and purposeful. As he went out of the door, he
called back over his shoulder, "Get your house in order,
Zoe."

She saw him through the screen door as he took the back
steps two at a time. Then he disappeared from her sight.
Slowly she stood up from the table, conscious of the stained
white robe, painfully conscious of her distaste for it. There
would be no party, no play, no night games, of that she was
certain. She glanced hastily about the kitchen. If she could
only find her clothes, she would offer to drive him into Whitney. There was a noon bus. He could be in Boston by one-
thirty. But even if she found her clothes, could she talk him
into leaving? And what would she do about the others who
apparently were already on their way? She sank sideways into
a near chair and stared blankly at the table. Without warning
she heard echoes of old voices:

A man's voice, angry, "For God's sake, get the child out
of here."

And a woman's, pleading, "She's hurrying as fast as she
can."

"Get her out of here. Now!"

"Don't. You're hurting me. Not in front of her. Please.
Wait—"

The voice dissolved into a whimpering sound. Zoe
closed her eyes. She bowed her head. Stillness lay all about.
The air from the opened back door was cool. A fly buzzed
close by. She felt something in her that was unassailable, a

space deep within her that continually apologized for what she was.

Quickly she sipped cold black coffee in an attempt to clear her brain. A strip of sunlight narrowed about the table. She felt her hair, loose and mussed about her face. Disorder everywhere. Well, the mess had to be cleaned up. Slowly, still struggling for a semblance of interior order, she carried the remaining dishes to the sink.

Beyond the dust-specked window, she looked out on the expanse of tangled yard. The rank woods pushing against it had almost devoured it. There was little here that was salvageable and less that was desirable. She leaned farther over the sink, spying to one side of the back porch a few persistent chrysanthemums. Her eyes moved slowly over the rest of the entanglement of green and brown, then stopped.

She saw him near the back of the yard, almost lost in shadow. He was on his knees and seemed to be working feverishly at something. She leaned still farther over the sink so that she might see through the smudges and stains on the window. Her vision impaired, nonetheless she caught specifics: a length of rope, a corner of a dark blue fabric, material of some sort. He seemed to be reaching continuously forward and withdrawing handfuls of strawlike substance, stuffing, pulling, rearranging something. Once she saw him stop to rest. He sat back on his haunches, pushed the hair from his eyes and appeared to be laughing uncontrollably.

Suddenly she saw him stand up. He stood back from the thing on the ground. Then with great effort he threw the length of the rope over a near branch of a tree. Quickly he ran to the other side and grabbed the dangling rope and stood a distance back from the tree and began to hoist something up into the air.

She stood absolutely still, holding her breath. The thing tied to the other end of the rope lifted, cleared the ground, swung crazily for a moment, suspended in air. She looked again. The thing was herself, a roughly filled form wearing her clothes, the dark blue suit, a headless, armless effigy with straw sticking out of the neck, grotesquely swinging from the rope that had been tied in the area of the waist.

She saw him tie the end of the rope to a tree and stand back, hands on hips, as though to admire the swinging form. He encircled it slowly, his expression clear even from that distance, alternately smiling and then striking out at the blue form, causing it to swing in a macabre fashion as if in agony.

Abruptly he lifted a hand to his waist and withdrew a knife. He started violently slashing, cutting, standing back, as the stuffing cascaded out and down until the thing itself fell from the tree and lay at his feet, an unrecognizable motionless lump.

For several long moments nothing stirred in her terrified mind except the need to escape. He was a madman who meant her harm. She knew it now. With neither excuse nor concession to logic and reason, paying no attention to the fact that she was without clothes except for the white robe, she turned frantically in the kitchen searching for a ready escape. Hurry. He might be coming for her, knife raised. Then she was running back through the shadowy corridor, past the rooms filled with ghostly furniture, running steadily toward the light at the front door.

The car had to be out front. After all he had told her that they had driven up. The car had to be there. She was caught in a nightmare and the car would provide her with an escape.

She pushed against the front door, then pushed again. Quickly she looked over her shoulder. Footsteps? Was he following her? In her terror, she battered against the hard oak surface, hurling herself forward again and again. Her shoulder throbbed. The pain cleared her head. Reason slipped in. Pull, don't push.

Quickly she jerked at the doorknob. The heavy door swung open. In the blaze of sunlight the porch seemed to be tilting dangerously. The hem of the white robe dragged and caught on rough wood. She took the porch, then the steps, and came to a stop on the gravel driveway. Empty. The car was gone. She looked desperately about in all directions and saw only empty space and the colored foliage of dying trees.

There was no escape. She could run. It was three miles into Whitney. She could reach the highway and flag a passing motorist. She could—

Suddenly she heard a footstep. She looked up and saw him standing a distance away at the corner of the house. She shook her head as though denying his presence and took one step backward. At that point of the horizon where earlier the morning sun had blazed, there now in silence crept dark masses of clouds which slowly consumed the blue spaces. The clouds boiled, pushed one another, slyly changed the contours of the sky.

She must have fallen for she was staring straight up at the clouds; she saw one tear itself away from the rest, drifting alone . . .

———————◆———————

He sat on the third step of the porch, head down, legs spread, the bottoms of his feet pressed together, his whole body drooping listlessly into the cavity of his wide-open legs. To one side rested the pile of slashed blue fabric.

Zoe sat a distance away in the center of the drive, sat cross-legged, one hand supporting her head, the other hand fingering loose gravel. The fainting spell had been mild and had not lasted long. She felt some discomfort sitting on the rough gravel but she could not summon the energy or will to do anything about it. He had been the one who had called

her out of the faint, apologizing profusely and promising to
stay away from her if that was what she wanted. Seeing that
he was once again harmless, she'd lost interest in cloud-
watching. She'd dragged herself up into a sitting position and
was now merely waiting. Her options were limited. She tried
several times in her mind to formulate other plans, but the
obstacles were too great. He could easily outrun her. Looking down into the area of her lap, she noticed a large brown
stain; looking closer she saw that it precisely resembled her
mother's profile.

"Then you'll be staying?" he asked almost timidly from
the third step of the porch.

She looked up. He seemed to have the ability to change
shape before her eyes. Now his black hair looked even more
deranged than usual and in the sun appeared to be lightly
powdered with silver. His dense beard resembled that of an
emir or a caliph.

The silence ran its course and in it she found a degree of
ease. "Do I have a choice?" she asked, returning her attention to the mindless activity of sifting gravel through her
fingers.

"I said I was sorry," he declared. "I don't know what
came over me. I really don't. I just wanted you to stay. In
fact, I couldn't bear to think of you leaving."

She didn't want to hear so she shut him out. Her mind,
left alone for a moment, moved with an air of selection to the
front of the house. She felt old. Thoughts kept coming into
her head and she was too tired to think about them.

The house looked dreadful. A half-decayed veranda encircled the front with missing slats in the railing, and chipped
and peeling paint everywhere. Rank creepers moved up the
slightly tilting trellis that once had supported prize morning
glories. Two windows were hanging disjointedly on single
hinges and the front screen door had been completely dis-

lodged and had fallen limply to one side. It had been an old house when her parents purchased it years ago, first as a summer place, then as a permanent retreat, a place to hide her father's encroaching madness. For a while her mother had painted and planted flowers. Then as the madness had become a contagion, even those activities had ceased.

Now looking up at it in the scudding light and shadow of passing clouds, the house seemed like a pitiful, half-wild creature begging for death.

A slight winter wind blew out of the north. She drew her robe around her and closed her eyes, hoping that her mind would follow suit.

He stood and advanced a few steps and sat opposite her at the edge of the drive. He appeared contrite, not out of any sense of making reparation for what he had done, but merely seeking the softening influence of an act of forgiveness. "I said I was sorry four times," he complained. "And you've said nothing."

"What do you want me to say?"

He edged closer, scooting across the gravel. "Say you forgive me."

She felt bereft of sense. It would be so easy to enter into his madness. For a moment she resisted. "What shall I wear?" she asked.

"Consider the lilies," he intoned. Then, apparently realizing that she was not in the mood, he added, "You look lovely."

She stared down at the bloodstain of her mother's profile. "I'm cold."

"Body temperature has nothing to do with the clothes you are wearing," he replied, implying it was something she should have known.

Incredible fatigue swept over her again. It was impossible to follow the antics of his mind. She looked at him now, almost pleading. "What do you want?"

He laughed outright. "Absolutely nothing." Suddenly he was on his knees before her, his face eager. "Did you happen to read about me last year in the New York *Times?* I was in an Off-Broadway play. I played a griffin. It was a lousy play, but a good part."

The wind lulled about her as though it feared to awaken her. She felt asleep and awake at the same time. Sleep was the relaxation of the conscious guard. Sleep was when all the unsorted stuff came flying out as from an overturned waste-basket. In sleep, time was divorced from the straight line of wakefulness.

Gripping gravel with both hands, she asked a question that both amazed and frightened her. "Am I asleep?"

He laughed outright. "If you are, I am. We both are, or aren't. Whatever goes for one goes for the other. Whichever the case may be."

The gravel felt sharp and solid in her hands. In point of fact she didn't feel asleep. She felt sensations clearly, heard the birdsongs that had first awakened her, smelled pine and dead leaves and the whole earthy brown odor of rank and undisciplined nature. She was awake and this confirmation allowed her to view her predicament with almost philosophi-cal calmness.

"Where is my car?" she asked.

"You don't need your car," he replied, and blew his nose in a wad of handkerchief.

She felt anger rising. "Why don't you let me be the judge of that?"

He stuffed the handkerchief back into his pocket and settled comfortably before her. "Why did your parents kill themselves?"

Tremors again, but minor ones and easy to control, although her head ached and she heard a ringing in her ears. "You'd have to ask them," she muttered.

The ringing became more persistent and was accompanied now by a low distant rumbling. She glanced up at the sky. Thunder perhaps. In an attempt to dispel the rumbling sound and to draw his attention back to the question at hand, she asked, a second time, "Please tell me where I can find my car."

But it continued, low vibrations accompanied now by distant voices and something else, a clattering as hooves on gravel. As the sounds continued to increase, she looked about in some uneasiness. The sound contained threats. Something was coming closer that she did not want to see, did not want to be forced to respond to. She begged openly, "I must go, please—"

If he heard the ever increasing rumbling, he gave no indication of it. He merely sat before her, cross-legged, with rapt attention, delighted with her every word, every movement.

Beneath her she felt vibrations, as if the earth were actually moving. The sounds were not coming from within her head. Her anxiety increased. "Do you hear anything?" she asked.

He turned his head to one side as though his ears were searching for the sounds. He smiled. "Yes, of course."

Still the rumbling grew louder, the voices more distinct, men and women shouting, the muted crack of a whip, someone urging horses onward.

She turned apprehensively on her knees, crouched down, as though she were ready to start a race. The direction was clear now. It was coming from the end of the driveway, although whatever was causing the commotion was still safely obscured by trees and brush. She stood up and reached out for protection against the ungodly clamor, which had now grown to almost deafening pitch. As she tried to withdraw to the porch, Bubs was on his feet beside her, holding fast to her arm, his face a blaze of light and excitement. "They've come!" he shouted. "They didn't need our flags after all. They're here!"

At the moment that she tried to wrench loose from his grip they appeared around the bend of the driveway, four large wooden carts, horse-drawn, people spilling out on all sides, laughing, shouting, prodding one another, the horses whinnying and shying on the gravel as the drivers forced them close to the house.

Zoe tried to look in all directions at once. Bubs still gripped her arm, not so much holding her a prisoner as intent on sharing with her the excitement of the new arrivals. All around her was a confusion of voices and dust. The large wooden carts rumbled to a stop less than five feet from where they stood. The lead horses bucked and whinnied. In the first cart she saw a familiar figure, blond wig, the woman herself dressed in peasant clothes with red-and-blue ribbons streaming from her hair, her face flushed with an almost hysterical excitement, shouting, "Aren't they marvelous?"

Zoe groaned and tried to pull away.

Bubs was scolding her, shaking her arm. "Your guests are here. Go and greet them."

"I didn't invite them," she protested, still trying to pull free from his hand. Suddenly she felt his fingers digging into the flesh of her upper arm.

Then the female voice was calling to her again. "Zoe! Zoe, come and look. Aren't they marvelous?"

He was now forcing her wrists together behind her back. He whispered close to her ear, so close she could feel his beard against the side of her face, "Smile and say welcome."

She held herself motionless. There appeared to be

twenty or thirty people milling about in the driveway before her. She recognized a few faces from the party the night before; the old woman in the flowing red robe, the two men from Logan Airport, Rich and Dempsey, the man in the chef's cap, and others she did not recognize, all silent now, all standing before her, waiting. Even Mary Lisa, still in the wooden cart, appeared frozen, her face creased into angles of hurt and rejection.

Zoe saw it all with perfect clarity, a dull red-and-brown background dotted with faces and flesh and brightly colored garments and the four curious carts and gently stamping horses. It was a nightmare scene in bright daylight.

Now Bubs renewed his grip on her wrist. She could feel his body behind her, pressing forward, threatening, twisting her arms back and up.

Yet for some minutes longer, she refrained from speaking. But as the discomfort in her arms and shoulders increased, and as he showed no signs of releasing her and as the others apparently did not know that she was being intimidated, she opened her mouth and uttered a sound which might have been construed as "Welcome—"

The single word was received with an incredible ovation. Suddenly there was a great shout and uproar of approval. Mary Lisa, totally enraptured informed them all at the top of her voice, "Isn't she marvelous?"

The milling, laughing crowd seemed to be shifting constantly before her eyes. Bubs still stood close behind her, although now he had released a portion of the pressure that he had brought to bear on her arms. He scolded her beneath his breath. "You knew they were coming. I told you so. Now behave as though you're glad to see them. They're human beings too. They have feelings." He released her, then called out to a few faces in the crowd, greeting them all warmly, exhibiting a sincere pleasure at their arrival.

Again Zoe considered running. But how far could she get? There were obstacles everywhere: people, carts, horses and always close at hand the man named Bubs. Resigned, she stood and watched the entire mad scene. Several of the women were now withdrawing large picnic hampers from the backs of the carts. Four men whom she had never seen before were unloading a curious item from the rear cart; from where she stood it looked like a long, slender, rectangular cabinet, about the size of an average man, quite bulky and apparently very heavy from the strain on the faces of the men who were trying to angle it out and down. It resembled a changeroom.

Bubs shouted at them, "For God's sake, why did you bring that?"

One of the men looked up, surprised. "You told us to."

Bubs scratched his head, then absentmindedly chewed the grit from his scalp out from beneath a fingernail. He shrugged. "Did I?"

Apparently his vagueness sufficed as an answer. The men continued to push and pull the dark wooden box, gripping it finally coffinlike, and carrying it carefully up the front steps and into the house. Several of the men were busily unbridling the horses. The animals were set free with a sharp slap on their rump; they pawed at the ground for a moment, not certain they could trust their freedom. Then they ambled casually over to the high grass growing on the far side of the driveway. The wooden carts were hand-pulled a distance away, two on one side, two on the other, neatly blocking both exits of the circular drive.

Zoe watched it all. She thought, curiously, how angry her father would be if he were to come home and find the driveway blocked. She continued to gaze out on the ever-moving, ever-shifting group. There seemed to be a camaraderie among them, a sense that they all had known each other for a long time in spite of their varying ages.

Suddenly Mary Lisa appeared close beside her, her face alive as ever, her eyes slightly manic. "Oh, Zoe," she exclaimed. "What a lovely robe! Really marvelous and you look exquisite in it." She lifted a fold of material as though to examine it. "Quite an unusual design," she murmured, studying the brown stains. "But then you always knew how to dress," she continued. "Even on cold rainy days, you always managed to look better than any of the rest of us. How *did* you manage it?"

Zoe could not quite bring herself to respond. Instead she tried to meet Mary Lisa's eyes, to communicate directly without words. But Mary Lisa merely turned away, talking even more loudly, cutting her off.

The woman was perpetual motion. She rushed out a few steps and for no apparent reason embraced a passing female in a long black woolen skirt with a high-necked white lace blouse. Then she came back to Zoe's side, gripping her hand. "You were so nice to invite us," she exclaimed. "You really were." She turned quickly and gestured toward the wooden carts which barricaded both sides of the driveway. "Aren't they marvelous? My father had them stored in his barn. They looked so useless, so pitiful, that we decided to leave our cars and make the carts feel good. Besides—" and she leaned close for an intimate giggle—"I always believe in making an entrance, don't you?" Her face was alive and close, babbling in a perpetual grin. "Did you ever know my father, Zoe? No, of course not," she rushed on, answering her own question. "You didn't have time, did you?" She stood back, shaking her head. The grin appeared fixed now, almost cold. "You were such a worker. I never knew such a worker. You set a fast pace for all of us, even though you knew that most of us couldn't keep up."

She started forward again, waving her arms at the women who were carrying picnic hampers. "In the kitchen," she called. "Follow me. I'll show you the way." She darted rapidly forward, the full peasant skirt billowing out behind.

Abruptly Bubs reached out for her and drew her close. "Have you come to make us happy?" he asked in a melodramatic stage whisper.

She whirled in his arms and cried out, "I've come to make everyone happy," and the group, which had been drifting off into private conversations, rallied and responded with shouts of approval. Mary Lisa repeated her promise three times, twirling all the while, the red-and-blue ribbons attached to the blond wig streaming out in all directions.

Finally, somewhat breathless, she stopped the mad pirouette. Bubs caught and steadied her, came forward and rested his chin on top of her head, a gesture of obvious and deep affection. The others seemed suddenly lethargic as well, as though they depended on Mary Lisa for their energy.

In this brief silence, Zoe stepped forward. "Mary Lisa?" she called, and her voice sounded as if she had run a great distance.

The woman turned, her eyes glittering unnaturally bright. The colors about her were soft and mistlike. For a moment, Zoe thought her the most beautiful creature she had ever seen. The thought caused disorientation, caused her to lose her already fragile sense of balance.

For an instant the two women stared at one another, one expectant, smiling, the other trembling slightly and hesitant. Now that Zoe had sought and won her attention, what was it that she had intended to say to her?

No matter how hard she tried, she couldn't remember. She faltered, her eyes down. Finally she muttered, "The fire last night? Was it bad?"

Mary Lisa returned her gaze with a quizzical expression. She seemed not to have understood the simple question.

Zoe was on the verge of repeating it when someone

appeared behind the broken screen door, shouting, "Wine and beer in the kitchen. Come and get it."

There was an incredible turmoil about her. Bodies pushed past, stumbling, jostling good-naturedly in their effort to reach the kitchen and the promise of liquid refreshment. A few called out warmly for her to join them. Hands touched her as an endless parade of painted, plain, sharp, angular, masklike faces pushed onto the porch. At some point Bubs and Mary Lisa were sucked into the current. Zoe saw the blond wig with red-and-blue satin streamers, then the black beard passed through the door and disappeared into her house.

Rich, the wheel expert from Logan Airport, was the last in line. He stopped before her. She noticed that he had changed clothes. He was now wearing faded coveralls and no shirt. His ruddy, freckled face was nicked, as though he had recently cut himself shaving. He squinted at her as though she were difficult to see, then he shook his head at her disapprovingly.

Still condemning something that he saw, he said, "Once, a long time ago, I went out into the street. In December it was, and I found a wino, a poor, shivering wino damn near frozen to death. I took him home and laid him on my own bed and covered him with my own blanket and sat with him all night until he stopped bawling." He leaned forward and whispered triumphantly to her, "He didn't bug me after that, didn't bug me a bit."

She listened. Something was ceaselessly murmuring inside her brain.

Slowly he leaned forward, his face twisted in curiosity. "Were you really responsible for killing a cow when you were a little girl? Mary Lisa says you were."

Before she could respond in any way, he lifted one hand

to the front of the white robe, almost reverently, pulled back the garment and peered at her left breast.

"It looks okay to me," he soothed, still looking.

It occurred to her to object, but there was something almost hypnotic about his movements, and by the time she had summoned a will strong enough to conquer her inertia, he had tenderly patted the opening of the robe back into place.

His eyes, meditative now, drifted over her face. They seemed to convey a sort of wistful compassion, as though she were a helpless victim. Someone shouted at him from inside the house. He turned away without another word and disappeared through the broken screen door.

For several moments Zoe held herself with great care. Breakage seemed imminent. She glanced slowly about at the now empty driveway. She felt a strong need to hang on to something, but she was several feet away from the porch railing of loosened, rotting wood. Still she missed support, felt it necessary to cling to something lest she shiver into pieces. Her breast ached from the man's eyes.

Dead Cow.

An unceasing wind wrapped around her and she felt with a strange listlessness a sense of doom. She was Zoe, she told herself with a kind of demented simplicity. She was Zoe and she belonged here. This was her home and there was no reason why she couldn't rid herself of these trespassers anytime she wished.

She moved slowly over to the edge of the porch to touch a dead pine tree. Somewhere in the back of her mind there surfaced a thought of a man, a husband, and two young children, sons—

Out of the corner of her eye, she saw faint movement coming from the rear of one of the nearby carts. She looked up. Briefly her eyes refused to focus. Then her vision cleared and she saw the old woman in the red robe sitting on the back of a cart, her bare feet swinging rhythmically in the air. The old woman was grinning at her; one gnarled paw lifted in a demure, almost timid wave.

Zoe took advantage of this fairly lucid interval to get control of herself. If they insisted on a party, then she would play along with them for a while. Again her options were limited. She tried to arrange her face into an expression of ease. She called out, "You don't care for wine?"

The old woman shook her head. "Oh, no, but I'm doing fine. Don't you worry about me. I brought my own."

The old woman reached for something behind her. Zoe started toward her, revived by the simple exchange. She thought with admirable calm, "These people are harmless. Pests, but harmless."

Without warning the old woman started laughing hysterically in a high-pitched shriek. She withdrew from a position of concealment beneath the red robe a round smooth object. It glistened eerily in the sun, caught the rays of light and hurled them directly into Zoe's eyes.

Momentarily blinded, she drew back as though under assault. She heard the old woman's cackle and now began to see the thing in her hand, an object which appeared to be the severed head of an infant, the top of the skull cut off, a plastic straw inserted into blood-red liquid. Still Zoe held fast even as she watched the old woman lift the skull to her mouth, clamp toothless gums around the straw and begin to drink in long, satisfying, gulping sounds.

The first major tremor came when she saw the old woman extend the grisly object to her as though to share its contents with her. Horrified, Zoe turned and started running down the driveway. The gravel cut into her bare feet. The white robe threatened to trip her. Still she ran. Midway down the drive the sun slipped behind a bank of clouds. The sky drew dark. A distance away in the underbrush a horse whinnied. As she ran, the white robe seemed to be growing longer. She tried to lift it up, but it seemed to have acquired a will of its own. It did not want to be lifted up or changed in any way.

Finally it conquered her. Tripping, she fell hard, knees and elbows scraping. She felt pure and precise sensations of pain. Stunned, she lay still for a moment, one hand moving aimlessly over loose gravel, the other crumpled beneath her hip.

Lying there, she knew for the first time that there was no escape, would be no escape, that no matter how hard she tried, she would not be able to send these people away, or dismiss them, or run for safety herself.

The realization was like a sentence passed on her. Above her, less than three feet away and perilously close to her head, a wandering horse stamped his right foot. As she looked up and felt the animal's eyes upon her, the feeling of disquiet increased, and she knew it would be a long time before anything was put to rights again . . .

———◆———

Bubs shook his head as if he were shaking water out of his hair. His face was disapproving. "I come in here looking for a party," he shouted, "and I find a wake." He was carrying a can of beer. He had taken off the white T-shirt and was now bare from the waist up. There was a luxurious and precise cross configuration of tiny, tightly curled black hairs on his chest.

"Come on," he shouted, anger rising. "What in the hell is going on?" He tipped his head back and took a long swallow of beer. He wiped his mouth with the back of his hand and burped pleasurably.

Zoe sat midway up the stairs, a safe position close to the railing, enabling her to keep an eye on all threats. Now and then she took a sip of harmless grape juice from the ceramic mug shaped like a baby's skull.

It was late evening. People roamed and ranged throughout the house. A few slumped dejectedly in the living room, collapsed, on the sheet-covered furniture, apparently satiated by the endless supply of food in the picnic hampers.

The old woman in the red robe had rescued Zoe from the end of the driveway and the stamping hoof of the curious horse. She had bent over most apologetically and had held out for Zoe's inspection a ceramic mug in the shape of a baby's head, a novelty item produced by the millions in Roxbury, Massachusetts. She had insisted that Zoe hold it, examine it, put her mind at ease. Now in the course of the evening, Zoe had grown quite attached to it. It enabled her to resemble the others drinking. It was an object to hold. It gave her hands something to do.

As she looked about her, she was convinced that in spite of Bubs's reprimand, the party had died before it had even been born. For a while, food and drink had sustained an atmosphere of merriment. But now all that could be said of the drowsy, drooping bodies was that they were there, totally uninteresting, equally harmless.

Now and then there was a distant voice coming from a room upstairs, a clatter of dishes in the kitchen. And occasionally in the hallway below her, people encircled the curious wooden cabinet which the men had brought in and which now stood propped up against the east wall. A few started to touch it, then quickly withdrew their hands. And of course there was the dull gathering in the living room, and Bubs, standing there, bare-chested in the doorway, viewing them between gulps of beer as though his heart would break.

Zoe watched it all and managed a thought of ironic humor. Even filled with people, the house was dead, as dead as it had been throughout her childhood, always a dead house. She smiled and took another sip of grape juice. The house was stronger than this band of raving, eccentric revelers. The house was defeating them. The house was her ally. Perhaps within the night, boredom would send them packing and she would be alone again in the house.

From the living room someone was complaining about the lack of television. A man's voice, flat and miserable grumbled, "We can't even watch the Patriots tomorrow."

She heard Bubs scold him. "What the hell? Did you come up here to watch football?"

And the man's voice again, disgruntled, "I don't know why I came up here. Another one of Mary Lisa's screwy notions."

Then a third voice, this one whining and female, "What *are* we going to do up here all week?"

Zoe sat a little straighter on the steps. All week? She listened more closely but no one was speaking now. All week? Were they insane? Surely they had jobs. Surely by tomorrow morning at the latest they would drag the wooden carts back to Mary Lisa's barn and go back to Boston.

Now the grumbling from the living room resumed, sounds of unrest, boredom. Zoe studied the ceramic infant's skull, a grotesque item, but it felt good in her hands. Suddenly Bubs appeared in the hallway below, confronting her. He stood with one hand on his hip, as a man does who has triumphed over another or as a vain lieutenant parades in front of his troops. He seemed visibly to enjoy the silence around him.

He announced, "Your guests are bored."

It was not anger she felt as much as indifference. "They are not my guests," she replied.

"They are in your house."

"I did not invite them, or you, or anyone else."

She placed the skull mug on the step beside her to terminate the conversation. The silence was unbroken save for a female laugh coming from someplace upstairs. Apparently someone was managing to have a good time.

Bubs continued to stare at her for several moments as if struggling to formulate a plan of action.

In the deepening silence, she heard footsteps running through the corridor upstairs. She turned backward to look and while she was turned away, Bubs moved up close, sat on the step directly beneath her, one hand resting on his knee, the other still holding the can of beer.

She signaled her distaste for his presence by moving to one side, pressing against the railing.

Undaunted, he simply moved up beside her.

She heard him draw a deep breath, saw him throw his head back and close his eyes. In a mixture of curiosity and repulsion, she stared at the tightly curled hair on his chest.

With his eyes still closed, he smiled. "You may touch it if you wish."

She turned away, embarrassed. "I don't wish. I don't wish for any of this."

He sat up suddenly, leaned forward. In a quick movement the side of his leg came to press against hers. "What was the happiest day in your life, Zoe?" he asked. The leg applied subtle pressure.

She wasn't interested in his questions or his games.

He repeated the question, his mouth drooping sadly, as though he knew he would not receive an answer. "No happy days?" he asked softly.

"None that I care to share with you."

He laughed outright. "A happy day has no other purpose, none at all." He put his arm around her, pressed even closer. She could smell beer on his breath. With the barrier of railing on one side and his pressing closeness on the other, she was trapped.

She looked down through the railing to the floor a few feet below. She whispered, "Please leave me alone."

At that moment Mary Lisa came out of the kitchen. She was wiping her hands on the peasant skirt. Looking up at the two on the steps, she grinned. "Isn't that marvelous? You make a lovely couple, you two. You really do."

Zoe reached forward and grabbed for the hand railing, tried to pull herself up and out from the entrapment, from the pressure of his body. But he held fast; quickly he put down the can of beer and restrained her with both hands.

Again Mary Lisa giggled. "Don't fight him, Zoe. Give him a chance and you'll find him irresistible. Every woman does. No reason why you should be any different."

Zoe continued to struggle but it was useless. Fear vaulted again. She heard her own voice, begging, "Mary Lisa, please. When do you plan to leave?"

Suddenly Mary Lisa erupted into laughter. She clapped her hands together. "Leave?" she exclaimed. "We just got here. My goodness, look at all the work that needs to be done in this place. We've come to help you. We want to help you get your house in order, Zoe. We've only come to help—"

Then the struggle was on again, Zoe trying to remove herself from the wedge of his body and the sharp edge of the slats, which were cutting into the flesh of her shoulder and arm.

The mute conflict of wills seemed to amuse Mary Lisa. She called for the others to come and watch. Within the moment, the dull-eyed, slack-jawed parade had filed out of the living room and were now standing about in the entry hall, varying expressions of amusement and curiosity on their faces.

Someone asked impersonally, "What's the trouble?"

Mary Lisa shook her head. "I don't know. I was intimately acquainted with her all through school and thought I knew her as well as I know myself. But would you believe what she asked me just a moment ago? She asked me when we were going to leave?"

The others reacted with expressions of hurt and shock and indignation. Another voice shouted encouragement. "Hang in there, Bubs, old boy."

As Zoe tried to flail out at her captor, their voices rose and blended in excitement. Once or twice her fists found their marks against the side of his head. But he simply stood up and grabbed her arms in midair and held them tightly suspended above her head. Then he moved forward and straddled her with his legs.

The entrapment was complete. Struggle was useless. Unable to match his strength, her head fell backward. She heard a female voice ask with concern whether or not she was crying yet.

No, she was not crying and she would never give them that satisfaction. She was angry that she had permitted herself to become their sport, their amusement. The entire party seemed to have gathered in the area of the stairs, rejuvenated by the struggle.

Suddenly the old woman in the red robe broke through the crowd. She came laboriously up the stairs and stood very close as though to assess what she saw, Zoe trapped, Bubs standing over her. She rubbed her wrinkled, parchmentlike brow, trying to collect her thoughts.

Zoe, in a daze of anger and determination, heard the silence of the group. No more shouting, no more laughter, everyone seemed to be poised, waiting expectantly for a decision from the old hag.

Finally the old woman asked sternly, "What did she do to deserve this?"

Bubs asked, "Do you want a complete list of her offenses or just the latest?"

The old woman looked impatient. "A complete list? At my age? You would have to shout them into my next grave. Just the latest will do nicely."

Bubs obliged. "Well, I came in here and told her that her guests were bored and she did exactly nothing. In fact she even had the nerve to ask Mary Lisa when we were leaving."

There was a strong murmur of disapproval from the crowd. Mary Lisa stepped forward, twisting and untwisting a golden curl around her finger. "I don't really think she meant anything by it," she said, apologetically.

"The hell she didn't," Bubs scoffed and tightened his grip on her arm.

Zoe's back, pressed against the sharp tread of the step, began to ache. Her suspended arms were beginning to turn cold from lack of circulation. She tried to hold her head erect, the better to let them see that she was not intimidated, but her neck ached and her throat and lips were dry. Almost in spite of herself and certainly to her surprise, she murmured a faint, "I'm sorry."

Mary Lisa was delighted. "There! You see? She didn't mean it. She didn't mean it at all." Her face grew hopeful. She ventured hesitantly as though she too were frightened, "Why don't you let her go now, Bubs?"

Zoe raised her head on a surge of hope. She saw indecision in the black bearded face hovering over her. Now Bubs looked to the old woman for the final decision.

Thought seemed to be crawling across the furrowed and beetling brow. Penetrating black eyes slid the length of Zoe's body and slowly crawled back up again. Finally she waved a bony hand at Bubs. "Let her go. She's our hostess. We'll perform for her shortly. Then we'll allow her to play our games. That's when she'll do her penance."

Within the instant, Zoe's arms fell limply against the steps. Bubs moved to one side. He picked up the can of beer and edged a distance away, saying something to the old woman under his breath as he passed.

The excitement over, the group disintegrated into various rooms. Mary Lisa scampered up the steps and sat close beside Zoe. She appeared to be trying to comfort her. "You musn't pay any attention to Bubs," she whispered. "He means nothing."

Zoe wrapped her still-cold arms around her body and drew the robe closely about her legs. She put her head down on her knees and made of herself an enclosed fortress.

Mary Lisa continued to inquire in a soft, concerned voice, "Are you all right?" Blithely she answered her own question. "Of course you're all right. You've been all right for as long as I've known you."

With her head down, Zoe did not care to respond. Her exhaustion and fear felt dull upon her. The grape juice left a curious taste in her mouth. Her arms still ached. She wondered, if she escaped, how long she would have to stand on the highway before someone stopped to help her. She wondered too if she would be better or worse off. Her mother had run from terrors in the house once, in a nightgown, in the dead of night. They had threatened her with the asylum.

From a distance, Bubs voice cut teasingly through the silence. "She's scheming again," he warned, "and we are not included."

"Nonsense," scolded Mary Lisa.

The old woman said, "It's the house that's doing it. First thing tomorrow morning, we probably should find a new place."

Within the fortress of her enclosed arms, Zoe held her breath. Perhaps they would be leaving. A new place implied not here. She looked up, spoke faintly, "It *is* the house," she confirmed. "You would all be better off someplace else. Back in Marblehead or Boston. There's never been a party here. Never. Not for as long as I can remember."

Throughout her brief speech, the others had given her close attention. Now she was embarrassed to find the hall filled with silent watching faces. Perhaps she had been too insistent. She stood up, wavered a moment, gripped the handrail for balance and announced as affably as possible, "I'll be leaving myself tomorrow. So there's really no need to—"

Mary Lisa interrupted her. "That's not true. You told me that you would be staying here all week. Besides, we could never think of going off and leaving you alone."

Zoe protested. "But I won't be alone. I said that I'm leaving too." She looked pointedly and a little fearfully down at Bubs. "That is if I can find my car," she added.

Someone in the group called out helpfully, "Oh, we saw it when we came in. It's down at the end of the drive, hidden in a grove of birch."

Zoe searched for the face that went with the voice. She was very grateful for the information. While she was still searching, Mary Lisa stood up as if possessed by a need for movement.

She smoothed and straightened the peasant skirt. "No more talk," she exclaimed. "And no more talk about anyone leaving." She ran a few steps down and posed prettily near the bottom of the steps. "It's time for the play. After all, it's what we came for."

The others applauded approvingly. A few performed quick and affected little dance steps reminiscent of Vaudeville. Within moments, the entire hallway was a twirling, preening, pirouetting mass of color, bodies and faces. Shouts of "A play! A play!" filled the air.

Zoe continued to watch from her position halfway up the stairs. She had never known such people. She saw the old woman lift thin, blue-veined hands up into the air and dance around. Two men in the far corner were now performing heated Elizabethan dialogue, arms flailing, imitating sword-play. A young woman near the bottom of the steps curtsied prettily to no one in particular. Near the living room door a man and a woman were slapping each other's faces in mock blows. Close by a man was crawling about on the floor on his hands and knees barking like a dog.

In the exact center of the chaos, Zoe saw Bubs and Mary Lisa in huddled conference, both as excited as children, their faces alive with plans. They were possessed, all of them. They were not children.

Fascinated in spite of herself, Zoe continued to watch. Now she saw the old woman leading several other women to the front door, where they fell into close examination of the faded lace curtains at the two long rectangular windows flank-ing the door. Costumes were being considered. From her position on the steps, Zoe saw two men roughly removing the white shrouds which covered the living room furniture. She looked around at the perpetual motion, but wanted no part in it. She felt as though she, too, were being examined and assessed for potential use.

Once Bubs pointed directly at her. Mary Lisa nodded and giggled.

Now he called up to her. "Are there any trapdoors in the house?"

She gazed blankly down, hearing, but not understand-ing.

He explained patiently. "Trapdoors leading to a base-ment perhaps." When she still did not answer, he explained

further, slightly impatient now, "The Greeks used them."
His impatience turned to anger. "For God's sake, are you
awake up there?"

Quickly she nodded, still not certain what it was that he
was raving about. Dust from the raised shrouds filled the air,
gave the teeming hallway below a filtered, misty appearance,
as if someone had already manned an invisible special effects
machine.

She had seen enough. Her nightmare had become too
convincing. She started to retreat to her upstairs bedroom.
But two steps up and she stopped. Someone had laid a fire in
the fireplace of the living room. From her position on the
steps she could see it, smell it. The little dancing flames had a
curiously soothing effect on her spirits. Now she noticed that
the others were gathering in the living room around the fire.
She found herself alone in the hallway.

Suddenly the lights went out. She glanced behind her
into the darkened second-floor corridor. Hazards there. Outside night pressed against the front door. When had night
fallen? A few moments ago, or so it seemed, it had been
morning. The two flanking windows, now naked, their lace
curtains pressed into some new service, resembled two elongated and saddened eyes. On the other side of the windows,
she knew that all was darkness and cold. There were hazards
there as well; barricades of wooden carts, free-ranging horses
and a deserted highway along which no one passed. A bitter
October wind had arisen, viciously slapping at the dead trees.

But in the living room, all harshness and darkness were
gone. There was relief in the warmth of the fire, even a degree of relief in the huddled shadowy figures who continued
to move and bob, voices muted now.

Still Zoe stood on the steps, foundering. Her interior
compass was broken. The entire house seemed to be holding
its breath.

A voice—Bubs, she felt certain, although he was speaking out of sight—was saying, "Suppose, in these sobering days of solved mysteries and bad dreams, some of the stories which have sustained mankind for centuries were to be retold. Suppose they were re-created nearer to reality, as the events they relate in all probability happened, and not as human imagination has embellished them."

Zoe listened in the cold darkness. Much to her surprise she discovered that she really did want to join them. But would they have her? She decided no. Then too, she always felt better, more at home on the outside; it was like slipping into classes after the roll had been called, leaving when someone asked her name. Now she lowered herself carefully onto the step and sat alone in the darkness.

The voice was saying, "Would it not be more likely to bring the troubled spirits the comfort and peace they now lack. The truth faced. Hard but ultimately beneficial and healthy."

From her position on the steps, Zoe saw Bubs move into view to a position directly in front of the fireplace. The growing flames behind him obscured his features and left a black silhouette. From the position of his head, however, she was certain that he was looking directly at her. With his hands behind his back, he rocked on the balls of his feet as he spoke. "You know, what frightens children most in nightmares is that they are so different from the beautiful stories of love and valor and nobility with which they were lulled to sleep. Perhaps what we need is to make our daydreams more like our nightmares instead of continually flogging the poor nag of reality to reach the heights of our dreams."

He had built to an effective dramatic climax and his skill was rewarded with a polite rustle of applause. Zoe saw him lift his hands modestly to discourage admiration. The fire behind him was in full blaze. A hush fell on the room. The voice that had been speaking to them was ready to make an announcement of paramount importance.

Bubs took full advantage of the silence. He seemed to preen before them. As he lifted his head the firelight caught the specifics of his bearded face, his bared chest. We have selected the play for this week's performance," he announced.

Zoe crouched on the steps, listening with ever-growing interest.

He went on. "We shall do a performance of an obscure, little-known theatrical oddity entitled—" He paused. Suddenly he lifted a hand and pointed a finger directly at her. His voice rose: "—entitled *Zoe Beginning and End.*"

Approval from the group was slow in coming. There were a few grumbles. A man scoffed, "Whoever heard of that?"

A woman whined, "I was hoping we would do *Peter Pan.*"

A third voice suggested, "What's the matter with *Marat/Sade?* We do that one beautifully."

Another whispered, "What did he say the name of it was?"

But Bubs appeared adamant. When he said nothing further and did not alter the announcement in any way, they began to confer softly with one another. Slowly one by one all turned until they were looking directly at her.

Zoe shook her head in silent protest and started backward up the steps. Her foot caught on the hem of the robe. Quickly she jerked the cumbersome material up and fled toward the darkened upstairs corridor. Every step was an obstacle that had to be negotiated. Behind her she could hear them stirring, voices rising, parts being assigned.

She reached the top of the steps and looked back. She thought she saw a shadow following her. Her flesh began to crawl. Beyond her in both directions stretched the pitch-black upstairs hallway. No protection there. She should have run the other way, down to the front door and out to the car, which she knew now was waiting at the end of the drive.

But in a very real sense the brain had ceased to work. It was no longer capable of putting thoughts together.

"Zoe?" The voice which moments before had been forceful and commanding was now a whisper. "We have saved the lead role for you," Bubs coaxed. "There is no one else quite as suited for it."

The shadow was even with her now. "Come along," he pleaded. "We're all ready and waiting." She felt his arm about her waist. "You must do your part. A play, like a chain, is only as strong as all of its links."

She did not resist the arm that was guiding her back down the steps. What good would it have done to resist? Resistance was foolish, accomplished nothing, served no purpose. Never once in her entire life had she successfully resisted anything.

The others looked up as she entered the room under Bubs's guidance. There was a rustle of respectful applause. Mary Lisa, visible on the front row whispered, "Isn't she marvelous?"

Two women sitting close by the doorway took her by the arm and led her to a chair beside the fire. She felt herself being arranged in the chair. Hands smoothed the white robe down over her legs. Fingers pulled back the hair from her face. She sank almost immediately into a heavy silent reverie.

Bubs took his place before the fire. He crossed his arms over his chest, threw back his head, shook the shaggy black beard and intoned, "Act I!"

At precisely that moment, a young woman near the back of the room stood up. As she approached the fire, Zoe noticed that she was dressed to resemble a bride. She was wearing a long white lace skirt which earlier had been a window curtain and her hands were clasped in front and she was holding the bouquet of dusty dried flowers from the hall table. Over her head was draped another panel of lace curtain. Her hair was dark and long and she looked frightened. Twice in her slow walk to the fire, she hesitated. But each time hands reached out and held her steady. Without a word, she came forward until she stood before Bubs. He whispered something in her ear. Without a sign of protest, she placed the bouquet of dried flowers to one side and lay quietly down on the floor before the fire.

Zoe saw Bubs reach into the darkness on the other side of the fireplace and withdraw a silver cylinder, about ten inches long, resembling the airtight container for a large cigar. He examined the cylinder for a moment, turned it over and over in his hand. Then he took the fireplace pincers, and reached into the fire. A moment later he drew out a small piece of burning red-hot ember. This too he examined carefully, turning it over in the pincers, and suddenly held it close to Zoe's face.

"This is you," he said. "In the beginning. A small lump of hot life. An inconvenience. A form of revenge for your father. A most effective form of torture for your mother." He shook his head sadly. "Remember, no romance now. No diverting melodrama. Only the truth of the dream."

The entire room was still, apparently as fascinated as Zoe, all held enthralled by Bubs's deliberate slow movements.

He held out the cylinder for all to see. Then carefully he dropped the hot ember into the round opening.

Still the bride-woman waited on the floor at his feet, placidly lying in the conception position, her hands folded benignly across her breast.

Bubs stepped forward, cylinder in hand. Zoe noticed his

chest rising and falling, his rate of breathing increasing, eyes enraged as though the submissive woman had angered him in some way. Quickly he knelt at her feet. The woman shivered, experiencing a mild tremor. Bubs moved forward on his knees. He lifted the long white skirt.

The entire room seemed to be holding a collective breath. In the red glow of the fire, Zoe saw their expressions, like children watching a puppet show.

Bubs crouched forward, lifted the long skirt until it covered his head and shoulders. From where Zoe sat he resembled a monstrous, headless bug, joined mutant fashion to the torso and head of the woman.

There was a single moment's silence. Then suddenly the woman wrenched backward. A shattering scream widened and distorted her mouth. She arched her body upward, arms flailing, legs struggling as though to dispel the pain.

Quickly Bubs reemerged from beneath the skirt, his face blood-red in the flickering fire. He closed her legs and held them secure by leaning over her with his entire body weight. When her strength, under the duress of agony, threatened to surpass his, he motioned with a frantic bob of his head for assistance from the front row. Two men scrambled forward, each reaching for and securing a flailing arm.

Thus secured, the woman continued to arch her body, her head twisting from side to side, eyes alternately pinched shut, then flung wide open. Her ordeal lasted only a few minutes. Then she grew quiet, though she was still trembling, her body now was wracked by the remembrance of pain.

Gently the two assistants replaced her arms across her breasts; one lingered a moment to brush a long strand of black tousled hair from her eyes.

Bubs gradually released his hold on her legs and moved back a few feet. His expression grew gentle, almost morose.

Zoe found herself peculiarly excited by the spectacle. It

was only a pantomime. True, at the exact moment of the woman's first scream, Zoe had turned away, her imagination supplying in abundance the hot penetration. But as the woman's agony had subsided, so had her own. Now she sat on the edge of the chair, concentrating on the pale still face.

Slowly Bubs stood up. He looked as if a genuine love of voluptuousness had laid hold of him. He preened before the prostrate woman. Arrogantly he walked about in a small circle, a cock parading, the most insufferable of male egos. Then he stepped close to Zoe and, taking her hand, spoke in quite a different tone, sincere, almost tender. "Your mother had never received a man before her wedding night." He shook his head compassionately. "Poor thing. She never received a man again. Her frigidity led to his impotence, twin curses, the decay of mind and body."

He encircled her chair twice, bending low the final time to see if she had understood. Embarrassed, she made her face a mask and gave him neither acceptance nor rejection.

Suddenly he stepped forward and began to kick at the woman on the floor, sharp pointed jabs aimed primarily at her back and buttocks. She rolled to one side and drew herself into a tight knot, arms over her head as though for protection against the strength of his foot.

A female voice protested from the back of the room. Other females joined in. Zoe lifted her head in the direction of the protest, saw the audience stir, shift. On every woman's face was indignation and censure.

Bubs, in the role of father, grew defensive. He stalked, paced, encircled the cringing woman on the floor. "And why not?" he shouted. "I have rights."

An enraged female cried out her objection. "No! You have no rights other than the ones she willingly grants you."

This was greeted by a round of applause. Zoe watched

and listened. The audience was entirely caught up in the conflict.

Bubs continued to stalk, shouting at the top of his lungs, his mouth twisting beneath the black beard in a series of reckless statements. "Where she is concerned, I have *all* rights. She was born inferior to me!" He stood erect before the group, arms outstretched, allowing them to relish his superiority. Then the mad raving continued. "Now she tells me there is something growing inside her." His voice filled with derision. "A dead woman can produce nothing alive." Suddenly he turned and delivered a stunning blow to the woman's back in the area of her kidneys.

She cried out, straightened her body against the pain, then coiled again into a closed knot.

Someone was sobbing in the audience, a female voice weeping. "You put it there, you son of a bitch. Whatever is growing inside her, you put it there."

Bubs appeared to contemplate the accusation. His face appeared to be almost devoid of color. "Then I curse the thing I put there," he said. Roughly he jerked the woman onto her back and began pounding on her abdomen with his fist. On his knees at her side, he pounded and pummeled, apparently oblivious to the woman's screams. Struggling, she dragged herself out from under the blows, half sat, half crouched at the foot of Zoe's chair.

Bubs, still kneeling, muttered, "Whore! I hope the thing dies and you with it."

Zoe stared at the two kneeling a distance apart, considering each other with hate and contempt. *She* was the thing growing inside the woman.

Bubs sat back on his haunches now, arms spread. He appeared to be sinking into a kind of complacency. The woman scrambled off into the darkness. Zoe heard her being received and consoled by other sympathizing females. The audience shifted on the hard floor but never once took their eyes off Bubs.

Still on his knees, forming a penance of confession, he spoke now of degradations. "I learned to masturbate," he whispered. "I learned to whore. I hid in urinals and watched young men. There is a bar in Boston with rooms above and a black male and a white female." He looked up, grinning. "The combinations are dazzling." His voice was calm, almost a monotone. Still on his haunches, he shook his head like one weary beyond words and passed quickly from horror to horror, lacking the will or the power to pause and examine a single detail.

Once his voice rose in a kind of astonished pride. "I *did* commit a clever crime," he smiled. He appeared almost dreamy now, his eyes floating unseeing over the ceiling of the room, a benign madman, recalling a moment of glory. "Over the course of years," he began, almost childlike, "I embezzled over seventy thousand dollars from the firm for which I was working." He repeated the sum gleefully, stretching out the words, "Seven-ty-thousand-dollars." He giggled and clapped his hands over his mouth and looked slyly out at the audience. "I'll tell you how if you won't tell. Anyone can do it."

He leaned forward, quite excited now, eager to share the details of his crime. "You see, what you do is over a period of years you fake death claims on life insurance policies. After the corpse is cold, you extend the insurance for a year, but"—here he raised his hand, coming to the best part —"but you change the beneficiary by forging a fake name."

Suddenly he bent over in convulsive laughter. "For years, I was George Wilson of Keene, New Hampshire." He burst into gales of new laughter, slapping his knees, tears rolling down his face. Near the end of the seizure he looked out at the audience as though in a state of rapture. "And then

I was Henry Pruett of Dublin and then I was Sebastian Mc-
Guire of Manchester. And they never found out. Never!"
He emphatically repeated it in an effort to repudiate the truth
of what he was saying. "They-never-found-out!" he exclaimed, incredulously. He grinned, arms outstretched, like a
kneeling frozen crucifix. The amusement on his face faded.
The smile appeared fixed. He began to tremble and shook his
head. He inquired of the audience. "It was only a small
crime. I wasn't wrong, was I? Only guilty men go to prison
and I never went to prison. So I wasn't guilty."

Now he began to crawl toward the front row, begging
for their forgiveness. "You see," he whimpered, "I needed
the money to support the black man and the white woman. I
needed the money to support the thing growing inside of
her."

Zoe had heard and seen enough and stood up to leave
the room. It was pure fabrication, all of it. She wanted no part
of it. But as she turned toward the door, she saw in memory
the stern, brutal, idle, withdrawn man. Even the corridors of
the house seemed to confirm the confession.

Near the door, she stopped, her attention drawn back to
Bubs crouched on the floor. He leaned forward, gesturing
for her to return, his face filled with a maniacal grin, building
to the best part of the drama.

"Worse than that," he grinned. "On the day of your
birth"—and he pointed a finger directly at Zoe— "On the
day of your birth, I was in the room over the bar off Scully
Square. Yes," he exclaimed. Suddenly he jumped to his feet.
"On the exact day of your birth, I was in the room over the
bar, and I—"

From out of the shadows near the back of the room, a
young girl appeared. She was wearing a short tight skirt, her
pretty dark hair piled carelessly on top of her head. Vaguely
Zoe remembered seeing her in one of the wooden carts

when the party had arrived. Now she walked jauntily past Bubs, one hand on her hip, chewing gum, tossing her pretty head from side to side.

Bubs appeared to freeze when he saw her. Twice she encircled him, thrusting forward her pelvis, her hands continuously massaging her breast in calculating professional movements.

The third time she passed before him, he grabbed her wrist and jerked her down onto her knees before him. The wide painted smile did not alter in any way. Rather she approached him eagerly on her knees, her tongue licking out at the front of his trousers. For a few moments, he pressed her face against him, his own head upraised in an enraptured expression.

The audience perceived what was happening and registered clearly their disapproval. Zoe tried to avert her eyes, but the degradation held her fascinated. She wanted to join with the audience in its censure.

Suddenly Bubs shuddered. His hand appeared to encircle the girl's head. He stared down at the upturned, passive, grinning face. Then slowly his fingers slid down the sides of her head and gripped her throat.

The female smile faded. The heavily made up eyes stretched open. The mouth trumpeted.

He leaned forward until she was bent over backward, channeling all his strength into his hands, pressing into the flesh of her throat until his fingers resembled steel rods twining themselves around her neck, pressing, pressing.

The lips became dry. The eyes fluttered. The hands weakly flailed at the air, then flailed not at all. The body went slack, but still he held on, shaking her now, his face obscured by long strands of black hair.

Someone in the audience whispered, "My God, she's

already dead. Does he want to kill her some more? He's overacting again. Someone had better tell him."

Only then did he let the body drop. The girl fell backward, her legs twisted beneath her. In the firelight her face appeared bloated, swollen.

Bubs studied his hands, pleased with their accomplishment. Slowly he lifted his head. He seemed to be undergoing rapid changes of emotion. He stepped toward the fire and turned his back on the group, shutting out their condemnation. He spoke quite calmly to the fire. "The balance of whores in this world must be kept even. If one is born, one must die. Otherwise they will take over the world." Abruptly he laughed. "A murder without motive. Of course I was never found out. No one came to me demanding my confession. I waited and waited. But no one came."

From where Zoe stood she could see his face. It looked pitiful as though he had been offended in some way. "They might at least have done me the courtesy of asking questions," he mourned. "But no. I merely walked out into the street and they didn't even find her body until it began to stink. No questions asked. A dead whore." He shrugged. "What can you expect?" His refrain became a soft, pathetic wail.

Still Zoe gazed down at his face, struggling against the threat of recognition. Suddenly she realized what it was that the countenance reminded her of, something quite familiar, of a particular winter evening. Once—Zoe was then about seven—her father had slipped on newly formed ice and Zoe, who was smaller even when standing than her gigantic father when kneeling, had held out her hands to help him. And the very same expression with which her father had risen to his feet now shown on Bubs's face, an expression which was wrathful and at which she shuddered, an expression which seemed to say, 'Don't help me. I have committed crimes for you and you never even asked questions.'

Zoe had no desire to see or hear any more. Yet as she turned away, she noticed that she was now the focus of attention. All eyes in the audience were on her; even the dead whore had lifted herself from the floor and was staring directly at her, awaiting a line of dialogue, a comment, a reaction.

Suddenly everything in her head began to dissolve in a torrent of protest. She had seen an extraordinary spectacle, but none of it had been true. How could they know? How could they possibly have had access to information that was unknown to her? It was merely a piece of theatrics, effective, but still illusion. Games. Nothing more. Safe in this conclusion, she sat rigidly on the edge of the chair to let them see that she was unmoved, unimpressed.

Someone muttered, "My God, she's deaf, dumb and blind."

Another voice warned, "Not really. Look closely at her face."

Quickly Zoe straightened her expression, whatever it was that was betraying her. She was under the impression that she had called out for someone, had literally spoken a name. Her lips were parted, the echo of the word still fresh in her ear.

A moment later, the mother-woman in the white veil stepped forward until she stood before Zoe where she sat in the chair. The woman's face appeared heavy with grief, her eyes glazed. Tenderly she put her arms around Zoe and drew her close. She pulled her blouse to one side and guided Zoe's face to her breast.

At first Zoe resisted. A low humiliated moan left her lips. She put both hands up to block the breast. Her eyes swiveled sideways and saw that everyone in the room was watching. Throughout the surrounding darkness, rising and falling, Bubs continued to whimper.

In an attempt to blot out the sights and sounds around her, Zoe opened her mouth. The sucking sensation soothed her.

She tasted sweet warm milk . . .

———◆———

The spot was singularly wild and impressive, a wooded amphitheater surrounded on three sides by precipitous cliffs of naked granite sloping gently toward the crest of another precipice that overlooked the valley. Upon the instant of awakening, Zoe knew where she was. She looked at the encircling pine and birch around her, at the sky, impressively blue overhead, at the valley a distance below, and heard her own name being called.

"Zoe! Good morning. You're late."

She raised her head from a grassy bed. Bubs stood several yards above her. Some of the others sat around him on the green slope that served as natural seats for the amphitheater. Their heads were down. They appeared to be reading or praying.

She nodded in response to the cheery greeting and since nothing more was demanded of her, at least for the moment, she raised up on her elbows and looked carefully about.

There was a remembrance of all this from her childhood. Countless times she had fled here to escape the hate of the house. Here in this green theater everything had been possible. On the hottest of August days, she had been able to conjure whirling mists of snowflakes. Depending upon the ugliness she had left behind, she had discovered that the landscape here could be magically changed to suit any purpose. And the variations of their hate had been dazzling.

They had been artists of hate. Just when she had been certain that she had seen every variety of hate they were capable of, they had always shown her yet another.

Now she sat sleepily up, ignoring the statuelike people sitting a distance away. She had not consciously thought of this place for years. The mystery of how she came to be here did not cause any great concern. Anyone strolling in a westward direction away from the house would have found it and surely its natural design would have caught the fancy of these people. Now with her legs curled demurely to one side, she glanced down at the white stained robe, recalled vaguely but with extreme pleasure the taste of warm milk, recalled less pleasantly the almost drugged heaviness that had caught her off guard and had sent her into a deep sleep.

Quickly she looked up at the gathering in search of the woman who had played her mother. She saw that Bubs was engaged in a conversation with a young man who kept insisting that the others would never find them here and that all would have to go without lunch. The old woman in the red robe looked up and told them both to shut up. The whore-woman, sitting at the edge of the group, readjusted her somewhat bedraggled hair with a feeble coquetry.

Zoe rose to her feet and prepared to climb the soft grassy incline to join the others. She did not like the sensation of being "onstage" with the others watching. Apparently while she was asleep someone had placed her on the stage area, apart and isolated from everyone else. To her surprise, she was no longer particularly agitated over their presence here. It was merely the sense that there was little she could do about it. Not that she was completely at ease. More accurately it was a state of guarded resignation.

Suddenly Bubs extended his right hand, palm toward her, like a traffic policeman. "Don't come any closer," he ordered. "You're late."

Zoe stopped, attempted to brush the hopelessly tangled hair from her eyes. "How can I be late?" she asked. "I don't even know how I got here."

"You lie!" he accused.

The old woman in red looked up. "Don't bully her," she scolded.

"Why not?" Bubs demanded. "She deserves to be bullied."

It was hopeless. Her momentary desire to penetrate the mysteries of their personalities rapidly faded. If they did not want her to be on the slope with them, then so be it. While Bubs did not exactly frighten her, his expression was sufficient to discourage her from coming any closer. Very well. She would stay here and they could stay there. It really didn't matter. She knew the direction of the house, knew the woods better than any of them. She felt safer here than she did enclosed in the walls of her house. Whatever madness they had planned for the morning, she would hear them out.

A few moments later something impelled her to look again at the familiar surroundings. The density of the enclosure made it difficult for the sun to penetrate. She was unable to remember the thick foliage from her childhood. Then it had seemed a sunny open place. Now points of light were all about her, but they were diffuse and scattered. Even the little group on the slope sat mostly in shadow too dark to reveal the nature and origin of their indolent attention. A few looked down on her, then quickly sent their eyes back to the cavities of their laps.

She sat cross-legged on the flat grassy floor, looking up at the others, in particular at Bubs, who seemed to be standing guard over her.

Slowly she shook her head and closed her eyes and rested her forehead in the palm of her hand. Of course the place had changed. Nature grew. The trees and surrounding brush had quite naturally increased with seasons of rain and sun. Still it did seem different in some way, as though this particular spot in nature had taken on some of the eccentricities of the group which now inhabited it. Perhaps it would be the wisest course to give up trying to make sense out of the events as well as the surroundings. Although it caused a feeling of shame within her, she had rather enjoyed the sight of her ritual conception the night before, had even enjoyed Bubs's reenactment of her father's fictional crimes. And of course they had been fictional. She suspected that Mary Lisa knew more about that than she cared to admit. But even Mary Lisa could not have access to facts which Zoe herself did not have.

Now she called out to Bubs, her voice only slightly mocking, "Are you still my father?"

He looked angrily down on her. She had disturbed him in some way. "That's none of your business."

"Where are the others?" she asked, shading her eyes against a direct ray of sun.

Bubs laughed derisively. He leaned over the young man sitting at his feet. "She misses her mother, do you hear? She enjoyed the nipple. The little girl misses her mother."

The others smiled and nodded. Zoe turned away, embarrassed. She felt childlike. She *did* want to see the mother-woman.

Someone in the group asked rather sleepily, "Isn't it about time to start?"

Bubs replied, "We're waiting for the others."

As if on cue, Zoe heard voices on the path at the top of the incline. The others turned their heads in the same direction where laughter and shouting now was heard.

Zoe got eagerly to her knees, watching expectantly along with the rest of them. Through the foliage, she caught sight of a bobbing blond wig. A few moments later, Mary

Lisa appeared at the top of the path, her face radiant, shouting, "Isn't this marvelous?"

Following close behind her came the rest of the party. Several of the women were carrying picnic hampers. In the constant movement of the group, Zoe caught a brief glimpse of the mother-woman. She tried to catch her eye and failed. The group mixed and mingled with warm familiarity, greeting each other as though they had been separated for a long time.

Still on her knees on the stage area, Zoe watched the comradeship wistfully. Once again she started forward and once again Bubs took a step in her direction, his eyes warning her clearly to stay where she was.

The laughing chatter continued, a continuous swirl of voices and faces. Zoe ached to join them. Her isolation was growing increasingly painful. She wanted to talk with the others, chat with Mary Lisa, to perhaps inquire how she had known about the wooded theater. And she wanted very much to see the woman who had played her mother.

Suddenly, unable to bear the exclusion any longer, she started forward. She was about halfway up the grassy slope when Bubs shouted angrily at her, "Get back! I said get back!"

The voice, so strong and out of key with the others, caught everyone's attention. All fell silent and looked around and down. Mary Lisa's smiling face clouded. Mildly she scolded Zoe. "You'd better do as he tells you."

But Zoe held her ground. Defiantly she asked, "Why? This is my place. I found it first. If you're here at all, you're here at my invitation." She moved forward another few feet.

Within the instant Bubs was at her side. He reached sharply out for her arm, missed, and reached again.

She recoiled from the bare chest, the black bearded

countenance. "Leave me alone," she whispered, backing away.

At that moment his manner changed. He became conciliatory. "Come on now," he soothed. "We've given you a place. Down there," and he pointed back toward the isolation of the flat earth floor.

She had been spoken to as a child and she responded childishly. "I don't want to stay down there," and at the moment she said it, she heard clearly the pouting quality in her voice. She felt that she no longer inhabited herself, that someone else had moved in and was speaking for her.

Slowly Mary Lisa approached, her face somber. "You'll be happy down there, Zoe," she soothed. "You were always happier down there."

Zoe shook her head again, a weak, childlike protest. Beyond Mary Lisa she could see the others eating quietly but hungrily from the picnic hampers. She too was hungry and said as much.

In answer to her announcement of hunger, Bubs said, "That's easily remedied." He scrambled up the grassy slope and returned with a waxed-paper-wrapped sandwich. "Here," he smiled. "Now take it back down there and eat it quietly like a good girl."

But again Zoe objected. It seemed to her that they were trying to break down her resistance, isolating her and setting her apart for their own purposes. If she wasn't careful she would fall into the worst sort of confusion. No more. She had a will of her own and she intended to use it.

Suddenly she scrambled around Mary Lisa in a furtive movement. She heard a brief outburst from Bubs, a string of obscenities, and she knew without looking back that he was pursuing her. She moved as fast as she could toward the silently staring group at the top of the incline. In her hand, she held the sandwich, crushing it in her haste.

Now as she drew near the top of the slope, the others looked up at the peculiar pursuit, Zoe, silent, struggling with the incline and the long uneven hem of the robe, and Bubs, equally silent, scrambling after her. There was a resigned expression on her face. She knew that capture was inevitable.

He caught up with her several feet short of the top of the incline. Gently, almost delicately, he took her by the hand and she permitted it, permitted him to remove the crushed sandwich and replace it with another. Then, because the others were watching, she allowed him to guide her back down the incline and permitted him, with only a slight whimper of protest, to arrange her, seated, cross-legged upon the ground at the center of the earth stage.

Mary Lisa, who stood to one side, grinned through orange lips. "We're going to have such a marvelous time today."

From the top of the incline, the old woman in red shouted down on them. "It was the house. I told you all along it was the house. Everyone feels better here."

Zoe listened. Everywhere new thoughts beckoned, new possibilities of why she was here, what they intended to do with her. Was she their prisoner or their guest?

Bubs was still scolding. "If you're going to cry, cry, but not with that cheap silent sob you picked up in the movies."

"I'm not crying," she protested and lifted bone-dry eyes to prove it.

At the top of the incline, the eating was drawing to a close. Apparently all had had their fill. The remainder of the food was replaced in the picnic hampers and the hampers themselves stored to one side of the path that led back to the house.

Zoe tasted her sandwich and found it peculiarly lacking in flavor, a chalky, bitter mayonnaise filling of some sort that caused her to experience a slight nausea. She set it quickly to one side. The effort of trying to understand and failing had exhausted her. She continued to sit, head down, in isolation, vaguely aware that the others were now taking seats on the grassy incline of the wooded amphitheater, waiting, watching her.

There was a continuous feeling of embarrassment within her, that she was somehow taking a witless part in her own humiliation. These people to whom she felt absolutely superior had somehow managed to get the upper hand.

Suddenly it got very silent. She looked up. They were all seated, staring down at her. Bubs stood to one side, ready to orchestrate the silence.

Now the woman who had played Zoe's mother started down the incline toward the stage. She was carrying a bucket. She leaned away from its obvious weight, moving carefully, steadily, down the hill.

Bubs called out a warning to her. "Be careful. You can't trust her."

The woman smiled her gratitude at his thoughtfulness and continued on down the slope until she stood directly before Zoe. She placed the bucket heavily to one side.

Zoe was glad to see her. She asked softly, "What are we doing here?"

The woman smiled warmly. "You brought us here last night. Don't you remember?"

The others laughed. The morning had taken an unexpected comic turn. Zoe heard someone repeat her question, mimicking her voice. Certainly she was now well awake. The surrounding faces were becoming faintly recognizable, like people you encounter on the same bus every morning or over coffee in a restaurant. She knew that the rough ground upon which she sat was earth, and the low, gray-rolling mass overhead was sky. For the moment that seemed to be all that she was permitted to know.

Suddenly Bubs announced in loud, slightly melodramatic tones, "Let us begin!"

Zoe looked up to see precisely what the beginning process was. The woman standing before her moved the bucket closer. She spoke quietly, her eyes filled with what appeared to be sudden fatigue. "Why did he have to bring home a cow," she asked, projecting her voice as though she were reciting a line.

Zoe looked blank. The question seemed to have been addressed to her. Once, a long time ago, her father had brought home a milk cow. "To save money," she replied effortlessly.

Bubs broke into brief applause. He leaned against a near tree, watching closely, apparently delighted with her response.

Now the mother-woman knelt before her, her eyes beseeching. "But who will do the milking? I've never milked a cow in my life."

Again they all seemed to be waiting for Zoe's response. She felt their eyes upon her, and rather than bear the weight of eyes, she replied, "I will. I can learn."

The mother-woman patted her hand gratefully. "You're a good girl." She shook her head sadly. "There's not one earthly reason why you should be a good girl, but you are and for that I'm grateful." She leaned forward and kissed Zoe lightly on the forehead.

She stood up then and backed away, calling a warning over her shoulder. "You'd better get it done before he comes home. You know how he can be. The bucket's just there. Take care."

The mother-woman rejoined the others on the slope. Zoe leaned forward and peered into the bucket. It was filled with cold creamy milk. As the silence and the waiting grew, she looked to Bubs, awaiting his direction.

With his arms still crossed, leaning against the tree he asked, "And did you milk the cow?"

Zoe nodded. She thought; Mary Lisa could have known about the cow and the accident. Everyone in town had known about the accident.

Bubs asked, "Was it difficult? The milking, I mean?"

She shook her head.

"What happened?"

Zoe shifted upon the hard ground. What was the point? It had happened years ago. Without looking at him, she replied, "I left the pasture gate open one night."

"And?"

"I forgot to put the latch down."

Bubs stepped forward, still questioning relentlessly. "What happened?"

Zoe shook her head. The past was too easily becoming the present. "I said I was sorry," she murmured.

Someone called out, "What happened?"

"She'll tell you," Bubs replied with confidence.

Zoe felt a faint chill about her face, like the chill on a frosted window.

Mary Lisa said cheerily from the front row. "I remember exactly when it happened. It was terrible. Blood everywhere."

This image seemed to stir interest among the others. Several voices now called out, "What happened? Tell us!"

Then Bubs was at her side. He lifted her head by pulling her hair back. The gesture was not particularly forceful; it startled her more than anything else.

Beyond the wall of trees, she saw a piece of blue sky with gold-veined clouds. "You're hurting me," she said, trying to keep her voice even.

"Then tell them," he commanded. "It's your line. Tell them what they want to know."

From the front row, Mary Lisa offered to help. "I will. We all went out to see it. The whole town. It was terrible. There was even a photographer from the newspaper." She giggled. "I slipped in the blood."

Zoe tried to pull away from the hand that forced her head up at a distorted angle. At the first sign of her resistance, he jerked again, harder this time.

The mother-woman protested. From the grassy slope she called out, "You're hurting the child. Let her go. She said it was an accident."

Bubs gazed very deliberately up at the intruding voice. Then carefully he twisted Zoe's hair about his hand and gave it a sudden wrenching jerk.

The force of the gesture brought her flat against the earth. Her scalp stung. As she was about to protest this offense, he quickly released her hair and placed his foot flat against the side of her face.

Taken off guard, she closed her eyes against the pressure, against the humiliation and rising fear. He was insane. They were all insane. Perhaps this ritual theatric would eventually lead to bodily harm. Or worse. In this state of panic, she thought of other kidnapped victims, other captives. Cooperation was her only chance.

She heard through her fear the mother-woman protesting again, this time more violently. "You have no right," the woman cried out. "No right at all."

"I have every right," Bubs countered. Zoe felt the pressure of the foot against the side of her face increase. Bubs shouted again, "It was her fault and she must pay."

As Zoe tried to shift her position, the foot became vicious in its insistence that the head not move. "Are you ready to tell us what happened?" Bubs demanded.

She tried to nod, but the force of his foot against the side of her head prohibited movement. She had been here before, had at some time lain with a foot pressing her face to earth. A peculiar feeling of quiet stole over her. If she had survived it once, she could survive it again.

"I'll tell," she murmured.

Mary Lisa squealed, "Oh, good. Let her up now, Bubs."

Slowly the pressure against the side of her head subsided. Slowly she pushed herself up, tasting dirt in her mouth.

"Well?" Bubs demanded, arms crossed in a stance of mindless male authority.

Vaguely she shook her head. Her fingers brushed dirt from her hair.

Bubs stepped forward again. His eyes were like quartz, dull and rounded. She looked at him and for the first time suspected that he was capable of anything. Cooperation might lead to survival. It was a chance.

"I left the pasture gate unlatched," she said, dully.

"And what happened?" The threatening hands held her fast, a human crutch, lifting her shoulders into an unnaturally raised position.

A ray of sunlight came from the side of the arena like a spotlight. To her surprise, she saw the unlatched pasture gate, saw the great lumbering, trusting animal wander out in search of tender grass, heard the truck while it was still a distance away around the curve. She tried to call out to the cow, but the cow had no name, was a great senseless wonder with all its brains in its monstrous teats. As in a slow-motion nightmare she saw herself trying to run for the cow, felt herself clawing at space, heard the screech of brakes, and at that moment saw the cow shoot up into the air, actually clear the ground, a hurtling, trumpeting hooved thing suddenly airborne. It seemed to her that the cow spun endlessly around. Blood splattered over her face. The animal landed less than five yards from her, an exploded, shattered mass of flesh and bone, the teats broken open, white milk blending with blood. And there were other noises too, the spinning wheels of the overturned truck and the wheezing of the dying driver. The last thing that she saw clearly was a cow hoof imbedded in the ground before her.

She shuddered, remembering, and closed her mouth as though she had been speaking, although she had felt no sensation of speech.

Bubs muttered, "So much for the cow." He walked toward the bucket of milk, slowly, deliberately lifted his foot and pushed it over. White spilled out over brown grass.

Mary Lisa giggled. "She's right. That's exactly the way it happened." She scrambled down toward the stage to share with Zoe the excitement of the tragedy. "Do you remember Willie Mitford, Zoe?" She grinned. She was on her knees now, hands clasped. "Well, before the police arrived, he cut off one of the teats and took it home and kept it in a cardboard box in the back of his closet until it began to smell so bad his mother made him throw it out."

Bubs kept repeating, "So much for the cow."

Zoe, standing alone, suddenly discovered she had no more strength for standing and slipped into a sitting position. "I said I was sorry," she murmured, rubbing the side of her face at the remembrance of splattered blood. She looked up at the faces of the audience. They were clearly condemning her. It was strange, but she was not particularly disquieted. The recall of the event had been vigorous, but it was now gradually disappearing again.

Bubs walked to a near tree and started to beat out a light rhythm against the bark with the palm of his hand.

Zoe felt a need to explain further. "It happened so fast."

"It might have been avoided," Bubs replied, not looking at her. "That is, unless you meant it to happen."

"No!" Zoe's protest was sharp and sincere.

Bubs broke off his drumming. "Were you punished?"
She shook her head.

He seemed stunned, then he grew expansive. He began to encircle her, arms outstretched as though entreating heaven for understanding. "No punishment?" he repeated, incredulously. He whirled quickly to the audience. "Did you hear that? No punishment at all. Here this careless girl leaves the gate unlatched, destroys a magnificent animal which I purchased with stolen money so that she might have milk, and no punishment!"

He dropped his arms to his sides, signifying disbelief. He glanced hopefully over his shoulder. "No beating?" he asked, lightly.

She shook her head.

"No forfeited meals?"

Again, no.

He confronted her directly now, turning his back to the audience.

"Then what in the name of God did your father do?"

Zoe fell into a close study of her hands in her lap. Her personality was dissolving like a grain of salt in water. It was so hard to remember. The grain could no longer be localized. "He-did"—she hesitated—"nothing." She shook her head, disbelieving her own statement.

Bubs stared mournfully down on her. "How sad for you."

Zoe nodded.

Mary Lisa whispered from close by, "Poor thing. I never knew. My old man beat me regularly." She smiled through orange lips. "It was marvelous."

Bubs knelt before Zoe and took her hands in his own. He asked softly, "Would you like to be punished now?" Quietly the others took up the refrain, chorus voices repeating his question.

The mother-woman whimpered, "No, please."

Suddenly Bubs looked angrily up at her. He ran a few yards to where she was sitting and confronted her. "You silly bitch," he scolded. "You don't know your lines at all."

The mother-woman dabbed at her eyes with a handkerchief. "She's just a child," she protested.

"She's a half-dead child," Bubs shouted. "Do you want to keep her that way?"

The mother-woman shook her head. In a whining voice, she said, "I only do what I think is best."

"Bullshit!" Bubs exploded. "You hate her as much as we all do, which is almost as much as she hates herself."

The mother-woman stood up and faced him directly. "At least I don't have to watch," she said defiantly. She swayed, a little dizzy, then turned and walked wearily up the incline to the path at the top. There she sat on the ground near a tree, closed her eyes and stuck her fingers in her ears.

"Good riddance," Bubs muttered. "Mothers!" he cursed and the word came out an obscenity.

Zoe was aware of what was going on about her. There were threats everywhere. Again she considered escape and again dismissed the idea. She was their sport, their amusement. Obscure facts from her life were being trotted out for their amateur theatrics. She had no choice but to play her role. How far they would go, she had no idea. She had already suffered a degree of humiliation at their hands. In anticipation of what might be in store for her, she looked up at Bubs. "Please," she begged. "It was an accident."

He responded with a burst of energy, running back down the incline, rubbing his hands together as though warming to the task before him.

"Yes, punishment." He returned to the stage floor and paced quickly for a moment, stroking his beard, his eyes lost in thought. "But what kind? We must make the punishment fit the crime." He called out to the audience. "Any suggestion?"

No one answered.

"Oh, come now," he scolded. "Don't leave it all to me. Why must I always do everything?"

Zoe watched and waited in a state of growing agitation. She tried twice to speak on her own behalf, but both times Bubs ignored her.

Suddenly Mary Lisa started forward in excitement. "I have it," she exclaimed. "Since she was responsible for the death of the cow, make her take the place of the cow."

The group fell silent, all considering the possibilities of her suggestion. Bubs stopped pacing. His eyes became pale and delicate. His face lifted. He looked at Mary Lisa admiringly. "Yes," he said, quietly. "Yes, of course. Why didn't I think of it?" The others joined in with their general approval. As the projected image grew clearer in their minds, a few scrambled down the grassy incline as though to get a better seat.

"I need a rope," Bubs shouted.

The man named Dempsey ran up the hill to one of the picnic hampers. He returned with a length of rope. As he passed by Zoe, he patted her on the head. "Nice Bossie," he grinned.

Her heart was beating too fast. Already she felt the heat of shame on her face.

Bubs, the executioner, approached her with great dignity. He took the rope and tied it loosely about her throat. Once she tried to remove it, but he merely pulled it tighter. She closed her eyes, felt the rough hemp against her neck.

When the rope had been secured, Bubs ordered, "Get on your knees."

Slowly she did as she was told. Her hand moved self-consciously up the rope around her neck. The movement seemed to anger Bubs. "Leave it alone," he snapped. "Cows don't examine their bondage. They accept it."

Thus reprimanded, she knelt before him and shut her eyes, not wishing to witness her own humiliation. With her eyes closed, she felt the white robe being pushed from her shoulders. The garment fell backward and was stopped at the cord which was tied around her waist. Instinctively her arms moved up to cover her breasts.

Again Bubs scolded her. "Cows don't suffer from modesty. A clothed body means nothing to them."

She was breathing very quickly now. All about her stood thirsty and dying gray-green alders and smooth-leaved willows and the piercing, curious, consuming stares of the audience. Bubs's eyes were directly above her, looking down; they were large and wise with a wisdom that never reached the surface to be expressed in speech.

She considered begging and dismissed the notion. She would not beg.

He stood before her, contemplating, and in his silence and in the silence of the others, on her knees with the rope around her neck, she felt herself becoming possessed of certain bovine qualities.

"On your hands and knees, please," he ordered now, his manner almost polite.

She looked downward. She was as common and as undistinguished as a cow. For a brief instant, before she obeyed his last command, she saw a Zoe, hatted and gloved for church, saw a Zoe of maddening refinement and control, saw a Zoe who carried, poised on two feet, a turbulent chaos of nightmares and guilt.

When she was on her hands and knees, Bubs took the end of the rope and led her around the stage floor in a little circle, always coaxing, always calling to her, "Here, Bossie, come on, Bossie, follow me like a good cow."

She tried to hold her head erect, but let it droop finally between her shoulders. She watched the passage of grass beneath her, countless tiny colored wild flowers she had never seen before, wincing now and then as her bare knees landed heavily on a stone invisible in the grass.

Mary Lisa on the front row clapped her hands in delight. "What a marvelous cow, but will she give milk?"

Bubs answered brightly, "We'll soon see," and he continued to lead her around in a circle, jerking now and then on the rope when she didn't move as rapidly as she should.

Dazed and humiliated, Zoe accepted her role in the animal kingdom. She saw a cleared space in a woods, a woman becoming a cow, a cow a woman, the white robe trailing behind, still tied at the waist obscuring her flanks and tail. They were trying to make her a madness, and willingly she followed, feeling only the jerk of the rope around her neck.

Finally Bubs shouted, "Milking time!" He led her back to the center of the arena. Fatigued, she tried to sit back on her haunches. The blood was beginning to race through her head. Her neck ached from its downward battle with gravity. Quickly he jerked at the rope. "Cows don't sit up," he informed her. "Dogs do, for a reward, but not cows. Cows have no brains, no feelings. They're good for only one thing."

She raised her head to the eyes staring back at her from the slope of the hill in search of one who might come to her aid. But they seemed just barely able to stay in their places, so great was their excitement. Mary Lisa appeared totally transfixed, her mouth open.

Zoe lowered her head again because she had seen enough and because there was no more strength in her for holding her neck erect. She had killed a cow and now she had become a cow. She felt half-human.

Bubs reached out for the empty bucket. He slid it beneath the arch of her body. He sat cross-legged at her side, facing the audience. "Now we'll see if she's a good cow."

She closed her eyes as the pulling motions on her breasts commenced. Her head fell farther down between her shoulder until she could see his hands, upside down, spreading and closing over her breasts.

A green light seemed to slant in on her brain; it appeared to be streaked with yellow. Circles of mild discomfort spread over her. A curtain of her own hair fell over her eyes, blessedly blocking her vision. There was a flashing of nerves, a tensing of muscles, and still the hands enclosed her, still pulling, working with greater exertion now.

Zoe turned once to look at him, to consider begging him to stop. She saw only the lower half of his face, a cow's view, saw his tongue move around his mouth until his teeth were bare. His jaws clenched, his chin sank, the rhythm and effort of his hands clearly recorded in the tautness of his face.

He jerked angrily at her neck rope. "Stand still!" he commanded. "Cows don't watch while they're being milked. They mind their own business."

Her head drooped; her body struggled for balance against the pulling motions. For a moment the ground beneath her was rising and falling. The discomfort was increasing.

Finally he sat back on his heels, his hands opened at his side, his voice weary, disgusted. "No milk," he muttered. "Not a trace of milk."

Someone from the audience urged him on. "Try again. I hear some cows can be very stubborn."

Another male voice called, "If she don't give milk, what in the hell is she good for?"

Bubs's hands expanded and closed around her. Every time he pulled, he cursed at her. Shouts of 'Harder!' filled her ears. Her arms and legs were trembling. The humiliation and pain was there to be examined. The dead cow was being paid for.

Then he too was beginning to see the futility of the effort. He sat back a final time, muttering, "Still no milk." He lifted her head by the back of her hair and mourned, "What *is* she good for? Woman or cow? What *is* she good for? What purpose is she supposed to serve?"

She tried not to look at him, but he insisted, asking her to assess her own worth. She tried to crawl forward but couldn't. She could neither rise nor fall nor move in any direction save for the one he had selected for her. She felt a separation then. The instant of terror and humiliation was over, but the darkness of separation went deeper than that. It was a gap of nonbeing, neither cow nor woman.

He released her finally, permitted her to scramble backward, to feverishly restore the robe to her shoulders. She covered her aching breasts and dragged herself a few feet away and took in with a single glance sky and trees and condemning faces.

Bubs stood a distance away, still muttering, "What *is* she good for? Woman or cow, it comes to the same thing."

Several members of the audience took up the refrain now, a slow drone of voices asking one another, "What *is* she good for? Woman or cow? What is she—"

Zoe closed her eyes against the rising human sound. There was no one there she knew or cared about, no one to report on her humiliation in this world to that other world. She began to burrow her fingers into the dead leaves around her. She wrapped the white robe around her and lay down. The blue-black sky weighed heavily upon her. But still it was a good moment.

The cow had been paid for . . .

A narrow ribbon of smoke wound its way lightly up out of the fire and rose in the misty autumn dust. The sun was just beginning to set. This time Zoe was aware of the passage of day and the beginning of night. She pretended not to be aware of it, but she was.

The dead cow had been left where it had fallen. She had been partially aware through closed eyes of Bubs removing the neck rope, had been aware of the group dividing into teams for the purpose of playing innocuous childish games. All afternoon they had raced and darted about in variations of blindman's buff, wood tag, punch the icebox, allee-allee outs in free, a harmless bacchanal. Zoe had watched them, heard them shrieking with delight as a few of them had passed close to her and looked sympathetically down at the "dead cow."

At some point in early evening, she had dragged herself to the far side of the arena, the better to be out of their way. Every movement had been misery. She felt she had been beaten. Finally she propped herself up against the tree trunk to watch the games, to assess once more her chances for escape. She was tempted to think that they were paying absolutely no attention to her. But near the top of the incline she spotted the two shadowy male figures of Rich and Dempsey, who seemed to take no part in the games, who appeared to serve as guards to the path which led back to the house. In the opposite direction was sheer granite cliff. She dismissed the notion of escape.

She brushed the matted hair from her eyes and leaned her head back against the tree trunk and watched the games, the curious lilting joy of voices shouting at one another, freely playing, gloriously enjoying themselves.

Once the mother-woman, running close, stopped to look down on her. She cried triumphantly to the others, "Look! Zoe's back!" Then she swooped low and smoothed the white robe over her shoulders, her mouth moving continuously, "Oh, my dear. Terrible things happened while you were gone. Don't ever leave again. Promise me that you'll never leave again."

At that moment, a young man with long blond hair leaped out from the dense underbrush nearby. "I see you," he shouted.

The mother-woman shrieked and dashed up the incline with the young boy in wild pursuit. Others came and went in this fashion, a few stopping, all welcoming her back.

Then it was dark with a suspect suddenness as if they were controlling nature as well as everything else. Three of the men fed the fire in the center of the arena. The warmth of the blaze drew all of them down from the wooded amphitheater. From her place of isolation near the far edge of the stage, Zoe watched them as they warmed their hands and backsides, a few munching on sandwiches and fruit left over from the picnic hampers.

She too was hungry and cold but she did not dare move from the protection of shadows. As far as she could tell all were present and accounted for. With one major exception. Bubs. He was nowhere in sight.

This alarmed her. She was totally defenseless against threats she could not see, could not even imagine. Still it was quiet at least for the moment, and she continued to lean against the tree trunk, exhausted from her ordeal of the morning. She felt intense humiliation now, like a delayed reaction. She saw too clearly the spectacle of herself being led around by a rope. Suddenly she closed her eyes against the remembered horror. Why had she permitted it? And a more valid question, why at the moment of greatest degradation had a portion of her being welcomed it?

She leaned her head forward against her knees and felt

the sharp chill of early autumn. With her head down, eyes closed, she heard their voices.

"Oh, clever, clever, clever. You're so bloody clever."

"What are we doing tonight?"

"Shhhhh! The dead cow is sleeping."

"Don't be ridiculous. How can the dead cow be sleeping? She's dead."

"I don't think so. I think she enjoyed it too much to be dead. One doesn't die from ecstasy. One dies only from despair."

"Is there a difference?"

"Shame on both of you. That's not a dead cow. That's Zoe, our hostess."

Zoe heard them clearly, multiple voices, male and female, high-pitched and low. She dared not look at them. She felt certain that if she made eye contact, they would involve her again in their madness. Curious ambivalence there. She did not want to be involved with them, but neither did she enjoy sitting alone in the cold darkness.

Suddenly the chattering group fell silent. There was a rustle of commotion on the path high above the steep incline. She raised her head and blinked in an attempt to focus her eyes. Between where she sat and the top of the ridge there was a valley of darkness. But high on the path she saw Bubs. He was standing in the center of a strong flashlight beam. Around his bare chest he wore a cape of some sort. Even from that distance, Zoe looked closer and recognized the faded, wine-colored brocade of her mother's living room drapes. Apparently they were stripping the house for their mad charades. On closer examination she observed that he had pulled back his long hair and had secured it at the base of his neck. He looked shorn.

All the others looked up now in wonder and admiration.

They broke into hearty applause. A few shouted, "Your majesty!"

Bubs smiled and swirled the cape around him and bowed low from the waist.

At his side and holding the flashlight was Mary Lisa. She turned it on herself for a moment, but quickly he reached out and refocused the beam on himself. Mary Lisa seemed to bask in his reflected glory and reached forward to straighten the folds of his cape.

After standing and preening at the top of the incline, they started regally down, Mary Lisa leading, throwing the flashlight beam backward so that he might have a lighted path. The others continued to approve heartily of what they saw, and several now scrambled about, placing the upturned bucket before the fire, preparing a throne.

Zoe, still in the shadows, watched it all, mildly repulsed, mildly intrigued. The man was insufferable. She saw him lift his beard to stroke it, arrogant, pompous gestures, chief madman in a group of madmen.

The royal procession had reached the arena floor now. The others rushed about admiringly, a few daring to touch the faded brocade cape. One minute he looked irresistibly powerful, the next merely ludicrous.

"It's a fine evening," he intoned to one and all, sweeping in a wide circle around the fire.

They murmured in agreement and backed away to give him all the room he needed. He walked around and around the fire in massive sweeping movements, nodding royally from side to side. Mary Lisa trailed after him as though he were the most marvelous creature she had ever seen.

Zoe noticed for the first time that Mary Lisa had changed clothes. She wore blue jeans and an oversized white shirt. The blond curly wig had been discarded and her own faded dark hair had been pulled back into two stubbly ponytails which stuck out on either side of her head. On her face, which appeared to be freshly washed, she wore not a sign of makeup.

As Bubs continued to pace, tension seemed to be building in the group around the fire. They knew that at a given moment the pacing would stop and something would be required of them.

Suddenly he broke the rhythm of his pacing and strode directly toward the tree beneath which Zoe was sitting. Instinctively she drew back.

Mary Lisa followed after him with a flashlight and now shone the harsh beam directly down into Zoe's face. The light was blinding, causing her to shield her eyes.

With a tone of disgust in her voice, Mary Lisa murmured, "It's just the dead cow."

But Bubs did not agree. "Oh no," he said softly. "You're wrong. It's my queen."

Mary Lisa lowered the flashlight and turned upon him immediately, offended. Her hands were on her hips and the flashlight beam was dancing eerily across black trees. "What do you mean, she's your queen?" she demanded. "She's a dead cow. You said so yourself this morning. If anyone has a right to be your queen, it should be me."

Bubs tried quickly to pacify her. "No, Mary Lisa. You've been a queen so many times before. You're Queen of the Hayride, Queen of the Barn, Queen of the Locker Room, Queen Beneath the Stadium, Queen Under the Table in the Makeup Room, Queen in the Choir Loft, always a queen." He gestured expansively, then pointed a finger down on Zoe. "But that poor creature," he went on, "has never been a queen of anything."

Again Mary Lisa protested angrily. "Then if that's the case, I'd say she didn't know how to be a queen."

"How do we know if she's never had a chance?" asked Bubs.

Mary Lisa appeared to be truly offended. "She doesn't want a chance. Ask her. Go ahead. I dare you. Just ask her."

Zoe was aware of Bubs on his knees before her. His voice came soothingly through the brilliance of the flashlight. "Do you want to be a queen, Zoe?" he asked softly.

Instinct advised her to play along. But before she had a chance to answer, a voice she recognized as the mother-woman's spoke for her. "Of course she wants to be queen. Who wouldn't? She's just never had a chance. She's my daughter. Just as good as anyone else. Of course she wants to be queen."

Again Mary Lisa objected. "She didn't say that. Why don't you let her answer for herself?"

At the moment when the madness seemed to be reaching fever pitch, when all fell silent awaiting her response, Zoe was aware of someone behind her in the darkness, someone crawling toward her. Before she could turn and look, she felt strong hands clamp themselves on either side of her head, felt the hands guide her head up and down in an affirmative motion.

"There!" Bubs cried exultantly. "She *does* want to be queen. You could see for yourself."

Zoe looked quickly over her shoulder to see who it was who had helped her with her reply. But there was nothing behind her except darkness and the density of foliage.

Still Mary Lisa was suspicious and said as much. "I don't think she moved her head at all. Dead cows don't move their heads. Someone did it for her."

But Bubs was determined. He stood up, adamant in his decision. "She shall be my queen. But you must clean her first. She's filthy. Look at her."

Again the flashlight beam moved over her, not just her

face, but down the length of the white soiled robe, lingering
for a moment on her bare feet curled to one side, then moving rapidly to the top of her matted hair. She shut her eyes
and tried to protect herself from their close scrutiny.

Someone muttered, "How repulsive."

Bubs ordered, "Women! Get to work. Make her pre-
sentable for court. A dress rehearsal for the true crucible yet
to come."

Zoe tried to protest. But it was futile. Within the instant
she felt hands lifting her to her feet. She tried to signal her
disapproval, but it was lost in the explosion of energetic activity around her. Again something unknown and incomprehensible was happening to her. As the females swarmed over
her, she felt herself dividing. She wanted no part of the hands
that were manipulating her, steering her toward the fire. But
on the other hand, Bubs had been right. She had never been
queen of anything. The realization was not joyful, but neither
was it particularly sorrowful. It was a dead realization. It had
no eyes that it might by a look reveal its source, and no
mouth that it might explain itself by words. It was just there,
a foolish, senseless, terribly important desire to be queen of
—something before she died.

Now she felt herself being guided into a position close
to the fire. The upturned bucket that was to have served as
Bubs's throne now served as her own. There were only
women around her, eight or ten of them as well as she could
see. Mary Lisa, no longer pouting, was now grinning radi-
antly at her. And the mother-woman was there, and the old
crone in red who seemed to be issuing most of the orders,
and the whore-woman as well, and several others whom Zoe
vaguely remembered having seen before. The men had disappeared. She could hear them talking a distance away but
she couldn't see them.

Mary Lisa leaned close and whispered, "It'll be better if you close your eyes. We can work faster."

The old woman cackled, "You listen to her, honey. She's the Queen of Queens. She knows what she's doing."

Zoe obeyed because she had no desire to watch them and no alternative other than to obey them. They frightened her, their irrationality, their whimsical changes of moods. Perhaps the queen role would be a safe one. Queens were not degraded and humiliated.

With her eyes closed she felt the robe being lowered from her shoulders again, felt a glorious sensation of a warm cloth moving over her body. Female hands gently massaged her back. Her arms were lifted, then replaced, her head moved from side to side. She felt doll-like and pampered. A cool oily substance was rubbed over her face and down her neck and throughout the ritual no one spoke. They were as quiet as she was, although all about she could hear their breathing. Their hands upon her were extremely pleasurable. Several worked on her hair, pulling gently but firmly at the tangles, easing out the snarls. Finally they were able to brush it back in long continuous strokes.

Last of all she felt a piece of material being guided down over her head, felt the white robe fall away beneath. Then another garment of some sort followed it and sat lightly on her shoulders. Her new clothes were perfumed, a delicate odor of flowers. Even with her eyes closed, she knew that she looked nice.

As though to confirm her thoughts, Mary Lisa giggled prettily. "Doesn't she look marvelous?"

Zoe opened her eyes. She was wearing Mary Lisa's peasant skirt and blouse. The fabric felt soft and clean about her body like garments that had been warmed before a fire.

The other women stepped back to admire their creation. They walked in small circles about her, stopping to flounce the skirt here, smooth it down there. Clearly they were pleased with what they saw.

The mother-woman stood on one hip, a hand massaging the back of her neck. She asked curiously, "How come you've never been a queen before? Just how come? You're beautiful."

Zoe blushed and played her role. "No one ever asked me," she said.

"Idiots!" grumbled the mother-woman.

Mary Lisa suggested, "Let's call the others. Bubs will be so pleased."

A strong-looking young girl standing a few feet away suggested, "I think we should keep her for ourselves. After all, we did the work. And she smiled at me. I think she would like me."

Mary Lisa looked with alarm toward the suggestion. "Oh no, we couldn't do that. That's a whole different game, another play. It doesn't belong here. Besides, Bubs would be—"

"Screw Bubs," the firm young voice said.

The old woman interceded, scolding, "Mind your tongue. We'll perform your play another time. I promise."

Then there was no further discussion. The men were returning. Zoe could hear them scrambling down the grassy incline, heard their exclamations of approval as they first caught sight of her.

In the last moment, Mary Lisa leaned forward with a smile. "You're going to love it. Being queen, I mean. You're just going to love it."

Zoe nodded in spite of herself. "What do I do?" she whispered as the male voices grew nearer.

Mary Lisa looked suddenly stricken. "Oh my God, that's right. You've never been queen before, have you?"

Zoe shivered and shook her head.

"Well, don't worry," Mary Lisa soothed. "You'll do just fine. Always remember that queens exist only for the pleasure of kings. They serve no other purpose." She added lightly, "And relax. It always helps to relax."

The hands in the lap of the peasant skirt were trembling. Zoe was trying very hard to play her role, but she did not know her lines or understand the character, had not the faintest idea what was expected of her.

Then out of the deepest shadows, she saw Bubs walking toward her. The others fell back. The purpose of the evening was about to be realized. Noiselessly he drew nearer, drawing his cape about him, head erect, appearing taller than usual in the firelight, broad in the shoulders, a serene, almost feminine grace, the part of his skin not covered with black hair appearing dazzling white. He wore neither shoes nor socks, wore only the faded blue denim trousers and bogus cape. He stood directly above her now, looking down, studying her with intense scrutiny. Under the weight of his eyes, she looked away.

The others were silent, awaiting some monumental judgment. Quietly he moved behind her, lifted her hair and touched the back of her neck. She closed her eyes as she felt the hand move down her neck. She stiffened, every fiber of her being rejecting the hand and the touch. It stayed flattened there for a moment as though testing something, then suddenly it withdrew itself, brusquely pushing her forward at the same time. She struggled for balance on the upturned bucket, drawing the blouse around her shoulders for protection against future contact.

Quickly he moved around in front of her, examining his hand as though it had been injured in some way.

Mary Lisa stepped forward, alarm on her face. "What's the matter? She's your queen. You asked for her. Well, there she is."

But Bubs shook his head angrily, blowing on his hand now as though to warm it. "She's a cold queen," he muttered. "I want no part of her."

"She's not!" Mary Lisa protested. "Give her a chance. You said yourself she didn't know how."

"Queens are born," he said imperiously, warming his cold hand before the fire. "There's no possible way to educate them to that position. She's cold, you can feel for yourself. She was born cold, will die cold, stone dead cold."

He moved behind her and touched her back again, rough almost slapping motions which caused her to dodge the onslaught of his hand. "A turnip queen," he exclaimed. "No real blood, just red juice. Not fit for male consumption."

Mary Lisa protested again. "That's not fair. You picked her."

"I didn't know," he pouted.

"Well, what do we do with her now?" Mary Lisa demanded.

Several others picked up the question. Grumblings were heard. The audience had been deprived of their entertainment.

Zoe felt fresh humiliation. It was so easy to fall into their charades. She offered a weak defense. "I'm not cold," she murmured.

"The hell you aren't," Bubs exploded. "Look at my fingers," he demanded, standing directly before her. "They're frostbitten. There are only two kinds of queens, warm queens and cold queens. And you definitely are a cold queen, a remnant of the Ice Age, a glacier. I'll have nothing to do with you."

The disappointment of the group was obvious. A male voice asked dejectedly, "What in hell do we do now?"

Bubs shrugged indifferently. "What we always do with cold queens. We leave them alone."

Mary Lisa shook her head wearily. "All that work," she sighed, "for nothing."

"It isn't your fault," Bubs comforted her. "You tried to tell me. I should have listened." He slipped away into the shadows for a moment and returned with a long crooked stick. He thrust it into Zoe's hands. "Your scepter, your majesty," he said, bowing low from the waist. "Cold queens are allowed only to watch. It's forbidden that they take part lest they freeze the entire world. Then where would we be?"

Zoe took the crooked stick, aware of her foolish posture on the upturned bucket, clearly aware of the condemnation coming from the others. She felt that she had been wrongly condemned but in a way she welcomed her role as mere witness. She might look and feel ridiculous on the upturned bucket, but at least it promised a degree of safety. She could survive their condemnation. It might have been interesting to see what was expected of a warm queen. But then it was true, she had never been queen. Of anything.

Bubs turned his back on her and walked toward the fire. He stood for a moment looking about at the other females, appraising them. Finally, predictably, he held out his hand to Mary Lisa.

She giggled and ducked her head. "I told you," she smiled. "I told you all along." She went to his side and slipped beneath his arm. He pulled her close and led her off into the shadows on the far side of the arena.

A laugh of approval went up from the group. Others now were pairing off, males selecting females, all disappearing into the dense foliage, men soothing, reassuring, women giggling.

Zoe sat alone in her queen clothes on the upturned

bucket holding the crooked stick. They had no right to condemn her out of hand. Incredibly the rejection actually hurt.

Softly from the front row came a strong female voice. "Do you enjoy being alone?"

Startled, Zoe blinked at the darkness and tried to see who was speaking to her. She saw only a crouched form. Lifting her eyes, she saw a second outline near the top of the path, her guard, still on duty, cutting off all avenue of escape. She looked back at the figure in the front row. "Who is it?" She whispered.

"I asked you a question," scolded the voice.

"I can't see."

"It isn't necessary that you see. Do you enjoy being alone?"

Zoe lowered her head. It occurred to her to drop the stick and leave the bucket, but she had been placed there and she was accustomed to staying where she had been placed.

The female voice from the front row was insistent yet kind. "Do you know how ridiculous you look?"

Zoe nodded. She glanced up at the faceless shadow. "Why didn't you go with the others?"

"I wanted to stay here with you."

The kindness moved her, made her feel vulnerable. "Go and join them if you wish. I'm not going anyplace."

The female voice laughed softly. "I know you're not going anyplace and I have no more desire to join them than you do." The shadow seemed to change positions. "Just listen to them," she whispered in a tone of disgust.

Zoe lifted her head. Imperceptibly at first, then growing louder, out of the shadows she heard sounds of human coupling. The night was alive with sexual activity. The sounds stretched mercilessly across her ear. Groans now, close by, pantings, and now and then sharp cries of pain and pleasure. The sounds became suggestions causing localized discomfort.

She dropped the stick and clapped both hands over her ears. Still she could hear them. Suddenly defiance flared. She didn't have to stay and listen to the sounds of her own rejection and exclusion. She left the upturned bucket and started running toward the top of the incline. She was vaguely aware of the female laughing in the front row, but she continued to run, struggling up the steep incline. Suddenly she stumbled over something. In the darkness, she saw a woman's bare legs straddling a man's flanks, fingers clawing. She drew back at the sight of the rhythmically entwined bodies.

Still struggling upward, she was determined to reach the safety of her home. There she would lock and bolt the doors. She did not belong here. She would lock herself in her room where she did not have to play the role of cold queen.

But at the top of the path, she felt the harsh force of the male guard as he reached out to restrain her. She flailed uselessly, recognized him as Dempsey, the mechanic from Logan Airport. She tried to speak his name, but he turned her effortlessly around without a word and headed her back down the incline toward the fire and the upturned bucket.

From the front row, the female voice called out, "I warned you, Zoe. You'd better come back."

She shook her head and again tried to bolt. But this time Dempsey merely escorted her back down the length of the incline, past the coupling forms, past the shadow in the front row, and sat her roughly on the upturned bucket.

It really didn't matter. Better a cold queen than a mad one. If what she heard around her was expected of warm queens, she wanted no part of it. Resigned now to her role, she sat on the bucket and wrapped her arms around her body in an attempt to shut out the chill.

From the front row, the female voice called out to her. "Have you ever made love with a woman?"

Zoe bent over and covered her head with her arms.

The voice from the front row continued to entice her. "Do you want to try it? It's really much better than with a man."

Zoe shook her head. "Please leave me alone."

The female voice became harsh. "You're hopeless, Zoe. You really are."

She discovered that she didn't have enough hands to shut out completely the sights and sounds that were going on about her. She was cold, colder than she had ever been before in her life. She raised her head and looked at the near fire, which seemed curiously to be withholding its warmth from her. The shadow in the front row drifted off, leaving her totally alone except for the guard at the top of the path.

In an attempt to conquer and dispel the cold loneliness within her, she studied the fire, saw an exquisite phallus in each separate flame, red tongues licking and penetrating the darkness. Instead of being identical in color and shape, she noticed that each level of the fire was made up of perfect geometric patterns with sharp angles which dissolved into liquid shapes and from each a brilliant spectrum of light exploded, not merely orange and red but green and blue and black as well. The patterns leaped upward, crisscrossed, merged, separated. Her rate of breathing increased. She felt hollow. Her discomfort crested with the tongues of fire. She turned away to digest her misery.

Sometime later she heard them drifting back. She had no desire to see them in their satiation. Instead she studied the darkness inside her lap, heard them laughing softly all about her, every female a coquette, every male a conqueror.

Someone called out, "Where's Bubs and Mary Lisa?"

A voice answered, laughing, "Working overtime, I imagine. They usually do."

A body passed close beside the upturned bucket. A hand

brushed roughly across the top of Zoe's head. A male voice cursed, "Cold bitch queen."

Someone warned, "Don't touch her. You'll freeze your fingers."

A female voice which Zoe vaguely recognized as belonging to the shadow in the front row informed them all, "Neither male nor female. She simply has no appetites. None at all. But then what can we expect? The dead seldom have appetites."

Zoe looked up. They were seated about her in a rough circle. A few of the women were still adjusting their clothes, others gazing reverently at their male companions. Still more mortifying was the contrast between her sense of disgust and their self-righteousness.

The mother-woman spoke to her. "Shame on you," she whispered. "How you've disappointed me."

To the left of the fire, the whore-woman twisted sensually upon the ground, her hands starting at her breasts and running the length of her body in an effort to retain recent sensations. "What a waste," she murmured. "What a sinful waste."

"She is what she is," someone commented.

"A woman is nothing but an assortment of receptive openings."

"Then she is nothing."

Zoe was on the verge of closing her eyes again when suddenly someone shouted, "Look! There she comes."

All heads swiveled toward the far edge of the arena. A slight figure appeared, wavered, then fell forward onto its knees. For a moment it did not move. Rather it continued to sit on its heels, its arms wrapped around its body, rocking back and forth in a gentle, self-soothing motion. The head was bowed, the body naked. Something wet and slimy had caused the stubbly mouse-colored hair to mat and cling to the skull like a grotesque cap. Around the shoulders, neck and breasts there were dark smudges like bruises. One eye was swollen shut and a thin trickle of blood slipped from the corner of the mouth. It was Mary Lisa, the warm queen.

Suddenly the entire group broke into spontaneous applause. Several of the men rose to their feet in a standing ovation. Mary Lisa tried to cover the aching eye with one hand, but apparently the effort of supporting the arm was too much and she let the palm fall back to her knee.

Stirred to compassion, Zoe hurried to her side and knelt down. Up close she saw new bruises on the hips and thighs. The grisly script was clear. A great deal had been asked of the warm Queen and she had obliged.

Mary Lisa kept her head down. She didn't want Zoe to see. One hand fluttered self-consciously about the butchered hair, moving gingerly around the slime, trying desperately to arrange it into some semblance of order.

Zoe tried to catch the hand, to hold it, to assure it that restoration was not necessary, was indeed impossible. "Don't," she whispered. "It'll be all right."

Someone from the group called angrily out, "For God's sake, leave her alone."

Someone else added, "You're just jealous. It could have been you."

Zoe turned on the barbaric words. While she was searching for the one who had spoken them, Mary Lisa tried to rise to her feet. She stumbled forward, falling again to her knees, perilously close to the fire, one hand clutching at her stomach tolerating unendurable pain.

Zoe had seen enough. The woman needed medical attention. Her mind stopped on the last thought, then surged ahead on a thread of hope. Medical attention, the need to see a doctor might provide her with a means of escape. Surely they would not deny their warm queen the assistance that she obviously needed. Now quickly Zoe went to her side and tried to lift her up.

But the protest was immediate and strong. Several of the men started toward her. Even Mary Lisa objected. "No," she whispered, trying to shake off Zoe's hands. "I—am the Queen," she added proudly and lifted a distorted purple face.

"But you're hurt," Zoe insisted. "Please, let me take you back to the house. You're cold and—"

But Mary Lisa would have none of it. She scrambled weakly away to the other side of the fire and licked her lips, enjoying the taste of blood. She shook her head and through spasms of chill murmured, "He said—wait here." The words were blurred as though it pained her to speak. Softly a smile broke across her lips. She lifted her battered face to Zoe. A thin trickle of blood seeped down from one nostril. "Isn't he marvelous?" she smiled.

Zoe stared helplessly. She tried again, escape paramount in her mind. "Mary Lisa, please, you can't—"

Suddenly a strong, slightly amused male voice cut through the protest. "She can't what?" he demanded.

Zoe looked up. It was Bubs standing a distance away at the edge of the dark trees. He still wore the foolish faded cape; his arms were crossed before him, his feet spread.

Immediately Mary Lisa crawled toward him. When she reached his feet, she hugged his legs and held fast for protection.

Zoe met his eyes and tried to stare him down. "Where are her clothes?" she demanded.

Bubs dislodged the woman clinging at his feet, shook her off as though he were walking through a pile of dead leaves. He strolled out onto the arena and toward the fire, totally unconcerned. "I'm not responsible for her clothes," he said, grinning at a few of the men. "She took them off.

She can go and put them on." He warmed his hands at the
fire, still grinning at the men and women, who were watching
him with expressions of mixed fear and admiration.

Zoe held her ground, trying to cope with the variety of
feelings: desire to escape, concern for Mary Lisa, deep rage at
the man who was standing so confidently before the fire. To
remain silent was a confession of weakness. She had to speak.
"What did you do to her?" she asked.

Without looking at her, still preening for the benefit of
the others, Bubs replied lightly, "Only what she wanted me
to do." Now he glanced at Zoe over his shoulder, smiling
with unfailing charm. "Only what she wanted me to do," he
repeated. "Nothing more. I do try to oblige."

Zoe glanced down at the shivering, bruised bleeding
woman in the shadows. Her hands were still examining the
butchered hair, her swollen eyes fixed upon him.

Bubs moved about the fire very deliberately, playing to
the audience, swirling and lifting the cape. "That's all we can
ever do, isn't it, men?" he asked broadly. "We just give them
what they want."

The men snickered their approval. Bubs continued to
encircle the fire, talking all the time. "She loved it," he announced, "loved every minute of it. Ask her yourself if you
don't believe me. Go ahead, ask her." He pointed toward the
collapsed woman. "Or better still, ask her if she wants more.
She was begging me a moment ago, but she was so unappetiz-
ing. I was the one who said no. Go ahead, ask her. Just look
at her. She's ready. That one was born ready." Now he asked
the group a direct question. "Do you want to see? Do you
want to make a bet?"

The audience, even the women, stirred to excitement.
They pushed closer to the fire, jockeying for a better view. A
male voice confirmed the bet. Other voices urged him on.

Only Zoe protested. She stepped between Mary Lisa and Bubs. "Leave her alone."

Bubs smiled at her with an expression of mock politeness. "You are in her way," he said quietly. "She's coming to me. I'm not forcing her. Look if you don't believe me."

He pointed down toward the scrambling female. On her hands and knees, Mary Lisa crawled painfully around Zoe and rejoined him near the fire. She sat, looking up, her hands moving over her breasts, her lips moving ever so slightly, her face set in a look of pure ecstasy. Slowly she lay down, totally submissive, wholly willing.

A round of applause came from the audience. Weakly Mary Lisa acknowledged their approval, then looked up at Bubs, who was standing over her.

Zoe felt sick. It was no business of hers, but she did not have to stay and watch. All eyes seemed to refocus on her, awaiting her next move. Even Mary Lisa was watching her from the ground.

Slowly Zoe backed away. "I'm going home," she said and started off in the darkness.

Bubs called after her. "I wish you wouldn't."

Zoe did not reply. She was intent on putting as much distance as possible between herself and the insane scene below. She dug her heels into the incline and tried to blot out the image of Mary Lisa lying battered and submissive by the fire. So intent was her concentration that she failed to see the three figures waiting for her at the top of the path. With her head down in the dark, she walked right into them, three male figures who silently closed around her, their hands on her arms and back, turning her around, forcing her down the hill toward the fire and Bubs.

He called out cheerily to her. "It won't take long. I don't know why you're so shocked. It goes on all the time, night and day."

She tried twice to break free of her captors, but it was useless. The men simply tightened their circle around her and guided her back down to the fire.

Bubs smiled. "I'm glad you have changed your mind," he said. "Mary Lisa would have been so disappointed. After all, this is for your benefit as much as hers. She worries about you."

Zoe quickly covered her mouth with her hand to stifle a scream. Pressing her lips together, she drew a deep breath. The point now as always was not to let them see or know her true feelings. To reveal herself made her even more vulnerable. She tried to close her eyes, but when she did she felt she was slowly falling forward into the fire.

The men retreated and left her alone near Bubs, who continued to stare at her. He seemed to feel almost sorry for her. "You really don't want to see, do you?"

She shook her head, not trusting herself to speak.

Amused, he said, "Mary Lisa doesn't mind. Why should you? It's perfectly natural. It's what she does best. She's built for it by nature, as you are. Why deny your purpose?"

"She's hurt," Zoe protested, wanting only to flee. She looked behind her for an escape route. But the entire audience had quietly regrouped about her. Escape was impossible.

Bubs suggested, "Why don't you sit down? You'll enjoy it more. Besides, you're blocking the view for the others."

The suggestion struck Zoe as absurd. "Please," she begged, "Let me go." Her voice falling, she added, "Why are you doing this to me?"

Bubs placed his hands on her shoulders and gently pushed her down to the ground. "I'm not doing it to you," he smiled. "Besides, it'll only take a minute. She's fast, that one is, almost too fast. She has no finesse, just sacred animal

energy." He looked down at the woman who was still waiting submissively at his feet.

Zoe was aware of sweat on her forehead. She was
trapped, but still she did not have to watch and she put her
head down and covered her face with her hands.

Suddenly on either side appeared the mother-woman
and the old crone in red. With gentle shushing sounds, they
removed her hands and held them tight, forcing her to
watch. She struggled briefly and lost and tilted her head back
and glared rigidly up at the starless night.

Bubs shook his head, disappointed. "We're doing this
for your benefit. So much trouble for another human soul,"
he scolded. "Now watch! And learn!"

Again Zoe struggled for possession of her outstretched
arms. Her head twisted. Suddenly strong hands clamped
down over her skull and held her head fast.

The entire audience seemed to be growing annoyed
with her. Warnings of "Sit still!" reaching her ears.

Thus secured, she had virtually no choice but to watch.
She tried once to focus on the fingers of fire and on the dark
trees beyond the arena. But the moaning woman attracted
her attention and held it.

Bubs had not touched her as yet but continued to stand
over her, looking thoughtfully down as though trying to
assess how he would launch his assault. Finally with great
deliberation, as though he were performing a sacred ritual,
he knelt between her legs and crawled forward.

At the first touch, Mary Lisa's head dug backward into
the ground. A trembling passed over her body as though it
were readying itself for the invasion. Bubs hesitated only a
moment, then penetrated forward.

The group became silent, intensely watching, a few
mouths slightly open, eyes staring as though they were witnessing a splendid miracle. Zoe tried to close her eyes but

couldn't. She saw a tiny paw claw at his back, saw Mary Lisa glance sideways at the group, her face a delirium of contortion, the rocking motions increasing, both hands clawing now, the purple bruises on her face glistening with sweat and effort.

Without warning, Zoe's eyes filled with tears. She tried again to turn away, but the hands holding her would not permit it. She felt fingernails digging into the flesh of her arms as the women continued to hold her fast.

The creature on top lost his identity. His broad back and shaggy head became part of the tormented woman beneath, a two-headed monstrosity locked together against its will. Mary Lisa's mouth fell open. Silver threads of saliva mixed with the blood.

The humpbacked thing continued its assault, releasing, advancing, a devastating rhythm, exploding finally in a full-throated gasp that caused the woman to wrench backward, the arch of her body lifting them both, mouthing nonsense sounds of pure gibberish, her bruised eyes completely closed.

Zoe groaned, experiencing the sensation of orgasm herself. She shut her eyes and struggled with the hands that held her. The churning in the pit of her stomach increased.

The two-headed creature was quiet now. The audience sat in silence, transfixed by the spectacle.

Through her agony, Zoe continued to feel rising nausea. What she had been forced to witness had been barbaric. In the continuing silence, she saw that Bubs was on his feet, looking down on Mary Lisa as though she were a trivial matter.

Mary Lisa lay shivering. Her body yielded to the shudders, but between bouts it lay still. Her mouth was opened and her eyes stared dully into the fire. Once she turned to one side. The mouth spoke. "Isn't he marvelous?"

Zoe felt as battered and abused as though she had suf-

fered the assault. Nausea continued to grip at her insides and
since the women refused to release her, she had no choice
but to lean forward and retch violently where she sat. Then
she felt herself being lowered gently onto the ground. Someone was cradling her head in their lap. Concerned voices
floated by overhead.

"Is she really sick?"

"What do you think?"

"Jesus, I guess we went too far, huh?"

"With one like her, you never know how far is too far."

"Well, we're doing the best we can do. That's all anyone
can ask of us."

Through blurred, frightened and sick eyes, Zoe watched
the faces swirl above her. She twisted her head to one side
and thought she saw Mary Lisa jump up from the ground,
thought she saw her take a towel from Bubs and wipe the
blood and bruised marks from her body, wipe them completely clean as though they had been merely painted on.
Zoe tried to refocus her eyes, the better to watch as Mary
Lisa adjusted the blond wig and pulled on the blue jeans and
white shirt, as strong and giggling as ever.

Fascinated, she continued to watch as Mary Lisa preened
and adjusted her clothes, saw her walk directly over to Bubs
and say matter-of-factly, "Well, that didn't work. Any other
bright ideas?"

Then she thought she saw Bubs, slouched against a tree,
looking totally exhausted, shaking his head, say, "She's beyond help. Absolutely beyond help. We offer a world of happiness and fulfillment and what does she do? She pukes."

Between the row of zombie faces on one side and the
madness of the man and woman near the tree on the other,
Zoe closed her eyes. She tried to lift herself up but couldn't.
Terror was becoming a constant companion. There were
times when she thought her unceasingly agitated mind was

laboring with some oppressive secret. The pressure was constant, the need to decipher what was and what merely appeared to be. She covered her face with her arms and thought consciously of her house in Newton, of her sons and husband, of the violets in copper pots that needed water, of the stray newspapers scattered across the lawn, of the cracked window in the back door that needed to be replaced. But the thoughts were not as real to her as the ghost people surrounding her.

She sank deep into a starless blackness where there was no pressure, no thought, just a sudden depth of green-rising forest, sculptured peaks, hills sloping down and other, darker mountains ahead . . .

—————◆—————

A male voice droned endlessly on.

"The effect of immediate and uncompleted experience is not easy to achieve. The victim is in the midst of the experience and at the moment has no way of knowing what will happen next."

Zoe's first impressions were similar to those of a patient awakening from surgery. She was in a bed, her own bed, she imagined, although she had nothing of substance on which to base the assumption.

The voice was nearby, speaking now in an instructional tone. She imagined other people listening carefully.

"Everything is in suspense and the victim uses for her immediate effects a recording of the unconscious. It is an effort to put into language not only what the victim thinks, but all of the impulses of her psyche, all the mysterious activities of her id. But the difficulty is nearly always a total inaction, a helpless stasis in which nothing of life exists but an overwhelming consciousness of the moment, or even a dreamlike semiconsciousness."

Words! Zoe turned on the pillow and gazed through the nearby window. It was autumn, she thought, about mid-October. Whether it was the same autumn, the same October, she could not say. She knew, without knowing precisely how she knew, that from early morning there had been an intermittent drizzle which now had been replaced by a warm sun. The weather was unsettled.

Still the voice pursued his lecture. Still she refused to turn her head in the direction that might bring him into view.

"The quest for new methods and new truth is urgent in our times, almost to the point of compulsion and even insanity. Every artist knows this. But drama is still most interesting when it is visible in action, when it is involved with events and consequences."

She listened. The leaves were making the faintest noise against the window. A breeze was barely creeping over the house.

"—so a life is nothing but an illusion of free and spontaneous and irresistible experience to be shared and lived by the victim in her own imagination. But life doesn't explain itself, nor does it present itself with unity and coherence. Our task is to inveigle the victim into sharing the mysteries and uncertainties of what seem to be true experience."

She heard a soft rustle of applause. The voice and the listeners seemed to be drifting away. She heard footsteps brushing softly down the hall, a body of life moving away from her.

Let them go. She felt no great urge either to identify them or to call them back. She felt comfortable, warm beneath blankets and sheets. Her head throbbed slightly but otherwise she was intact. She pushed back the blanket and noticed that she was wearing a soft flannel loosely fitting black garment of some sort, like an old-fashioned nightgown with long sleeves and high neck and ample folds of warm soft material about her legs and ankles. Only the color struck her as odd. Black.

She had no idea how long she had slept, or who had carried her to her bed, or even what day it was. She was lost in the freedom of one week that did not have to be accounted for. She was fairly certain that she was being held a prisoner in her childhood home by a party of mad men and women, that she was being manipulated for some purpose, but she wasn't certain what. What was now coming out of her brain was a trickle of the kind of consciousness which might help her to stay alive, but little more.

Suddenly she lay quietly in the bed, memory returning of certain degradations; the dead cow, the cold queen, the forced witness to a brutal assault. The rain was back and increasing; it struck against the windowpane in sharp staccato bursts. For a moment she listened intently without taking her eyes from the spot on the window where the sound of rain had first attracted her.

In a distant part of the house, she heard voices, human stirrings. She listened. She heard footsteps on the stairs, heard female voices laughing, chattering, drawing nearer.

Her eyes widened, then closed. She wasn't ready for them yet. She needed more time. But the voices were loud, directly outside her door. She heard a woman shout, "Keep up, you idiot!"

Then another female voice laughed derisively, "Look at him, just look at him."

Zoe slipped down into the bed and covered her head with the blanket. She wasn't ready. Whatever new madness they had in mind for her, she wasn't ready.

From beneath the blanket, she heard the door burst open. Within the instant Mary Lisa was beside her, jerking the covers back, grinning down, "You awake?" she called cheerily. "You've slept for ever so long. The rest of us have been up and busy for hours."

At the sight of the orange-painted lips and blond wig, Zoe turned away. However, she lingered in some fascination at the transformation now standing before her, the energetic woman who only the night before had lain as though brutally damaged.

Zoe asked weakly, "Are you all right?"

"I'm fine," grinned Mary Lisa. She stood back to demonstrate the truth of what she had said. Then she leaned closer, beaming, "We've brought you something." She gestured toward the door. "Look!" she urged. "Just look. Isn't he marvelous?"

Curious in spite of herself, Zoe raised up on her elbows. The area near the door was filled with women, their faces more or less familiar; the mother-woman, the old crone, the whore-woman, several young female faces all grinning back at her, awaiting her pleasure. But what caught her attention and held it was the male figure at the center of the group.

She sat slowly up, trying to clear the sleep from her eyes in an attempt to make sense out of what she saw. It was Bubs. He was completely bound and tied. The faded cape was gone and his bare chest was crisscrossed with ropes, his hands tied rigidly behind his back, his head held erect by the taut angle of his bondage. He kept his eyes down, obviously trying to bestow upon his helpless position a disdainful and bored expression. He was forever puckering up his eyes, making a wry face, letting the corners of his lips droop, affectedly yawning and with a not quite adroit nonchalance now tried to shake the long hair from his face. He was posturing insufferably.

Zoe noticed that Mary Lisa held the end of the rope in her hand. The other end was tied about his neck. Roughly she jerked on the rope as one leads a dog on a leash. With a slow rolling step he walked awkwardly to the side of the bed, stood unspeaking. He barely deigned to bestow a fleeting and apathetic glance at Zoe, then he turned his head away. Suddenly Mary Lisa gave the rope a second more powerful jerk. His head spun around and locked rigidly into a grotesque angle. Mary Lisa giggled. "Isn't he marvelous?" She jerked him a step closer now. "And he's all yours. We brought him to you so that you could decide on his punishment."

Zoe rubbed the ache in the side of her head. "Punishment?"

The mother-woman stepped forward to the opposite side of the bed. "Of course, punishment," she exclaimed. "What else? After what he did to you last night, I certainly recommend the sternest, harshest punishment you can think of."

"And not just last night," cackled the old crone in red. She moved close to the foot of the bed, the flesh of her face sagging and discolored by age. "He's responsible for everything. Why, he's done nothing but humiliate you since the day you entered our lives."

A young female with short curly brown hair said from the door, "He made you into a dead cow yesterday. Don't you remember?" She shuddered. "I've never seen anything so awful in my life."

"And worse," said another. "The cold queen. Surely you remember."

The mother-woman sat down on the bed beside her. Her breath was foul as she leaned close and whispered, "But last night, late last night, was the worst of all. Don't you remember?"

Zoe did not attempt a reply. She breathed deeply in an attempt to clear her head. She found it difficult to look directly at any of them. Perhaps their fantasies were contagious.

Perhaps if she recognized anything of what they were saying, she would fall under their spell and become one of them.

Still Bubs fascinated her, the strong, powerful body reduced to a state of helplessness under the bondage of the ropes. He stood beside the bed, his head twisted into a grotesque angle by the rope around his neck. His face was alternately vivacious and sullen. He appeared to be listening closely to the hollow-sounding accusations that were being leveled against him. It was good, amazingly good, to see the man helpless.

Now Mary Lisa shifted her attention from Bubs back to Zoe. She leaned close. "Do you hurt anywhere?" she murmured.

Zoe shook her head and pulled away from the hand that was reaching out to her.

Bubs laughed. "She doesn't even remember. Anything! She's so goddamn dead, she doesn't even—"

Again Mary Lisa gave a rough jerk on the rope. The suddenness caught him unaware. For a moment he appeared to lose his balance; he wavered forward, struggled to straighten his shoulders and finally righted himself, although his head was completely bowed now to accommodate the new angle at which Mary Lisa held the rope.

"He's really impossible," she scolded. "Completely impossible. Which is why we have brought him to you. While he has done damage to all of us, you are his most recent victim. Therefore we felt that your desire for revenge would be more effective than ours." She giggled. "We sometimes tend to forget. You know?"

Zoe shook her head and slipped back down into the safety of the bed. "I don't want him," she muttered.

"Don't want him?" shrieked the old woman. "After what he did to you?"

"He did nothing to me," Zoe said.

Bubs giggled. "See? I told you."

The old woman screamed at him. "You shut up. You hear me? Not another word out of you."

Now the mother-woman looked curiously down on Zoe. "Don't you remember? Anything?" she asked incredulously.

Zoe met her eyes and responded as evenly as possible. "No."

Several of the young girls at the door turned away in astonishment. All were staring at her. A spur of irritation surfaced within her. She said quickly, "Please just get him out of here and leave me alone. All of you. If you insist on staying here, then stay away from me. Just get him out of here and go play your games somewhere else." She slid back down beneath the blanket and closed her eyes, trying to make herself absent yet present all at the same time.

"Well, I never," gasped someone at the foot of the bed.

"She was to be the judge and pass sentence," complained another voice. "We even gave her the black robe. She's not playing her part."

Bubs snickered.

Zoe listened beneath the blanket with her eyes closed. "Just take him away," she pleaded. "All of you, just go away." She lay very still in the bed, on her side, her hands tucked between her legs. She could feel their eyes still upon her, could hear the weight of the silence.

Suddenly as though she had just solved the problem, Mary Lisa exclaimed, "She doesn't want to remember! That's the trouble. She's always been like that for as long as I've known her. She remembers, but she doesn't want to remember." The voice rose into a steady, high-pitched clamor. "She was like that in school, she really was. She never wanted to see or remember anything."

The mother-woman asked calmly, "What do you suggest

then? There's been a crime here. There must be punishment. It's the law."

Bubs offered lightly, "I could humiliate her again. Maybe this time she'd—"

"No," Mary Lisa said. "If we're going to help her we must do it in the right way."

"Which is?"

Again silence. Zoe pressed her eyes tightly closed as though the sound of their voices might penetrate her vision. She heard the rain against the window coming harder. The storm was increasing, the day growing colder.

Suddenly she heard a commotion around her. Bubs shouted, "Hey! What the—" There seemed to be incredible activity. She felt the bed vibrating, someone pushing against it. Footsteps slid quickly over the floor. She heard increased breathing as if something were being done that required great exertion. Not daring or wanting to look, she turned quickly on her stomach and buried her face in the pillow, still feeling movement about the bed, feeling the bed itself jerk.

Bubs continued to object to something, his voice low now, then rising in anger, shouting a string of oaths, a series of half-completed protests.

"Get that end," someone called. "Pull it tight."

"Goddamn bitches," he shouted. "Where does it say I have to do this. Let me—" Again he broke off, apparently unable to finish.

Suddenly all activity ceased. The chilled voice of the whore-woman announced with pride, "There!"

Mary Lisa giggled, "Isn't he marvelous?"

Bubs's voice, quite breathless now, cursed again, "God-damn good-for-nothing cunts."

"It's for the best," Mary Lisa soothed. "It's probably not exactly the way it happened that day, but I'll bet it's close to it." She giggled again. "Get her to tell you about it. It was all over school."

Still Zoe dared not look. The silence in the room was dense, interrupted only by the rain on the window. Softly she felt a hand on the back of her hair, soothing, inviting, "Look, Zoe, look how much he resembles Ben Frailly."

Inside the darkness of her pillow, Zoe's eyes opened. Her breath caught in her throat as though the pillow were suffocating her. But still she refused to look, refused even to acknowledge their presence. She continued to hear the sound of labored breathing, a husky rising and falling of someone under great duress.

"Please look, Zoe," begged Mary Lisa.

"She's stubborn," someone said.

"Who was Ben Frailly?" asked another voice.

"Bubs knows," Mary Lisa said confidently. "And Zoe knows. They're the only ones who need to know. Come on. Let's go. They can work it out for themselves. I have complete confidence in both of them."

Then it was silent again. Zoe was learning to fear the silences. There was a last rustle of movement, a whispered exchange of some sort. They were moving away from her again. A moment later she heard the door open, then close.

She waited for what she thought was a safe period of time. Once or twice she thought she felt the bed move. Cautiously at first she raised her head, then lowered it back onto the pillow, afraid to look. The first sound she heard was a plaintive plea, a male voice, very young sounding, coming from the foot of the bed. "Zoe. Please be my friend."

Slowly she looked over her shoulder. At first glance she gasped. They had tied him to the posts at the foot of the bed, a crazy crucifixion, arms extended, wrists and ankles tied to opposite poles, a distorted, spread-eagle position. In addition, his face had been blackened by some substance, causing his eyes and teeth to appear unnaturally white. The blackface stopped at his neck in a smudged jagged smeared line as though someone had applied the makeup in a hurry.

"No," she groaned. "Please go away. Please leave me alone."

Suddenly he laughed outright. "I have no choice, as you can see. You have no choice either, so let's get on with it."

Zoe stared at the calm reassuring tone. "Get on with what?" she asked. The outstretched male body filled the cavity at the end of the bed. He resembled a gigantic bird frozen in flight. She could not bear to look at his black face.

Suddenly she slipped from the bed and ran for the door. Even before her hand reached out, she knew that it would be locked. And it was. She heard him laughing behind her, heard again the male voice, which sounded incredibly like a young boy. "And don't bother untying me either," he warned softly. "They'll just come back and do it all over again."

She looked at him, at his broad back suspended awkwardly between the posts. His calmness, his reasonableness, was contagious. Slowly she walked past him back to the bed and sat on the edge of the mattress and asked almost coldly, "Then what am I suppose to do now?"

He shrugged. "You were there. I wasn't. You tell me."

"Tell you what?"

"About Ben Frailly. About what happened."

"I don't know anyone by that name," she said. "How can I tell you about someone I don't know?"

He seemed to grow impatient with her answer and tried to shift against the ropes. Once she thought she saw him wince in pain as the ropes cut into his wrists. She made a move toward the end of the bed with the thought of untying him. But he warned her sharply, "No! Stay away. We'll never get anyplace if I'm free."

Weary and confused, she sat back down. "Then tell me precisely what it is that we are supposed to do."

"You know that better than I do."

"I know nothing."

He laughed again. "I'm almost tempted to believe you."

She leaned forward and rested her head in her hands. Why was it that sleep never seemed to ease her fatigue? She looked up at his hands wrapped around the bedpost, then on up to his bearded face. Bubs returned her gaze. "Talk to me," he suggested kindly.

"About what?"

"I have no idea. I was hoping you would know."

She shook her head. "When will you let me leave?" she asked.

"You just got here. So did we all. There's work to do."

She looked at him again, at the black makeup smudged over his jaws, cheekbones, forehead. He lowered his head, aware of her close scrutiny. "I've looked better," he apologized.

At best it seemed a stupid remark. She left the bed and wandered aimlessly about the room, stopping near the window to study the condition of the dreary day. Beneath her on the dresser sat the line of dusty Barbie dolls. Mindlessly she fingered a tiny blond head.

Into this silence he spoke. "Did you invite Ben Frailly to come home with you that day?"

She started to reply but caught herself in time and instead looked blankly out the window. Through the tops of dead spidery trees, she saw churning clouds.

"Poor Zoe," he said, taking her silence for an answer. "What a hard time you've had of it."

She resented his condescension, the note of pity in his voice. "No worse than anyone else," she said, turning away from the window. She looked at his ridiculous black face and suspended position between the bedpost. "No worse than you," she said pointedly.

Again he laughed outright. "Oh, this isn't so bad. A bit undignified, but that's all. At least I'm not on my knees as you are."

She stared at him, not understanding, and returned to the bed to demonstrate her ability to move and function. In a way she felt safe with him thus bound. Daring to relax, she sat almost easily at the head of the bed, leaned back and reached for a pillow, hugged it to her. She studied him a moment longer. "Do you have any idea how ridiculous you look?" she asked.

He nodded. "Some."

"Why did you let them do it to you?"

He shook his head. "I had no choice. I was outnumbered."

In addition to the stupidity of the situation itself was now added the futility of a conversation. She felt sorry for him, felt certain that he must be experiencing a degree of discomfort. She shook her head, unable to understand anything. "Please tell me what it is that I'm supposed to do," she asked finally, "so that I can do it and we both can get out of here."

He frowned down on her. "That's not the right attitude."

"Then tell me what the right attitude is and I'll assume it."

"You're supposed to tell me about Ben Frailly."

Frightened by his insistence, she tried forcibly to remind herself of the rest of the world, of the village of Whitney less than three miles away where normal people undoubtedly were huddled inside store windows waiting for the rain to stop, or Boston, that larger world a hundred miles away with buildings and cars and people scurrying for shelter, unaware. Someplace beyond this room there were relatively safe worlds of lights and colors and sounds. She noticed now that Bubs was trying to flex his fingers, opening and closing them about the bedpost. "Can't you feel anything?" she asked.

He cocked his head to one side. "I was about to ask you the same thing. Are you certain, absolutely certain, that you don't remember Ben Frailly, because if you do, I'd be very appreciative if you'd remember it all as quickly as possible so that I can get down from this spider web." He pushed backward from the angle of the bondage; if the desired result had been relief, it failed. His black face contorted; his eyes closed, his hands went suddenly stiff as though in a spasm of new discomfort.

Zoe could scarcely bear to look at him. "I remember some things," she said hurriedly.

"Well, why in the hell didn't you say so?"

"Primarily because it was none of your business, not yours or Mary Lisa's or anyone elses." Brief anger flared. "Why don't you leave me alone? All of you. You have no right. Do you hear? Leave me alone." She was shouting. She hugged the pillow to her, leaned her face against it.

Suddenly she heard Bubs struggling again. His black face was distorted by pain, the long hair flung into disarray. After a few moments, his body went limp from the exertion; he hung between the two bedposts, head down, rib cage rising and falling.

"Don't," she begged. "It does no good. Please let me untie you."

He looked up at her, weary of the game. "I'm sorry, Zoe, I really am. They've gone too far." He stopped as though to consider his words, then laughed weakly. "No, that's not true. They probably haven't gone anywhere at all. They're probably right outside the door listening."

"For what?"

He shrugged. "They'll tell us when they've finished with us."

"And when will that be?"

He smiled. "They'll tell us that as well."

She closed her eyes, unable to understand any of it. Why Ben Frailly, she thought?

"Because something happened that day," Bubs suggested, watching her closely.

"Nothing happened," she protested. "My God, what could have happened? We were only thirteen."

"Age generally has little to do with it."

She had the feeling that their thoughts were running on two separate tracks which threatened to meet at any moment. She adjusted the pillow in her arms. If thinking about Ben Frailly would help her get out of here, then she would gladly do it.

"Good," smiled Bubs. "Remember everything and I'll listen carefully as the others are probably listening carefully outside the door."

Zoe glanced toward the door. She'd glanced toward the door that other day as well, her ears straining then as well as now to hear footsteps.

"Zoe, it's raining. Can I come into your house and wait?"

The voice had come from Bubs although it did not belong to Bubs. It sounded younger, much younger. Shocked at the mimicry, she looked up at him. His head was erect in spite of his bondage. The expression was constrained, painfully intelligent. Poor little black boy. How everyone hated him. What the town of Whitney would do without Frailly's Garage and Service Station, no one knew. But still they hated them. George Frailly, Ben's father, hated the town in return so he was safe. But Ben, standing there before her now at the foot of the bed, the black, moist-eyed little genius with the fine irregular features who spoke softly and who constantly and unwittingly reminded the Whitney High School faculty of its stupidity, had not yet learned to love hate and repentance, so he was despised openly with hardly any respite, a hated black boy, the only one in Whitney, his small frame racked and crucified daily. Like now.

Zoe shifted on the bed. Images blurred and mingled. The expression at the foot of the bed was the same, the eyes begging, offering her a depth of friendship she had never known in return for nothing or so little.

Her parents were gone, or rather her father was gone and her mother was looking for him as always.

"Zoe, I'll ride home on the bus with you, then walk back. Okay?" It was Bubs again, though not Bubs. Ben in Bubs, or the other way around. Whatever, the face was kind even in its agony.

"You can't stay," she warned him, "and if my father is at home, you can't even come in."

The helpless man between the bedpost nodded. The pain on his face seemed eased, as if her kindness had had a medicinal effect on him.

"Zoe, it's raining," he said. "I can't walk home in this."

She glanced out of the window at the storm. The dead trees were scarcely visible behind solid sheets of rain. "Listen!" she whispered. Quickly she moved to the door. Nothing. The house was quiet. "I think they're gone. Come on in. It'll be all right for a while."

Again the man-boy smiled his gratitude although his continuing discomfort was apparent. Every move no matter how small registered on his face. She saw the flesh of his hands turn white as the ropes tightened against the pressure. His head fell backward, then forward. His legs, spread-eagle to accommodate the bondage, collapsed altogether. For one hideous moment, he literally hung there, a crucifixion by rope.

"Please," she whispered, "let me untie you."

He didn't answer. He sounded suffocated.

He lifted his head. She saw his fingers clutching again at the bedpost, saw his body lift as once more the legs supported the distended torso. He succeeded in straightening his back, gaining a few inches in height, which released the pressure on his lungs. His hands were glowing patches of red as the blood flowed back and forth. He looked at her, his voice weak. "You can't release me. No one can. But you can be my friend."

Eagerly she nodded. "Friends." On her knees before him at the end of the bed, she comforted him, brushed back the long hair from his face, loved him with the mindless intensity of a first love, with the winged happiness that was the result of finding a comrade soul in the deceits and trickeries of her environment.

He responded. "You're beautiful, Zoe."

She'd never been called beautiful before.

"Is this your bedroom?"

She nodded.

"Is this your bed where you sleep?"

Again she nodded. As long as she was near him and touching him, he did not seem to feel his agony so acutely. There was a mysterious urge within her then to share more with him. Still on her knees before him, she slowly loosened the black flannel robe while Ben Frailly watched closely, not encouraging, but not protesting, as though to see more of her would help him to endure. As the garment fell away, she ran her hands gently up to her hair with a gesture that raised her child's breasts and gave her body a pleasing attitude.

Ben Frailly appeared intoxicated with her beauty. He

seemed content merely to watch, a degree of the pain on his face replaced now by rapture.

She laughed and preened for him, her eyes skittering across the top of the ceiling. She'd never known the effect of a man's eyes on her body before and it proved a potent intoxicant.

Suddenly she saw over his shoulder a dark figure standing in the doorway watching them. The figure, robed in black, appeared faceless, an atmosphere of cold about him, a caricature implacably hating life, a father-demon figure.

She scrambled backward on the bed, reaching frantically for the discarded gown to cover her nakedness. Ben Frailly was straining to see the threat for himself, his eyes wide with terror, still immobilized by his bondage. He was shouting something, but in her own terror, Zoe couldn't understand. In the next instant the room was filled with black-robed figures, all moving toward her.

A crone voice cackled, "There! I told you so. She's a whore just like the others. But you wouldn't believe me."

A male voice, his head obscured in the black folds of a hood, cursed, "You bitch." He reached out for her and roughly dragged her from the bed. "We turn our backs for a minute and we trust you and what do you do? You behave like a slut."

All the time that Zoe was pulling on the black robe, the others were closing in around her. Once she glanced back at Ben Frailly, but he was gone. The ropes were cut and dangling emptily from the bedpost. Angrily she pushed away from the hands that reached out for her. "Leave me alone," she protested. "I did nothing."

The male voice thundered down. "The hell you didn't."

A female voice was wimpering at the edge of the group. "Leave her alone. She's only a child."

"She's not a child. Do you call what we just saw the act of an innocent child?"

Zoe stood against the far wall beyond the bed, trapped. They had led her into remembering and she had been stupid enough to follow. Nothing had happened that day or now. She tried to regain a semblance of control, although the black hoods bobbed crazily about her in a nightmare of old guilt and fresh terror. "Leave me alone," she begged. "You have no right." She tried to gather courage about her but her hands beneath the black flannel gown were trembling. "Get out, all of you," she cried. "Get out. This is my house. You have no right. Get out! All of you. Get out now. I mean it. Get out. Leave me alone. Please leave me alone."

What had started on a burst of courage ended in an outraged cry. She closed her eyes in an effort to digest her fury and stood, slightly bowed, against the far wall.

A bent figure started toward her. "Calm down, Zoe. We're doing this for your own good. You may be finished, but we're not," she said. "There's work to be done in the kitchen. We can't leave out anything. We've learned our lines and besides it wouldn't make any sense."

Zoe continued to back away. Nothing she said seemed to make any difference to them. Over the old woman's shoulder she saw the others moving closer. Now she tried to escape over the bed, but it was useless. Black figures merely stepped forward to fill the openings. Two figures were on either side of her. One, a female leaned close with advice. "Be a good girl for a change. They just want you to come along with them to the kitchen. The others are waiting there."

In increasing terror, Zoe shook her head.

The bent figure looked sharply at her. "Everything happened in the kitchen, didn't it?"

Her final protest was weak, scarcely audible, "I did—nothing," she whispered. "You have no right."

But then they were guiding her out of the room, closing in about her, hands reaching forward when she faltered or appeared to draw back. The hallway walls looked freshly whitewashed, the ceiling vaulted. A temple of judgment. The staircase appeared to be lined with the flickering light of candles. From the top of the stairs, she saw in the hallway below two lines of black-robed figures, all carrying candles. She felt hands guiding her directly down the steps between the two rows of figures, leading her inevitably to the kitchen door.

She heard whispers as she passed.

"She's a born whore, you know. Bad blood always tells."

"What was the punishment?"

"My God, haven't you heard?"

As she passed between the rows of figures with candles, she heard a female voice giggling, "Isn't she marvelous?"

She stopped to look about in search of Mary Lisa. But she saw nothing but black hoods and featureless faces and the endless shimmering light of candles. Before she knew it, long before she was ready for it, she was standing before the closed kitchen door. The old crone, who had been her constant companion down the long stairs, jerked at her, scolding, "No tears. Don't try tears on us. Not after what you've done." She patted Zoe on the hand. "Besides," she said almost kindly, "it's for your own good."

Was she weeping? She was certain she was not, although her teeth were beginning to chatter. She begged a final time, "Not—the kitchen."

But the old woman gripped her by the arm and shoved her toward the door. "Go on in," she hissed. "He's waiting for you, just like he was waiting that other night."

Again Zoe considered escape. Suddenly she bolted backward away from the door. But as she turned, she faced a solid line of black hoods and blinding candlelight. She searched desperately for an opening through the impenetrable phalanx but there was none.

Her eyes darted from candle to candle. Her face felt hard things touching it, jabbing fingers, all accusing. The black wave moved forward. She was conscious of the near heat of candles.

Then she was aware that the kitchen door had fallen open and she was facing passage through the blackest hole of all. With careful vigilance, she measured the density of this enclosed world and realized that she was being forced to go to the one place she had no desire to go.

The others were pushing her along. In their eagerness to reach the promised spectacle they were willing to trample the central protagonist, for she had no doubt about her role in this next scene. She knew all too well what would be expected of her and accordingly, when she reached the kitchen, she took her place at the table in her black flannel gown, her hands folded primly in her lap, head down, waiting.

The mother-woman was weeping at the kitchen sink. The other black-robed figures lined the wall of the small room, their burning candles filling the air with noxious fumes.

Still Zoe waited. Despair seemed the only genuine response. Why were they forcing her back over old ground? She had managed thus far. There was no need, no point. It had been a common place incident, nothing more, a daily occurrence of paternal rage against the first stirrings of the female child to become a woman, the very response they desired yet condemned.

At that moment Bubs entered the semidarkened room. He was wearing a brown corduroy jacket over his bare chest, her father's, with patched frayed sleeves, or one very much like it. In his hand, tapping rigidly against the side of his leg, was a yardstick.

Suddenly the mother-woman interrupted her weeping long enough to protest. "Don't hurt her. You have no right—"

The slight tapping against the side of the leg went on, uninterrupted.

Zoe shifted in the chair. Her hands grasped the edge of the seat. First there had been talk years ago, an ugly exchange. She wondered if they knew their lines. The mother-woman turned back into the shadows, sobbing openly.

Bubs stepped forward. The candlelight caught the specifics of his face. She saw yet another transformation. He resembled her father, the eyes swollen from drinking, a heavy, rancorous moody face.

He stood directly above her. Slowly he lifted the yardstick with its metal tip and pressed it into the middle of her forehead, pinning her in the chair. He asked softly, almost sadly, "Why the nigger?"

Neither then nor now did Zoe brush away the tip of the yardstick, although it occurred to her to do so. It rested lightly on her forehead, a strange slight penetration. Then as now she answered truthfully. "He's my friend."

Bubs sneered, mimicking her. "He's my friend." To the mother-woman he demanded, "Did you hear? Did you hear what your daughter just said? The nigger is her friend."

Zoe tried to look up at him but he merely increased the pressure of the metal tip against her forehead.

Bubs moved closer, so close she could feel the corduroy jacket against her arm. He lifted the yardstick and placed it on top of her head as though he intended to penetrate her brain with it. The pressure increased. He asked again in ominous repetition. "Why the nigger?"

"Please," she whispered, then as now, "leave me alone. I did nothing."

"You did nothing?" he repeated incredulously. Suddenly he slapped the yardstick down against the side of his leg and circled angrily behind her. "What I saw was far from nothing. What I saw was a whore taking off her clothes for a dirty nigger." His voice rose. "What I saw was a slut, a flesh-eating, prick-sucking slut."

A murmur ran through the black figures behind her, a chorus of shock like a network of sound that wove itself into the atmosphere.

Zoe's pulse accelerated. She continued to grip the sides of the chair. In her terror she had assumed the exact position of the other Zoe.

The murmurs died. Bubs was standing directly behind her. She could hear his breathing, a rhythm building to rage. Softly at first she felt his hand on the top of her head. Slowly his fingers dug into her hair, gathered the strands together and knotted the long tresses around his fist. He pulled her head back until she was forced to view him upside down. She saw the beads of saliva in his beard, saw thin trickles of moisture at the sides of his mouth. Again he asked the same question as though exercising great patience. "Why the nigger?"

The mother-woman flailed her way out of the shadows. She appeared to be on the verge of hysteria. "What did she do to deserve this?" she cried. "You're terrifying her. She had her blouse unbuttoned. That was all. Please leave her alone. She's just a child."

"She's a whore," Bubs shouted. "I saw her. You didn't." As though he were re-creating the scene in his mind, he jerked harder on her hair, forcing her head back even further, a gesture so violent that the chair in which she was sitting tilted and threatened to tip over. For a moment, her hands flailed in the empty air, ready to break her fall.

The mother-woman cried out. From her upside down angle, Zoe saw the impending confrontation between the mother-woman and Bubs. He seemed to control her with his eyes alone, wordless warning that silenced her and left her standing helpless beside Zoe's chair, her face drained of color, an obedient, terrified mechanical woman.

Bubs spoke softly to her, certain of his control over her. "Surely you don't approve of what she did?" he asked, as though addressing a dim-witted child.

The mother-woman shook her head.

"And neither do you think that she should go unpunished?"

Again she shook her head.

Bubs still held Zoe's head at an extreme angle, his fingers tightening and retightening around her hair as he continued to question the mother-woman. "I wish you had seen her," he said sorrowfully. "I wish you could have seen her as I did." He shook his head and twisted the hair more tightly around his fist. "There's probably nothing in a man's life more disconcerting than to discover that his daughter is a whore."

Zoe closed her eyes against the realization of what was coming. They knew their lines all too well. "I did—nothing," she whispered.

He jerked on her hair; her scalp ached. He leaned close over her face, so close she could smell his breath, a sickening stench of alcohol and decay. "A woman," he began, "does not take off her clothes for nothing."

The chorus took up the refrain, a low angry repetition of his exact words.

"What we have here," he announced, his voice suddenly expansive, "is the town whore with a preference for niggers."

The chorus gasped.

"What we have here," he went on in the manner of an evangelist, "is a slut who undresses in broad daylight for the enjoyment of a scaly, slimy little nigger."

The murmurs of outrage increased.

The mother-woman stepped forward and leaned over Zoe's face. "Then she must be punished," she said, as though she were reciting a line.

A gust of wind blew in through the window, causing the candlelight to waver.

Zoe tried to send away everything within her that was important. She knew what was coming. There had been no defense mechanisms that first time. She had been too young to know about such things. But now she summoned everything at her disposal as protection against the inevitable. She knew precisely what was happening when she felt Bubs suddenly pull her forward, force her face down across the table, knew the sensation of her arms being jerked forward and her wrists held rigidly by the mother-woman, remembered all too well the peculiar sensation of moisture on her hands, the mother-woman weeping even as she was cooperating. She felt the cool air on her back as the black flannel gown was lifted and pulled almost over her head. And seconds before she felt the first stinging blow of the yardstick against her flesh, she knew what was happening and how long it would go on, knew the tremendous feat of endurance that was ahead of her, knew that she would lose count of the blows at twenty-seven, knew that the pain would increase beyond the point that she could bear it, knew that she would grind her forehead into the surface of the table, knew that the steel edge of the yardstick would open her flesh and there would be blood, and the swollen torn tissue would throb with each new blow and that ultimately the yardstick would break, leaving her father with a residue of rage that would have to be spent in some other fashion.

And it happened exactly as she knew it would happen, even to the point where the mother-woman, sickened by the sight, ran from the room and left her alone with the drunken, enraged man.

But she did not know everything, nor did she care to remember everything, how the heavily breathing father lifted her from the table and dropped her onto the floor as though she were refuse to be discarded. Neither did she know nor care to remember how he stood over her for a moment, seeming to enjoy her helpless stunned state. Neither did she know nor did she care to remember how he muttered obscenities at her, his breathing increasing, stopping to wipe the blood from his hands, his eyes wide and distended, telling her almost tenderly that since she had obliged the nigger, surely she would not deny her own father.

No! She didn't remember that, couldn't remember that, wouldn't remember that, not even when his strength was massed on her hips, his gaping jaws and mad eyes pressed against her face, her hands trying in a futile struggle to protect the rest of her body, the broad daylight of consciousness slipping away under his crushingly heavy weight, nonsensation flooding her outermost extremities with the exception of the penetration itself, the broken maidenhead, the certainty of her complete punishment.

Suddenly Zoe screamed. All about her was a fulmination of shouts and groans; sad faces appeared from behind black hoods, a rapid reverberation which seemed to undermine her on all sides until she was reduced to nothing but the essence of her own scream, a child gone temporarily mad under damning circumstances, a prolonged, senseless wail followed by shorter, piercing cries, her nerves, muscles, bones resisting the memory of the tyrannical rider who had shattered her, dragging the memory by the heels up the staircase of consciousness and exposing it to the light for the first time.

The earth itself seemed to shake at the terrible screams. She began to beat her head against the floor. Quickly Bubs stepped forward and pulled her away from her own destruction. He cradled her in his arms, his hands sheltering her. The black figures removed their hoods, eyes downcast as though in mourning.

Bubs murmured, "No wonder a cold queen."

In the darkness several of the voices echoed his words.

Gratefully Zoe accepted the comfort of his arms. One dark passage had been conquered. The hubbub was receding. One wall of blindness and deafness had been penetrated. She looked up through glazed eyes at the flickering of candlelight.

The thought of what had been done to her was no longer unthinkable. It was merely drab . . .

———◆———

She sat at the sun-drenched kitchen table, drinking hot fragrant black coffee with Mary Lisa. The morning was clear or at least what she could see of it. There appeared to be feverish activity all about; two women stood at the window, one inside, one outside, industriously washing the panes of glass, their heads bobbing together almost in unison with the scrubbing motions of their arms. Behind her, invisible, she heard the sound of hammering and sawing. Now and then she heard men calling for nails, for assistance. The smell of fresh paint was everywhere.

Time was out of joint. But she felt amazingly good, yet mysteriously hollow. She held the cup with both hands and let the steam drift over her face. She was vaguely conscious of the inexorable annihilation with which she had been threatened for the last few days. But her mind for the moment seemed to be enjoying a kind of self-satisfaction. It had at last grown tired of asking the same questions, of what species, what life form, what cosmos was she the secret and unappealing cipher?

Mary Lisa giggled suddenly. Beneath her small head and helmet of little golden curls, her eyes grew wide. "What *are* you staring at, Zoe?"

Zoe replaced the cup on the table and smiled apologetically. Looking down into her lap, she noticed for the first time she was wearing blue jeans and oversized faded blue workshirt. Her last conscious recollection was of a black flannel gown. "Where did I get these?" she asked.

Again Mary Lisa giggled, "You *are* a case. Where do you think you got them? From your closet, of course."

No, that wasn't true. Her closet was empty. But it seemed a minor point to pursue. Still she stared across the table, quietly alarmed by her lapses of consciousness. Slowly she went on taking personal inventory. Her feet were bare. Her hair hung down about her face in disarray; it felt matted, hopelessly snarled. She discovered further that any sudden movement caused a slight discomfort throughout her entire body as if she had recently been under great stress.

A man's voice shouted from the front hall. "What color do you want it in here?"

Without hesitation, Mary Lisa called over her shoulder, "White, of course."

The woman cleaning the inside of the window tapped frantically at the woman outside. "There's a spot you missed," she called, indicating the window glass. "Do a good job or I'll get someone else."

Zoe turned her head rapidly in several directions. Her right knee and thigh trembled slightly beneath the table. The mind was questioning again, although it knew it was useless. Still she had to try. "Mary Lisa," she entreated gently, "Please tell me—"

"Tell you what?" Mary Lisa's violet-encircled eyes grew wide with innocence. She became quite businesslike. "Look. We're all here together and we're all having fun and that's all that should matter, right?" Before Zoe had a chance to reply, she rushed on. "Look, if you're through with that"—and she indicated the cup of coffee—"there's really so much to be done. Your father and mother will be back shortly and the kids and I thought that—"

She faltered and studied her purple fingernails. "Well," she went on, "we just thought that maybe if we helped you get this place cleaned up, in order, you know, then maybe, just maybe they wouldn't be so hard on you." Her bright childlike face seemed alive with hope.

Zoe felt confusion descending again. Her parents were dead. Mary Lisa misread her silence. She leaned forward and extended a hand toward Zoe. "Look, I'm sorry, but we know what happened. Everything. All of us. When you didn't come back to school for four days, and when Ben Frailly disappeared, we just knew." She threw back her head and laughed. "You can't have any secrets in a town like Whitney. You should know that by now."

The hair on Zoe's arm bristled. Every cell in her brain reached out hungrily for a scrap of information. She stared blankly into the painted face across the table. She was aware that the woman at the kitchen window was listening closely. In embarrassment and confusion she closed her eyes and shook her head.

Mary Lisa reached across the table with both hands. "Please, Zoe," she begged. "Don't feel bad. I think what you did was marvelous, truly marvelous. We all do. You just played your role, that's all. And that's what we're here for, just to play our roles. No need to be embarrassed. Any of us."

Zoe studied the course wood grain on the table surface.

Her mind rushed headlong into a comforting darkness. Anything was better than the brightness of unmitigated chaos.

Mary Lisa was standing at her side now, her arm resting lightly on her shoulder. "Well, look, you just sit here and finish your coffee. You've been through a lot. I hear your old man really raised hell. When you feel like it, let me know. There's plenty of work to do." She patted Zoe lightly and turned immediately to the woman at the window. "If you're through with that one, don't waste time. There are plenty of others. Come on, let's do a good job for Zoe."

Zoe heard them moving toward opposite doors; the window washer toward the back door, Mary Lisa toward the door that led into the front hall. She waited for the confirmation of silence that told her that she was alone. Then she looked up.

To her surprise, she saw Mary Lisa still standing in the door, her usually vivacious face strangely still.

"I wouldn't leave the house today if I were you," she said secretively. "I hear your father's gone on an absolute rampage. Your mother's trying to find him and bring him home. But in case he decides to come back here, you'd better stay in the house. With the doors locked. You hear?"

Still Zoe did not respond in any way.

"We'll help you," Mary Lisa concluded brightly. "We've always wanted to help you. But you wouldn't let us until now."

Someone shouted for her from the front hall. She called out, "Be right there." Then she waved gaily at Zoe and disappeared.

Zoe stared at the empty doorway. Slowly she propped her elbows up on the table and cradled her aching head in her hands. They were still playing with her, manipulating her. Inside the blindness of her closed eyes, she saw the light of a void. Unhappy ghosts filed by in orderly procession. She wondered vaguely what day it was. Had she missed her family's return? Wouldn't Clay be looking for her, trying to call her?

Someone entered the kitchen. She looked up to see the old woman in the red robe walking briskly by, carrying in one hand a bucket of what appeared to be white plaster of paris. She stopped and leaned close over Zoe and whispered, "I'm really sorry about last night. If murder were legal, I'd kill him myself. If I were you, I'd make myself a shell for protection." She held up the bucket of white plaster for Zoe's inspection. "Cracks everywhere. Never seen so many cracks. A lifetime of cracks to be covered over and filled in." Then she hurried out of the kitchen, the red robe floating behind her.

Zoe continued to sit listlessly at the table as though drugged. Her mind progressed a few steps in one direction, then stopped. Why couldn't she just walk away from this place? What was preventing her from just walking away? She lifted her head to face the empty kitchen. A curtain, a fresh curtain, she noticed, swayed gently at the window. Beyond the window she saw the familiar woods and hills, the expanse of ponds and fields that turned into marshes in autumn. Perhaps she *could* just walk away. The back yard and the woods beyond appeared to be empty. There was a path she had known as a child that led through the pasture and down a steep incline, rejoining the highway on the other side. From where she stood at the window, she even saw the beginning of the path. Perhaps there was a chance.

But as she started toward the back door, she remembered Mary Lisa's warning to stay in the house. The thought stopped her. If everything had been planned, even the path and the hope of escape were perhaps part of the plot. She had walked into their games before. Now she stood indecisively at the window, looking over her shoulder toward the entry hall, which had become strangely quiet. No sounds of hammering now. No sounds at all.

She heard the apprehension in her own voice as she called out, "Is anybody there?" When no one answered, she walked slowly into the front hall. All about she saw paint pots and brushes, the bucket of white plaster and a scattering of hammers and nails. In the far corner she saw the curious wooden cabinet which the men had carried in on the day of their arrival. She stared at it intently and for no reason felt fear rising. On the edge of a step, she saw a lighted cigarette, still burning.

She waited, listening, then called out again, "Mary Lisa?"

Her voice echoed and bounced crazily back on her.

She moved more slowly, peered into the dining room. Someone had removed all the white shrouds from the furniture. The table looked polished. The crystal on the sideboard gleamed as from a recent washing. The brass bowl in the center of the table held shiny fresh red apples. The walls and woodwork had been painted white, dazzling, blinding white. She lifted her hand to the wall and discovered that the paint was still wet.

A few feet ahead she found the living room in the same immaculate condition, freshly swept and painted, the fireplace cleaned, new logs laid, the white shrouds gone. All the clutter of restoration seemed to be localized in the hallway. In the corner next to the slender cabinet, she noticed a pile of gauze cloths cut in strips, a can of paint remover and a black toolbox. On the stairs behind her, the cigarette still burned.

"Mary Lisa?" she called.

She looked up the stairs toward the skittering shadows caused by sunlight coming in through the window at the far end of the upstairs hall. In memory, she heard the old woman's suggestion, "I'd make myself a shell if I were you." She had been carrying the bucket of white plaster. Where was she now?

Zoe turned in a circle, trying to look in all directions. The house was empty, or appeared to be. She walked to the burning cigarette and ground it out on the edge of the step. She discovered that her hand was shaking.

"Is anyone here?" she called, sensing that they were, that somewhere behind the silence lay new and undreamed-of hazards. But the house gave back nothing in the way of a response. She started toward the front door, her hand reaching out for the doorknob. A slight noise in the kitchen caught her attention.

From where she stood, the long hallway stretched end-lessly to the back of the house. She saw from that distance that the curtains at the kitchen window were no longer lifting and falling in the slight breeze. She saw that the window had been closed. On the outer edges of the silence, she heard a faint grating sound. It seemed to be coming from the direction of the back door.

Stay in the house in case your father returns.

"Please," she called out. "Answer if you are there." Her voice sounded flat, unidentifiable. It belonged to someone else. Effortlessly she conjured up in the paint-reeking stuffiness of the front hall new threats, new assaults. Her lips were dry and tasted bitter from the residue of coffee.

The questionable silence spoke clearly to her. Run now, it said, while you still have a chance. She lifted her head toward the kitchen. The grating noise had stopped. She turned to face the front door. Her hand reached out for the doorknob while she was still a distance away. She peered through the rectangular windows on either side of the door and saw nothing but empty porch, empty driveway, empty wooden carts and empty woods.

Stealthily, she turned the doorknob. Her shoulders lifted

as she tried again. She pushed forward, pulled back, trying yet a third time. The doorknob would not turn. She jerked at it, her fingers gripping at the small knob, her palm damp.

In panic, she pulled with all her strength. Still the door did not move. She laid her shoulder against it and pushed, momentarily forgetting the order of the hinges. Her mind still felt drugged. Her mental movement was as jerking as her physical movement. The door would not open. The door must be locked. If the door was locked, she couldn't leave here. If she couldn't leave, she would have to stay.

All at once there seemed to be boundaries to her mental abilities. The waking dream was familiar, locked in the house, unable to escape. Always locked doors. Her parents had locked themselves in before they had gone up to the bathroom. The sheriff, she had been told, had had to break down the front door after the stench had spread to the highway and had been noticed by a passing hitchhiker.

These shifting gusts of memory lasted only a moment. *Make yourself a protective shell.* She stood back to examine the door that once had been broken in. Someone had repaired it with remarkable expertise.

Then she was moving again, alive on a thread of hope, remembering the back door. In the kitchen she shuddered at the sight of the large oak table on which she had relived her punishment. Two coffee cups sat there now in a harmless tableau. Quickly she ran through the small pantry, her hand extended as though her nerves could not wait for freedom. Fingers closed around the smooth surface of the doorknob, pulled.

She took one step backward and pulled again, both hands wrapped tightly about the doorknob, the fingernails of one hand digging into the flesh of the other.

The door was solid and unyielding. Glassless, it did not even afford her a view of the outside world. She flailed uselessly at the surface of the door, her mind yielding immediately to a new wave of terror. Her entrapment in the house was complete. The thought "Please help" was silent, addressed to no one in particular and therefore useless. Fear began to impede her breathing. Very faint in the distance, she thought she heard a step.

The battle was on. She ran back through the kitchen, calling, "Who is it? Is someone there?"

Finding no one in the front of the hall, she stopped to listen. The whole house seemed alive with unseen presences. She turned rapidly in every direction, once running halfway up the stairs until a new wave of terror stopped her.

Make yourself a protective shell.

The thought caused her to freeze at midstep, unable in her present frenzy to separate voice from echo. She peered upward into the hallway. Was something moving? She stood straight and stiff, incapable of moving forward or backward, her eyes wide. She brought her right arm up and grasped at the banister. But something was wrong with her muscles. They would not obey the signals from the brain. The fingers refused to grasp the railing as though they wanted her to fall. What little control she had left was now concentrated on keeping her balance.

Then that too was gone and she swung around and slumped heavily on the stairs. At the moment of no will, she heard someone calling to her from an upstairs room. She fought to answer, ordering her tongue to move, but it merely licked weakly at her lips, still tasting something bitter. She hung there on the steps, the voice behind growing more urgent, more demanding.

It was then that she had the sensation of being lifted up, of hands grasping her from behind and pulling her backward. She felt her legs bouncing against the treads, felt other hands now jerk at her arms, several someones dragging her up the stairs and into her parents' room at the top of the landing.

She saw everything as though underwater, saw a sterile, antiseptic white room, stripped of furniture with the smell of a hospital, of medicine and bandages and drugs. The hands that manipulated her seemed disembodied. She tried to turn her head to find faces to go with the hands. But significant movement was impossible. The mind still was not obeying.

She stood upright in the center of her parents' bedroom and felt the hands arranging her, lifting her head, raising her arms a few inches from the sides of her body, spreading her feet a distance apart to give her a base of support. And she endured it, lifeless as a mannequin, her eyes still seeing, her ears hearing everything, but her body and brain unable to muster any sort of viable protest.

She heard a voice ask as though genuinely interested, "Are you certain this is what she wants?"

Another replied, "Of course, it's what she's wanted all her life. Can you think of any other way?"

"But Jesus Christ, this seems rather extreme. Are you sure it won't hurt her?"

"Oh, I'm never sure of that. But I *do* know it's what she wants. It's what she's always wanted. You can't keep secrets in a town like Whitney."

"Well, then—"

All voices ceased. She felt nothing at first. Then slowly the sensation of a faint heat around her legs began to creep up, strips of something being wrapped around and around, a texture, almost soothing like bandages of some sort. She was aware of movement all around her as though several hands were busily at work. As the strips climbed upward, she felt the lower ones begin to harden, felt a mild constriction against her muscles.

The pressure increased as the strips climbed toward her

waist, an encasement of plaster covering now her breasts, the disembodied hands continuing to move around her body. When she realized what was happening, she tried to lift her head in order to let the scream in her throat escape. But the white, damp, antiseptic-smelling strips were climbing to her chin now. She set her teeth and closed her eyes as the whiteness covered her face, the strips being pulled tightly about her head, the wet surface hardening almost immediately upon contact with flesh, a grave, mummifying process, cutting off all warmth, all movement, leaving her encased in a cold, hard plaster shell.

A perplexed voice inquired, "Are you really certain that this is what she wants?"

And the calm reply, "Of course. Don't ask so many questions."

She felt the pressure moving down her arms. Instinctively her hands became fists. Before she could open her fingers, the wet plaster had covered everything. Her fingers were locked into permanent fists. She could not move. She felt nothing but the safe, cold hardness which encased her. She made no sound although she felt the sensation of air around the slit of her mouth. She looked out through narrow limited openings at the white room.

A voice was explaining in pedantic tones. "You see, this is precisely what she did after that night. I'm certain it seemed the wisest course of action at the time, all things considered, but still—"

The brain was crying out for a crevice through which it might move. But the cries were irrelevant. Apparently the disembodied hands and voices heard nothing.

Someone murmured incredulously, as though viewing its handiwork. "Goddamn! What a sight!"

"She looks like a mummy."

"But she's functioned like that for years, just like that."

"Incredible."

"But safe. You'll have to admit it's safe."

She tried to lift her face off the barrier of hard plaster. But there was another barrier of equal strength pushing against the back of her head. Her arms, extended rigidly in air, fought their encasement and gave up. Even the fingers inside the mummified right fist surrendered. One leg tried to straighten itself, but the plaster held it rigid.

Now the voices seemed to be drifting away. One said, "Well, she's got what she wants."

"I can't believe it."

"Believe it. It's true."

"Why is it what she's always wanted?"

There was no answer, or at least none that Zoe could hear. There were only hard surfaces confining every part of her body. She thought about movements that could not happen. She peered out through slits at the white empty room. Every now and then the swell of her heart thumped against the white encasement. Her mouth fell open like her eyes and she sucked breath through the narrow slit around her lips. Inside the skull, all was strangely quiet. The brain simply refused to deal with what had happened. It didn't have to worry anymore about footsteps and locked doors and punishments and disembodied hands or stench that had spread to the highway. In fact, it had no worries at all.

Resigned and convinced that nothing more could happen to her, the woman stood huddled inside the hard white shell, left cheek pillowed against cold plaster, hands drawn permanently into fists. Every now and then there was a faint scratching sound as the body shivered . . .

———◆———

Sometime later she heard them returning, heard first the pre-
dictable cry of Mary Lisa, "Oh, isn't she marvelous! Just look
at her!"

The voice came from the direction of the doorway. The
entire room seemed now to be filled with voices, laughing
and calling out to one another to come and look at the human
mummy.

Zoe in her confinement had lost track of time. She had
watched through the narrow eye slits the light of day fade
from the windows, had settled comfortably in with the darkness, had even managed to lose consciousness inside her
white tomb, a kind of sleep, partially induced by the absolute
certainty that she was at last safe.

Now the overhead light flooded the room and she
peered out through the plaster encasement at Mary Lisa's
rosy beaming face. In her arms she appeared to be carrying
boughs of autumn foliage and the flush on her cheeks suggested that she had just come in from outside.

"Can she talk?" Mary Lisa asked brightly, turning to
someone standing in the shadow of the hall.

"Of course she can talk, although I doubt if she has anything of importance to say." Bubs pushed past the confusion
at the door and into the lighted room. He came forward and
placed his hands on Zoe's shoulders and peered closely
through the eye slits. "Are you in there?" he called cheerily.

Zoe felt only the slightest pressure from his hands. She
considered speaking but decided against it and kept her eyes
downcast. A cold air from his breath lightly coated her lips.

Mary Lisa encircled her, tapping once on the plaster
back. The sound gave off a hollow reverberation. "Are you
sure this is really what she wanted?" she asked skeptically,
reemerging into Zoe's view. She hugged the brightly colored
autumn boughs to keep herself safe from a similar confinement.

"Absolutely!" Bubs answered with conviction. "She put up no struggle at all. Not a bit. Was as docile and cooperative as I've ever seen her."

Zoe watched the two watching her. She inched her arms up and down inside the encasement and vaguely wished she could flex her fingers. Let them look their fill, then maybe they would go away.

Mary Lisa moved closer and stared at her through the narrow eye slits. "Zoe," she whispered, "are you sure you don't want to come out? We're getting ready to have a party downstairs. We'd love to have you."

In an effort of will, Zoe tensed her muscles to keep back the deep shudders that were sweeping through her.

Mary Lisa looked suddenly stricken. "She *can't* talk," she said accusingly to Bubs.

"Of course she can. She just has nothing to say. Never has. All we've done is to relieve her of the pain of having to fake it."

He moved close to Mary Lisa, put both arms around her, crushing the autumn foliage. "Besides, she's out of our way up here. She can be quite a bore."

Mary Lisa struggled loose, giggling, "Not now, Bubs. We've got to get back downstairs. They're bringing her father in here in a minute."

The hoarded personality within the plaster encasement stared out with benign and unmoving eyes.

Bubs accepted Mary Lisa's rejection and transferred his energy to the stone woman. Suddenly he stepped very close and slipped his tongue into the narrow mouth slit.

She felt the prodding wetness trying to force her lips open. The cold and exhaustion and fear came back. She wasn't safe, not even now. She struggled against the encasement, trying to avoid the tongue that was invading her mouth.

Bubs stepped back, laughing. "You know, incredible as it sounds, I think she'd be happier if we sealed her breathing hole as well."

From the doorway, Mary Lisa giggled. "She'd die then."

"She's dead now." Bubs took a final look at Zoe. His face appeared to grow thoughtful, almost sad. "You sure you don't want to come out?" he asked softly.

Zoe said nothing.

"You can't stay in there forever, you know." He reached one hand up and stroked the side of the plaster face. "None of it was your fault. How can you possibly feel guilty?"

Mary Lisa called impatiently from the door. "Come on, we've got so much to do. I think the others are ready now."

"I'm coming." He shoved his hands into his pocket in a gesture of resignation. He smiled at Zoe a final time. Out of sight now, he shouted to someone, "I'm not going to enjoy this any more than you are. Just try not to take it all so seriously. We're here for just a fraction of a second. That's all. No more."

His voice trailed off as though he were passing through a tunnel.

With the absence of human company, Zoe dared to lean back against her encasement. She would not fall, could not fall. Her prison wouldn't permit it. It wasn't that there was muscular or nervous strength there that refused to be beaten, but rather that the echoes of certain voices were pushing against the sides of her encasement. There was in the middle of the skull a fact that was so nakedly the center of everything that it could not even examine itself. In the darkness of the skull it existed, the realization that this was happening to her, that in a way she was permitting it to happen, that somehow she had lost all contact with comprehensible events.

The thought lifted, crawled this way and that like a

worm slowly trying to eat its way through her brain. At last her lips stopped moving. The white prison held her tightly. Her eyes were opened and unfocused. She wished, really wished, that they had turned off the light when they left. Water ran from the corner of the right eye; it tickled inside the encasement. She had only a slight desire to comfort the tickling. So she endured it.

Then slowly out of the silence she heard a new commotion. Somewhere a man was shouting unspeakable obscenities while other voices rose around the curses. She heard a series of thuds in the vicinity of the stairs, a tremendous racket.

She struggled for broader vision, feeling certain that the threat of voices was coming toward her. The noise and confusion grew louder, right outside the door now, or so it seemed, someone being dragged or forced along against their will, a deep enraged male voice shouting in drunken slurs, cursing everyone, invoking Satan, screaming to be released.

Suddenly the door burst open. Two men dressed identically in olive green uniforms struggled into the room. They appeared to be policemen of some sort. Between them they were half-carrying, half-dragging Bubs. His arms were tightly encased in a heavy white canvas straitjacket. A foam of saliva spilled out from his parched lips and dribbled down into his beard. Almost on his knees between the two men, he struggled uselessly against the straitjacket when abruptly they thrust him roughly forward into a writhing heap in the middle of the floor.

Behind them came the mother-woman, her face white and drawn, a dark sweater thrown over her shoulders, her hand dabbing continuously at her eyes with a damp soiled handkerchief.

The scene was no longer beyond Zoe's vision. It was being enacted directly in front of her. She recognized the two bogus policemen: one was Rich, the other was Dempsey, the two mechanics from Logan Airport.

She saw Rich straighten up from the ordeal and wipe something from his face. "You sure you can handle him now, ma'am?" he asked the mother-woman. "If you want my opinion, I think he should be locked up."

"Oh, no," the mother-woman protested, "he's just had too much to drink. It happens. This time he had an argument with our daughter." She looked quickly at Zoe embarrassed. She added weakly, "He'll sleep it off. He always does."

The other officer seemed unconvinced. He straightened his tie, smoothed down his shirt inside his belt. "He's dangerous," he said flatly. "I wouldn't take that jacket off for a while if I were you."

"Oh no, I won't," agreed the mother-woman. She wiped at her face. "I can't thank you enough for helping me."

The man on the floor lay perfectly still, looking up at the three who were talking about him, cold rage in his eyes.

Zoe watched it all, curious as to why the officers did not comment on her presence. Both had looked directly at her and had said nothing. She was there. Why didn't they acknowledge her?

Now they were leaving. One officer, Rich, smoothed back his hair and readjusted his cap. Zoe noticed dark rings of perspiration on his olive green shirt as he lifted his arms. "You just calm down, buddy," he said sternly to the man on the floor. "You got a nice family here. Now treat them decent, you understand?"

Bubs struggled, rolled to the opposite side. His hands, Zoe noticed, were almost touching each other across his back, so tightly drawn were the buckles on the jacket.

Dempsey was patting the mother-woman's hand. "Just call us if you need us," he comforted. "And I'd get rid of all the booze in the house. Let him sweat it out. It'll do him good."

The mother-woman nodded, eyes down, embarrassed.

"By the way," Rich asked from the door. "Where's your daughter now?"

The mother-woman glanced almost shyly at Zoe, then shook her head. "I really don't know," she smiled. "He gave her quite a beating. She might have run off."

"Well, don't worry," Dempsey said kindly, "we'll keep an eye out for her. But it's my guess she'll be home in time for dinner." He grinned and winked. "I know kids," he beamed. "Got seven of my own."

The mother-woman seemed to want to respond to the man's kindness. But her eyes were fixed downward on the back of the man twisted into a knot upon the floor, lying absolutely motionless.

Zoe read the fear in the woman's eyes, knew precisely what she was thinking. Bubs's persistent silence after the seismic convulsions could not be misinterpreted.

As the officers disappeared through the door, she felt a strong urge to call out after them. She knew what happened next and knew it was within her power to warn her mother. Suddenly she struggled against the white plaster shell, wanting out, wanting desperately to be a part of the scene, to have a voice that could warn, a cry that would alert. And still she struggled and now cried out. But no one heard her. No one paid the slightest attention to her.

The mother-woman appeared to be waiting. Her head was cocked to one side listening to the receding steps of the officers. Bubs too appeared to be in a suspended state of animation. He lay on his back, knees raised slightly, his imprisoned arms a white, useless mound upon his chest. From where Zoe stood, she noticed that his eyes were closed; the eyelids were a deceptive blank in the still face. He was resting, merely resting.

She heard the front door slam shut downstairs. She'd heard the sound before. A moment later, she heard the car cough, sputter, heard the engine turn over. Tires crunched gravel. She'd heard that before as well. The engine accelerated, then settled into a steady though diminishing hum. Then all sound was gone.

Still the tableau inside the upstairs bedroom held, no one moving, no one giving the faintest indication that they would ever move again. The mother-woman stood stiffly beside the door, her head turned to one side, listening to a sound that no one else could hear.

The only movement in Bubs's otherwise dead face was the slight, almost imperceptible twitching of his eyes beneath the closed eyelids, as though he were still watching everything closely behind his self-imposed blindness.

And Zoe was there, safe behind her white wall. She really wished that they had taken him someplace else. The house was large, there were countless other rooms in which they might have played out their scene. But they were here and they gave no indication that they would be leaving soon. So she settled down behind the white wall and waited along with them.

Suddenly the mother-woman buried her face in her hands and ran from the room, unable to bear any more. Zoe heard her outside in the hall weeping softly. How well she knew the sound and how sick to death she was of it. She considered calling for the mother-woman to be quiet. But she changed her mind. It would only transfer attention to herself and she had no desire to do that.

Bubs was stirring now, flexing his legs, struggling against the encasement around his chest and arms. He maneuvered himself around until he was facing Zoe, his expression alive with recognition. He blinked his eyes, trying to clear them and lifted his head at a grotesque angle. "You bitch," he whispered. "You're responsible for this."

She did not reply because she wasn't there.

Bubs continued to stare at her. He moistened his lips with his tongue and paused a moment to get his breath. Something was brewing behind the calm forehead, some new plan. Zoe knew the expression all too well and braced herself for what was coming.

Then he twisted his head upon the floor, pushed backward, lifting his chin, unable to breathe. His head continued to roll from side to side and he appeared to be breathing very shallowly now. He gasped, "Go get her. I can't breathe." And again he was writhing and twisting on the floor, his eyes alternately pinched closed, then wide open, his mouth agape, nostrils flared.

Zoe knew it. Another performance.

Suddenly he rolled over onto his stomach, his body hunched forward at an angle over the mound of bound arms. "Please," he gasped, "I'm—" But apparently the words were cut off in a new spasm of pain.

She continued to watch him, unmoved. It was a device to gain his freedom, nothing more.

He was pressing his forehead into the floor. His tongue hung limply out of one corner of his mouth. A gurgling sound came from the base of his throat. Suddenly his legs relaxed and he fell backward. A foot twitched slightly, but otherwise he appeared lifeless.

Zoe was impressed, but not enough to call for help. Let him play his scene. He was much safer dead and in a way more tolerable.

The mother-woman came back into the room. She was still wiping at her eyes. But when she saw the lifeless man on the floor, she screamed.

A crawling sensation ran down Zoe's back. When she saw the mother-woman run to the still figure and start frantically to undo the complication of straps and buckles, she cried out for the first time, "No!"

But the mother-woman seemed impervious to her cries. Her hands worked feverishly at his back, jerking, pulling at the straps, all the while weeping uncontrollably, "I'm sorry, I'm so sorry."

Zoe moaned and struggled inside the white encasement. She called out, "Don't do it. He's only pretending. Can't you see?" But the mother-woman continued to work until the straps were undone. Then she stood above him and jerked at the straitjacket. His arms fell free.

He lay absolutely motionless on the floor like something dead or broken. The mother-woman continued to hover over him, stroking his face, smoothing back the long dark hair, weeping her apologies.

Slowly, almost imperceptibly at first, the man moved. He stared up at the mother-woman. Zoe found herself flinching from the implacable stare.

The mother-woman smiled as though grateful. She knelt lovingly beside him. "Thank God," she whispered, "you're all right. I would never have forgiven myself."

His right arm, newly released, started up toward her face.

Zoe cried out, "Run! Please run."

But they both seemed not to hear her cries. Bubs spoke very gently. "Why did you call the police?" he asked, his hand stroking her face.

The mother-woman leaned into the caress, grateful for it. "I didn't know where you were. I wanted to find you. I didn't want you to hurt yourself."

Bubs, still feigning weakness, continued merely to touch the side of her face. The mother-woman was leaning over him, continuously whispering, "I'm sorry. I won't do it again."

Bubs appeared to receive her affection. Carefully he put his arms around her and drew her down. "They hurt me," he murmured.

"Who, my darling?"

"Those men."

"I'm sorry, so sorry."

He closed his eyes, suffering fresh humiliation. "They embarrassed me," he murmured.

"They didn't mean to—"

"They wrapped that thing around me so that everyone in town could see."

"They were only worried that you—"

"What did I do to deserve that?"

"Nothing, my darling, nothing. But it was for your own good."

"Everyone saw—"

"They'll forget."

"It's hard to forget. I was bound. Like an animal."

They continued to whisper breathlessly to each other, the mother-woman covering his face with light kisses, Bubs's arms enfolding her, pulling her down, down.

Zoe closed her eyes. It was only a matter of time. She remembered now the terror of no sound coming from the upstairs bedroom, then the rhythmic rising and falling of something being beaten, like a rug hung in the sun to air. Groans then, as though someone were refusing to cry aloud. She remembered the way she had pressed against the side of the house after her futile run through the woods, remembered the way she had clutched handfuls of gravel, concentrating first on the way the sun cast patterns about her feet, then later watching the stars shine through leafless branches, hearing an occasional car pass by on the highway, still waiting, growing chill, wondering how long the prolonged punishment in the bedroom would last.

Suddenly her muscles struggled against the white encasement. She did not want to know then or now why the back of her mother's dress had spotted red for several days.

The tender scene on the floor continued, both murmuring into each other's ears, a suspect display of affection that Zoe knew was only prelude to something else.

Then suddenly their positions on the floor were reversed. The mother-woman lay on her back, her eyes inflamed from the recent tears, looking up at him with a mixed expression of fear and obedience. Bubs straddled her on his knees. Slowly he began pulling the thick leather belt from the loops around his trousers.

The mother-woman pushed backward. "No, please," she protested weakly. "Zoe might come back."

Bubs shook his head and looked directly toward the white plaster figure standing nearby. "She won't bother us," he said. "I just want to make love to you. Husbands have that right."

The woman on the floor was clearly terrified. She struggled to free herself from the weight of his body. "I can't," she gasped.

"You never can," smiled Bubs as though he knew what her reply would be. His voice was cold, all vestiges of weakness were gone. He continued to slide the belt through his hands, watching her, repulsion gathering in his eyes. "Bitch," he muttered.

Suddenly the mother-woman lay absolutely still. The tears subsided. Her mouth gaped, lips distorted, a poorly done death mask taken at the moment of greatest agony. She opened her eyes; the lips moved. "Beat me," she whispered as though offering him a viable alternative. "Beat me," she suggested again. She ground her teeth together; the flesh on her face seemed to shudder as she begged still a third time, "Beat me. I'd rather the beating than—"

They held each other in a locked gaze as though in spite of everything they were communicating, understanding each other.

Watching them, Zoe wished fervently that the white plaster shell covered her eyes. It wasn't necessary to see. She didn't want to see.

But she saw everything, saw Bubs stand up, saw the deliberate, almost choreographed movement of the mother-woman as she sat erect and gracefully unbuttoned her dress, like a woman preparing for the act of love, baring her back. She observed, too, the final, almost deliriously happy expression on the woman's face as she prostrated herself on the floor at Bubs's feet, lying facedown, her arms extended rigidly in front of her, her legs stiff, toes pointed.

Bubs pulled the belt through his hands, stroking it, a sensuous gesture, feeling its texture, concentrating on the pointed edges of the heavy metal buckle. He stepped back a few steps and aligned himself with the bare back at his feet. Then he lifted the belt high into the air over his head.

At the first dull report of leather striking flesh, Zoe moaned. She looked down and saw a narrow red welt rising on the expanse of the white skin. She lost count of the number of times the belt was lifted into the air and brought down with stunning accuracy against the back. Like a delighted child, Bubs went about his task. His face bore a fixed smile. His brow glistened. Now and then his eyes lifted and fell with the belt as though the act of striking were of much greater importance than the object which was being struck. At first the rhythm was steady, an almost peaceful rising and falling of his arm, the sharp stinging report a kind of counterpoint to the labored but steady breathing. Then all at once the rhythm increased to a frenzy. His jaws clenched. His arm, moving up and down, whipped the belt through the air until it became a blur of continuous motion. Finally he staggered backward, looking up at the ceiling. He spun crazily around and brought the belt down a final time. He collapsed on his knees a distance away, groaning, clutching his groin in the throes of sexual agony.

The beating over, Zoe dared to look down at the mother-woman. What she saw on the floor was a red and living horror, the back a grisly script of livid lacerations criss-crossing in an endless pattern of rising, swelling flesh, punctuated here and there by torn flaps of skin where the sharp edges of the buckle had penetrated. Throughout the entire beating, the mother-woman had neither moved nor cried out. Now slowly she lifted her head although it required energy from the outermost fibers of her being to do so. Her hands struggled to support the weight of her shoulders and failing, she fell back down, her head turned sideways toward Zoe, a faint, slightly beatific smile on her lips.

Zoe struggled with all her might against the shell that imprisoned her. She'd seen enough. Yet the two on the floor were motionless, frozen in a tableau for her benefit, forcing her to study the specifics of the scene, commit it to memory so that she might take it with her everywhere. She noticed an odor in the room now, a corpse smell.

Why didn't they move? Were they the corpses? She cried out for help but no sound left her lips. She tried to turn away from the sight but couldn't. She tried to lift an arm to cover her eyes, felt her muscles doing battle with the hardened plaster. It occurred to her to call a name. But whose name? Who was there to hear? She thought of red-cellophane-wrapped candy drops and a little boy's face. But the main problem was passage from this world back into that one. Unable to find the proper road, she merely clawed mechanically at her prison.

Then a face appeared directly in front of her eyes, someone crouching at her feet out of sight all the while. Through
the narrow slits she saw orange-painted lips and a blond wig.

"Aren't they marvelous?" grinned Mary Lisa.

Zoe pushed against the imprisonment, startled, but re-
lieved by the sudden appearance. "Please," she begged
weakly, "let me out."

The orange lips narrowed into a thin line. "Proof of
identity," Mary Lisa demanded.

Zoe's entire body felt numb from the prolonged confinement. "Please," she whispered, "just—"

Mary Lisa was moving away from her, her usually warm
face as stern as Zoe had ever seen it. "No proof of identity,"
she called back briskly. "Can't help you."

Zoe cried out, "Please. I can't move."

"You don't want to move."

"I do. Help me."

Mary Lisa stepped across the bloodied prostrate woman
on the floor. "We're having a great party downstairs," she
smiled excitedly. "Wish you could join us."

Zoe cried out again. "Please don't go. Help me. I don't
want to stay here. Please—"

"Oh no," Mary Lisa said almost flippantly. "You have no
name, no proof of identity. You're much better off where you
are. Nameless, faceless people suffer so much. They're in
constant need of reassuring. It's such a drag."

"No!" The cry was sudden and piercing. Zoe's knuck-
les, beating against the plaster, felt wet. She tried to bend her
body, to incline her neck forward, but the plaster caused her
to choke.

Mary Lisa watched the frantic movement from the door,
her face creased with pity. She shook her blond curls. "Poor
Zoe. Never satisfied. In. Out. In. Out. If you don't know
what you want, how do you expect us to know?"

Zoe moaned again, "Oh, God, please."

Apparently something in her tone caused Mary Lisa to soften. She walked back and affectionately patted the white plaster prison. "It won't be long now," she whispered, "just one or two more scenes. Then we'll be finished." She leaned close to the eye slits. "I promise. It's almost over. You've done your part very well. Don't let us down now."

As Zoe watched her walk away, she felt an explosion near the top of her skull. Numerous pieces of splintered glass seemed to be raining down upon her, penetrating the plaster exterior, imbedding themselves in her brain. Even the corridors and staircase of the house seemed to reverberate with someone's frightened cries. The fury of the inside body spread; the head made a tiny bobbing motion each time the heart beat.

The claustrophobia was complete. She could not breathe, could find no air with which to fill her lungs. The plaster seemed to be shrinking. She felt incredible pressure over all her body. She jerked her head upward in an attempt to expand her lungs. But there was no room for expansion. She had the sensation now of water lapping at her face as though she were drowning. Her lips whispered a final desperate plea for help. But the slightest of breezes blew the word away.

The two on the floor held their positions. Zoe's voice sank into a deliberate and mindless repetition of one word, repeated over and over again, a soft, continuous, boneless nonsensical muttering. There was the light of madness in her eyes. Her skull was a globe of darkness. Somewhere there was an instrument of examination, a point that knew it existed. But it was sleeping now; incredibly there were still sounds that came out of the lower part of the face.

But they had no meaning attached to them. They were useless . . .

"Well, it worked in *Gaslight.*" Bubs explained irritably. "We did a production of it in '43 at the Berwick-on-Tweed Rep Company. For the soldiers. Bombs falling all over. A smashing production really. You see, the man kept turning the lights up and down and drove her completely insane."

Mary Lisa said, "I thought the point was to drive her sane."

"I know," snapped Bubs. "That's what I'm saying. We must try something else."

They sat around in the living room in various states of relaxation, Bubs with his legs swung over the arm of Zoe's father's gray leather chair, Mary Lisa on the floor at his feet, her knees drawn up, the blond curly head resting on her hands. Others spilled about on the floor and in chairs, looking exhausted.

Only the old woman in the red robe stood alert, accusing. Now she raised a finger and pointed it through the archway and looked out into the hall where Zoe sat alone on the stairs and isolated. "Well, just look at her now," she demanded. "She's completely mad. How do you expect us to enjoy ourselves if our hostess is completely mad?"

Zoe's lips moved. "I'm not mad," she said dully. She looked about at the vacant air, hoping it might provide her with some clue concerning how she had traveled from upstairs to down. Recently she'd been confined somewhere. She couldn't remember. Something white. She looked down at the blue jeans and workshirt. They were dotted here and there with what appeared to be small white flecks of plaster. Her fingernails, she noticed, were thick with the substance. Nearby, standing now in the exact center of the hallway, she noticed the slender cabinet which the men had carried in some days ago. Heat seemed to be emanating from the side. She looked back toward the people who were watching her so intensely from the living room. "I'm not mad," she repeated. Then, in order to relieve herself of the burden of their eyes, she began mechanically to pick off the clinging pieces of plaster.

A voice shouted at her, "For God's sake, don't drop that stuff on the floor. I just swept."

"She's looney all right. Just look at her. She looks like a monkey picking fleas."

Mary Lisa stirred restlessly from her position on the floor. "Why don't we test her then? I guess there are ways to find out for certain whether or not a person's insane."

"Won't do any good," grumbled the old woman. "You've got eyes. Use them. She's beyond our help."

"How do we know until we've tried?" protested Mary Lisa.

Bubs sat up on the edge of his chair, the light of interest moving across his face. He chewed at his thumbnail and gazed at Zoe, still sitting alone and isolated in the hall. "It might work," he muttered, his eyes narrow and calculating.

Zoe moved backward on the steps. She knew the expression on his face, knew from experience that it preceded hell. She shook her head, protesting, "No more." She wrapped her arms around herself and in the process spilled the handful of tiny white plaster particles on the floor.

Suddenly the mother-woman flew at her from out of the shadows. "Goddamn you," she cried. She emerged from a semidarkened corner of the living room and stood directly in front of Zoe, her face angry. "I told you not to drop that stuff on the floor. How many times have I told you? You have no consideration for me at all. No one does. My life isn't easy. I've already swept that floor a dozen times today and I don't intend to sweep it again."

She gestured wildly, her hands a blur as she pointed first at Zoe, then to the floor and the scattering of plaster particles. At the height of her rage, something caught in her face. She gasped sharply and grimaced, her eyes shut tight.

"Pick it up," she concluded weakly. "Pick up every last bit of it." She looked at Zoe as though pleading. "Don't you think I have enough to do with him in there?" She inclined her head toward Bubs. "Don't you think that's enough for one soul?" she asked almost pitiably.

Pity or no, Zoe had had enough. "Damn you," she cried out. "Damn you all. You have no right to be here, to do what you are doing. You have no—"

Suddenly her words seemed so impotent. Nothing was registering on those blank faces. Then she ran toward the front door and for one blessed second she was out of their range of vision, though coming up rapidly behind her she heard a rush of heavy footsteps and looked back in time to see Rich and Dempsey overtake her.

Dempsey reached out one beefy hand for her shoulder. She fell back against the door, turned her head to one side and bit down as hard as she could on the flesh of his hand. She saw him recoil in pain and heard his curses as he started up toward her a second time. And now she lifted her right knee in one well-aimed blow to his groin and again he fell backward, howling, clutching his injured area, yelling for Rich to "get her, get the slut—"

As Rich was angling himself into position for the third attack, Zoe struggled for breath as well as freedom and saw Mary Lisa appear from the living room and start slowly toward her, soothing, "Come on, Zoe, this isn't necessary. We're trying to help you is all—"

Bubs was right behind her, looking hurt. "Why are you running for the door, Zoe? You don't have the key. You've never had the key. To anything. You don't even know what a key looks like."

Still angry, still longing to bolt free of this madness, Zoe saw the two of them approaching on either side, and then Mary Lisa was directly in front of her. "Come on back, Zoe. I thought we were friends. We'll go if you want us to, sooner or later, in a minute or two."

Zoe lowered her head, embarrassed. She thought she heard snickers coming from the living room. There were visionary horrors before her eyes from which she could not escape. She had the feeling that there were necessary conditions she had to fulfill before she could pass through the door. But what? Somewhere beyond the barrier of the door was the reassuring banality of everyday life. The choice apparently was not between heaven and hell, but rather between hell and hell.

"You coming?" Bubs called out cheerily. "We have a test for you."

She turned away from the locked door, weary of being shuffled back and forth between them. She felt hands on her shoulders. Bubs was there, smiling down on her with an expression of pity. "You don't really want to go out there anyway," he said softly. "You came here to escape, remember? One week of freedom? At least something is happening here. And that's a vantage point, really, something happening." He smiled. "Maybe it's not always pleasant, but at least it's movement. Exactly how long has it been since you have experienced significant movement?"

She obeyed his hands and listened to his voice because she had no choice. The sense of her consciousness was like a lump of undigested matter in her system. Her body seemed to be growing progressively more dense, more tightly packed. She had suffered at their hands, yet not suffered. Always at the moment of greatest distress she had felt, paradoxically, dead and alive. A sudden weakness swept through her, causing her to slump lightly against him. Without warning he enfolded her in his arms and held her close.

"Well, isn't that sweet!" the old woman cackled from the living room. "Lordy! Lovers! That's all we need now. And we haven't even rehearsed *that* script." She called back to the others. "Look! We've got a pair of bloody lovers on our hands."

"Not true," said Bubs, abruptly disengaging Zoe from his arms. "We must remember that it doesn't hurt now and then to be kind and human."

"You can't be kind to an insane woman," snapped the old woman peevishly. "She doesn't know the difference."

Standing alone again in the hall, Zoe noticed that all about her now there appeared to be preternatural light. It seemed to come from the baseboards of the slender cabinet, as though a sun were rising beneath it. She looked quickly about to see if anyone else had noticed it. Apparently they hadn't. She heard Bubs inquire softly, "Are you ready?"

"For what?" she asked, trying to shade her eyes from the incredible illumination.

"For your test," he answered. He leaned close and whispered, "It won't be hard. Just answer the questions honestly and you'll do fine."

Again she felt his arm around her shoulder, felt herself being guided back into the living room. She felt a chair behind her and sat down, still trying to shield her eyes from the intense light in the hallway. She half listened to an argument which seemed to be going on around her, heard chairs being scraped across the floor. Someone was moaning in the far corner, the mother-woman she imagined. Her mother had moaned for days after the officers had brought her father home. She felt grit in her hand and looked down at the residue of plaster particles in her palm. Suddenly she saw the exquisite beauty of each grain, saw that every particle was made up of a perfect geometrical pattern with sharp angles from each of which a brilliant shaft of light was reflected, causing the tiny crystals to shine.

"Don't fool with that now," Bubs scolded. Roughly he grabbed her wrist and brushed the beauty from her palm like a scolding father.

She mourned its death and tried to look up at the blinding light. Now the illumination seemed to come from two powerful spotlights which stood on poles about three feet in front of her. The others had moved to the far end of the room and had left her alone, sitting self-consciously on the chair in the dazzling light. She could not see faces or figures, but she could hear their voices chattering lightly.

"The schizophrenic is not merely unregenerate but desperately sick from the bargain."

"Hospitalization?"

"Perhaps. For her own good."

"Is she schizo?"

"What do you think?"

"In a way, I think she's enjoyed everything."

"Not really. She's just stubborn."

"She was an excellent dead cow."

"Her true role."

"She can't keep away from evil. I've watched her closely. A psychological suicide if I've ever seen one."

"What do you know about anything?"

"Nothing, really."

"Then shut up."

Zoe sat with her head down, her hands folded obediently in her lap, listening to the voices behind the lights. She felt that if she attempted to communicate with them, she'd be communicating with another universe. Her mind seemed to have its place apart and separate from theirs. Yet somehow they were pooling information about her, manipulating her with little or no common ground of memory to serve as a basis for understanding.

She glanced up at the lights and beyond. All chatter ceased. Between the lights, she saw Bubs standing, his feet spread, hands on hips, a mere outline but recognizable. Suddenly he demanded, "What's your name?"

"Zoe Manning."

"And what was it before that?"

"I don't remember." She heard a murmur run through the audience.

Bubs cleared his throat to signal for silence. "Who owns you?" he demanded.

"No one," she replied.

"Bullshit. Who owns you?"

She lifted her head. "No one owns me. I own myself."

"You're lying!" Bub's voice thundered down upon her, unable to control his rage. "You can't even see yourself, let alone own yourself. Ownership is a serious matter. The delusion that you own yourself is just that. A good whack on your head may help to clear it. Do you want one?"

She shook her head, embarrassed, and looked about at the floor. The carpet was the same, fading yellow roses trailing on a bilious green background, brown smudges for leaves and vines. It had not been attractive twenty years ago and it was still not attractive.

"Pay no attention to the rugs," Bubs scolded. "It's not the rug that's on trial here."

A female voice protested sharply from the audience. "And it's not a trial, you jackass. It's just a test. Stop bullying her."

Zoe heard mutters of agreement. She squinted up at the blinding lights and saw Bubs pacing, trying to digest the reprimand. Suddenly he grabbed the heavy metal standards on which the strong lights were mounted and moved them closer until their broad round bases were only inches from Zoe's feet. Two enormous eyes of light rained down on her, so close she could feel their heat. It was impossible to look up. The retinas would not endure it.

His action provoked another slight murmur of disapproval from the audience. But no one called for the lights to be moved back. So they stayed where they had placed them, all their awesome power focused directly down on Zoe, a merciless assault of wattage.

"Now!" Bubs said, satisfied with this new arrangement. "You say you're not owned by anybody. Is that correct?"

Zoe nodded, her head down, eyes closed against the blinding lights.

"Could you tell me then how you got here?"

"You drove me up in my car, or at least that's what you said."

"I don't mean that," Bubs snapped irritably. "And why don't you look at me? People who own themselves usually have direct vision."

"Because I can't," Zoe said. But at that moment she did look up. Her eyes felt as if they were being penetrated by a thousand needles. She leaned her head forward and covered her eyes with both hands. She struggled with the discomfort, then murmured angrily, "You know I can't see. Why do you insist on playing these games? Just let me go. You have no right."

There was a sharp gasp from the audience. Someone whispered, "The bitch is insolent."

"I told you she hasn't changed. Not really. In spite of everything."

"It won't get her anyplace. Is she stupid in the bargain?"

"He doesn't like it. Look! You can see."

Zoe rubbed her eyes and shaded them with her hands

and waited out the voices. She heard movement behind her, recognized bleakly the presence that was encircling her. Suddenly she felt strong hands on either side of her face, felt those hands force her head upward. Even with her eyes tightly closed, the powerful rays penetrated like twin suns which had fallen and were now setting directly on her face. She struggled, but the hands holding her head merely renewed their grip and held her fast. She felt moisture slipping down her face. Her eyeballs were being seared.

Someone from the audience called out, "All right. That's enough."

The hands slipped down her head, tightened briefly about her throat, then were gone.

Quickly she leaned forward in the chair and buried her face in her lap. Even there in that mild darkness she still saw a thousand suns. The flesh around her eyes ached, the eyes themselves felt burned.

"No more impudence," Bubs warned. "Do you understand?"

She nodded but kept her head down. She blotted the moisture from her face on the blue jeans. She opened one eye and looked down at her bare feet, soiled, dirt-encrusted.

Bubs confirmed her thoughts. "You're filthy and deserve to be. And these are not games we are playing. Ask the mother-woman." At that moment Zoe heard a groan coming from the shadows; she remembered the bleeding back, the red lines across the dress.

"Ask yourself," Bubs added. "How do you feel? Good? I daresay not. These are not games. We've worked very hard for you. All we want is a decent display of cooperation. Is that clear?"

Zoe nodded.

"All right then," he said in a tone of resolve, "let's try again." She heard him pacing a few feet in front of her. She kept her head down, eyes safely closed against the hot rays of the light.

"Now, you say you're owned by no one. You say you own yourself. You say further that I brought you here in your own car. Yet I say I did not. I say I have never seen you before in my life. And if I brought you here in your car, where is that car now?"

Zoe thought for a moment. "You told me that you had hidden it."

Bubs laughed outright. "Now why would I want to hide it?"

"To keep me from getting away."

Several others in the audience laughed openly.

Over this laughter, Bubs said, "You couldn't get away if there were ten cars out there, all running with keys in the ignition and ready to go."

Zoe sat with her head propped up in one hand. "I want to go home," she begged.

Bubs replied with feigned shock. "Well, my God, I thought this was your home. Where in the hell are we if this isn't your home? I hope I haven't trespassed. I'd hate to be arrested. I've never been arrested in my entire life. Not once."

There was a soft scattering of applause for this pronouncement. Zoe spoke above the noise. "This is my parents' home. Not mine."

"And where is yours, if I might ask?"

"In Newton."

"Do you live there alone?"

"No. With my husband and two sons."

"Why do you hate them?"

"I don't hate them."

"Then why didn't you go with them?"

Zoe rubbed her forehead. She wished that she might

straighten her back, might look her inquisitor in the eye. "I don't know," she muttered.

"I assume you didn't go because you didn't want to go."

She sighed and said sarcastically, "You're perceptive."

"Don't get smart," Bubs warned. "You should know by now what can happen."

She heard him pacing beyond the lights, heard a slight rustle as the audience shifted in their positions. From the sound of his voice, he seemed to be ranging throughout the audience now. From some distance, he called back to her, "Do you make love with that man in Newton?"

Zoe looked at her fingers, which had been pressed tightly against her lips. A tiny silver thread of spittle joined them.

"I didn't hear you," Bubs called again.

"Yes," she replied angrily, "although I don't think it's any of your business."

"Everything is my business," he said flatly. "Do you enjoy it?"

"Yes."

"You're not telling the truth."

"I am telling the truth."

"You don't enjoy it with me."

She looked furiously up at the light and instantly regretted it. Quickly she bowed her head and waited out the pain in her eyes. "I've never made love with you and I have no intention of doing so," she replied.

The audience snickered. Bubs was quite close to her now. "The hell you haven't," he murmured. "I've come to your bed every night and broken open the locked door behind which you keep your hoarded virginity."

Zoe shook her head. "I'm not a virgin," she said.

"Yes you are," Bubs replied, almost tenderly. "You've opened your legs for a man. You've given birth. But you're still a virgin in your heart, passionless, wholly self-absorbed. But that's old ground. We've covered it before. What I'm primarily interested in is the now of things."

She felt something in her head grating and thumping against her skull. She felt pinned, like a specimen. "Leave me alone," she murmured.

"I don't want to leave you alone," Bubs said petulantly. "I just want to know why you make love with him and not with me. A woman is only three things, two breasts and a vagina. To deny that is to deny your only purpose. You have no other reason for existing. To deny it is to deny your right to life." His voice grew expansive as if a certain thought had amused him. "In this age of rising crime, if I had valuables to store, I'd hide them between your legs because I'd know they would be safe there."

The audience laughed heartily at this. Zoe felt humiliated, her eyes like dull stones. She wrapped her arms around her body and began to rock slowly back and forth. Her shirt was wet through with perspiration. She heard the derision in their laughter. "I love him," she insisted softly. "I don't love you."

Bubs ordered the audience to stop laughing. "What did you say?" he demanded.

Zoe repeated dully, "I said I love him. I don't love you."

"Then why didn't you go with him?"

Zoe moaned, her brain felt like soft pudding. "I don't know. I wish I had."

Suddenly the audience gasped. Someone whispered, "Look! Is she crying?"

Zoe sat in a submissive position in the chair, head down.

"She's really survived a great deal," someone whispered.

"But has she survived?"

"I think so—look at her."

"She always was the smartest one in the class. A little strange. Haughty, aloof, you know."

Bubs thundered at the whisperers. "Tears don't mean a goddamn thing and you know it. We are dealing not with exceptional facts which might justifiably be overlooked, but with a general human phenomenon which cannot be disregarded by any of us who are trying to discover what the human soul is."

There was a scattering of applause. Someone said, "Very pretty speech."

Zoe listened. It was unimportant that she see anything. Slowly she lifted her head. They did not intend to let her go. Ever. Hopelessness moved in. The smooth hot rays from the lights stabbed her eyes. Beyond the initial pain was a numb blindness which she welcomed.

Bubs shouted triumphantly, "You see? She's allowing herself to be blinded. Not even a mild sense of virtue or obligation is stopping her. She is openly courting disaster and loving every minute of it. Look!" he cried exultantly. "Look at her eyes. She is deliberately blinding herself."

Zoe was aware of the excited rush of voices but concentrated instead on the fire in her eyes. Flames seemed to be licking at her face. She thought she smelled flesh burning. The lights blurred, faded. With what was left of her vision, she saw the edge of a dark cliff. It was a sheer, almost unbroken descent. The ledge of the precipice was coming toward her, a world on fire danced before her eyes, and in order to escape from the heat, from the hideous sight of people aflame, she fell forward on her hands and knees and crawled toward the black edge.

"Look! You see?" Bubs shouted again, pleased. "The lump has fallen! Look how instinctive it is. Look how it crawls into the corner. At last it knew its rightful place. What do you suggest we do with it now?"

Someone whispered, "She's a cooked goose."

"And blind at that."

"A poor, blind cooked goose."

Bubs muttered derisively, "She's never been happier. Just look how she sits in her corner. Incredible, really incredible. She is absolutely of no use to anyone now."

A female voice begged, "Cover her eyes, please. I can't bear the sight of them."

What they were saying was at least partly true. Zoe had crawled into a corner, fleeing from their madness as much as the heat of the lights. She felt a solid intersection of walls behind her. It was also true that her vision was gone. She saw merely shadow. It was an extraordinary experience, not particularly agonizing now that the worst was over. It was almost pleasant in the darkness. She felt a piercing sweetness as she realized that she would always be an object of pity.

Bubs said in a loud, near voice, "She sickens me, she really does. She's actually enjoying herself."

A female voice whispered again, "Please cover her eyes. I don't want to see."

Zoe heard footsteps approaching, felt hands moving about her head, felt a soft, fragrant cloth being wrapped around her eyes and tied firmly in back. A double blindness. Good. She tried to thank someone for their kindness, but her lips were dry and stuck together.

Bubs muttered, "She should be deaf and mute as well. Then we could burn her with the other garbage."

A female ordered, "No! Leave her alone. You've done enough. It's your fault anyway. If you hadn't asked her such stupid questions, if you hadn't moved the light so close, she'd be able to see now."

Another female said accusingly, "You forced the blind-

ness on her. You gave her no alternative. You moved the
lights too close. You embarrassed her."

And still another, "That's all you've done from the beginning."

"Just used her—"

"On the pretext of helping her."

Zoe heard a slow shifting of movement. The audience
seemed to be taking sides. She heard no male voices at all,
not even that of Bubs, just the slow steady accumulation of
female accusers.

"From the very beginning it was you."

"Now you say burn her with the other garbage. There's
worse garbage in this room if you ask me."

Their voices were cold and without inflection, a dirge
that Zoe somehow suspected had been rehearsed.

Now a female was mimicking him. " 'Let us help her,'
you said. 'She needs us,' you said." The voice was acid in its
sarcasm. " 'Let us soothe her,' you said—"

Another female voice rose in anger. " 'Let us destroy
her' is what you meant. It's what you always mean."

"Your protection suffocates."

"Your name chokes."

"She was not inferior to you. She was superior and that
was what you couldn't stand."

The sound of movement was shifting radically, several
were advancing, someone retreating. Zoe tried to push farther back into the corner to avoid all contact with them. She
had no strong feeling in the conflict one way or another. She
was safer now, safer even than she had been inside the plaster
shell. Not to see was the greatest of blessings.

Someone stopped directly in front of her. The voice was
male, scratchy and slightly breathless. "You're defending
that?" it demanded.

It may have been Bubs, but she wasn't certain. If it was,

his voice had lost all its resonance. "Look at her," he went
on. "The best role she ever played was that of a dead cow."

"You made her a dead cow. You assigned the role to
her."

"I didn't. She came equipped that way."

"And you exploited her."

She felt movement against the side of her leg, someone
seeking protection in her same corner. The female voices
were drawing nearer, closing in.

"You speak of the soul's needs," said one derisively.
"What was she supposed to do? Pattern hers after yours? Is
there no other way?"

"She had a choice," Bubs offered weakly.

"She had no choice, has never had a choice except those
you deigned to offer her."

"She could have run."

"Where? You would have found her and brought her
back. You always do."

The female voices seemed to be standing directly above
her. Zoe raised the bandage from her eyes, trying to see. As
well as she could tell, Bubs was crouched in the corner beside
her. She felt his arm next to hers, heard him whisper, "Leave
me alone, bitches. I did what I thought was best for her."

She heard the females laughing. "Well, what do you suggest?" one of them asked.

"Burn *him* with the garbage."

"He doesn't burn."

"Then what?"

Someone, perhaps Bubs, groaned. He was so close.
"Oh, for God's sake, you bitches. I'll service all of you if you
like. I know what you want, even if you don't." A portion of
the old arrogance had returned.

A storm of laughter arose from the females.

"Well, I can, you know," Bubs shouted above the laughter. "I can make all of you and not even stop once for breath."

The laughter ceased. Shock waves seemed to be moving out in concentric circles of female voices. Someone gasped, "Did you ever—"

"No, I never—"

"The nerve—"

"The gall—"

"God damn him."

"I have! Just now."

"Then it's settled?"

"Yes." The voice sounded breathless.

"Who will do it?"

"We all will do it."

The arm pushing against Zoe was trembling.

"We'll need a sharp knife."

"Use his own. It would be poetic justice."

"This one?"

There were murmurs of approval. Bubs pushed back farther into the wall. The trembling of his arms seemed to have spread to his entire body. A residue of the old arrogance flared briefly. "You wouldn't do it," he muttered. "You can't get along without me. You wouldn't dare."

"We'll need ropes," a female said, impervious to his boasting. "He'll have to be restrained."

Zoe closed her eyes behind the bandage. Inside the darkness she saw a row of batlike creatures. They were perched in a solid line across a field of gray. They were quiet, watching for her. She heard footsteps scurrying off, then a moment later heard them returning.

"Ropes!" someone announced.

"I'm so glad you remembered to bring them. I had no idea we'd use them so often."

"Where shall we do it? There'll be blood. Quite a mess."

"Right here on the floor. We can clean it up."

"Shall we make it complete or partial?"

Someone giggled, "Who cares?"

Zoe felt Bubs pushing against her shoulder. She felt his beard against the side of her face, his hands clawing at her arm, terror spreading. "Don't let them do it," he whispered. "A word from you and they would stop. They've gotten completely out of hand. Please speak to them."

The female voices hummed around them and then fell silent, all listening. Zoe bowed her head and stuck her fingers in her ears so she wouldn't have to hear the silence. But she still heard. Apparently Bubs was on his knees before them. He was begging pitiably. "You musn't do it. Where will it get you? You'll want it again. Then where will you be?"

A female voice laughed. "No worse off than we are now and perhaps better off."

Bubs grasped Zoe's hands and pulled them away from her ears. "Can you see me?" he whispered. "I need your help. We've had some good times, haven't we? It hasn't been all bad, has it?"

A female snickered. "You have the nerve to say that to her? Look at her. Forget your own problems for a minute and just look at what you've done to her."

Now they came forward. She felt Bubs push against her, struggling to get away. There was movement all around her, scrambling feet, hands flailing, bodies swerving close, the air heavy with the labored breathing of exertion.

"Get his other leg," someone gasped.

"He's strong."

"He won't be in a minute."

They set upon him again and again, trying to pull him away from the safety of the corner.

"Need more room," someone gasped.

"Bring him out into the open."

"His arm, grab it!"

"Where's the rope?"

Throughout the struggle, Bubs was strangely quiet. Zoe assumed that he had nothing to say and was for the moment channeling all his energies into escape. Her darkness sorted itself into near and far, and at the high point of the gray field, the bats were scurrying for safety.

He groaned, his breath coming into sharp spasms over the humiliation of his capture. Gradually the activity diminished. Zoe discovered that she could extend her arms out in either direction and touch nothing but empty space. There was considerable commotion in the center of the room, female voices rising and blending in a series of suggestions, confirmations, approvals.

At last there was a substantial silence. Someone had been tamed, secured, rendered helpless. Zoe sat listening, at first with doubt, then with terror to the descriptions the females breathed at her. A dawn faded out the gray field and at last light filtered inside the shelter of her blindfold. She began to stir under the dread of returning vision. The place where she sat was impossibly dangerous. She saw shapes hovering over a bound, motionless figure.

"What if he screams?" someone asked.

"It's very likely that he will."

"We need a gag."

She heard footsteps coming near, felt hands roughly jerking the bandage from her eyes. She tried to protest, tried to reach up and claim what was rightfully hers. But they were paying no attention to her. She considered crawling out of the room but there was an unpleasant sound coming from the bound figure and she would have to pass right by it, a male voice choking on his own saliva, a gurgling, wet terror that simply repeated dully over and over, "Don't—don't—"

Zoe tried to cover both her ears and her eyes. A single bat flapped upward inside her mind with a hoarse cry that was echoed by something in the center of the room. The shapes knelt around the still figure.

"Remove his trousers," a female ordered.

"It's too bad she can't watch. It's for her that we're doing it."

"She can see everything she wants to see."

"Where to start?"

"Take it all. Complete castration. Only then will the world be entirely safe."

Zoe jammed her fingers into her ears. This dulled her hearing, but her vision was growing clearer. She had the sense of someone watching her. As the gray field lifted, she saw the gagged bearded face looking in her direction, the eyes entreating. All attention was now focused on the lower half of his body, leaving his chest and face exposed. He lay on the floor, his mouth gaping around the white gag, his arms tied tightly beneath him.

"Are we ready?" a female voice asked, almost reverently.

A beast with claws was scratching at Zoe's eyes. She shuddered, still fighting the return of vision. She saw Bubs's face, tight and pale. Suddenly he sucked in breath with a gasp. He pushed his head backward against the floor. His chest sank, then lifted. The pupils of his eyes disappeared, leaving two white ovals. He thrashed, made sucking sounds around the gag. Then suddenly he made a thunderous half leap upward in spite of the ropes. His lips tightly compressed around the gag, his eyes closed beneath the dark moist fringe of his hair. His body was stiff yet quiet; one hand clawed feebly at the floor. Then it too fell limp.

"Is it done?" a female whispered.

"It is."

"So quick."

"Is he dead?"

"Oh, my no. He'll survive. Just altered, that's all."

"Stop the bleeding," someone said casually as though it were the thing to say, perhaps the thing to do.

"What are we supposed to do with *this?*"

Someone giggled. "It looks absolutely harmless now."

"God, what a mess."

"Is he out?"

"Cold."

"Poor Bubs," another muttered.

"It really was very easy, considering—"

Someone started humming a low tuneless sound, trying to comfort themselves.

"It's a shame. In a way," a female murmured. "When he was good, he was very, very good."

"There are others. An endless supply of them," someone said harshly.

"Should we have gone this far?"

"Ask her. She's the one who wanted it."

As the females turned to stare at Zoe, she eased slowly backward into a corner. Her vision and hearing were completely intact now. She saw their bloodied hands, saw the man, bare-legged, lying in a pool of blood. She offered a weak protest. "I didn't want it. It wasn't my idea—" Her voice faltered and stopped. She could not discipline her eyes to stay away from the bleeding torso. Hemmed in by walls, she tried to scramble backward. She looked solemnly at the staring females. They seemed to be awaiting her orders. "You're insane," she whispered. "All of you."

"That's beside the point," one said coolly. "He's all yours now. What do you want to do with him?"

"He's not mine," Zoe protested.

"He's still bleeding," someone announced. "He may die."

This caused a young female to turn away. "We shouldn't have done it," she moaned. "What will we do when we want him?"

"You should have thought of that," snapped another.

Gradually the old woman in the red robe materialized out of the circle. "Take him upstairs and put him to bed," she ordered. "Then clean yourselves up. He'll probably need a doctor after your butchery. I'll call one."

Slowly they responded to her strength. Four of them lifted Bubs from the floor and carried him laboriously from the room. The others followed, some sniffling, a slow, mournful procession, each indulging in innumerable separate gestures, weak attempts to clean their hands, to help with the heavy burden. As they passed by Zoe, she noticed that Bubs's head was moving slowly from side to side. He appeared to be breathing heavily around the gag; his eyes were open but unfocused.

"Where shall we put him?" a female asked weakly.

"Put him in her bed," the old woman grinned, pointing at Zoe.

A near female smiled sweetly. "Of course. Where else? Perfect justice."

Zoe watched them up the stairs, saw them adjust to the complication of the upward angle and the leaden weight they were carrying. They left a trail of blood all the way up the steps.

She was alone in the living room. Exhaustion and terror spoke directly to her. Leave at once, they said. Break the window by the door if you must and take your chances outside in the night. There is nothing here but madness. Leave!

She glanced toward the door as though the door had

spoken to her. Where were the men, her constant guards? They had been here earlier, but now the house seemed to be filled only with women. She listened. There was no sound coming from upstairs. The mournful procession was strangely quiet.

Abruptly, interrupting her thoughts, she heard footsteps on the front porch. It was beginning again as she knew it would. She looked up and saw the doorknob rotating, heard the hinges give.

A man in a white suit stepped through the door. He closed it immediately behind him. He was carrying a black bag and seemed to be in a terrible rush. "I heard there's a man here who needs medical attention," he said roughly.

Without waiting for a reply, he rushed past Zoe and took the stairs two at a time. She felt the vibrations of his speed. At the top of the steps, he called angrily down to her, "Which way? Good God, I've never been here before. Help me."

Incredulously she stared up at him. The black beard was the same, the eyes were the same, as well as the long shaggy black hair. When she failed to answer right away, he cursed her, "You dumb bitch! You really want him to die, don't you?" He shifted the black bag to the other hand and again demanded, "Where is he? We're losing precious time."

Slowly she pointed down the corridor in the direction of her bedroom. "Bubs?" she questioned softly, still struggling for recognition.

But he had already gone off in the appointed direction. She continued to stare at the empty spot at the top of the stairs, trying to pit her knowledge against the certainty of what she thought she had seen.

So intent was her concentration that she failed at first to hear the other men filing silently in through the front door. Two of them moved the slender enclosed cabinet which they had brought with them that first day to the center of the hall while the others took their places around the wall. Then all gazed on her wordlessly, their faces pale and sweating . . .

———◆———

"Well, he's dead," Bubs announced soberly from the top of the steps.

He had been gone only a matter of seconds. Zoe was still trying to determine if it was Bubs when she heard his footsteps returning. At the same time she had at last been aware of the silent men who had arranged the cabinet in the center of the hall. A moment later she heard from the upstairs bedroom a chorus of weeping, wailing women. Trying to look in all directions at once, she ultimately gave up and now sat on the bottom step, listening to the sounds of mourning.

Bubs gazed down on her, held by an ancient recognition. "Did you hear me?" he demanded. "He's dead. Do you feel safer, stronger, more content?"

The wailing upstairs did not sound like a performance. Someone, several someones were suffering the agonies of outrageous grief. Zoe tried to speak above the sound. "How did he die?" she asked, not looking up.

"Simple," Bubs replied. "He bled to death. It doesn't take long. The body's life juices slip out with appalling ease. And considering the butchering that you did—"

"I didn't do it," she protested.

One of the men standing around the wall cursed as though enraged by her denial. She glanced forward and saw their intense and communal expressions, not varying from face to face.

Behind her at the top of the steps, Bubs again demanded, "Why did you do it?"

"I didn't do it," she repeated. "It was the others."

"You're not telling the truth," he shouted. "Have you ever told the truth? Just once in your entire life?"

"I am telling the truth," she insisted. "I had nothing to do with it. It was the others. They were the ones."

"What others?" he asked. "Can you identify them?"

Wearily she turned away. Her neck ached from looking up at him. "You know them better than I do," she muttered. "They're your friends, not mine."

Upstairs the female mourning continued, a howling lament. Zoe closed her eyes against the sound. In the interim Bubs started down the steps toward her. As he drew even with her, he said, "There must be punishment, you know."

One of the men called out, "There has to be a trial first. It's the American Way."

"Screw the American Way," thundered Bubs. "She doesn't deserve a trial. A trial is conducted when there is doubt. There's no doubt here."

Zoe glanced down over the bannister into the kitchen. If the back door were open—Escape through the front door was out of the question since a solid line of men stood between her and the door.

From upstairs she heard a sustained guttural note of extraordinary purity. It ended in a series of modulations at once joyous and heartbroken.

"Well, it's over," Bubs said quietly. "He's given up the ghost."

Again Zoe protested her innocence. "I didn't do it. The others did it."

From the top of the stairs she heard a cold female voice. "That's not true. It was all her idea. We did it for her."

She looked up and saw Mary Lisa standing there, her eyes red and swollen from weeping. Behind her were the other females, all dabbing at their eyes, all dressed in immaculate white robes.

The announcement seemed to please Bubs. Roughly he jerked at Zoe's arm and dragged her to the center of the hall less than three feet from the slender cabinet. "You're guilty," he said quietly. "It's plain as day."

Still a male voice protested. "We need a trial here."

The old woman called down from the top of the steps. "No trial. They're all rigged anyway. Just be a waste of time."

Zoe looked up and saw the hem of the red robe beneath the outer edges of the white one. All of the female faces were becoming recognizable and all were pushing against Mary Lisa at the top of the stairs, shouting, "No trial. Just punishment."

Zoe stood alone in the center of the hall, facing her accusers. Now and then her attention drifted toward the cabinet. From where she stood, it appeared solid. There was still the peculiar sensation of light and heat emanating from it, but she could find no heat source and ultimately her attention was drawn back to her now silent accusers. Her feet felt heavy and swollen. Even if she wanted to run, she would not be capable of escape. She felt stupid and self-conscious and tried repeatedly to think of something reasonable to say in her own defense. But she was certain that no one was interested in listening.

Bubs stood a few feet away, his arms crossed, one hand stroking his beard, a slight smile on his face, as though he had at last brought her to a highly desirable place and state of mind. He asked quietly, "Shall it be punishment or execution?"

No one answered right away. Clearly they were mulling over the alternatives. Finally the mother-woman called from the top of the stairs, "There's been enough death here. No execution."

A male voice protested. "How do we know she won't try to castrate all of us? None of us are safe while she lives."

A female voice answered, "I don't think she'll try it again."

"She did it once, didn't she?"

Zoe was aware of their voices, plotting her future. She fell into a kind of stupor, conscious of her existence only from the throbbing of arteries.

Finally Bubs announced soberly, "I think execution. She's a very real threat to us. Look at her. An inferior creature in every way, yet causing havoc wherever she goes."

The light seemed to be fading. Although Zoe could no longer see each specific face, she felt their condemnation. Bubs continued to stand a distance away, incorporeal, a shadow between the flickering light at the top of the stairs and the night outside the window.

Mary Lisa started down the steps. "Maybe we've done enough," she ventured reluctantly. "When you consider what we've put her through—" She shook the blond wig until the curls bounced, remembering specific horrors.

"Done enough?" Bubs exclaimed. "If we'd done enough, she wouldn't be standing there in the middle of the floor looking as she does. If we'd done enough, there wouldn't be a dead man upstairs in her bed."

Mary Lisa tried to comfort him. "It isn't your fault, Bubs. You tried, you really did."

The old woman, sitting midway up the steps, suggested, "How about a partial execution? Kill her slightly and let her live." She cackled into her hands. "Half-dead victims are beautifully disfigured and malformed. They make up the bulk of the world."

Bubs shook his head. "Not that one. She'd just learn to love her scars."

Zoe stood quietly in the center of the hall and listened to the voices whirl about her. Now and then she glanced over at the cabinet. She wished they would move it away.

Mary Lisa whispered softly. "What are we going to do, Bubs?"

No answer.

A male voice asked almost flippantly, "What do you have in mind, old man?"

Still no answer.

Zoe was aware of him standing a distance away and she was clearly aware of a growing apprehension in the others. All of the females had ventured down the steps, a strange disquieting expression on their faces. One begged, "Tell us what you're going to do, please?"

Mary Lisa was begging openly. "Bubs, please don't just stand there. Tell us. We have a right—"

Suddenly her voice broke off. Zoe looked up and saw the expression on her face, an expression that seemed to suggest a grinding pain. Zoe saw her start to back away, slowly shaking her head in futile protest against an unnamed horror.

Even the men seemed visibly upset. One said sharply, "She won't survive it. Few do."

Bubs walked around in front of Zoe. He lifted her face, forced her to look at him. "This one might," he said quietly.

The females were still protesting. Mary Lisa called out, "You have no right."

"I have every right," he countered.

A male voice said flatly, "Well, I want no part of it. There's a limit."

"Not where this one is concerned," Bubs snapped.

Zoe, her head still held rigid by his hand, was forced to

look into his eyes. She met his gaze, feeling that it was important not to let him know that she was afraid.

"Look at her," Bubs muttered. "It's my belief that it
won't even faze her."

"That's what you said the last time," a male voice commented, "and I still haven't recovered from that one."

"I'll take full responsibility," Bubs said.

Zoe watched and listened to the exchange, but the bulk
of her attention was concentrated on the strange cabinet. It
appeared to be made of dark-grained wood, completely enclosed top and bottom, a long narrow closet of some sort. A
peculiar light struck it from all sides, highlighting the wood
grain. It struck her as ominous, a sealed-off thing.

She took a step backward. Quickly the females closed in
around her.

Bubs grinned. "Oh, she's a smart one, she is. She's beginning to stir. Hurry. Take off her clothes." As the women
closed in around her, Zoe tried to object. But it was futile.
There were too many of them. They were too insistent.

A few moments later, she was naked. Embarrassed, she
tried to cover her nakedness.

She felt the women draw away and scatter out among
the men who were sitting around the wall. A numbness
seemed to be invading her body. Her skin tingled as if it had
been asleep.

Bubs stood a few feet away, studying her, a peculiar look
of pity on his face. He said, "I'm sorry that it had to come to
this."

Zoe bowed her head under his close scrutiny. Even with
her head down she still could see the cubicle to one side. She
wondered where it had come from, what was its purpose.

Bubs approached her. "Don't be afraid." He lifted her
face. "You're really overdue, you know. We should have

reached you when you were twelve. At the latest twenty-two. But thirty-two—" He shook his head.

A male voice against the far wall muttered, "Get it over with."

Zoe raised her head in an attempt to see who was speaking. But the light had changed again. It was dark around the edges of the wall where the people were. The only illumination seemed to come from directly overhead, a single beam of light which shone directly down on the top of the cabinet.

She felt suddenly self-conscious in her nakedness. Everyone could see her but she could see no one, could see nothing really except the slim upright cabinet, which bore no resemblance to anything she had ever seen before.

The whispering in the shadows continued. A female voice protested, "You're going too far this time. She'll never survive it."

Another woman added, "Then what will we do with her? We can't leave her here."

Still another, "She's due at the airport on Saturday. You know that as well as we all do. If she isn't there—"

The voices were so close they seemed to be coming from inside Zoe's head. They did not vibrate and disappear but rather seemed to hang there, caught on a portion of her brain.

Then she heard Bubs's voice, low, calm, coming toward her at an angle. "Look at her," he whispered as though he were certain she couldn't hear. "She's not nearly as alarmed as all of you."

"She doesn't know—"

"And it's the not-knowing that will keep her safe. For a while." He chuckled. "She's dead anyway. What difference will it make? She's been dead for years. Her perceptions are devoid of all significance." He lowered his voice, speaking confidentially to only one or two. "Consider the night games we've put her through and consider how far they have gotten us. Then tell me again that I'm wrong."

This time there was no response, no challenge. She studied the base of the cubicle, saw solid boards securely joined to other solid boards, no convenient slit for peering inside, an impenetrable construction in which something awaited her.

Then Bubs was beside her, one hand pressed against her back. "People think it's too late," he whispered, "once they've embarked on a course. But it isn't."

A female voice whispered, "For God's sake, get it over with."

Bubs held her at arm's length. "Are you ready?" he asked.

She was shivering visibly. She did well to nod.

"Well, then," he said. He stepped away from her. He bowed his head, then walked toward the cubicle.

A female prayed softly, "Dear God—"

Zoe watched as he ran his hand along a sharp edge of the wood. He leaned forward, examining the intersection of two narrow walls. Suddenly his hand stopped. She heard a small click and saw one of the walls swing open. She saw him standing beside the open door, motioning for her to come forward.

Someone near the wall was weeping audibly now. She went forward until she stood directly in front of the open door. She peered into blackness. Bubs took her arm and indicated that she was to enter the cubicle. "It's dark now," he soothed. "But in a moment you will see."

She paused. Her hands reached out to grasp the wooden enclosure. The cavity ahead was pitch-black.

Bubs warned, "Watch your step!"

Slowly she lifted her foot and stepped over the threshold into blackness. The moment she was inside she reached out and felt three walls only inches away. It was an enclosure large enough to accommodate one. She turned in the narrow confinement and saw Bubs standing outside, his hand still on the open door. He looked unbearably sad.

In the darkness in which she was standing, she saw that his face seemed to have lost all its detail. His shadow loomed behind him on the wall, an enormous bearded shape. She'd been in the cubicle four seconds and already she wanted out. Whatever was in store for her, she didn't have to go through with it. She'd played their insane games long enough, had amused and entertained them with her cooperation. Now she had had enough.

She was on the verge of saying all of this when, without warning, Bubs slammed the fourth wall shut. Suddenly her heart raced against the blackness. She leaned with all her strength against the fourth wall. But it would not give. Reaching out, she struggled against the other three walls, against the suffocating enclosure filled with no sound except that of her own rapid breathing.

There was no way out. She closed her eyes, then opened them, but it made no difference. The conditions of blackness were not altered in any way. She called Bubs's name twice, but there was no sound to her voice. The enclosed darkness had captured the sound waves. Slowly she turned around, feeling always the confinement of the walls. She reached up to the top with the hope of finding a weakness in the wood through which she might escape. Then she inched her arms down on either side and found the floor as smooth and solid and unyielding as the ceiling. As she squatted, her knees pushed against the opposite walls. The confinement was such that it did not even permit her to sit, a skillfully designed cubicle which forced the victim to stand throughout the ordeal.

Now she leaned against one wall and pushed with all her

strength against the opposite ones. She felt no give at all to the wood. The strain tightened her face. What was the point? How long was she supposed to stand erect in total darkness? She felt her heart beating and slumped forward against her confinement and covered her face with her hands.

With her eyes closed, she did not at first see the light, the peculiar illumination that had no source. Only when she felt its warmth did she look up. She was staring into her own face. As the light increased, she turned in a rapid circle and discovered that the interior walls of the cubicle were solid mirrors, floor to ceiling. She reached out a hand to the four Zoes, appalled and embarrassed by their nakedness. Astonished, she gazed upward at the upturned Zoe face which stared down on her, her shoulders, the tips of her breasts reflected in the mirror overhead. And beneath her there was another mirror reflecting knees, thighs, groin, the rising and falling of her belly. In all directions, including up and down, there were only Zoes, seven in all; one at the center, four surrounding her, one above and one below. Slowly she moved around while they in turn rotated and looked back at her. The source of the light confounded her. She reached up to the ceiling, trying to determine if the lights were inset.

Suddenly she realized that the other Zoes were reaching up with her, clearly imitating. For one irrational moment she caught herself resenting their mimicry. Yet when she turned angrily to face them, they faced her just as angrily. When in mild desperation she leaned in on one wall, the Zoe there leaned out to meet her. Their shoulders touched. Repulsed, she drew back and collided with the Zoe behind her, a sniveling, tearful Zoe who peered back at her.

It required a conscious effort of will to remind herself of the principle of reflection. Mirrors gave back the images of what they saw, nothing more. Armed with the logic, she stood stiffly in the exact center of the cubicle, facing a stiff-standing Zoe who stared critically back at her.

Suddenly she groaned. All the Zoes groaned with her. For a moment there was a quadruple silence. The picture steadied. She stood suspended in a circle of identical women. She dredged up from her splintered wits a portion of reason. She was surrounded by mirrors. Quite logically she would be surrounded by images of herself. There was no need to struggle or flail out. It was merely a fun house. All that was required of her was the ability to survive. She wrapped her arms about her and closed her eyes so that she wouldn't have to see the gesture multiplied by four. She tried to think rationally but her thoughts were laborious and disconnected.

Presently they will let me out.

I must act disturbed because obviously they expect me to act disturbed.

It is important that I be someplace on Saturday.

She roused herself with a surge of feeling. It would be an easy matter to control herself. It was the other images who were causing the difficulty. She let her arms fall away and forced her head back in order to avoid the glimpses of self-images. Above her was an upturned Zoe looking down. There were dark circles about the eyes. The hair was straight and unkempt.

Annoyed by the face looking down on her, she reached up to blot it out. She pushed upward at the woman suspended above her. But she wouldn't go away.

Perhaps it was the angle that was so ugly. She stooped downward and struck her head on the Zoe in front of her. Her eyes lifted to Zoe eyes. She raised slowly up. The whiteness surrounding the pupils was flecked with red, the pupils were brown with tiny gold flecks in them.

Fascinated, she leaned closer. The eyes were incredible, like flat brown pebbles, lusterless, without movement, the red lines no larger than twisting red hairs cutting into the pupils. She blinked. The eyes blinked back at her. She pressed both hands against the surface of two identical hands. As she squinted, she noticed small crevices near the corners of the eyes deeply cut into the surface of the skin, thousands of finely chiseled erosions fanning out over the flesh of the cheekbone. Incredibly ugly.

She blinked again and observed feathery black lashes opening and closing, separate curled hairs which fanned out and up from the eyelid. A small feathery extension encircled the lower part of the eyes, like two miniature bearded mouths.

The eyes gazed calmly at her. A speck of gold in the left eye caught a beam of the unknown light and sparkled brilliantly for a moment. Remarkable. Microscopic eye-doors opened and closed, opened and closed, smooth flaps of flesh alternating light and dark, vision and nonvision. Truly remarkable. She leaned so close to the mirror that her breath left a circle of white fog. A moment later it was gone.

Suddenly water welled up in the corners of the eyes, came just like that, two underground springs accompanied by a stinging behind the bridge of the nose. Two solitary drops of water rested in the corners of the eyes. She watched the water, still fascinated. Then she blinked and the water spread throughout the eyes, causing her vision to blur.

She stepped back and put a short distance between herself and the eyes. The eye-worlds had been fascinating but dangerous. She closed her eyes and shut out the eye-worlds. She leaned forward with her arms raised. The Zoe before her did the same thing. She rested her forehead against the upraised arm and looked down at the floor Zoe, who looked up at her.

The face on the floor seemed grotesquely unreal, a self-styled image, a clockwork dummy going through her motions, yet always a beat behind somehow. Slowly she pushed away from the mirror and looked directly down at the floor Zoe. The robot was nothing if not versatile. Over the length of the body she saw little of the face but the forehead, the outcropping of a nose, all nostrils from that angle. The chin was missing, lost in the angle of the breasts.

What she saw clearly from that angle was two legs, blue-veined in places from the weight of two pregnancies, the dark mound of pubic hair below which the pregnancies had commenced, the loose belly flesh where the pregnancies had grown and lived, had finally pushed violently out in the form of two strangers complete with the necessary equipment to repeat the entire procedure on other females. She rubbed her hands down over her stomach, remembering. Her face sagged. She saw clearly the torture chamber of stirrups and straps, of cold prodding instruments, sets of impersonal eyes, the hanging screams, blood gushing, the tremendous pressure, flesh-splitting pressure as the things angled down and out.

She moaned. One hand covered her stomach while the other hand moved down between legs as though to block any future penetration. The distorted position was recorded before her with complete accuracy. She looked up, scanned the length of the crouching, terrified Zoe before her. She looked merely ridiculous.

Slowly she straightened up, her hands wandering aimlessly over her body as though assessing the flesh there. She stood erect, made an attempt to accept the purposes of her body, its weaknesses and its strengths.

Out of the silence, she heard a soft noise. She looked over her shoulder. The Zoe behind her was not following her lead anymore. That Zoe was standing in the mirror silently weeping. Quickly she looked away and tried to clear her vision. An illusion of some sort, she was certain. But when she looked back, she saw the Zoe reflection grip both breasts as though she wanted to rip them off. She continued to watch, horrified as the hands clawed at the flesh, the fingernails leaving long red marks, the woman in the reflection howling like an animal, her head upturned, her eyes shut as though she were suffering unendurable pain.

Zoe looked about at the other Zoes. They were still following her obediently. But the fourth Zoe had broken away, had arranged herself in the mirror in an outraged, pitiful position, her arms outspread, palms up entreating Zoe to help her. She cried out repeatedly in the echoing hole of the mirror, shrill, sharp screams that forced Zoe back into the intersection of mirrors, three Zoes huddling together watching the fourth Zoe in agony.

Finally the maverick Zoe slipped to her knees. Her breasts were bleeding from the repeated clawing of her fingernails, her long hair tumbling over her face obscuring her features.

Zoe pushed farther back into the corner of the mirrors. What she saw had no basis in logic or reason. Perhaps she was hallucinating or perhaps they had at last driven her as insane as they were. But the equation didn't work. *They* were noplace in sight. As she was sealed in, they were sealed out. There was no way they could manipulate her inside the cubicle. Then what was it that she saw on the floor of the fourth mirror? How could the image have fallen when *she* was still standing upright? There were no answers to her questions. And when the fallen Zoe stirred and look pitifully up at her, she felt that something needed to be said and a hand went pleasantly forward to offer aid and comfort. "Are you all right?" she whispered, keeping her voice down, afraid that someone might hear her talking to her reflection.

The prostrate woman neither stirred nor replied.

Zoe bent over as far as the confinement would allow. "Can you hear me?" she asked.

Slowly the woman pushed herself up from the floor, hung there for a moment, her face wet with tears. She cast a hate-filled glance at Zoe and muttered, "You make me sick."

Alarmed, Zoe squatted down until she was wedged into the base of the cubicle. "Why?" she asked, concerned. "What have I done?"

The Zoe image pushed herself up into a sitting position. Her head wobbled slightly. A few of the lacerations on her breasts were deep and small rivulets of blood seeped down the white skin. Her lips were dry and she appeared to be having difficulty in speaking. "You make me sick," she repeated dully, shaking her head.

Still concerned, Zoe reached out a hand in an attempt to touch the unhappy image. "Can't you tell me what I've done?" she begged.

But the image merely shook her head as if her personal sorrow was too great to talk about. She sat now with her legs curled demurely to one side, her head downcast, studying the damaged breasts. She wiped away the blood with the back of her hand and shook her head, still weeping. Words were beyond her. "I don't understand," she wept.

Zoe leaned closer. She wanted to share in the sorrow. She looked briefly at the other three Zoes squatting with her. Then she invited, "Please talk to me."

The Zoe image looked up at her angrily through her tears. "You complain about men and yet you do everything in your power to attract them." Her voice rose. *"I'm* the one who has to endure it. I'm the one." Furiously she brushed the hair from her face as though she were warming to the subject. "You attract them, then go off and leave me to finish the job. You go off someplace where they can't hurt you or touch you and leave me to digest their slobbering lips, their prying

hands, the weight of their bodies." She shuddered and
looked directly at Zoe, her eyes cold in spite of the tears.
"Well, I'll tell you one thing. I've had enough. I'm tired of
being your body. I've endured more than enough. Look!"
She pointed at her bruised and bleeding breasts. She lowered
her voice, imitating a man. "Get on your knees, Zoe. Let's
try it that way." She gestured broadly, arms outflung. "Well,
I'm the one who gets on her knees. Not you. You go off
someplace and leave me alone. Lift up, Zoe. Now, over
here." She raised up on her knees, shrieking, "I'm the one
who goes over there. I'm the one who is told to be quiet
because I might wake the children, and I'm the one who gets
filled up every night. I'm the one who is pushed and pulled
and arranged and manipulated. I'm the one. I'm the one!"

She was screaming at Zoe now, her fingers jabbing at
her own breasts as she emphasized the words, "I'm the one,
not you." She stopped short, struggling for control. Finally
she sat heavily back down in the reflection, her head drooping listlessly, her hands resting limply in her lap. "Please,"
she begged, "cut off my breasts. Please, no more. I can't take
it." She looked up at Zoe, entreating. "I feel battered, used
up. I have never enjoyed it. I do it only for you, to try and
help you." Her voice fell until it was scarcely audible. "If
you'd only stay and help sometime, absorb some of the sensations. I don't know where you go. But you're never there."
Through her tears she looked up at Zoe, her face ravaged.
"You have no idea what it's like." She shuddered horribly.
"None at all." She wrapped her arms around the abused
breasts and folded herself into a tight knot. Slowly she began
to rock back and forth, a humming sound escaping through
her lips like a continuous shudder.

Zoe crouched before her, watching and listening closely.
Once she tried to reach out and touch the reflection who had
endured so much for her. But her hand merely collided with

the solid surface of the mirror. The huddled, rocking, fallen image could not be touched. Wedged into the narrow cubicle, surrounded by herself, Zoe had no choice but to watch. "I'm sorry," she murmured.

She looked again at the fallen image, then slowly she began to ease herself upward. The backs of her legs ached from squatting. Her hands reached out to the other Zoes for support. Once erect, she looked down on the fallen image. That woman had not moved. She still sat on the floor of the mirror, her face set in an expression of agony.

Slowly she lifted her face. Her eyes met Zoe's. "No more," she warned through her tears. "No more men. Ever. Do you hear?"

Zoe could think of nothing to say in her own defense, certainly nothing that would assuage the woman's feelings or alter her memories.

Softly behind her she heard giggling. She looked quickly over her shoulder and saw another Zoe-image lean lightly against the surface of the mirror, one hand on her hip, the other hand sensuously fondling her breasts. One leg was cocked at an angle behind her, the other leg supporting her body weight. The image crooked a finger at Zoe, motioning for her to come closer.

The disintegration around her caused her to shiver. She gaped at the phenomenon of the second independent image, who was moving and speaking without her permission. "What do you want?" she whispered, hoping the fallen image at her feet would not hear.

The giggling woman motioned for her to come still closer. She put her hand to her mouth, her words were intended for Zoe's ears alone, "Are you really going to listen to her?" she asked.

As Zoe faced her, she noted with relief that the other two images were still obeying her. They moved only when she moved, one on one side, the other giving her a shoulder to lean against. To the giggling Zoe, she whispered, "I don't know what you mean."

The image shifted positions within the mirror, stood now with both hands on her hips, her feet spread. "You know damn well what I mean," she said. "What am *I* supposed to do? If you pay any attention to what she says, what in hell am I supposed to do?"

"I don't understand," Zoe murmured. "She seems to have suffered a great deal. I think I should at least listen—"

"Hell!" snorted the opposing image, "Suffered my ass." Now she imitated the woman's plea of "Cut off my breasts." She signaled her contempt with a sharp explosion of air. "I mean, after all, how melodramatic can you get?" Slowly she cupped her hands beneath her own breasts, lifted them as though displaying them; the hands moved down to caress her body; she arched and preened, her hands coming at last to rest on her groin. She grinned. "Now, I mean, really, what else does she think all this is for?" She lowered her voice, speaking for Zoe's ears alone. "We learned a long time ago what the female body could do. Remember? I think it was little Ben Frailly who first taught us. Oh God, the way he looked at me. You *do* remember that, don't you?" she gasped, a sharp intake of air, a dazzling smile on her upturned face. "For the first time, I knew." She lifted her arms high into the air, laughing openly. "I knew! What's more, since that time, I've never been able to get enough. Never. You'd know the feeling too if you'd let me be honest with yourself."

She glared at Zoe. "But no, you listen to her." She pointed a contemptuous finger at the fallen image in the opposite reflection. "You let her fill your head with all sorts of guilt. You've never paid the slightest attention to me. How many times you've denied me. You closed me in and locked

the door and you thought I'd gone away." She raised slowly
up. "But I haven't gone away. I'll never go away," she giggled. "Clay likes me, when I can get out, when you turn your
back for just a minute and let me be what I was meant to be.
Do you remember those months before you married him?
Oh God, a golden age of sexual passion if ever there was
one. You remember, don't you? You have to remember.
You'd sent *her* away then and good riddance, I said."

She called angrily past Zoe to the fallen image in the
opposite reflection. "Why don't you die?" she cried, "Do
you know what you are? You're the world's greatest curse."
She was screaming, as though what she was saying sprang
from the deepest rage. "I'll tell you what you do. You cause
wars, you cause murders, you cause whores, you cause rapes.
It isn't politicians or armies that cause the sorrow in the
world. It's you, the frigid wife, the denying, self-righteous,
self-seeking, self-serving cold bitch who condemns the world
to death by frustration."

Zoe looked from one image to the other, a contemptuous stern, puritan face on one side, a blissful, enraptured face
on the other. She leaned sideways against a still-cooperating
Zoe, wanting to escape from both images. Bewildered, she
covered her face with her hands and a cooperating Zoe did
the same. She heard pleasurable groans coming from in front
of her as masturbation commenced. She could see out of the
corner of her eye the writhing body, the back arched, ready
to receive the entire world.

Zoe wanted out. The cubicle was becoming unbearable.
Her shoulder pushed uselessly at the unyielding mirrored
surface. Everywhere she looked she saw another Zoe staring
back at her; two still obedient, but one looking up at her with
condemning eyes, the other crawling to her knees, babbling
about the ingenious ways she had devised to fill the emptiness.

Suddenly Zoe shouted at both of them. "Stop it!" She felt a convulsion through her body, a trembling that threatened to split her in half. She collapsed against a cooperating Zoe behind her and shut her eyes and covered her ears with her hands, trying to close off the squabbling images before and behind her.

Without warning and softly into the silence there came another voice, a calm, authoritative commanding voice. "Well, I think we've had just about enough of this," the voice said, "There are other, more important things with which we must concern ourselves."

Zoe was afraid to look. She knew that another image had rebelled, had broken free. But which one? She felt the Zoe image next to her still cooperating, still supporting her. Then it must be—

"Don't *you* think we've had enough?" the voice asked sternly. "Look at me. You can't hide forever, you know, from your responsibilities or from yourself."

Slowly Zoe lowered her hands. There on one side of her was a stern mother image, her arms crossed, her feet planted in a base of strength. Her head was erect and she was piercing Zoe with two judgmental and condemnatory eyes. "I'm ashamed of you," she said, "I really am." She lifted her arm and pointed a finger. "You're a mother. You've brought life into this world. Now you have a responsibility to that life which takes priority over either of these silly women."

Already Zoe had heard enough. She sighed and started to turn away. But the mother image stopped her. "I wouldn't do that if I were you," she warned. "You're in enough trouble as it is."

"What have I done?" Zoe asked wearily.

"It's not what you've done," the mother image explained imperiously. "It's what you haven't done."

Zoe protested. "I've tried—"

The image cut her off. "You've tried nothing and you've accomplished nothing." She stepped closer to the surface of the mirror. "You have two children. I know they're monsters, but what else are they? Boys or girls?"

Zoe tried to answer, but the mother image cut her off again. "What are their names then? If you don't know what they are, maybe you at least know their names."

A third time, Zoe tried to reply, but again the mother-image cut her off. "Good heavens, things are worse than I thought. She doesn't even know the names and sex of her own children."

Zoe protested. "Why don't you give me a chance to answer? It's almost as if you don't want me to know."

The mother-image sneered, "Typical excuse. I expected it of you."

"It's not an excuse. Their names are—" Within the gray haze of Zoe's brain, something stirred, then went back to sleep.

"Well?" The mother image demanded again. "Not the most difficult question in the world," she snapped, "to ask a mother to name her children and identify their sex. After all, it is life that came from her body."

The intense light inside the cubicle was beginning to bother Zoe. There were no safe shadows for hiding, no ready garments to cover her nakedness. If she moved so much as an inch in either direction, she ran the risk of colliding with another image. She turned her back on all three images and rested her forehead against the forehead of the last, still cooperating Zoe. She felt so tired. Her legs ached from standing. She was sick to death of her naked body. She pushed against the fourth Zoe, hoping the panel would give and she might escape.

The mother image laughed sharply. "Up to your old

tricks, aren't you? If you can't handle it, run away. My goodness, that could be the story of your life. In one brief line."

"I've done the best I could," Zoe murmured.

"Well, it's not good enough," said the mother image.
"Obviously you have no conception of what is expected of
you and on that basis alone, I forgive you somewhat."

Zoe pressed closer to the fourth image until their bodies
were touching at all points. She felt flogged by the voice
coming from behind her. She gulped in air in an attempt to
conquer momentary dizziness.

"Help me to get out of here," Zoe begged.

The mother image smiled. She spoke with such calm
reassurance and began to pace back and forth within the confines of the reflection, her hands clasped behind her back.
"You must understand what you have never understood before, Zoe," she said, her voice clear and brisk. "When a
woman marries and brings life into the world, from that moment on, she has no right, no right at all, to think of herself.
All of her energies, all of her time and all of her talent must
be devoted to the new life. She must dedicate herself wholly.
Her one, her only purpose in life is their comfort, their well-
being."

Suddenly she stopped pacing and turned to face Zoe.
"You must kill any needs, any desires within yourself. You
must kill all awareness of self. You must kill all dreams, all
hopes, all plans." Everytime she said kill, she brought her fist
down against the palm of her hand, powerful blows to demonstrate what she was saying.

Zoe pressed hard against the fourth image, flinching
slightly every time the fist struck the hand.

The mother image went on with evangelical zeal. She
was so close to the surface of the mirror now that she appeared to be trying to break out. "Listen to me. You've done

enough damage. You must understand once and for all exactly what is expected of you."

For a moment, Zoe was distracted by the whore image. The groans were increasing. She was rolling about on the floor in the worst sort of agony. The fallen image was praying audibly. There were drops of sweat on her forehead.

The voice of the mother image cut powerfully through the confusion. "Kill them both," she ordered and struck her fist against the surface of the mirror. "They have no right to your life now. You have only one cosmic responsibility. You must cook hot meals. You must darn worn socks, you must wash and iron bed linens. You must do nothing except those acts that contribute to their comfort and well-being. In short, you must kill yourself and be reborn in your husband and children. You have no right to a life outside them. You are permitted to live for one reason alone, to serve and comfort them, to nurture them, to be obedient to their demands, responsive to their wishes, and considerate of their needs. You must be totally subservient to them. They give you your identity. They save you from being nothing for without them, you serve no purpose. You are nothing. Nothing!"

The mother image was pounding with both fists on the surface of the mirror. Zoe listened, horrified. She felt the side of her face go dead. Her confusion and fear were a double confinement. She looked up so that she would not have to see the contorted face of the mother image. Instead she saw the Zoe above her looking down. All the images were speaking at once, a steady and unbearable assault of whispered prayers, of sexual agony, of an enraged scolding, condemning her for her many failures.

They were all her enemies. They all meant her harm, all except perhaps— She turned slowly to face the last Zoe. It was with no great surprise that she saw this Zoe sitting cross-legged on the floor in the mirror, sucking childishly on a

strand of hair, her fingers wandering aimlessly back and forth
across the mirror.

The image looked up at Zoe. "I hate you," she announced in a childlike way. "I really do hate you." The child
image scooted furtively back, an expression of secrecy on her
face. "You never play with me," she pouted. "You make me
go cold and hungry." The child image smiled pallidly up at
Zoe. "I'm hungry now. Will you feed me?"

The dark center inside Zoe's brain turned over once,
then stopped. She was forced now to stand absolutely erect in
the center of the cubicle. Movement in any direction would
bring her into direct contact with another warring Zoe.

The child image twisted a strand of hair around the finger. There were constant gurgling and sucking sounds com
ing from her throat. She smacked her lips in a ruminative
swallow. "You never pay any attention to me," she complained. "Once I asked you to play dolls and you said no and
I wanted to kill you." She grinned prettily. "I want to kill
you now. I really do."

Zoe held herself rigid and looked down on the pouting
child. "I didn't hear you," she apologized.

"No, you never heard me. You still don't hear me."

Zoe felt strangely moved by the small, helpless face.
"That's not true," she said. "I've always known you were
there. There just wasn't any time for you."

"Isn't there time now?" she asked eagerly. "Look! We
could still play. Can you do this?" Quickly she hopped up,
held her arms out on either side of her body and walked
slowly toward the front of the mirror as though she were
balancing on a high wire. "It's fun. It really is. You pretend
that you are three miles above the earth and if you slip, you
fall and smash into a million pieces."

Zoe felt herself caught up in the contagion of the child
image. "I can do that," she smiled. As she raised her arms for

balance, she struck the images on either side. The fallen image cried out as though wounded. The whore image ran her hands down the spot on her breasts where Zoe's hand had made contact. She groaned pleasurably.

In an attempt to move away from them, Zoe struck the mother image before her. A stern cold whisper filled her ear. "You are nothing without your husband and children. You have no right to exist without their permission."

The child image started shrieking. "See? See? You never do anything with me. Never pay any attention to me at all." She was weeping bitterly, rubbing her eyes with two tight small fists. "I'm so cold," she sobbed, "so lonely. All I want is for you to see me, to play with me."

Zoe moved toward the child, her hand out to comfort her. "Please don't cry," she begged. "I won't pay any attention to the others. Please believe me." She ached to touch the child image, but she could not reach her.

The child fell into a soft heap on the floor, one arm cradling her head. She looked up at Zoe through one tear-stained eye. "You've promised before," she whispered. "You never keep your promises."

Zoe knelt down as close as she could to the weeping child. "What do you want to play now? I'll keep my promise. Give me another chance, please."

The child-image wiped her nose on the back of her arm. The lips were petulant, her eyes clouded with tears. "Don't want to play nothing," she muttered.

"Then what?", Zoe asked. "Tell me. I'll do it. I promise."

The child image squirmed uncomfortably. "I have to go to the bathroom." She looked slyly up at Zoe. "Will you take me?"

Zoe closed her eyes in frustration. "How?" she begged. "How can I take you anywhere? I can't get out myself."

The child image clutched at her groin, her face screwed up in discomfort. "Yes you can. You just don't want to." She started whimpering now, her eyes closed against the discomfort of a swollen bladder. "Oh, I have to go so bad. Please—"

Zoe was on her knees, frantically trying to make her understand. "I can't," she said. "If I can't get out of here myself, how could I—"

Suddenly the child image bowed her head. She tensed her legs and bent double. A small damp circle appeared beneath her buttocks. She stared at the spreading water, then sobbed, "Now look what you've made me do. I'll get all chapped and stinky. It's all your fault." The child image was weeping hysterically. On her knees, she lifted her face and howled in anguish, a lonely, bereft, animal cry.

Zoe begged repeatedly for her to stop, but she wouldn't. The ungodly noise seemed to rouse the others; the whore image began to cry out for help, twisting upon the floor, begging for satiation. The mother image started to scold again. "You still haven't learned, have you? You are nothing. You exist only for them." The fallen image commenced flagellating herself, delivering hard, stinging blows to the side of her face, head-jarring blows that caused a trickle of blood to appear in the corner of her mouth.

The voices rose still higher, striking Zoe on all sides. She tried to cover both her ears and her eyes and in doing so she lost her balance and fell on all fours in the narrowest part of the cubicle, wedged in by walls. She opened her eyes and breathed wetly as foam streamed down her face. A lock of hair was plastered just above the bridge of her nose like a jagged scar.

Now the floor image seemed to be pushing against her. She felt the surface grow suddenly hot, then hotter and still hotter as though she were kneeling on an open fire. She cried out as heat seared the flesh on her hands and knees. She tried to lean forward and straighten her legs. Her face moved up against a near mirror; the image there chattered and danced around her and grinned down on her, delighted with her suffering. She forced her hands behind her back in an attempt to form a barrier between her flesh and the increasing heat. The floor image gave a sideward lurch and sucked her down against the hot surface and held her firmly.

Her cheek, now pillowed against flesh-searing heat, saw the floor image looking up at her. This image smiled and calmly suggested, "There *is* a way."

The other images fell suddenly silent, listening. The heat seemed to subside. Zoe knelt quietly, breathing heavily, her eyes wide and unfocused.

The floor image spoke again, suggesting slyly, "There *is* a way if you want to take it."

Zoe tried to move her lips, but they felt dry and bleeding, her right arm was bent double beneath her body. The discomfort was intense.

The floor image spoke again more urgently. "Do you want to know or don't you?"

By channeling all her concentration into the slightest of movements, Zoe managed to nod.

The floor image giggled. "Simple. Don't be Zoe anymore. Don't be the Zoe of everyone else. Be your own Zoe. Get rid of that face and you can become anyone you want to be. I'm the foundation of everything. I ought to know what I'm talking about." This voice spoke quite matter-of-factly. "You're connected with those other bitches because you've allowed them to become extensions of you. It's so simple. Then don't be you any longer. Remove their faces and become yourself again, as you were born."

Zoe heard what had been said. She began to think very slowly. I have fallen into myself, she thought. In order to pull myself out, I must not be myself any longer. I must remove the Zoe masks that are causing the trouble.

Slowly she struggled to an upright position and sat on the foundation. Carefully she placed her fingers at the top of her forehead and dug with her nails into the flesh of her face. The other images were all on their knees, watching her, horrified. There was a descending scream in the air. Still she tore angrily at the stubborn features, trying to raise a flap of skin. She longed for a knife, something sharp with which to gouge out the eyes, remove the nose, mutilate the tongue and mouth. Her fingernails dug deeper. The hysteria around her increased as each image begged her to stop.

But there was no pain sharp enough to compel her to cease. The pain was outside her head and the persistent image of being multiple Zoes stung her even more than the lacerations. She felt a smooth wetness running down her cheeks and spat out blood. She saw little now of the images around her, but only flashes of an intimate being, a hands' investigation that told her the face was still Zoe.

"I can't," she moaned. "I can't change it."

But the floor image was gone. It was merely a mirrored floor now, spotted with blood. Even the heat was receding.

The image above her looked down with interest. What life was left was concentrated in the crawling right hand that continued to examine the unalterable specifics of her face. The hand found the bleeding lacerations about the eyes, the narrow ridge of nose, the gaping terrified mouth. The body lifted a few inches and waited motionless. When the frustrations subsided, the hand went up and tapped blindly on the mirror overhead.

She lifted her face and considered the image above her. A firm, whole, undaunted and undamaged Zoe face stared down on her.

The knees gave way. A cry started low and climbed upward. The right leg buckled. The shoulders let go and came down to the knees. The arms moved wide in an all-encompassing arc as though, faced with no other alternative, she wanted very much now to gather the images about her, pay attention to them, recognize them, accept them, comfort them. The body went limp. But the hands moved back once more in a beckoning gesture to all of the images.

Last of all the face changed, not dramatically, but changed slowly from within. Under the persistent light of the new whole Zoe, in the corners of the mouth and eyes came a slight muscular shift and ease of complicated tensions until the face rearranged itself and bore the expression of acceptance.

The mouth opened. The irreversible knowledge stirred in the dark center of the brain. Simultaneously, as though the thought had just occurred to the other images, she watched them turn away and take her acceptance to the far corners of the mirrors where they arranged themselves into relaxed positions and fell instantly to sleep.

Last of all, she heard the dark center of the brain whispering in a mixture of astonishment and acceptance.

She was . . . Zoe.

———◆———

"Is it the sight of life or death?"

"A bit of both, I'd say."

"It took longer than I thought."

"Who can say what long is? A day? A century? What does it matter?"

"She must meet the plane."

"She will. The older ones always take longer. But in all my years of experience, it's never failed to work."

"Oh, my God. Look at her."

"You've seen worse, and so have I. Come on now, help me get her out."

Zoe was first aware of a rush of cool air. Then she heard voices. Delicately, almost caressingly, she felt hands lifting her out.

"Be calm," someone soothed.

She felt calm. Her eyes were closed. The hands felt like feathers about her, barely supporting her, but with no touch of substance. Memories churned in her mind. She saw her husband, the house in Newton, her two sons, the airport where she had last seen them. For a moment she was afraid that she had drifted into madness and would never see them again.

A voice in her ear continually soothed her. "It's all right. The worst is over."

She sighed and gave herself up to the voices and the hands supporting her.

"What shall we do with her?"

"Take her upstairs."

"It's her face that's the worst."

"It will heal. She can always say she got caught in thornbushes."

"Are there thornbushes around here?"

"There are thornbushes everywhere."

She felt her body being tilted upward, felt the cold draft that always swept down the staircase to the hall below. She tried to distinguish the voices, but she couldn't.

Near the top of the steps, the hands that supported her legs and feet slipped. She felt her entire body lurch downward, felt a wrenching beneath her arms as someone tried to keep her from falling.

Someone shouted, "For God's sake, watch it!"

A whining voice protested, "Well, she's wet."

"Move back. I'll take her the rest of the way. Get that

mess cleaned up down there and bring me her clothes, do you hear? Hurry!"

She felt strong arms lift her up into the air, felt just the whisper of a beard against the side of her face. A voice from the bottom of the hall called up the stairs. "Where's her car?"

The voice behind the beard answered. She could feel the vibrations of his chest next to her arm. "It's in the thicket near the end of the road. Bring it up and leave it in front of the house."

There seemed to be a flurry of activity in the other world. She heard footsteps running, doors opening and closing, shouts and cries, male and female voices blending.

But within the confines of the arms that carried her, it was silent. She felt the steady rhythm of his body as he carried her into a room, felt the slightest urge of effort as he leaned over and placed her gently on a bed. She sank relaxed into soft cool comfort. With her eyes still closed, she enjoyed the freedom of movement after the confinement of the cubicle. She considered opening her eyes, but decided against it.

She felt a warm cloth on her face, heard him constantly soothing her with murmurs of, "There, there."

She considered speaking but changed her mind. What could she say? What needed to be said? She was aware of others in the room now; she heard a whispered exchange by the door, someone reassuring someone else that she was just fine. She felt a soft, sweetly smelling sheet being pulled up and around her shoulders.

In a strong way she wanted very much to respond to all the kindness. But she was so tired. She couldn't remember when she had felt such exhaustion. She wanted only to sleep.

Several seemed to be standing directly over her now, a male and a female voice predominating.

"Do you think she'll remember?"

"Of course she'll remember. They always do."

"Everything?"

"No. Not everything. Enough. The important parts."

"I really didn't know her very well. She wouldn't let anyone know her very well."

"Do you blame her?"

"Did all that really happen to her?"

"What do you think? It's not an unusual case."

"I'd call it unusual."

"Happens everyday."

"Poor Bubs. You worked so hard."

"Let's go. I'm starved and sick to death of peanut butter sandwiches. Besides there's so much work to do, so much work."

"Isn't she marvelous? Look at her. And you say her face will heal?"

"In no time. Let's go."

"What would we do without you?"

"Try it sometime."

The whispers ceased. She was aware of eyes looking down on her. Then she heard footsteps, muffled, someone walking on tiptoe, not wanting to disturb her. She heard them leave the room, heard them going down the stairs and out of the front door. A moment later, she heard horses and a rumbling like wooden carts being drawn away.

At last she was alone with only a complete and glorious silence. She turned comfortably in the bed. She wondered with no great urgency whether it was night or day. Once she thought she felt sun on her face, but wasn't certain whether it was an external or internal warmth. Again, it really didn't matter.

She was warm and dry and comfortable and sleepy and at peace. She had no conscious recollection of ever having felt so good. The aches, the bondage, the abuse, self-imposed and otherwise, had diminished from solids to vapors. In the absence of cold, everything could be inspected, not merely with eyes, but with understanding.

She rubbed her legs against the softness surrounding her. She moved a hand over her breasts and seemed to draw actual strength from the awareness and sensations of her body.

She was Zoe, not by education or intelligence, but by a much greater force that could not be altered or changed in any way.

Even while she slept, her mind was active, like that of a woman who has a willing audience and who realizes for the first time that she wants very much to say something . . .

———◆———

In the short chill of dawn, she awakened. Gray feathery light skittered around the edges of her vision. She lay expressionless for a moment in the pleasant fog of semiconsciousness. She listened carefully to the silence coming from the old house, to the birds lifting and singing out from treetops.

She stretched beneath the sheets, enjoyed a moment longer the warm indentation caused by the night's sound sleep. Her hand brushed across the empty pillow next to her. She paused lamely and studied the emptiness. An image flickered in her brain. She wished that Clay were here with her, and in so wishing, she turned on her side in a minor agony of longing.

From her position in the bed, she could see the world outside the window, a gray chill October morning with a hint of an orange sun which promised to burn off the damp cold before noon. She thought how much her sons would enjoy this house, how very much she would enjoy sharing it with them, the countless melodramas they could enact in her wooded amphitheater, the fun of gathering pinecones in win-

ter, colored leaves in autumn, wild violets in spring and blue-
berries in summer. Every season had its unique richness and
all were waiting for her. Her sons would flourish in the freedom of the woods, in the comfortable, abused quality of the
house itself.

Suddenly she sat up, alive with plans. Like a delighted
child she gazed around her upon the ever-moving firmament
of unlimited possibilities.

Then she remembered. She had to meet a plane. How
she knew for certain that she had to meet a plane, she
couldn't say. But a sense of urgency overtook her. Quickly
she glanced about the room, awaiting the next unspoken order. She saw her clothes hanging neatly on a hanger on the
back of the door. Without warning a sharper vision clouded
her brain. She thought she perceived from somewhere a blur
of a knife, a hand lifting and slashing at the dark blue material. She noticed that the door was slightly ajar and cold air
streamed into the room. There was silence; an air of watchful
expectancy seemed to be moving around her. She drew a
deep breath in an attempt to dismiss the image and carefully
left the bed. She approached the dark blue suit as though it
were a specter. For a moment an old unidentifiable fear
washed over her.

Carefully she examined the fabric. It was not whole
cloth. It had been mended, skillfully mended, but mended all
the same. She held the fabric in her hand and stared down on
it. A shadow of an old defeat passed over her. The trouble
was, she could not place the knife in specific hands, could not
even see very clearly the knife itself. The image or memory
seemed to float disembodied in her mind.

Finally it seemed unimportant that she remember. The
clothes were certainly wearable and she needed clothes in
order to meet a plane. She examined them a final time,
amazed at the artistry in mending. There was always the pos-

sibility that she had torn them herself. The woods about the house were thick and overgrown. She tried a final time to place the meaningless image in time and place, but could not.

Still the house was silent, a peculiar stillness that seemed filled with listening ears. What had happened during the week? Had she accomplished anything at all? She could remember so little.

She was bent over in the process of stepping into the slacks when her head lifted and her eyes met the eyes of the reflected image which stared back at her from the mirror. Slowly the slacks dropped back down to the floor. She raised up from the crouched position and confronted the image. Instantly her hands lifted, wanting to touch the reflection. Then they settled back at her sides and she stood motionless. The scratches on her face caught and held her attention. One superficial but elongated mark started at the tip of her left temple and extended the length of her face, disappearing finally beneath the line of her jaw. Around the top of her forehead where her flesh met the hairline were several shorter marks. Something sharp had tried to separate flesh from bone. There was a lesser mark on the right cheek, like one half of a set of parentheses. All were dried now, thin, narrow, healing marks, looking almost as if they had been painted on her face.

Again she raised her hand. She felt a perilous necessity to examine the marks carefully. They would heal within days. But the source and cause of the scratches was another matter. For a moment her confusion grew dense. She shivered in the cold room and moved back a step from the full-length mirror. She was drifting again. She would have to watch that. If the marks were not understandable, they were at least bearable.

She shook her head. What had happened? How had she arrived at this place? She had a sensation of events transpiring that she had both feared and enjoyed. But this was foolish.

She knew where she was, thought she remembered how she had arrived at this point. She vaguely remembered encountering an acquaintance in the airport, a childhood friend. She remembered a night drive to Marblehead. And she remembered—nothing more.

Well, so be it. Perhaps more would return later. Still standing before the mirror she accepted the fact of the mirror, accepted the fact of her scratched face, accepted the fact that for now her memory was flawed. Perhaps someday she would remember it all.

She completed the dressing process, stopping now and then to listen, to pay serious attention to the blurred images that filtered across her brain. Dead cow. That was one. Stone woman. Another. Curious words.

Finally she stood fully dressed before the mirror. The reflection was coherent if nothing else. It was all she had to go on, so it had to be enough.

Moving slowly, thinking that at any minute something more might be revealed to her, she went out into the hall and started down the long corridor. She paused before the closed bathroom door. Nothing to mourn there. Suddenly she stepped forward and flung open the door. It was over and now the door would remain open.

She turned away from the white-tiled surface and proceeded on to the head of the stairs. She grasped the railing and started down. The house seemed to be breathing heavily, suffering her confusion with her. But it was endurable confusion, merely fragments of old nightmares, completely unrelated to today and certainly having no bearing on tomorrow.

Moving faster she rushed past the hallway and threw open the front door. A brilliant sun greeted her. A residue of dampness glistened on leaves and bushes. With neither shock nor surprise she saw her car waiting for her in the driveway. She knew it would be waiting for her.

She paused, hand on the doorknob, listening to a sound that was a rare and forgotten thing. Then immediately she closed the door, continued to pull against it long after the lock had clicked, as though she were closing up the past and making way for a beginning, the source of all that had at last come to be. There were a thousand lives between her and childhood. What possible difference could it make? She tested the door to make certain it was locked, then she went down the steps.

Inside the car she found her purse and shoes aligned neatly on the seat as though someone had arranged them for her. She slid behind the wheel and sat for a moment and took from her purse keys and compact. A light patina of powder helped to cover the scratches in case Clay asked and he was sure to ask. Of course she could always say she had stumbled into thornbushes.

Are there thornbushes around here?
There are thornbushes everywhere.

She looked up as though someone had spoken to her. Only the wind. She brushed the hair back from her face and let it fall loose around her shoulders. The tiny round image in the compact stared evenly back at her.

With a snap, she closed the compact and swung her legs into the car. She glanced up. A rectangle-shaped Zoe stared down on her from the rearview mirror. She returned the gaze, met it eye to eye. Not the best, she thought, certainly there were better, but perhaps not the worst. Certainly there were worse, assuming of course that one could define better and worse, which she couldn't so she was stuck with it.

Carefully she backed the car around and headed it toward the end of the drive. She glanced over her shoulder for a final look at the house. It was silly that they should not use it. She could handle the ghosts.

She stepped on the accelerator. The car moved forward

slowly for the brief length of the driveway. As she broke speed near the end of the drive for passing traffic, she spied Rick's baseball cap on the dashboard. With one fluid movement she scooped it up and plopped it on her head at an absurd rakish angle.

All the way back to Boston she hummed nonsensical, childish songs, a chorus of Zoes taking all the parts, indulging in amateur but passable harmony.

Only occasionally did the image in the rearview mirror look down on her, interrupting the song patterns, coming at random, obeying no law of life, facing her with the soluble, bearable, even joyous problems of her existence . . .

———◆———

Fortunately the plane was late. She encountered fierce traffic on Route 128. When she arrived at Logan, the monstrous parking lots were filled to overflowing. She circled in and out between solids lines of cars and finally found an empty space and abandoned her car. She had two immediate goals. First, meet Clay and the boys, then seek out Mary Lisa and thank her.

She fell into the flow of fast-moving foot traffic entering the terminal. She went directly to the airlines desk. A dark brooding young man informed her rather irritably that the plane from Los Angeles had been about an hour late, but that it had just arrived.

She thanked him with a smile and his irritability seemed to diminish.

She waved back at him, then began to dodge her way down the long concourse, part of her vision trained on the near hazard of oncoming traffic, the other part thrown a distance down the endless concourse.

In spite of her haste, she felt strangely relaxed. She

pulled to one side near the wall and made a halfhearted attempt to straighten herself. Her hands moved in a token circle around her hair. There was no gold clasp so there was nothing to pull back and tighten. Where had she lost it? Probably in the wooded amphitheater. Without warning another image moved across her mind. Something had transpired in the woods. But she couldn't remember exactly what. Then she was back within the urgency of the moment. She pushed off from the wall toward the open sea of traffic.

Two gates later, she saw him. He stood a good head taller than the crowd, his face, even from that distance, almost blotted out by fatigue. On a surge of excitement she broke into a run, calling out his name. She saw her two sons now, sitting wearily on the floor at his feet, surrounded by bulky, colorful Disneyland shopping bags, looking satiated by overindulgence, by too many sights and sounds, bored at seven and ten by life itself. She called out four times before Clay finally heard her. Suddenly he looked in her direction. She gave a quick prayer of thanks that they had returned safely to her. Then she was in his arms, almost before he was ready for her to be in his arms. With her eyes closed she felt the familiar contours of his body as he embraced her, tentatively at first as though she had caught him off guard. Then she felt his arms tighten about her, felt his hand as it found the small of her back, felt the subtle but significant pressure as he drew her still closer. Willingly she gave in to the fragrant deep hollow of his neck, feeling an incredible and powerful response of body, mind, nerves.

All the while she felt the boys scrambling about her waist, struggling for a way into the exclusive embrace, calling her over and over again, shrieking greedily for her attention, as greedily as the male arms which held her close and refused to let go.

Finally Clay stepped back and held her at arm's length.

His face clouded, grew stern. He faltered, "What in the hell happened to you?"

It was her face, she was certain, the scratches. Self-consciously she touched her cheekbone. "Thornbushes," she smiled. "The old place is overgrown with them."

Whether he believed her or not, she couldn't tell. Then the boys would not be put off any longer. She bent over and hugged both of them to her, an armful of wriggling, convulsive life. With the exception of Clay's stern glare, it was a good reunion, the four of them huddling together, the boys talking at once of the glories of Disneyland, the fishing trip, and the tall slim woman who had fixed pecan pancakes for them every morning.

Finally she raised up and looked directly at Clay. "I'm glad you're home," she said quietly. "I've missed you."

He continued to stare at her, clearly seeing her for the first time. "You look terrible," he scowled. His eyes made a slow critical trip around her face, hair, the length of her body. "What in hell happened to—"

"Nothing," she replied, perhaps a bit too quickly. She shrugged vaguely. "The house is a mess, but I think we'll enjoy it."

Her two sons were looking at her now, the same critical expressions on their faces. Robert asked, "What happened to your hair, Mom?"

She laughed. "Nothing happened to my hair. I just lost the clasp, that's all."

The three males were still examining her critically. In an attempt to dispel the small defeat that was forming in their eyes, she lifted her head and tried to stir them into action. "Come on, let's go."

But they held their positions, clearly aligned, mouths agape. She *was* different, and this difference was upsetting them. Rather dismally she began to finger her hair self-consciously. The scratches on her face felt alive suddenly as if they were freshly bleeding. Off in one corner of her brain, she heard an animal howling. The bondage was still there, waiting for a vulnerable moment. The gloriously alive week was over. Within moments they were on the verge of converting her back into that dead mass of rejected and rejecting images.

"No!" she said abruptly. She backed away from them. Then, seeing the confusion in their eyes, she smiled. "Are we going to go home, or are we going to stand around here all day?"

Clay squinted down on her, confident that if he just looked at her long enough, she could be solved. Slowly the boys began to gather their treasures in Disneyland shopping bags, glancing warily up at her now and then as though they knew instinctively that the changes in her would sooner or later require changes in themselves.

She returned Clay's gaze and started to inquire politely whether or not he had had a good week. But she changed her mind. Instead she walked the short distance to his side and guided his arm around her shoulder. There was always the outside chance that what had happened to her was contagious. With help, perhaps he could learn how it must be if either of them was to survive.

"Come on," she urged again. "I want to make a brief stop at a newsstand, then we'll go home."

All the while he gathered up his luggage, he never took his eyes off of her. She was the one who led the way back down the long concourse. As she approached the intersection that led to Mary Lisa's newsstand, she waited for them to catch up. Three males, one large, two small, all struggling under the weight of their heavy luggage, their faces weary and strained from traveling, a tense, confused look in their eyes. She was a stranger and therefore a threat.

Feeling a surge of compassion for them, she promised, "I won't be a minute. Right over there, that newsstand. I want to make a quick stop, all right?"

She hurried on ahead, confident that they would wait for her. While she was still several yards away, Zoe recognized the unhappy Flossie who a few days earlier had insulted Mary Lisa and for her troubles had been showered with love.

Cautiously Zoe approached. She glanced over her shoulder and saw Clay and the boys waiting by the far wall. Then she focused all of her attention on Flossie, not certain that she could react with the same maturity as Mary Lisa. "I—beg your pardon?" she called out, hesitantly.

The old woman looked sharply up. "What?" she demanded, without a trace of a smile.

"I'm—looking for Mary Lisa," Zoe went on, searching the newsstand even as she asked. "Mary Lisa Fletcher. She works here. Could you tell—"

"No, I couldn't," the old woman interrupted. "This here isn't an information desk, this here is a—"

"I know," Zoe said, beginning to lose nerve as well as patience. "But she works here, Mary Lisa is her name and I met her here not—"

"Who?"

"Mary Lisa Fletcher."

"The whore, you mean?"

The old woman's cruel voice seemed to lift and carry across the crowded concourse. Zoe looked over her shoulder. Clay was hidden behind a wrinkled copy of the Los Angeles *Times* and the boys were on the floor, fishing through their Disneyland shopping bags.

"Please," Zoe began again, keeping her voice down, hoping the old woman would follow suit.

"Please what?" snapped the old woman. "Who you're looking for ain't here and never will be."

"I don't under—"

"Her with her fancy ways and notions and all her screwball friends. Act-ors was what they called themselves. Scum is what I called 'em. A bunch of freaks, if you asked me, parading around like they was God's gifts to the world. I mean, who asked them, you know what I mean?"

Her incoherent anger and bitterness seemed to be aimed at Zoe, who was ill-equipped to receive it. "Look, all I want to know is if she isn't here now, when will she—"

"She *was* a whore, you know, plain and simple, call it anything you like, dress it up or down, she was, is, and always will be a slut. Nuts attract nuts, you know, and she also was Queen of the Nuts, what with all her act-ors, traveling all over New England, performing their little plays and night games, that's what they called them, you know, and all I can say is, who asked them, you know what I mean? 'Oh but I do love troubled children, Flossie, yes I do, I mean, isn't all this really marvelous?' "

The old woman broke into a shrill imitation of Mary Lisa, her wrinkled face contorted with resentment and hate.

"Slut, that's all she was—"

"Please, could you tell—"

"Carried that magic box with 'em, least the slut said it was magic, can you imagine. Lined with mirrors. Now does that make sense? The slut said the children liked to step inside and get to know themselves. What a goddamned bunch of—"

"Please!" This time Zoe stepped forward until she confronted the old woman head on. "Look, all I want is some information. If Mary Lisa isn't here now, could you tell me when you expect her?"

"Never."

Zoe blinked at the one-word response.

"I—don't understand?"

"I said never. How much plainer do I have to make it?"

Still struggling for understanding, Zoe faltered. "H-has she quit?"

"She's dead."

The words hung on the air between them for a moment. Zoe blinked once and tried to repeat, "D-dead?"

"I said so, didn't I?"

Suddenly old Flossie seemed bored with the encounter. She turned back to the pyramids of Planters Peanuts and Mars Bars. "So the slut is gone and good riddance."

"H-how?"

Flossie gave a massive shrug. "It was that curve on the south side of Dublin Lake. Slick as hell with October rain. The brakes on that old van didn't hold and van and all slid right off into the lake. Everyone drowned. Every last one of them. All them act-ors and the magic cabinet as well. Gone, gone and good riddance."

Zoe lifted a trembling hand in an attempt to stop the never-ending flow of words. She shut her eyes, then quickly opened them. "When?" she asked with held breath.

Flossie looked up at the long blue tubes of fluorescent light, thinking. "Three years ago—this month. This very month, yes sir, that was it. Look, I got business, so I've wasted enough time—"

And with that, the old woman turned away and left Zoe gaping after her. Twice Zoe tried to call her back but either the old woman didn't hear or wasn't paying any more attention to her.

Dead. Three years ago. It wasn't possible—

"Zoe, is anything wrong?"

At the sound of the familiar voice, she turned and saw Clay just coming up on her right.

"Nothing," she said quickly, knowing full well she

could never explain to Clay, could perhaps never explain it to herself.

"Mama?"

Then the boys were at her side, one on each hand, tired of waiting. "Can we go home now?"

"Home," she repeated, thinking on Flossie's words, trying desperately hard to understand.

"Do you know that woman?" Clay asked, still puzzled, nodding toward Flossie who was busily occupied with several customers.

Zoe shook her head. "Last week I met a woman here I had known in Whitney. We went to high school together. I just wanted to see if she was still here?"

"Was she?"

"No, but I must have the wrong newsstand." Over her words, Zoe heard Flossie's voice in echo: Dead—three years —a troupe of act-ors—

Clay was now close beside her, keeping pace as they walked down the concourse toward the large glass doors. "Zoe," he said softly, "I—missed you—"

It was such a vital confession, such a sweet one.

"And I you," she said, leaning close for a kiss. "Come on," she said, enlarging her invitation to include the boys.

She slipped her arm around Clay's waist and pulled him close. She was still struggling for understanding. What had happened to her? What had happened to Mary Lisa? Maybe one day she would understand. All she knew for now was that while there were still problems ahead for all of them, she felt more confident of herself than she'd ever felt before. And for that she was grateful.

"Come on," she said to all of them. "Let's go home. I've so much to tell you about the house in Whitney, so much more to show you. Perhaps we could drive up this weekend . . ."